Dear Reader,

Welcome to two fantastically emotional books in one satisfying volume! These two stories by Janice Kay Johnson and Margot Early have a common theme—marriage of convenience. But in addition to that, both heroes are single fathers.

These men are faced with tough but quite different situations and it's interesting that they both see one just solution—marriage! They're basically prepared to do anything for their children and in our book that makes them truly fabulous fathers.

Happy reading!

The Editors

*First published in Great Britain 2000
by Harlequin Mills & Boon Limited,
Eton House, 18-24 Paradise Road,
Richmond, Surrey TW9 1SR*

WHOSE BABY? © Janice Kay Johnson 2000
MR FAMILY © Margot Early 1996

ISBN 0 373 04672 3

20-1000

*Printed and bound in Spain
by Litografia Rosés S.A., Barcelona*

Whose Baby?

JANICE KAY JOHNSON

TORONTO • NEW YORK • LONDON
AMSTERDAM • PARIS • SYDNEY • HAMBURG
STOCKHOLM • ATHENS • TOKYO • MILAN • MADRID
PRAGUE • WARSAW • BUDAPEST • AUCKLAND

Dear Reader,

I'm sure it won't surprise you to hear that the idea for *Whose Baby?* came to me when I was reading about the recent case in which it was discovered that two little girls had been switched at birth. All of us, I'm sure, were transfixed when reading about this horrifying mistake. I'll bet every parent thought immediately *'What if…'* Perhaps our deepest instinct is to protect our children. And yet…which child? If I found out one of my daughters wasn't biologically mine, I'd feel no less fiercely protective, no less loving. And yet…I could easily come to feel the same about the child I'd carried for nine months.

Any time I read or hear about something so emotional, the writer part of me kicks in and also wonders *'What if…'* What if the hero had lost his wife, and their biological child is all he has left of her? What if the heroine fears he wants *both* girls? Talk about conflict!

I don't know that I've ever written a story with so many layers of painful and exhilarating emotion. Sitting in front of the computer each day, I felt as if I were unwrapping a gift from someone I'd loved and lost. Each layer was poignant, making me grateful for my own family.

See if you don't feel the same!

Best,

Janice Kay Johnson

CHAPTER ONE

$O + O$ DOES NOT $= B$. So why was she even nervous?

Oblivious to the salt-scented breeze and the familiar whoosh of the broken surf, Lynn Chanak stared at the envelope in her hand. *Open it,* she told herself. *Then you can quit worrying about nothing.*

And nothing was just what it would prove to be.

That Portland lab had mixed up somebody else's blood with Shelly's. It was dumb to let the results shake her even for a minute. Poor Shelly had had to endure being stuck with a needle again, which still made Lynn mad, but it was done, over with, and now with the results from the new lab she'd be able to refute her ex-husband's ridiculous accusation.

There was no way a second lab would make the same kind of mistake. Lynn and Brian both had Type O blood; heaven help her, she'd once been foolish enough to think that meant they were made for each other.

With both parents having Type O blood, Shelly had to have the same.

So why not open the envelope?

"Mama!" Lynn's three-and-a-half-year-old daughter tugged at her sleeve. "See what I found?"

The small hand cupped a flame-red, wave-polished

chunk of agate that beachcombing tourists would have killed for.

Lynn smiled in delight and hugged her daughter. "That's a pretty one! You've got sharp eyes!"

She sat on a gray, winter-tossed log on the beach, the pile of mail in her hand. This was a daily ritual for her and Shelly when the shop was closed. Wait for the mail, don sweatshirts against the sharp breeze, and then walk the two blocks from home to the rocky beach, famous for the sea stacks that reared offshore. Otter Beach had been a tiny lumber town until the Oregon coast became a favorite tourist destination. Now streets were lined with art galleries and antique shops, and prime beachfront real estate was taken by inns and bed-and-breakfasts.

Lynn's bookstore was one block over from the main street. The upstairs of the old house was home, the downstairs her business. During tourist season, she stayed open six days a week. By the time winter storms pounded the coast, she only bothered to open from Thursday through Sunday for locals and for the few hardy souls who came for romantic weekends and beachcombing after storms deposited Japanese floats and agates on the shore.

"I'll give this to Daddy next time he comes," Shelly announced. "C'n you save it for him, Mommy?"

"You bet, sweetie," agreed Lynn, hiding her dismay. How was she going to explain to a three-year-old why Daddy wasn't visiting anymore?

Giggling, Shelly wormed her hand into the pocket of Lynn's faded, zip-front sweatshirt to deposit her find. The chunk of agate joined the crab claw and the mussel shell entwined with dried seaweed that she'd already collected.

For a moment Lynn watched as Shelly wandered away. She looked so cute in her denim overalls and rubber-toed sneakers, her mink-brown ponytail straight and sleek. Lynn tried hard to see what Brian did, but how could she? This was her *daughter*.

So what if her own hair was a warm, wavy chestnut-brown, if Brian was blond? So what if Shelly's eyes were brown, while Lynn's were green and Brian's blue? Kids didn't always look just like their parents. In fact, they hardly ever did. The genes that created a person were like…like the threads of color in a Persian carpet, thousands of bits of wool, woven together with a complexity that defied any ability to say that a certain blue came from such and such a sheep. Shelly might look like some forgotten great-grandmother. Did it *matter* that her face wasn't a reflection of her father's?

Apparently it did to Brian. He'd always been unreasonably jealous, both before they were married— when Lynn considered possessiveness romantic— and after. The marriage had been a mistake, a terrible mistake. Guilt ate at Lynn every time she thought about Brian, because she knew the failure was hers. She shouldn't have married him. He was right, when he had believed she didn't love him enough.

But she had never been unfaithful. There hadn't been another man; probably never would be, now that she knew she wasn't capable of the kind of passion a lifetime commitment required. She hadn't given Brian any reason to suspect she was seeing anyone, so it outraged her that now he should claim Shelly wasn't his.

Lynn bitterly resented having to put a three-year-old through the scary process of having blood drawn, but she'd done it. Not just because she needed Brian to keep paying the child support, but also because Shelly needed her dad.

So why wasn't she tearing open the envelope? Lynn wrenched her gaze from Shelly, crouched on her heels ten yards down the beach staring with intense fascination at something, and studied the return address on the envelope. McElvoy Laboratories, Seattle, Washington.

A different lab. Lynn hadn't taken Shelly back to their regular clinic for the second blood draw. She'd driven to Lincoln City. Of course she should have marched back into their doctor's office, waving that stupid piece of paper and proclaiming her indignation at the mistake. She shouldn't have had to pay for the second round of analysis. But she'd felt…cautious.

She made a face. Gun-shy. Brian had made her paranoid. She didn't want to give him any ammunition. If he knew about the first results, he wouldn't believe the second ones. He'd want more, instead of accepting the truth when she handed it to him.

Anyway, a voice whispered, *what if it* wasn't *a mistake? Shelly* doesn't *look like either parent.*

"Oh, right!" she said out loud. For Pete's sake, she'd been awake and present during her awful labor. Sure, because of the hemorrhaging, she hadn't seen her newborn daughter for the first hours, but then they'd laid the tiny red-faced baby at her breast, and she'd held her and loved her ever since. And, damn it, so had Brian! Only, now he had to get suspicious. Or cheap. He was late sometimes with the child-support check. Think what a good excuse this would be not to pay at all!

Lynn glanced up again; her daughter was in the exact same spot. A miniature tide pool, probably. Shelly had learned not to take living creatures from them, only to observe. She'd seen the difference between the rich color of a sea star clinging to a rock beneath the water and the dull hard body of a dead preserved one. She loved the scamper of tiny crabs, the dart of brown sandpipers, the hoarse roar of sea lions on the rocks offshore. This was home, magical and familiar at the same time.

Like having a child. For fleeting moments, Lynn saw through her daughter's eyes and became three years old again. Wondering, awed, frightened, reassured by simple comforts.

Other times, Lynn was perplexed by this complete, small person her daughter seemed to be. It was as if she'd been born whole, finished, and all Lynn could do was open the world to her. The idea that a parent could shape her child was as silly as believing the same blood type meant two people were mysteriously akin.

Open it.

Lynn couldn't understand her reluctance. She kept fingering that damned envelope. She'd peeked at all the bills, even flipped through a couple of publishers' catalogs as if their spring lists mattered more than the blood that traced pale blue lines beneath the translucent skin of her daughter's wrists, that beaded crimson when Shelly skinned her knee. Lifeblood.

Still Shelly crouched in the same spot, her attention span astonishing for a child her age. She didn't need her mom right now, except as home base. A pocket and a smile and a hug.

Lynn tore open the envelope and pulled out the single sheet of paper. Unfolded it, and stared down at the bald black letter *B*. There was more, but she didn't see it.

Her heart pounded so hard she wouldn't have heard Shelly scream. Her vision misted, and she had the eerie sensation of being alone on the beach after a late-afternoon fog had rolled in. Everything was gray, indistinct, abruptly looming in front of her and then swallowed behind her.

Oh God, oh God, oh God.

There had been no other man. Only Brian, ever. If Brian wasn't the father of Shelly Schoening, then she—Lynn—wasn't her mother, either.

How was that possible?

She moaned and hugged her knees. *How?*

She could think of only one answer. Somehow, two babies had been switched in the hospital. The little girl laid to nurse at her breast wasn't the one she'd carried for nine months. Her own baby had been given to another mother.

Somewhere, a toddler with bright blue eyes like Brian's or chestnut-brown hair like Lynn's called another woman Mommy.

Lynn whimpered again.

"Mommy?"

Swallowing her terror, Lynn looked into Shelly's frightened brown eyes. "Yes, honey?" She sounded only a little hoarse.

"Is Mommy sick?"

To death. Her whole world was her daughter. Not that unknown child somewhere, the one who might look like her, but *this* child—the one she'd nursed and diapered, whose toes she'd tickled and counted, the one who squeezed her hand and waited for an answer.

"No," she said. "Yes. Mommy's tummy felt funny for a minute. Like this." She burrowed her hand inside the OshKosh overalls and tickled until Shelly's elfin face crinkled with a giggle.

Shelly wrapped her arms around her mother's neck and pressed her cold, plump cheek against Lynn's. "I wanna cheeseburger," she confided. "And chocolate milk."

Lynn hugged back. Hugged until the toddler squeaked with alarm.

"You know what?" Lynn said. "A cheeseburger sounds good to me, too. *And* chocolate milk. What do you say we go home?"

Shelly nodded vigorously. Lynn rose from the log, feeling as stiff as an old woman. She collected her pile of mail and took her daughter's small hand. Feeling numb, she turned her back on the waves, her sneakered feet accustomed to the way the beach stones and sand gave with each step. One forward, half back. A struggle that strengthened the body.

Her daughter chattered. Lynn heard not a word, although she smiled and agreed.

She focused passionately on only one thought: Shelly was *hers*. Nobody must ever know that maybe, somehow, she wasn't.

After lunch, while Shelly napped, Lynn sat at the

kitchen table and convinced herself that Brian couldn't insist on this blood work. She'd give up the child-support money first, tell him he could think what he liked. Even agree that he was right, although she hated the idea of letting him believe she'd sneaked around and had sweaty sex with some man she hardly knew—because, after all, she had no real friends who were male.

It took until five o'clock for Lynn to get angry. She put water on to boil for macaroni and went to check on Shelly. She was curled at one end of the shabby velveteen couch watching Dumbo for the thousandth time. Her flowered flannel blanket was tucked under one arm and her thumb was in her mouth. On the dentist's advice, Lynn had been trying to break her of sucking her thumb, but tonight she didn't say anything, just kissed the silky top of Shelly's head and breathed in her essence before going back to the kitchen.

Things like babies getting switched in the hospital didn't happen! she thought incredulously, then more firmly. Parents were always afraid they would, but hospitals took such precautions these days. Lynn still had the plastic band that had been around Shelly's plump wrist when she was released from the hospital. It had exactly matched Lynn's.

No. There had to be some other explanation.

This lab was wrong, too?

She poured the macaroni into the boiling water and frowned.

Wait! Could Brian have lied about his blood type? She stirred the macaroni and tried to remember. Had she said what hers was first? It would be like him to try to create a fiction to make it sound as though they were destined for each other. He'd wanted her from the first time they'd met, in the bookstore where she'd worked after she graduated from college.

Closing her eyes, Lynn tried to replay the scene. A popular professor at the university had been in a car accident, and the English department had held a blood drive. She'd been resting after giving a pint, when the nurse pushed back the curtain and said, "If you've finished your juice, you're all set!"

And there Brian was, on the next gurney. Still lying down, he'd turned his head and grinned. "Hey, they've been sucking blood out of you, too, huh?"

He'd come into the bookstore for the first time just the previous weekend. Or, at least, she'd noticed him for the first time. And how could she not have noticed him? He was six feet two inches, with short sun-streaked blond hair and bright blue eyes. He was tanned from skiing at Mount Hood. She'd asked, because it was winter and most people in Portland were pale. He looked like a surfer, broad shouldered and athletic and golden.

"Well, it was voluntary," she'd said shyly.

"Yeah, so they say." He waved away the orange juice and sat up without taking it slowly. How like a man!

Somehow they ended up walking out together. And...yes! He'd asked, "What type blood do you have?"

She did volunteer the information first. She distinctly remembered the way he'd turned and said, so seriously, "That means the same blood runs through our veins. We must be meant for each other."

She'd made it a joke; they'd both laughed, but a small thrill had run through her at the idea, presented with the intensity and gravity of a marriage proposal.

The more fool her!

She dumped the macaroni into the waiting colander, jumping when the boiling water splashed her hand. She should have known better. The single, chipped porcelain sink was shallow, and she was always careful.

Tears sprang to her eyes. "Damn, damn, damn," she muttered, turning on the cold water and sticking her hand under it.

Why, that creep! All this anguish, and he'd lied!

She told herself she was furious, but really relief flooded her in a sweet tide. Such a simple explanation! And after she'd come up with such a convoluted one.

The relief lasted all evening. She played Chutes and Ladders with Shelly, then told silly stories and every knock-knock joke she could think of at bedtime, buoyed by that wash of exquisite release from fear.

She thought about calling him, the scumbag, and saying, "I might think about checking our daughter's blood type, if I knew what yours *really* is."

But, although she should be madder than she was, Lynn still thought she should cool down before she confronted him. Besides, she wanted to be sure of herself.

She could ask his mother. No, better yet, she could call the blood bank and say that he'd been in a car accident, and she didn't remember his blood type but she knew he'd donated.

That was the moment when she remembered. There she was, checking to be sure the bathroom door was open enough to cast light into the hall so Shelly wouldn't get scared if she woke up later. One part of Lynn's mind thought, six inches, that's perfect, and another part was wondering if she shouldn't add more books on tape to her stock downstairs—a man, a tourist, had asked for them Sunday, and left without buying anything after looking at what she did have—and oh yes, she had to pick up peanut butter at the store tomorrow, since Shelly practically lived on it.

Through all her other preoccupations, she felt the onset of fear and the prickle of goose bumps on her skin even before a memory came to her. A woman from the blood bank had called, not long after Lynn and Brian got married, and she'd asked Lynn to encourage her husband to donate blood again.

"He's got Type O, you know," she said, "and we're terribly short."

Lynn had said helpfully, "My blood is O, too," and she'd promised she would ask Brian, but she'd definitely come down to the blood bank herself. She had, and he must have, too, after work, not romantically together this time. That part didn't matter; what did was that the blood bank had specifically wanted him to come in because he had O.

Instead of going to bed, Lynn felt her way back along the narrow hall to the kitchen, with its tiny refrigerator so old she had to regularly defrost the freezer part, the linoleum with the pattern worn to a blur, the brand-new shiny white stove, bought when the old one gave up the ghost at the worst possible

moment, the way it always went. In the brightness
when she switched on the light, the cheery yellow
she'd painted the cabinets looked garish, a disguise
as obvious as a clown's red nose.

The living quarters of the house were crummy;
she'd put all her money into the downstairs, the
bookstore. She'd had to. She and Shelly could make
do, Lynn had told herself. Until the store became
really profitable. If bookstores ever did.

But now she couldn't help looking around and
imagining what other people would think. If, for example, Shelly's real, biological parents were trying
to take her back.

I wouldn't look very good, would I? Lynn thought.
Her knees crumpled, and she sank onto one of the
two mismatched chairs that went with the tiny,
scarred Formica and metal kitchen table. *I don't have
much to offer Shelly materially, and I'm divorced,
and my ex-husband thinks I must have cheated on
him.*

Those other parents, they could take Shelly away
from her. She remembered a photo from some horrible child custody case, when the little boy was
screaming and reaching for the only parents he'd
ever known while the biological father carried him
away. How painfully easy it was to transpose faces:
she was the one trying to be brave, make this seem
like the right thing, while Shelly was ripped away
from her like one of the beautiful sea stars from a
slick wet rock.

Oh God, oh God, oh God.

She drew up her knees and hugged herself and
shook, panting for breaths. She could hear herself

gasping. She must be in shock, she felt so strange. Cold, and frightened, as if an intruder had crept in and violated her, as if she would never feel safe again.

Nobody must ever know. That was her only hope. *Nobody. Ever.*

Eventually the shaking passed, and she saw again her kitchen, tidy and spotlessly clean, however shabby, and on the refrigerator Shelly's bright crayon drawings that were supposed to be sea stars or seals or horses, those inner imaginings that her short fingers were not yet capable of rendering. It was home: loving, safe, clean and ordered. What else mattered? Certainly not money.

Nor blood. She didn't care whose ran through Shelly's veins. She would never let it matter.

But first, she had to be sure.

The blue plastic clock on the wall said eight-thirty. Not too late to call Brian's mother.

Ruth Schoening's voice held caution, once she knew who was on the phone.

"Lynn. My, it's late in the evening to be calling."

Not: *Oh, gracious, Shelly is all right, isn't she?*

Lynn noticed the lack, and decided on honesty. "Brian's told you he doesn't think Shelly is his daughter, hasn't he?"

The pause resonated with awkwardness. "He did say something."

"I would never…" The automatic denial caught in Lynn's throat. Oh, God. She might someday have to claim she *had.* She took a breath. "You don't believe that, do you?"

Really, she was begging, *You* know *me.* Please say

that you have faith in me, that you love Shelly no matter what.

"It's not really my business," her ex-husband's mother said, the constraint in her voice obvious.

"She's your granddaughter."

"Is she?"

She had begun to shake again, Lynn noticed with peculiar detachment. "This is so ridiculous," she exclaimed, trying to laugh and failing.

"I hope so," Ruth said. "But, you know, he's right—Shelly doesn't look like anybody in the family."

"When my grandmother was a little girl…"

"Brian said he'd looked through your family album, and Shelly doesn't look like anybody on your side, either. She's so…so dark, and with that pointy chin she makes me think of, oh, a pixie from a fairy tale. *My* children were round and sturdy and blond. Like little Swedes."

She always said that as if Swedish children were fairer than any other kind. She never addressed the fact that Schoening was a German name, not Scandinavian.

Obviously, there would be no assurances of unfailing love no matter what. Shelly would lose her grandparents, too, if it came to that.

"Well," Lynn said, "the reason I'm calling is that I'm considering having Shelly tested so we can lay this foolishness to rest. It makes me mad to have to subject her to needles and all that scariness, but I might do it. So what I wondered is, do you remember what Brian's blood type is?"

"Oh, yes," his mother said promptly. "He's O

positive, just like me. What a good idea, Lynn! Doubts should always be laid to rest, don't you think?''

Fury kindled in her breast. Now that she'd gotten what she wanted, she let anger have its rein, sharpening her voice. "What I think is that all this is incredibly insulting. I understand that Brian's still angry about our divorce, but you know me better than to believe this...this hogwash. You claim to love Shelly. You always say I should bring her for visits more often, that she's adorable, that I should send pictures so you can show all your friends, and now you talk about her as if she's tainted and you've always known something was wrong with her. She's...she's a bright, beautiful child whose eyes don't happen to be blue. Well, I'm not *Swedish,* and I don't expect my daughter to look like she is!'' Lynn ended with a snap. "*That's* what I think.''

She didn't wait for a response. She hung up the telephone in a righteous rage that deserted her too quickly. How could she get mad, when Shelly *wasn't* Brian's daughter? Maybe she was the one who was blind! Maybe she should have realized immediately that something was wrong, that the baby the nurses handed her was a changeling.

But she hadn't, oh, she hadn't. Instead, the connection had been deep and instant, a mother's love for this child and only this one.

Well, the fierceness of her love hadn't diminished. She would tell Brian that she wasn't going to get Shelly tested, and if he cut his daughter off, so be it. She would let him live with a creeping feeling of shame. It would serve him right.

She stood up, as wearily as if she'd just overcome a violent bout of flu, and turned off the kitchen light, using the glow from the bathroom to find her way to her bedroom.

Life might get harder; Shelly would be hurt that her father didn't want her. *But no one must ever know.*

THE DREAM CAME EVERY NIGHT from then on. She was searching desperately for someone. For her little girl. First she was on the beach, and she'd been reading her mail, and the fog had rolled in, and she looked up suddenly and realized she couldn't see her.

"Shelly!" she began crying. "Shelly, where are you?" She leaped to her feet and spun in every direction, crying over and over, "Shelly!"

She began stumbling toward the water. Boulders reared from nowhere, tripping her. The roar of the surf filled her ears, and she knew with sickening certainty that Shelly had been caught by a wave.

But, no, she wasn't on the beach at all. She was in a city, although the fog still played tricks with her eyes. The sound was from traffic. Oh, no! How could she have looked away, even for a moment? The sea was merciless, but cars were deadly.

She searched the sidewalks frantically for a bright chestnut head. People passing ignored her. Then she saw her, out on the median, cars racing by without slowing at all for the toddler who teetered there. She wore rags; she looked like Cosette in *Les Misérables,* wretched and unwanted. Brimming with tears, her bright blue eyes met Lynn's momentarily through a break in the traffic, but without recognition.

My daughter doesn't know me, Lynn realized with horror.

"Stay where you are!" Lynn screamed. "Wait! I'm coming!"

But her voice meant nothing to this child, and with greater shock Lynn discovered she didn't know her own daughter's name.

Sobbing, the little girl stepped from the curb.

And Lynn awakened, as she did every night, her screamed "No!" trembling on her lips and tears running down her cheeks.

With a moan she curled into a ball and shuddered. At last she went into the bathroom and splashed cold water on her face, then stared hopelessly at herself in the mirror.

Of course she was having dreams; their content was hardly subtle.

Somewhere out there was another little girl, one she'd carried in her womb. How many promises she'd made to that baby as she dreamed of the future! She sang to her and laughed and tickled her own belly when a tiny toe or elbow surfaced. She played music and danced and read aloud, just so her child would know her voice, would know she was loved.

But, through no fault of her own, she hadn't kept those promises. Her baby had never heard her voice again. Someone else had taken her home. Did these other parents love her and sing to her and tickle her toes? Or had she gone home with a teenager who hadn't really wanted to get pregnant? Perhaps she was in a foster home, or had an angry father who shook her when she wouldn't quit crying. What if she was slow to develop, but nobody was patient?

Or what if they loved her, these parents, but they were raising her the only way they knew how, by spanking her when she got cranky or broke something, by screaming at her with the anger of their own childhoods in their voices?

"If only..." Lynn breathed soundlessly. If only she could *know*. See that this other little girl *was* loved and cared for, read to and hugged, that *her* artwork was on the refrigerator for all to admire.

If she knew, the dreams would go away.

But how could she ever find out, without contacting the hospital and telling them? Without taking the chance of losing Shelly?

That was the torment. Risk the little girl who was the center of her life, who meant everything to her, for the sake of one who couldn't possibly remember her voice. Who would have forgotten her songs and the stories she'd promised to finish someday, when they could giggle together.

She crept down the hall like a ghost to her daughter's room, hovering in the doorway because the bed nearly filled the space, which in a house of this era had probably been meant as a sewing room or a nursery. Sunny yellow and black cats frolicked among sunflowers on the wallpaper that climbed the slanted ceiling. Yellow curtains covered the tall sash window. Under a pale lemon-yellow and white comforter, Shelly slept peacefully. Lynn could just make out her face in the glow from the hall, and thought, Ruth is right. She looks like a Celt from old stories, a fairy child, with that small, pointy chin, that high curving forehead and glossy brown hair as straight as promises that were kept.

Risk her, for the dream child?

Lynn closed her eyes on a soft, agonized exhalation. How could she?

How could she not?

CHAPTER TWO

LATE AGAIN.

Adam Landry swore at the driver of the car in front of him, which hesitated just too long and missed the one and only opening to make a left turn before the light became red.

Damn, he thought bitterly. They'd both be sitting through another full light. And he was already—he snatched an edgy look at the clock on his dash—ten minutes past the closing of his daughter's preschool.

This was getting to be routine, and if he wasn't careful they'd ask him to make other arrangements for Rose. But the Cottage Path Preschool and Day Care was the best.

Oh, hell, why lie to himself? He didn't know if it was best. He didn't know a thing about it, except that Jennifer had chosen it, an eternity ago when she was pregnant and joyful, not planning to go back to work but figuring she'd need a place for drop-in sometimes.

Over dinner, she'd told him about it, her eyes sparkling with pleasure. "It's the Cottage Path Preschool. Isn't that perfect? Can you believe it? Our Rose will trip up the path to the cottage. Oh!" She shivered in delight, and he'd momentarily seen the vision that had become the center of her life: a little girl with the same mahogany brown hair as her mommy, her legs skinny, dimples flashing and her giggle a trill like a flute solo that reached for heaven and found it.

Their child.

And him? What had he said? A gruff, "You're not letting the name of the place suck you in, are you?"

She'd only laughed at him, her joy undimmed. "Don't be silly. It's a wonderful preschool! The director's written a book about early childhood development. They have animals—chickens and goats and this big lazy dog that lets kids climb all over him and only grunts. And puzzles and books and blocks and puppets! It's wonderland."

Pain stabbed now and Adam rubbed his chest. He'd never considered any place else for Rose. He was trying to raise their daughter as Jennifer would have wanted to, which meant he scraped his memory for nuggets his wife might have dropped, perhaps in bed when he scanned the financial news a last time while she chattered on in her light voice as if oblivious to his lack of attention.

Adam took another savage look at the clock and swore. Was he screwing up one more thing Jennifer had wanted for Rose?

But maybe it wasn't the best choice now. Maybe he should go for a nanny.

He tensed when the light turned green and willed the driver of the Buick to make a dash before cross-traffic began. But, hell, no. The car didn't even inch forward. The heel of Adam's hand was on the horn when he clenched his teeth and made himself wrap his fingers around the wheel again. *Shit.* If he hadn't stayed for that last goddamn phone call, he wouldn't be in such a hurry he wanted other drivers to take their lives in their hands just to get out of his way. Why hadn't he walked out, ignored the ringing?

He couldn't do everything.

He had to try. He owed it to Rose. And to Jennifer.

An interminable five more minutes had passed before he barreled into the parking lot, yanked on the emergency brake and killed the engine, slamming his door before he strode in.

The director of the preschool, a woman of his own age named Melissa Gearhart, waited in the entry, eyes cool.

"Mr. Landry. Rose has been worried."

His intense anxiety made itself felt in a long huff of breath. "God, I'm sorry. I've done it again."

"I'm afraid I'm going to have to start charging you when staff has to stay late, like today."

"I understand." He swallowed. "Where's Rose?"

The dark-haired woman with tired smudges beneath her eyes turned. "Under the climber."

He stepped past her into the main activity room, where the floor was covered with bright mats to pad falls from the slide and wooden peg climber. He had to circle a playhouse before he saw his daughter, lying on the mat with her thumb in her mouth.

Wearing clothes he'd never seen before. Ill fitting and mismatched.

"She had an accident again," Melissa said softly behind him. "No big deal. I've got her clothes in a plastic bag for you. Just bring those back when you've washed them."

He closed his eyes for a moment, acknowledging

more failure. Or maybe not—he hadn't had the guts to ask the mothers who picked up their three-year-olds whether they had potty accidents still, too. Or the occasional father, none exclusive parents the way he was. Adam didn't even like to ask Melissa, because he didn't want to know something was wrong, that he'd already warped his beloved child.

If only he knew what the hell he was doing.

If only Jennifer were alive to help him do it.

"Hey, Rose Red," he said softly, crouching. "Ready to bloom?"

"Daddy!" She erupted to her feet and into his arms, her sky-blue eyes flooding with tears. "You're late, and I'm hungry, and I had a accident, an'…"

He stemmed the flow. "I'm sorry, I'm sorry. Here you were, all by yourself."

"Except for Lissa," Rose mumbled against his shoulder. She snuffled. "Lissa didn't leave me."

He felt the crushing addition, *Like you do.* Every day.

She'd taken lately to holding on to him and screaming when he tried to drop her off in the morning. He felt like the worst parent in the whole damned world when the day-care workers had to pry his daughter's fingers off him and haul her away, when the last thing he saw was Rose's round tear-streaked face. Those desperate, pleading eyes haunted his days, gave him a feeling of self-loathing.

But, goddamn it, he had to work!

Rationally he knew that other kids cried in the morning, too, that it was probably just a stage. Reason didn't quell the guilt that ate at his gut like too many cups of coffee.

She needed her daddy, and he wasn't there.

He hustled her out to the car, belatedly grabbing the white plastic garbage sack that held Rose's own clothes. That meant laundry tonight. He didn't want to leave these for Ann, their twenty-something housekeeper-cook. When Rose wet the bed, he always changed it, too. Three and a half wasn't so old, he tried to tell himself, but he hadn't seen those discreet plastic bags go home with Rose's friends Rainy and Sylvie, either. Not in months.

His daughter fell asleep during the drive home, worn out by a ten-hour day, and more guilt stabbed him. Poor Rosebud. How did a little girl grow into a woman without a mother to lead the way? What did he know about girlish secrets or adolescent crushes or makeup or menstrual cramps?

Well, he'd damn well learn. He was mommy and daddy both, determined not to foist his daughter's upbringing on a series of nannies. Jennifer wouldn't have wanted that.

I didn't mean it, he said silently, speaking to her as if she were listening. *No nanny.*

A nanny would be a replacement. A substitute mother. No one could be Jennifer, petite, quick moving, eternally optimistic, *alive.*

Dead, in every meaningful way, long before her daughter was cut from her belly.

He hadn't even looked at Rose when doctors performed the C-section. He'd been holding Jennifer's hand, although Jennifer didn't know it, would never know it, because she was brain-dead. He'd been saying goodbye, because the shell of her body had no purpose anymore, now that it wasn't needed to sus-

tain her child. He had agreed that she would be un-
hooked from machines as soon as the baby could
survive on her own.

"I'll do my best," he had whispered to the love
of his life. One last promise, he thought, praying she
didn't know how he had dreaded the birth because it
meant severing any last wisp of hope that the doctors
were wrong, that she would yet wake up.

How could she be gone? He had gripped her hand
so hard it should have hurt, but she only lay there,
eyes closed, breast rising and falling with the hissing
push of the respirator, unaware of her daughter's
birth, of his tears and whispered, wrenching, "Goodbye, Jenny." Unaware when he blundered from the
room.

Unaware when her heart stopped, when the last
breath caught in her throat.

His bright-faced, pretty, otherworldly wife was already dead when her daughter began life.

He named her Jenny Rose, and called her Rose,
this little girl who showed no signs of looking like
her mama, to his relief and disappointment both. Her
hair had developed red tints and curls, and the deep
blue of her eyes never changed, as everyone said it
would.

Some days, Adam was intensely grateful that he
didn't have to think about his lost Jenny every time
he looked at his daughter. And yet, he'd wanted to
hold on to a part of her, remember her, never lose
sight of her pixie face, but sometimes now he had to
pick up the photo that sat on his bedside table in a
silver frame to remember her. Sometimes she faded
to the point that he thought perhaps her face *was*

round, like Rose's, or her nose solemnly straight; perhaps her hair had a forgotten wave, or she had moved or talked with a deliberateness that spoke of long thought.

But the sight of her face, even in the photograph, reminded him of her high cheekbones and pointy chin, turned-up nose and full yet delicate lips, always parted as she breathlessly waited for the chance to launch into speech. How often she'd had to crinkle her nose in apology, because she had been untactful or indiscreet, words flowing without thought. Even when she was hurtful, he'd found her spontaneity endearing, innocence to be treasured and guarded.

Adam had wanted the same for Rose, that she should grow up free to chatter. He wanted her to believe, always, that what she thought and felt was valued.

Instead his Rose was a quiet child, as thoughtful as her mother had been airy. Their daughter was in personality more his than Jennifer's, although she didn't look much like him, either.

He paused at the curb long enough to grab the mail from the box, then drove straight into the garage. Rose didn't stir when he turned off the engine. When he went around to unbuckle her car seat, he set the mail on the car roof. A card for her from Jennifer's parents, he noted with one corner of his attention. Good, Rose loved to get mail. A credit card statement, probably a demand for money from the utility company, the usual junk hoping he'd buy a new bedroom suite or refinance his house, and something from the hospital where Rose had been born.

The bills for Jennifer's protracted death and Rose's

birth had been horrendous. But paid, every last one of them. The insurance company, bless them, hadn't balked at a one.

The doctors and nursing staff had been compassionate, patient, gentle and kind. And he never wanted to see any of them again. Never wanted to walk those halls, smell cleansers and death. He'd go to any other hospital in the city in preference.

Unless perhaps, he thought, easing his sleepy, grumbling daughter from her car seat, Rose was seriously ill or hurt. Then he could endure the memories, for her.

In the house, Adam plopped her on the couch and put on a video. *Winnie the Pooh,* her current favorite. Hurrying to the kitchen, he took a casserole covered in plastic wrap from the refrigerator and put it straight into the microwave. High, twenty minutes, Ann had written on the sticky note attached to it. She was a gem. The kitchen sparkled, as always, and her cooking was damned good.

The one thing she didn't do was child care. She'd made that plain from the start. Her disinclination suited his reluctance to pass any part of his job as parent onto someone else, even though it would have been handy to have a housekeeper who would watch Rose when she was sick and couldn't go to day care, or to pick her up when Adam had to stay late in the office. But he'd known how easy it would be to slide from that into having Ann pick her up every day, feed her dinner, then perhaps make her breakfast and drive her to the Cottage Path Preschool, until in the end he wasn't doing much but kissing his daughter good-night.

So he and Ann had a deal: in return for weekly checks, she was like the shoemaker's elves, invisible and indispensable. Rose had scarcely even met her, and Adam and she communicated by sticky notes left on the fridge, but the house was clean and she always had dinner ready to go in the oven or microwave. Saturdays he cooked himself. Sundays, he and Rose usually went out for dinner, her choice, which meant McDonald's or Renny's Pizza Parlor, but he didn't mind.

While the microwave hummed, he thumbed through the mail and discarded three-quarters of it, setting aside the card for Rose when she was a little more alert. The envelope from the hospital Adam fingered. He was strangely reluctant to open it. Some kind of follow-up, he supposed, or maybe they wanted him on their board of governors, or…

Well, hell, find out.

He read the letter through the first time without understanding it. A distressing discovery had been made. At this point, hospital officials didn't know where to assign blame. He could be assured an investigation was under way. In the meantime, Jenny Rose Landry should undergo testing.

Testing for what?

He knew and wouldn't let himself see the sentence that began, ''Because of unusual circumstances, the mother of a girl born on the same day as your daughter in this hospital has found that she has been raising a child who is not a biological relation to her.'' The letter continued by raising the possibility that two of the six baby girls born that day had been switched in the nursery. Administrators were asking that parents agree to blood tests to determine whether this was, indeed, what had happened. He was particularly urged, because his child had been born within twenty minutes of the girl in question.

When Adam did, finally, make himself see, and when he grasped all that this could mean, anger roared through his veins, darkening his vision.

Could they really be so incompetent as to make a mistake of this magnitude? Babies were supposed to be tagged immediately so this wasn't possible! Hadn't they put a wristband on Jenny Rose while she was still bloody, still giving her first thin cry?

He hadn't seen. Adam bent his head suddenly and gripped the edge of the kitchen counter as panic whipped around the perimeter of his anger, as if it were only the eye of a hurricane.

They might not have followed the usual procedures, because the circumstances were so unusual. Respecting his grief, nurses might have carried the infant girl straight to the nursery before taking the Apgar and banding her wrist.

Even then—his anger revived—how could they screw up so royally? What did they do, leave babies lying around like Lego blocks in a preschool? Had the nurses wandered by sometime later and said, "Oh, yeah, this one must be the Landry kid?"

But the panic was more powerful than the anger, because his basic nature wouldn't let him be less than logical. If a mistake had been made that night, his daughter had all too likely been part of it. No mother or father had been hovering over her; she had never been placed at her mother's breast, and she wasn't held by her father until hours after her birth. Adam inhaled sharply, swearing. Hours? God. He hadn't thought about Jenny Rose until the next day, when his grief had dulled and he'd remembered that his wife had left a trust to him.

Only, by that time, the baby that had been lifted, blood-slick, from Jennifer's belly might have accidentally been switched with another little girl born the same hour.

Where had *her* parents been? he raged. How could they not have paid more attention? Why hadn't they noticed the switch?

He breathed heavily through his mouth. The microwave was beeping.

"Daddy?" Jenny Rose was saying from the kitchen doorway, the single word murmured around her thumb.

Think, he commanded himself. Then, *Don't think. Not now.*

"Yeah, Petunia?" He sounded almost normal.

She gave a hiccuping giggle. "Rose, Daddy! Not Petunia."

It was an old joke. "Oh, yeah," he agreed. "I knew you were some flower or other."

"Daddy, I'm hungry."

"Lucky for you, dinner's done." He hadn't put on a vegetable, but right now he didn't care.

He dished up the casserole in bowls and carried them out to the family room where he joined Rose in watching Tigger and Pooh Bear try to patch up Eeyore's problems, in their bumbling, well-meaning way.

Like the damned hospital officials.

Why contact me? Adam wondered. Was that

mother dissatisfied with the child she'd been given? Did she want to trade her in for another one? Fresh anger buffeted him. Wasn't his biological child good enough for her?

Not just his. Jennifer's.

That's when it hit him: In this other home, there might be a little girl who *did* have Jenny's pointed chin and quirky smile and ability to flit from idea to idea as if the last was forgotten as soon as the temptation of the next presented itself.

He groaned, barely muffling the sound in time to prevent Rose from wanting to know if Daddy hurt. Could she kiss it and make it better?

His Rose. By God, nobody was taking her from him.

But. Jennifer had left their baby in trust to him, and he might have lost her. He hadn't even looked at her. If only he'd seen her tiny features, he would have known, later, when they handed him Rose.

He made his decision then, as simply as that, although not without fear greater than any he'd felt since the phone call telling him his wife had been in a car accident.

Nobody would take his Jenny Rose from him. But he had to let her be tested, and if she wasn't his daughter, wasn't Jennifer's...

Well, he had to see the child who was. Find out what he could do to make her life right, from now on. Earn the trust he'd been given.

ADAM DIDN'T TAKE his Rosebud to that hospital. He didn't trust them, although he never defined the sins he thought them willing to commit. He only knew he had to protect Rose. So he took her to her own pediatrician for DNA testing. And then Adam went to the hospital with the results in his hand.

The results that had told him Jenny Rose was neither his daughter nor Jennifer's.

There, he listened to repeated expressions of regret, saw in their eyes the intense anxiety that meant officials had lawsuits dancing in their heads at night like poisonous sugarplums. He didn't quiet their fears. Hadn't made up his mind about a lawsuit. They deserved to pay until they hurt. But he didn't want or need blood money. And no justice he could exact on them would make up for what they had done to him and Rose. To his other daughter. And perhaps, to Rose's biological parents, although it wasn't yet clear to him whether they shared his agony, or were hoping to steal Jenny Rose.

They talked of an investigation. They were interviewing nurses, although it was taking time, they said, sweating. Several on duty that night no longer worked there, or even lived in Portland. But babies were always banded in the birthing room, that was hospital policy. Somebody would surely remember why, on this occasion, policy hadn't been followed.

Adam knew why it hadn't, in the case of his daughter. Although it should have been. How could the nurses and doctors not have realized how doubly precious his daughter would be to him, once the lines on the monitors flattened, once the machines were unplugged and the illusion of life was taken from his wife? Seeing his grief, how could they have been so careless?

And how the hell could two mistakes so monumental have been made on the same night?

The other mother—the hospital's representatives cleared their throats—Jenny Rose's biological mother, that is, had been hemorrhaging. Doctors had feared for her life. Had been concentrating on saving her. Thus, in this case, too, the baby had been an afterthought. Nurses had hustled her away, so she didn't distract the doctors. Neither parent had looked at her; the father had been intent on his wife, and she had been semiconscious. The mistake was inexcusable, but—ahem—they could understand how it had been made. Or, at least, how it had been set up, they said. Two bassinets next to each other in the nursery, two baby girls born within twenty minutes of each other, both brown haired. And newborns could look so much alike.

He vented his rage at this point and they quailed. But what good did his rage do? What satisfaction could he take in frightening a bunch of lawyers and administrators who hadn't been there that night, probably hardly knew what wing of the hospital housed the delivery rooms or the nursery?

None.

"The future," they suggested tentatively, and he bit back further rage even he recognized as naked fear. Nobody had said, *She's not your daughter. It won't do you any good to go to court and fight for custody. The biological parents* will *win, given that this situation is not their fault any more than it's yours.* But they were thinking it.

"All right," he said abruptly, voice harsh. "I'll meet with these other parents."

It would be only the mother, he was told. She was divorced, and the biological father was not at this point interested in custody. She was anxious to talk to him, they said. Could he please bring a photograph of Jenny Rose?

The hospital set it up for the next afternoon. Each parent could bring an attorney. Adam chose not to, although he knew it might be foolish. Right now, he just wanted to see what he was facing. He expected the worst.

The woman had begun this horror in a quest to find her natural daughter, apparently never minding the cost to the innocent child she had raised.

Adam fully expected to detest her.

A nearly sleepless night followed a half-a-dozen others. He'd forgotten how to sleep, except in nightmarish bursts from which he awakened to the sound of Rosebud screaming. But when he rolled from bed and stumbled into the hall, he invariably realized the sobs, the terror, were in his head. She slept peacefully, he would see, standing in the doorway to her room, able to make out her round, gentle face in the soft glow from her Pooh Bear night-light. He hadn't told her about any of this. She didn't know that a woman she'd never met wanted to tear her away from her home and her daddy. He might not be the best parent in the world, he thought in anguish, but she trusted him. He'd given her that much.

He left her that morning at the Cottage Path Preschool and let her cling longer than usual before he handed her, crying, to a day-care worker. Navigating Portland's old freeways like an automaton, Adam arrived at the hospital early. His eyes burned from lack of sleep, but he otherwise felt numb. He wanted to see her before she saw him, before she knew who he was. As he locked his Lexus and walked toward the entrance, he searched the parking lot for any woman who could possibly be the mother of a child the age of his daughter. Daughters. Of Jenny Rose and... Shelly. Shelly Schoening.

But of course he was denied any kind of anonymous entry. A receptionist was poised in wait to usher him onto an elevator with murmurs and more regrets and an "Oh, dear" when she got a good look at his face just before the elevator doors shut.

A lawyer took over when the doors sprang open on the third floor. "The conference room is just down this way."

They were so damned helpful, Adam was reminded of an old football trick: help your opponent up as fast as you knocked him down. Never let him rest.

The carpet up here was plush, the plants glossy, the artwork hanging on the papered walls elegant. This part of the hospital was completely divorced from the trenches, where babies were born and surgeries performed, where death happened. Up here they knew bills and statistics. He could have been in a law firm.

The conference room was smallish, holding one long table and eight chairs upholstered in an unobtrusive oatmeal. The air had that hushed quality that told him the room was well soundproofed. A place where grieving parents and spouses could be persuaded to sign away their loved ones' body parts. He might have been here, back then. He didn't remember.

Not even this air could muffle the anxiety crackling from his escort. It warned him before he saw her, sitting alone at the table, facing the door.

This slender woman with curly auburn hair had also wanted to be here early; wanted to see him before he saw her. She, too, clutched at any minor advantage.

This round, she'd won.

Poleaxed, he was barely aware of walking to the other side of the table and pulling out a chair. Sitting down, gripping the wooden arms, and looking a hungry, shocked fill.

She was Jenny Rose's mother. He would have recognized her in a crowd. A round, pleasant face, pretty rather than beautiful, a scattering of tiny freckles on a small nose, a curve of forehead and a way of tilting her head to one side…all were Rose. And that hair. God, that hair. Shiny, untamable waves, brown lit by a brushfire. He'd shampooed that hair, eased a brush through it, struggled to braid it. Kissed it.

"What," he asked hoarsely, "do you want?"

CHAPTER THREE

HE STRODE IN, just as she'd feared, a big angry man with a hard face. From the moment he sat down, she felt his hostility like porcupine quills jabbing and hooking her skin.

"What do you want?" he asked brusquely.

No preambles. No introductions. No "we're in a tough spot, aren't we?"

Through her exhaustion and dread, Lynn said, "I want this never to have happened."

His eyes narrowed a flicker.

Lynn had completely forgotten they weren't alone in the room until one of the lawyers cleared his throat. "Ms. Chanak, let me introduce Adam Landry. Mr. Landry, Lynn Chanak."

His mouth thinned, but he gave a brief, reluctant nod in acknowledgment of the formal introduction.

She swallowed. "Mr. Landry."

He looked past her. "I'd prefer to talk to Ms. Chanak alone. If—" the coldly commanding gaze touched her "—she doesn't mind."

In the flurry of objection, she caught only one phrase, which annoyed her unreasonably.

"The hospital's interest is in seeing us come up with an amicable future plan." She'd memorized that phrase: amicable future plan. Was there such a thing?

"Only we can decide on the future of our daughters. We need to get to know each other. Please."

She had hoped, heaven help her, for approval. He only waited.

The lawyers offered their intervention if it was needed. Adam Landry said nothing. Lynn stared at her hands. After a moment, the two men backed out, shutting the door behind them. The silence in their wake was as absolute as any she'd ever heard. The courage that had gotten her this far deserted her. She couldn't look up.

Her nerves had reached the screaming point when Adam Landry said at last, "Perhaps I phrased my question incorrectly. Why did you start this? Did you suspect your daughter..." he stumbled, "Shelly, wasn't yours?"

"No." At last she lifted her head, letting him see her tumult. "No. Never. It was my ex-husband. He...he didn't want to pay the child support anymore. He claimed I must have had an affair. That she wasn't *his* child. But it wasn't true! I never..." She bit her lip and said more quietly, "I wouldn't do something like that. So I took Shelly to have a blood test to prove to Brian that she was his. Only..."

"She wasn't."

"No. Which meant—" she took a deep breath "—that she wasn't mine, either. Unless you believe..."

"In immaculate conception?" His voice was dry.

"Yes. And...and I don't." She tried for a smile and failed. "I wasn't going to tell anybody. Only, then I started worrying about the other little girl. The one who was really my daughter."

The dreams wouldn't impress him, not this man. He reminded her too much of the lawyers. His gray suit cost more than she spent on food and mortgage in a month or more. His dark hair was clipped short, but by a stylist, not a barber. She could easily picture his big, capable hands gripping the leather-covered wheel of an expensive sedan, or resting on the keyboard of a laptop computer. Not changing diapers, or sifting through the sand for a seashell, or brushing away tears.

Who was raising Jenny Rose Landry? A grandmother? A nanny? Anxiety crimped her chest.

Softly she finished, "I wanted to be sure she was all right. Loved."

"And that's it. That's all you want." His tone said he didn't believe her for a second.

Lynn didn't blame him for his skepticism. Already, if she was being honest, she'd have to admit that she wouldn't be satisfied with that modest goal.

"I don't know." She held his gaze, although she quaked inside. "I'm not sure anymore. I suppose I'd like to meet her. And…perhaps get acquainted. Now that I know she doesn't have a mother."

"What makes you so sure she needs one?" Landry stood abruptly and shoved his chair back. Looming over her, hands planted on the table, he said tautly, "Is it so impossible to believe I'm an adequate parent?"

Her breath caught. She'd obviously struck a raw nerve. "No. Of course not. I'm a single parent myself, and I think I'm doing a fine job." Naturally she would say that; did she really expect him to believe her? More uncertainly, she continued, "It's just that…'' For all her rehearsing, she didn't know how to express these inchoate emotions, these wants, these needs, these fears. "She's my daughter," Lynn finished simply.

A muscle jerked in his cheek. "You suddenly want to be a mother to *my* daughter."

"Aren't you curious, too?" How timid she sounded! No, perhaps *hopeful* was the word. Could it be that he didn't want Shelly, wouldn't try to reclaim his birth daughter? That she'd never had to worry at all?

He swung away in a jerky motion and took two steps to the window. Gazing out at—what? the parking lot?—he killed her hopes in a flat, unrevealing voice. "Yes. I'm curious. Why do you think I'm here?"

Lynn whispered, "Is that all? You're just… curious?"

He faced her, anger blazing in his eyes. "My wife died and never held her baby. Now I find out that neither have I. Does 'curious' cover my reaction? Probably not. But we have to start somewhere."

He sounded reasonable and yet scared her to death. She'd hoped for a completely different kind of man. Perhaps a car mechanic, struggling to make ends meet, grease under his fingernails and kindness in his eyes. Or a small-business owner. Someone like her. Ordinary. Not a formidable, wealthy man used to having his way and able to pay to get it. Someone she could never beat, if it came to a fight.

Make sure it doesn't, she told herself, trying to quiet the renewed panic. *You can work something out. Go slowly. He may not be that interested in parenting even one girl, much less two.*

"I brought pictures," she said tentatively. "Of Shelly."

He closed his eyes for a moment and rubbed the back of his neck. Lynn could tell he was trying, too, when he said gruffly, "I brought some of Rose, too."

They stared at each other, neither moving. *I'll show you mine if you show me yours,* she thought, semihysterically. How absurd. Make the first move.

Lynn bent down and took the envelope from her purse, which sat on the floor by her feet. Slowly she opened it, her fingers stiff and reluctant. She felt as if she were sharing something incredibly private, pulling back a curtain on the small, sunny space that was her life.

He came back to the table and sat down. As she removed the pile of photos from the envelope, he pulled a matching one from the pocket of his suit jacket. When she pushed the photographs across the span of oak, he did the same with his.

Lynn reached for them, hesitated.

"She looks like you," he said, startling her.

"What?"

"Her hair." His gaze felt like a touch. "Her nose, and her freckles, and her chin. But her eyes are blue."

"Brian's…Brian's are blue."

Her hands were even more awkward now. Did she want to see the child's face? There might be no going back.

She turned the small pile of four-by-five photographs, peripherally aware that he was doing the same. And then the fist drove into her belly, bringing a small gasp from her, and Adam Landry vanished from her awareness.

She saw only the little girl, grinning at the camera. At *her*. My daughter, Lynn thought in astonishment.

He was right: Jenny Rose could have been Lynn at that age, except for the pure crystal blue of her eyes. The little girl's face was round, solemn in the other pictures Lynn thumbed through. She was still plump, not skinny and ever in motion like Shelly. The freckles—Lynn touched them, almost startled by the slick feel of photographic paper instead of the crinkling, warm nose she saw. How like hers! Rose's mouth was sweet, pursed as if she wanted to consider deeply before she rendered a judgment.

There she was in another photo, on Santa's lap, not crying, but not entirely happy, either. And younger yet, a swimsuit over her diaper, the photograph taken as she stood knee-deep in a small backyard pool filled by a hose. Why wasn't she smiling more often? Was she truly happy?

Lynn looked through the pictures over and over again, beginning to resent the meager number, hungering for more. What was she really like, this little girl who had once been part of her? What made her sad? What did she think was funny? Did she suck her thumb? Have nightmares? Wish she had a mommy?

At last, at last, she looked up, aware that tears were raining down her cheeks, that Adam Landry had made a sound. Like a blind man, he was touching one of the photographs she'd given him. His fingers shook as he traced, so delicately, her daughter's face.

She saw him swallow, saw the emotions akin to hers ravage his features.

"Jenny," he whispered.

"Does she look like your wife?"

His hand curled into a fist. "It's…uncanny."

For the first time, Lynn understood. "This must be almost worse for you, with your wife dead."

He looked up, but his eyes didn't focus; he might have been blind, or seeing something else. "Our daughter was all I had left."

She couldn't draw a breath, only sat paralyzed. He saw the wife he'd loved and lost in Shelly's face. *He would want her.* She could even sympathize with how he must feel. She had to meet Jenny Rose, answer the questions the photographs didn't, hold her, hug her, hear her voice, her laugh, feel her warm breath. She had to be part of her life.

As he would, somehow, have to be part of Shelly's life.

"I want to see her," he said, a demand not a request. "Where do you live?"

Her sympathy evaporated at his assumption that he could bulldoze her. She wanted suddenly to lie, or refuse to answer, or…but what was the point? People were easy to find, particularly one who hadn't been trying to hide. A few phone calls and he could be knocking on her door.

"Otter Beach. Over on the coast. I own a bookstore."

"Did you bring her with you?"

"No. She's…she's home. With a baby-sitter." Lynn lifted her chin. "What about Jenny Rose? Where's she?"

As impassive as his face was, still Lynn saw his initial reluctance give way to the same begrudging acceptance. "She goes to a preschool Monday through Friday. While I'm working."

"You don't have a nanny, or someone like that?"

"No." He caught on, and a flush traveled across his cheekbones. "Is that what I look like? A man who takes care of his personal life by writing a check?"

Yes. Oh, yes, that's exactly what he looked like.

But she couldn't say so, of course. "What do you do for a living?"

"I'm a stockbroker."

"It's just that it's hard to be a single parent. Most of us do everything because we have to. You don't."

"You assume I'm wealthy."

She raised her eyebrows. "Aren't you?"

"I make a decent living."

Ten or twenty times the one she made, if Lynn was any judge.

"Couldn't you afford a nanny?"

"I don't want someone else raising my child." He said it in a hard voice.

The words sliced like a switchblade between the ribs. *She* was someone else.

He swore. "I wasn't talking about you."

"No?"

"When you contacted the hospital, what did you have in mind? That we trade kids?"

Trade kids? Lynn stared at him in shock. Was that what he had in mind?

"You don't love your—" she corrected herself "—*my* daughter at all, do you?"

Neither his voice nor his expression softened an iota. "I wasn't talking about me. You're the one who started this. I'm asking what you thought you'd get out of it."

She squeezed her fingers on her lap. "What I'd get out of it? You think I'm using this mix-up to gain something?"

"Why not?" He sounded grim. "You know the hospital is prepared to pay a fortune to shut us up."

"I don't want money." Shaking, she gathered the pictures of the daughter she'd never met and pushed them heedlessly into her purse, then snatched it up and stood. "I told you what I wanted. That's all I have to say. My attorney will be contacting you about visitation rights."

"Stop," he snapped. "Sit down."

"Why?"

"We have to talk." He shut his eyes again for a moment, then opened them and let out a ragged breath. "Please."

Lynn bit her lip, then slowly sat again. "What is there to say?"

"I don't know, but these are our kids. Do we want the courts mandating their futures?"

"No." Lynn sagged. "I didn't bring a lawyer today. I hoped…"

"I hoped, too." After a long silence he sighed. "Where do you suggest we go from here?"

"I'd like to meet her. Jenny Rose. And I expect you'd like to meet Shelly." When he nodded, Lynn said fiercely, "You can't have her, you know. She's my daughter. I love her. I'm her world."

Adam Landry's hard mouth twisted. "It would

seem we have something in common. I'd fight to the death for Rose. Nobody is taking her. So you can put that right out of your mind.''

Had she imagined raising both girls? "Then what?'' she asked in a low voice.

He shook his head. "Visitation. We can take it slow.''

"Have you told Rose about me?'' Lynn asked curiously. "About what happened?''

"No. You?''

"No.'' She made a face. "It's a hard thing to explain to a three-year-old.''

"On Rose's nightstand is a picture of her mommy, who she knows is in heaven. How the hell do I introduce you?'' Bafflement and anger filled his dark eyes, so like Shelly's.

"All we can do is our best.'' How prissy she sounded, Lynn thought in distaste.

He didn't react to her sugar pill, continuing as if she'd said nothing, "It's going to scare the hell out of her if I suddenly announce she isn't my daughter at all. And, oh yeah, here's your real mommy.''

Lynn had imagined the same conversation a million times. To a child this age, parents were the only security. They were the anchor that made exploring the world possible.

"Maybe we should meet first,'' she suggested. "Would it be less scary once they know us?''

"Maybe.'' He made a rough sound in his throat. "Yeah. All right. We'll all just be buddies at first.''

She let his irony pass, giving a small nod. When he said nothing more, Lynn clutched her purse in her lap. "Shall I bring Shelly to Portland one day?''

"Why don't I come there instead? Rosebud would enjoy a day at the beach. It might seem more natural."

Rosebud. She liked that. She liked, too, what the gentle nickname suggested about this man. Perhaps he wasn't as tough as he seemed.

"Fine. Saturday?"

They agreed. He wrote down her address and phone number, then gave her a business card with his. It all felt so…mundane, a mere appointment, not the clock set ticking for an earthshaking event.

He escorted her out of the conference room and, with his hand on her elbow, hustled her past the cluster of lawyers and administrators lying in wait.

Over his shoulder, he told them brusquely, "We'll be in touch once we figure this out."

Lynn imagined the consternation brewing at their abrupt departure. Together.

She and Adam Landry rode down silently in the elevator, Lynn painfully conscious of his physical presence. She caught him glancing at her once or twice, but each time he looked quickly away, frowning at the lighted numbers over the door. Of course, he couldn't help being so imposing at his height, with broad shoulders and the build of a natural athlete. Nor could he help that face, with Slavic cheekbones and bullish jaw and high forehead that together made him handsome enough to displace Mel Gibson in a woman's fantasies.

She was glad that Shelly looked like her mother and not her father. It would have been too bizarre for words to see her daughter in this stranger's face. As though they must have had sex and she just didn't remember it, or else how could she have breast-fed his child, raised her, loved her?

Heat suddenly blossomed on her cheeks. Had he had the same thought, she wondered, about her? As though he must know her on a level deeper than he understood? No wonder he didn't want to look at her!

When the elevator doors opened, he gripped her arm again as if she wouldn't know where to go without his guidance. Habit, she gathered, when he was with a woman. "Where are you parked?"

"My car is right out in front."

He urged her forward, his stride so long she had to scuttle along like a tiny hermit crab just to avoid falling and being hauled ungracefully to her feet. Outside the hospital doors, Lynn balked.

Adam Landry looked so surprised when she pointedly removed her elbow from his bruising grip that she might have been amused under other circumstances.

"My car is right over there." She gestured. "I don't see a purse snatcher lurking. I can make it on my own, thank you, Mr. Landry."

"Adam."

"Adam," she acknowledged. "I'll see you Saturday."

The lines between his nose and mouth deepened. "We'll be there."

Neither moved for an awkward moment. Then he bent his head in a stiff goodbye and stalked away across the parking lot. With a sense of unreality she watched him go, wondering how she would have viewed him if they'd passed in the halls earlier, before she knew who he was.

I would have thought he must be a doctor, she decided. He had that air of money and command, as though he could make life and death decisions before breakfast and assume it was his right.

He would be a tough opponent, way out of her league.

Then she didn't dare let him become an opponent, Lynn thought again. Although she disliked the idea acutely, she must accommodate him, coax him, play friends—do whatever it took to stay out of court.

Her stomach roiled. It was bad enough that a divorced woman with a child had to spend the next twenty years somehow getting along with her exhusband. Now she, Lynn Chanak, had gone one better: she had to get along with a man she hadn't chosen, even if foolishly. A man she'd never married, never made love with—a total stranger. All for the sake of the child they shared.

For better or worse, they were tied together until Shelly and Rose were grown.

How bizarre did it get?

LYNN MADE THE LONG, winding trip back over the coastal range to the Pacific Ocean and home. Her instinct was to collect Shelly right away, to reassure herself by her daughter's presence that nothing would ever change, that they were a family.

But there were things she didn't want Shelly to hear, and she should make some phone calls first.

She got Brian's answering machine and started to leave a halting message, feeling like an idiot. Why was she always taken aback when the beep sounded and she had to talk onto a tape? But this time she'd barely begun when he picked up the phone.

"Yeah, I'm here."

"I, um, I told you I'd found her."

"Our daughter."

"Yes." She took a breath. "Today I saw pictures of her. She has your eyes. And my hair."

Strangely, what flitted into her mind at that moment wasn't the photo, but rather the potent way Adam Landry's gaze had touched her and the grit in his voice when he said, "She looks like you."

"How do you know this is the right kid?" her ex-husband, the true stranger, said with an audible sneer.

Closing her eyes, Lynn said evenly, "We've had DNA testing done. And you'd know, if you saw her."

He grunted. "So what do you want from me?"

"Nothing." How glad she was to be able to say that! "I thought you should know. That's all."

"Uh-huh. Well, you do what you want." His tone changed. "Hey, my call-waiting beeped. Hold on." When he came back on a minute later, Brian said, "You don't have her there, right?"

"The man who has been raising her didn't hand her over to me, if that's what you mean."

Brian being Brian, he stayed focused on all that he cared about. "Well, I'm not paying any more child support. I mean, Shelly's not my responsibility. And I'm not paying this other guy, I can tell you that."

How could she ever have married this man? How

had she deceived herself, even for a while, into thinking she loved him?

"You held Shelly and kissed her and changed her diaper. She thinks you're her daddy. After all these years, don't you love her at all?" Lynn asked, trying to understand.

"She's not my kid," he explained, as though she was an idiot not to grasp the concept immediately. "Maybe it's different for a woman. But for a guy…hey, we want to pass on our own bloodlines. I mean, sure, Shelly's a sweet kid. But she's got a dad now, right?"

"That's lucky for her, isn't it?" Lynn carefully, gently, hung up the telephone receiver.

However much she feared Adam Landry, he had to be a better father than the man she'd married.

She picked up the phone again and dialed quickly. Her mother answered on the second ring.

"Mom, I saw her picture today."

"Oh, honey," her mother said, compassion brimming in her voice. "I wish we were there. I can hardly wait to meet her. And to cuddle Shelly and make sure she knows we'll always be Grandma and Grandpa."

Just like that, tears spilled hotly from Lynn's eyes. "Oh, Mom." She sniffed. "I wish you could be here, too."

Her mother had raised Lynn alone, but she'd remarried right after Lynn left home. Hal would never feel like "Dad" to Lynn, but he was a kind man who loved to be Grandpa. Lynn was grateful her mother had found him. She only wished his work hadn't taken them to Virginia.

"For Christmas," her mother said. "I promise we'll come for Christmas."

She gave a watery laugh. "I'll hold out until then. No, really we'll be fine."

"Do you need money? We can help more than we have been, you know. If we have to, we'll take out a loan."

Lynn's mother and stepfather had loaned her the seed money for the bookstore and her mortgage on this old house. She wasn't going to take another cent from them. She knew darn well they didn't really have it.

"No, money's not the problem," she said, meaning it. "It's just…everything."

"Then tell me everything," her mother said comfortingly. "And we'll see which parts of it really count."

Lynn saw herself suddenly, a child. What grade had she been in? Third or fourth? The teacher had accused her of cheating, and she hadn't been! Goody Two-shoes that she was, she never would. She'd been humiliated and hurt that Mrs. Sanders hadn't believed her. All the way home, she'd dragged her feet. What if Mom didn't believe her, either?

She found her mother in the kitchen. Unable to speak, she began crying. Funny how clearly she remembered every sensation of her mother's embrace, the soothing warmth of her voice. "Tell me what's wrong," Mom had murmured, "and we'll see which parts of it really count."

Mom had always said that, when troubles seemed overwhelming. And her analysis invariably did help. She brought problems down to size.

Well, not even Mom was going to be able to shrink this one.

But she told her mother everything anyway, the way she always did.

THIS WAS THE SECOND toughest phone call Adam had ever had to make. Both to his parents-in-law.

He probably should have told them these past weeks what was going on, so that they could absorb the shock slowly, as he apparently had.

But he hadn't wanted to alarm them. It might all come to nothing. Jenny Rose was all they had left of their Jennifer. They always called her Jenny, and sometimes he was sorry he'd named his daughter after her mother. He'd turn, half-expecting to see Jennifer. Besides, Rosebud shouldn't have to live up to such an intense emotional demand. She wasn't her mother, and shouldn't have to fill Jennifer's shoes. Her own were enough, right?

So he hadn't told them. Unfortunately, the time had come. Some things couldn't be avoided forever.

"Mom," he said carefully, when Angela McCloskey answered the phone.

"Adam, dear! Oh, I was just thinking about you. And Jenny, of course." She chuckled. "Christmas is coming, you know."

It was barely autumn. Adam was interested in how retailers did in November and December, but he didn't do his own shopping until the last week or two before Christmas. How hard was it to take a day and fill the trunk of his car?

He made a noncommittal sound. "Mom, something has happened." At her intake of breath, he regretted his choice of words. "Rose is fine. Nothing like that. The thing is..." Oh, hell. He didn't know how to be anything but blunt, but instinct told him he needed to edge into this.

"What?" His tone had given something away. His mother-in-law sounded scared.

"There was a mix-up at the hospital."

"Not Jenny's...Jenny's ashes."

"No," he said hastily, then closed his eyes and squeezed the bridge of his nose. "Not Jenny. Rose. We've, uh, had DNA testing done. Rose isn't my biological daughter. Or Jennifer's."

"Rose isn't...I don't understand." She was pleading with him.

How well he knew the feeling. He'd begged God himself. Some prayers weren't answered.

"The other mother and I met today. We... exchanged pictures."

"You've found her, then?" Angela latched on to the idea with frightening, pitiful eagerness. "Our Jenny's little girl?"

"Yes."

"You'll be bringing her home, won't you?"

He pinched his nose again. "Mom, we're taking it slowly. This mother...she loves Shelly. That's the girl's name. Shelly Schoening. And I love Rose."

"We do, too, of course," she agreed, but he heard no conviction in her voice. "But...but Jenny's daughter. You can't leave her to be raised by someone else."

"How can I not?" he said brutally. "I wouldn't trade Rose away, even if I could."

His mother-in-law was crying now, he could hear

hitches of breath, the salty pain in her voice. "No...but our granddaughter..."

"I hope you'll still think of Rose that way."

"Jennifer was all we had."

How well he knew!

Gently he said, "I'll try to arrange for you to meet Shelly as soon as possible. The, uh, mother seems like a decent woman." He still had his doubts, but he wasn't sharing them with Angela, reeling from one blow already. "I can't imagine that she won't be willing to involve you in Shelly's life."

"Shelly! That wasn't even on Jenny's list of possible names."

"No, but it's pretty, isn't it?" he soothed. Had she even heard him?

"Yes, I suppose. Adam..."

"We have to take it slow. For the girls' sake."

"Does she know?"

"She" wasn't Rose, he guessed, anger stirring. "Neither Rose nor Shelly has been told. They're really too young to understand. We've agreed to meet, get to know the other child, so it's less frightening when they have to be told."

"You're just going to leave her?" Fixated, his mother-in-law made it sound as if he was deserting his own flesh and blood.

"I am not going to wrench her from the only home she's ever known, if that's what you mean," Adam said evenly. "We'll see what happens. You've got to be patient."

"We want to meet her."

He suppressed a profanity. "I'll try."

But he saw suddenly that he couldn't let them near

Shelly too soon. They couldn't be trusted not to tell her they were Grandma and Grandpa. And, God! When they saw her resemblance to Jennifer...

He got off the phone after a dozen more promises he didn't mean. He paced his office, anger and pity and intense frustration churning in his belly. Rose had just lost her grandparents, he knew. Angela and Rob McCloskey would say the right things, but without meaning them. He wondered about the other grandparents. Would they be as desperate to meet Rose?

His own parents wouldn't be, he knew. Not especially warm with him, they were pleasant and remote with Rose. One or the other might become interested when Rose reached school age if she displayed a real spark of artistic ability—Mom—or a powerful interest in anatomy or oceanography—Dad.

Adam made the call nonetheless. For better or worse, they were his parents.

His mother listened without interrupting.

Only when he was done did she ask, "Why didn't you say something sooner?"

He couldn't believe he'd hurt her feelings. "I wanted to be sure."

"Is going further with this a good idea?" she asked unexpectedly. "Rose is a sweet child. I don't see how this can end happily for her."

Adam assured her that he wasn't going to let anybody take his Rosebud from him. But she'd stirred a different kind of uneasiness that ate at him from the moment he set the phone down in its cradle again.

Saturday seemed a century away and, at the same

time, too close. What would he feel when he saw her, that little girl with his eyes and Jennifer's face? Would there be some instant connection? In a way, he hoped not. He didn't want anything to affect his love for Rose. To lessen it. Emotions shouldn't be so insubstantial. They shouldn't be dependent on blood tests or facial features.

It had unnerved him, though, to see how much of Rose had come from her mother. That hair. On the ride down in the elevator, it had been all he could do not to touch it, see whether the texture was the same as Rose's.

The sweetness of her face had stunned him. He'd arrived certain he would hate her, but how could he hate someone who looked like his Rosebud?

Now he didn't know what to think of her. Her ex-husband had thought her capable of having an affair, which didn't speak very well for her morals. And yet, she'd defended her Shelly as fiercely as he had his Rose. Whatever her other flaws, she seemed genuinely to love the little girl she'd raised.

Or had it all been an act?

He sank into the leather chair behind his wide bird's-eye maple desk and cursed. How could he know? How could he trust her?

Did he have any choice?

CHAPTER FOUR

OTTER BEACH REMINDED ADAM of Cannon Beach, just up the coast: charming, but self-consciously so. Inns, bed-and-breakfasts, bakeries, restaurants and shops lined the brick main street. It was one of those towns that existed for visitors, not for the people who lived there. Where did they buy groceries? he wondered. Or get tune-ups for their cars, or their teeth cleaned?

On the other hand, this was a hell of a beautiful spot. Maybe, living with this view, you didn't mind having to drive an hour just to go to a hardware store. Between shingled cottages that were now shops and restaurants, he caught glimpses of the pebbly beach and the two famous sea stacks just offshore. Bright, tailed kites rose in a brisk breeze, and beachcombers wandered. Tendrils of smoke gave away the presence of small fires shielded by driftwood. He cracked his window and breathed in the scent of the ocean.

Rose was sound asleep in her car seat, he saw with a glance in the rearview mirror. Good. He wasn't in the mood for her excitement. He'd told her only that they were going to spend the day with a friend who had a daughter Rose's age. They'd go to the beach, he promised. Maybe out for lunch. The trunk of the car was full of plastic buckets and shovels, sand molds and towels, plus an ice chest with drinks and snacks. Rose was ready for anything.

Adam wasn't. He was doing his damnedest not to think about what lay ahead, about why they were here. He didn't care about Otter Beach. If he let the crack in his self-control open, his mind filled with images, people—Shelly, Lynn, Jennifer lying in the hospital pale as marble. Questions. What would he feel when he saw Shelly? Would Rose notice how much she looked like Lynn? What would they talk about? And after today, what?

How the hell could they pull this off?

Sheer willpower allowed him to slam the crack shut. Brooding would get him nowhere.

Per her directions, Adam turned down a side street. Then right one block. He heard stirring behind him. The tires on brick had woken Rose. On the corner was an antique store, the windows filled with bottles and knickknacks. Next door, espresso was being served on the canopied sidewalk, where half-a-dozen wrought-iron tables jostled for room. Finally, the bookstore.

A simple, old-fashioned wooden sign declared, Otter Beach Books. Beneath it dangled a smaller sign, Open. The old house was painted butter-yellow with the trim deep pink—rose colored, he supposed, with awareness of the irony. The white picket fence was a nice touch. Yellow and white roses, fading now, scrambled over a broad arch. He could only see part-way up the brick walk, which led between tangles of asters and other flowers he didn't know to the porch steps. He did recognize the hollyhocks leaning drunkenly against the clapboard wall of the house. His grandmother had grown ones just like them.

Gravel crunched as he turned the Lexus into the driveway and joined one other car in the slot. Business didn't appear to be booming, or, come to think of it, most shoppers probably came on foot.

Ignoring the dread that sat like a heavy meal in his belly, he turned off the engine. "Hey, Rosebud, we're here."

She rubbed her eyes and swiveled her head. "Where's the beach? Is there sand?"

"I bet we can find some. In a few minutes. This is where my friend lives. She owns a bookstore."

"Oh." Rose momentarily gazed at the garden. "There's Tigger."

Good God, she was right. A garden statue of Pooh Bear's buddy Tigger looked ready to bound over a cluster of pansies.

"Hey, maybe Pooh's there, too."

She began to struggle. "I want to get out! I want to see!"

"Hold your bouquet, kiddo!"

He went around the car, aware of the house behind him and the small-paned windows. Was she looking out, even now? He was unsettled to realize that the *she* he imagined with such disquiet wasn't Shelly.

Well, that was natural, Adam told himself as he unbuckled his daughter. Lynn Chanak was the one who shared his emotional turmoil. The one who understood, the one who might turn out to be an enemy. He and she—Adam made a sound in his throat that brought a single curious glance from Rose before she scrambled under his arm and out of the car. His mouth twisted. He and Lynn Chanak were going to have one strange relationship.

Rose was quivering with eagerness, taking everything in, but she waited for him as she knew to do in a parking lot. When he slammed the car door, she snatched his hand. "Come *on,* Daddy."

A touch on Tigger's rough, concrete head, and Rose tugged her father under a second white-painted arch thick with huge blue saucer-shaped flowers—clematis?—and into the small front garden.

In its heart was a tiny brick-paved courtyard with a birdbath, a garden seat and Pooh Bear peeking shyly from a tangle of another bluish-purple-flowered perennial Adam didn't recognize. Rose squatted in front of Pooh.

Maintaining this garden must take time, but it was damn fine marketing, Adam decided. Any passerby would be seduced into stepping beneath the rose arch. Once that far, why not go in? The mood was set, the imagination captured. Lynn Chanak was a smart woman. It was a shame the store wasn't on the main drag.

"Let's go in," he said, suddenly impatient to have the first meeting over. Shelly would just be another little girl; he wouldn't feel anything but a sense of obligation and perhaps regret. Maybe he and Ms. Chanak would agree to leave things as they were. Stay in touch. He'd help out if she needed it. With her ex out of the picture, she wouldn't be able to put Shelly through college on the income from a bookstore, for example.

Someday Jennifer's parents would have to meet

Shelly, he remembered with a frown. But he could explain, refuse to tell them where she was.

"I like books," Rosebud told him slyly as they started up the steps. "I'm tired of all the ones I have."

Adam's mood lightened, even as that lump stayed, grew, in his stomach. "Then pick out a couple of new ones before we go to the beach. They'll give us something to remember the day by."

"Is...Shelly nice?" She stumbled over the name, although she'd asked the same question half-a-dozen times. "Will she like me?"

"What's not to like?" He scooped her up and settled her on his hip, liking the idea of walking in the door with her plainly claimed. *Mine.* "And I've never met Shelly."

A bell rang when he opened the door to a room filled with warmth and clutter and bright colors: a bookstore the way they were meant to be. Dark wood shelves, tables heaped with books, a comfy rocker in what had been a sunporch, a playhouse...and at least a couple of customers browsing, including a teenage boy with tattoos and a pierced eyebrow.

He heard her voice first. "Mary, can you help this gentleman find..."

They saw each other at the same moment. The words she'd intended to speak trailed off. He had a violent moment of reaction to that damned resemblance to Rose. After a moment, he recognized it as anger. He hated seeing his daughter all grown up in a woman he didn't know.

After that first shocked instance, Adam realized she was no longer looking at him. Her gaze devoured

Rose. The book she held slipped from her hand and slapped to the floor. Heads turned, but Lynn Chanak kept staring.

"Daddy?" Rose said uncertainly. "Is that lady your friend?"

Friend. The way she was looking at his daughter scared the hell out of him.

"Yeah." He swallowed. "This is my friend Lynn. Lynn, my daughter Rose."

"I..." Lynn couldn't seem to tear her eyes from the child. "I'm happy to meet you, Rose."

In a sudden bout of shyness, Rose buried her face in his neck. She whispered, "Why is she looking at me so funny?"

"Maybe," he whispered, too, "because your hair is the same color as hers. How many people have curls like my Rose?"

She giggled, but shakily, because even her three-year-old intuition knew something was up.

God, he thought with gritted teeth. They looked so much alike. Everyone in the store must notice. They probably all thought he was the proprietor's ex-husband, and this her daughter. How was she going to explain the resemblance?

"Rose is anxious to meet Shelly," he said, too loudly. He didn't so much want to meet his daughter, as he wanted this woman to quit staring at Rose as if she were royalty. Or, hell, a baboon. Something she might never see again.

"I..." Lynn blinked and turned her head, cheeks pale and her eyes unfocused. "I...I'm not sure..."

He glanced around and saw that the shoppers had gone about their business. A young woman behind the counter was ringing up a purchase. At the same moment, a giggle wafted from the sunporch.

"I'm here, Mommy! Remember?"

The playhouse. It must be two-story, because framed in an upper window of the fake castle was a little girl's face, flushed with delight because her presence had been a secret.

The rock that had been sitting in his stomach was suddenly a boulder, craggy and painful. It pressed his lungs until he couldn't breathe.

Rose was wriggling, so he set her down without tearing his gaze from the child. He felt his lips move, knew they formed a name: *Jennifer.*

Even the voice. Sounding confident and open, she invited Rose to come up. Shyly his daughter went, bending to crawl across the mock drawbridge and inside. As if Rose couldn't figure out how to climb a ladder, Shelly gave her directions and told her what she'd find up at the top and how Mom had said they'd go to the beach and did Rose like hot dogs 'cuz Mom said maybe that's what they could have for lunch. The words flowed like a stream over stones, making a kind of song, and all as inevitable as water finding its way downhill.

Jennifer, he thought in agony.

She peeked out the window at him, her face, alight with laughter, looking for all the world like a nine-teenth-century children's book illustration of an elf perched on a flower stem. Shelly's ears stuck out just a little. Jennifer had hated hers, though he had thought them cute. Just like Jennifer's, Shelly's face narrowed from high cheekbones to a pointy chin, and just like Jennifer's, her eyes shimmered with amusement and devilment.

"It's worse than seeing the picture, isn't it?" the woman beside him said softly.

Taking a ragged breath, he turned his head and met Lynn Chanak's eyes. "God."

She nodded.

"Do you see yourself?" he asked, keeping his voice low.

"I suppose." Like him, she gazed toward the playhouse. Neither girl was visible in the window, although whispers and laughter drifted out. "She does look like pictures of me at that age, but I don't exactly remember my face in the mirror from when I was three, so it's not quite as big a shock as Shelly must be for you."

He fumbled for his wallet and, with shaking hands, took out a photo of his dead wife and handed it to Lynn.

She looked at it for a long moment. When she lifted her head, her gray-green eyes were misty. "She was beautiful."

"Shelly is going to look like her."

A tear dropped, shimmering, from her lash. She wiped it from her cheek. "Oh, I wish..."

"This hadn't happened?"

She squeezed her eyes shut, as if willing back further tears. "No," Lynn said finally. "Because then I wouldn't have Shelly, and she's my life. No, I was going to say, I wish we'd never found out. But now..." She gazed again toward the playhouse where first one girl's laughing face, then the other, popped up. "But now, I'm not so sure."

"Jennifer's parents want to meet her," he heard himself say.

Lynn squeezed her hands together without looking at him. "I thought they might. But how can we do that, without Shelly knowing who they are?"

"I told them they might have to wait."

She smiled with obvious difficulty. "Thank you."

"What about your parents? And your ex-husband's?"

"My mother and stepfather love Shelly, and I'm sure they'll love Rose, if you give them the chance. They'll support whatever we decide. Brian's parents…" She hesitated. "I don't know. At the moment, he's washed his hands of the whole thing. My pregnancy wasn't planned, and…" She swallowed whatever she had been going to say, perhaps suddenly aware that she had been going to reveal too much that was private to a relative stranger. "Well," she said, a little awkwardly. "Certainly there's no rush, where they're concerned. Right now, it's just Shelly and me."

"Not anymore," he murmured.

Her startled glance became troubled, but she said nothing, although the small creases stayed between her brows. He understood how she felt. They were both between a rock and a hard place.

"Does Rose want to go to the beach?"

Adam cooperated with her desire to put their visit on conventional ground. "She can't talk about anything else."

"Then shall we?" Lynn nodded toward the register. "I have someone to mind the shop for me."

Belatedly he noticed that she wore jeans, faded

canvas sneakers and a T-shirt the color of the Aegean Sea. Her hair was gathered into a ponytail, making her look absurdly young, with that round face and sprinkling of freckles. The fact that he couldn't help noticing her full breasts and flare of hip was a useful reminder that her husband had suspected her of infidelity. He couldn't let her resemblance to Rose disarm him.

"Rose wanted to pick out a couple of books first," he said. "Maybe I'll do it for her. Any suggestions?"

Lynn led him into the children's area and offered several of Shelly's favorites.

"We've read this about two hundred times," he said, setting one aside. "I liked it the first hundred."

She grinned, her nose crinkling. "Yeah, me, too. But, hey, most of them wear thin after five or ten repetitions."

Damn it, under other circumstances he'd have been attracted to her, Adam realized in dismay. *Don't,* he told himself sharply. Talk about messy.

He grunted and probably glowered, and pretended to concentrate on the book he was flipping through. After a moment Lynn turned away and began straightening a rack of paperbacks for middle-grade readers, but he didn't forget her presence. He'd never be able to forget her, he thought grimly. How could he? She was the mother of his daughter. Of both his daughters, one way or another.

How many men could say that about a woman they'd never touched?

Irritated with himself at a thought that nudged uncomfortably close to sexual awareness, Adam raised his voice. "Rosebud, you want to go to the beach?"

He heard whispers above his head. Then Rose said, "Okay, Daddy. If Shelly can go."

"You bet." Lynn smiled as if she hadn't noticed his withdrawal.

The sounds of scrambling within eventually produced both girls, his Rose in her pink flowered overalls with matching shirt, and Shelly in a bright red dress—he thought it was a dress, made out of T-shirt fabric—over purple leggings.

"I know, I know," Lynn murmured, evidently seeing his astonishment. "She wants to dress herself, and mostly I let her."

"Ah." Rose accepted what he laid out. A difference in temperament? Or was Rose, as he feared, immature for her age? God! What if there was even something wrong with her?

But her language was well developed, he reminded himself.

"Hey, kiddo," he said. "You still want some books?"

She approved his selection and added two more with scarcely a glance inside the covers. He carried the pile to the register and let Lynn ring it up, not even wincing at the total.

"Let me give them to you at cost," she offered.

He shook his head brusquely. "Don't be ridiculous. This is your business. If I weren't buying them here, it would be somewhere else."

"I thought…" Her expression closed. "Thank you. No, I don't need to see ID."

She was a stranger, he told himself. He hadn't hurt her feelings in some way he didn't understand. How could he? She didn't have the power to hurt his.

Lynn smiled brightly as she came out from behind the counter. "Shelly, Rose, let's go use the bathroom before we head off." She raised her eyebrows at him. "Adam?"

"No. If you don't mind taking Rose..."

Her sidelong glance reeked of irony. Oh, no. She wouldn't mind taking his daughter. He couldn't help a minor feeling of loss when Rose willingly took Lynn's hand and went without a look back.

They returned hand in hand, the pretty woman, his Rosebud and Shelly, so much like Jennifer that his heart spasmed again.

His face revealed too much once more, because Lynn said in an achingly gentle voice, "Shelly, this is Rose's daddy."

"Hi, Shelly." He sounded gruff to his own ears. "I see you have a sweatshirt. Rose had better get hers from the car."

"I have buckets, too," Rose confided. "An' shovels, an' everything."

"Wow." Lynn's smile was wide and unaffected for the girls, tentative for him. "Then how about we go make some sand castles? Or chase crabs, or hunt for shells and agates?"

She and Shelly had both tied sweatshirts around their waists. He grabbed sweaters from the car for Rose and himself, as well as the beach paraphernalia.

Rose took his hand and they walked behind Lynn and Shelly the two blocks to the public pass-through to the beach. Rose stared at the tourists and shop windows. A toy store brought her up on tiptoes as they passed. Adam watched the pair ahead, the woman's springy auburn ponytail, the child's sleek brown one just as familiar to him. The way Shelly danced instead of trudging obediently along as Rose did. He loved every placid, thoughtful bone in Rosebud's body, but something in him ached at the sight of Jennifer reincarnated, a sprite in constant movement.

All that distracted him from this child was the sway of Lynn Chanak's hips, her faded jeans snug, or the sight of her pale, slender nape when she bent her head to listen to the little girl.

Dressed like this, she seemed not so much young as vulnerable, Adam decided. Here was who she was, how she lived. In letting him come to her home, she had bared herself for him, in a way. Their meeting at the hospital had had an anonymity, a sense of the impersonal, that was lost now.

At the ocean, broad concrete steps led from a paved boardwalk down to the pebbly beach. Once at the bottom, Shelly let go of her mom's hand and spun eagerly.

"Come on! I'll show you the best places."

Rose's grip tightened on her dad's hand. "The birds won't hurt me, will they?" she asked uncertainly.

Seagulls gathered only feet away, their beady eyes searching for handouts.

"Nah." He waved his arm, and the nearest hopped backward. "See? They're not interested in you. They want a peanut butter sandwich."

She giggled a little weakly. Instead of prying her fingers loose, he walked with her and Shelly, Lynn trailing. The gulls stayed behind, hoping for bread thrown from the diners eating outside just above.

At a safe distance from the scary birds, Rose proved willing to let go and join Shelly. The adults strolled behind as the girls ran ahead, scrambling up a favorite driftwood log and jumping over and over again to the forgiving pebbles. Finally Shelly took Rose's hand and led her onto slick rocks where they crouched to stare into a tide pool.

As Adam looked over their shoulders, Shelly was saying earnestly, "We can't take anything out. Sometimes I touch. See?" She dipped her hand into the cold water and let a swaying anemone brush her fingers. Her face scrunched up. "But if you take them home, they get icky. They stink and stuff. So we leave 'em."

Rose nodded, not wanting to admit she didn't have a clue what her new friend was talking about. Not two minutes later, she slipped over to her father.

"Why do things get icky if we take 'em home, Daddy?" she asked, not bothering to hush her piercing voice.

Death and decomposition was not what he wanted to talk about.

"Because those are sea creatures. They can't live out of the sea. Just like we need air, they need water."

"But they could take a bath with me." Her mouth was pursed with perplexity.

Lynn stepped forward. "They need this *special* kind of water. See? Put a drop on your tongue?"

Rose stuck her tongue out, then made a horrible face at the taste. When she could speak, she exclaimed, "They want *that* kinda water?"

"Just that kind." Lynn smiled at her. "And no

matter how hard we try, we can't make the bathwater right for them.''

''Oh.'' Rose thought it over. After a moment, her forehead smoothed. She nodded and went back to her friend, squatting beside her to stare down into the tidepool.

Adam stayed near Rose as Shelly led the way next across mussel- and barnacle-encrusted rocks to a blowhole. Each incoming wave rushed beneath the rock in a froth of white, sending a thin jet shooting upward through the hole like a geyser. Here the roar of the surf surrounded them and spray hung in the air, dampening their hair and filling their nostrils and lungs with salty wet air.

''Ooh,'' breathed Rose, clutching Adam's hand and watching with wondering eyes.

Eventually they made their way to a tiny cove of gritty sand between arms of basalt worn by the pounding of the waves. Adam dropped to his knees and helped build a sand castle, grander than anything the girls could have done alone.

He wondered wryly whether he was trying to make points with Lynn by showing what a great parent he was, or whether he was just avoiding having to talk to her.

She gave no sign she noticed either way. Instead, under her daughter's orders Lynn willingly ferried water by the bright plastic bucketful from the foamy fingers of surf. At the sound of her laughter, Adam sank back on his heels and watched her squelch back toward the construction site, her sneakers and the hems of her jeans soaking wet.

Like Rose, she wasn't a chatterbox, and her face

didn't have Jennifer's animation, but it was bright and good-humored.

"The wave got me," she announced. "I think the tide is coming in."

Sure enough, each wave licked onto dry sand and inched toward the tide pools.

"Let's dig a moat," Adam declared. "We can watch the water rush around the castle."

"Good idea." Lynn dropped to her knees and began hollowing out a trench with her hands, sand flying.

"What's a moat?" Shelly asked.

Adam grinned at her. "It's filled with water to keep the invaders away from the castle walls."

"Oh. What's 'vaders?"

"Um." Almost unconsciously, he looked to Lynn for help.

"Invaders are the enemy," she said in mock growl. "Like Ian and Ron at your play group, when they want to grab the dolls and run over them with their trucks."

Shelly's chocolate-brown eyes widened. "I don't like *them*." She began scooping sand. "Come on, Rose. We don't want no 'vaders in *our* castle!"

They stayed long enough to see the water fill the moat but not long enough for the girls to watch their magnificent castle crumple. By that time, the girls were getting tired anyway. When Rose whimpered after her foot slipped in the loose pebbles, Adam swung her up onto his shoulders.

Her mood revived. "Giddap, Daddy!" Her heels drummed his chest. "You're my horsie, Daddy."

Shelly stopped in her tracks. "I want you to be my horsie, Mama."

"Only if I can take you piggyback, punkin." For a fleeting second, Lynn's eyes met Adam's, revealing a complex of emotions he didn't know how to read. "I'm not big enough to lift you onto my shoulders."

Had he somehow made her feel inadequate?

Shelly's mouth trembled. "But I wanna ride like *her*."

"Her daddy's bigger than I am."

Shelly's expression became calculating. "Maybe *he* could give me a ride."

"But he's already carrying Rose—"

"Tell you what," Adam interjected. "We'll switch back and forth. Okay, Daisy?"

"'kay, Daddy," Rose agreed. "But I'm not Daisy."

He bounced her a couple of times. "Nope. Guess not. You have too many petals."

She giggled.

Shelly climbed onto her mother's back. "Why'd he call her Daisy? That's not her name. Her name is Rose."

"Her daddy is just teasing," Lynn explained. "It's like me calling you Belly when I tickle you."

"Oh." She booted her heels into her mom's hips. "Giddap, horsie!"

Halfway up the beach, Adam stopped. "Okay, Shelly Belly, your turn."

"Daddy!" Rose whined.

"Nope. Fair's fair. Besides, you want to try out the other horse, don't you?"

Rose being Rose, she didn't say any more when

he lowered her to the sand, but she clutched his leg, the afternoon's acquaintance not enough to let her go to this lady. Shelly, on the other hand, had already taken a handful of his shirt and was demanding, "Up! You're my horsie, now."

Lynn's smile never wavered as she said, "Do you think we can beat them to the stairs, Rose?"

But, damn, she had to hurt, looking at her own daughter none too eager to trust her. Never mind that Rose had no idea. He knew how Lynn must feel, because something in him had soared at Shelly's eagerness to climb onto his shoulders.

"I'll tell you what," he said. "Let me lift you up, Rosebud."

He set her on Lynn's back, where she had no choice but to wrap her arms around Lynn's neck. In the breeze both had lost tendrils of hair from their ponytails, and the two auburn heads looked so much alike, his heart squeezed. They looked up, reminding him of an advertisement for a skin-care product, maybe, their complexions both creamy with the delicate scattering of freckles, the shape of their mouths so much alike, even their eyes, although Lynn's were green and Rose's blue. Mother and daughter.

For an instant, he couldn't breathe.

"Up!" Shelly demanded again.

And a hint of mischief sparkled in Lynn's eyes.

"Race you to the steps!" she announced, and took off.

"Hey!" Adam protested. "No fair!"

She had a good ten-yard head start by the time he'd swung his daughter—his heart cramped again—

onto his shoulders and grabbed Rose's bucket and shovel that he'd earlier set down.

"Go! Go!" Shelly screamed in delight.

She was so light, as fine of bone as her mother, a wiry little bundle of energy. She twined her fingers in his hair and bounced, urging him on the whole way, her shrieks happy and uninhibited.

Shelly wasn't his Rosebud, but she was his, too.

He almost caught them, but not quite. Rose was quietly pleased by the victory, Lynn's face was alight with laughter, and Shelly giggled as he swung her onto the boardwalk.

"Mommy's fast, huh?"

"Yep," he agreed. "You've trained her well."

Shelly thought that was hysterically funny.

Adam had a flash of memory. Jennifer in jeans and a white T-shirt, lying back on their bed with her arms flung above her head, laughing uncontrollably until tears came in her eyes. He didn't remember what was so funny. Only that he had followed her down onto the bed and kissed her until…

He almost groaned. To hold Jenny again. To touch her like that. To see her laugh. He hadn't recalled her so vividly in a long time.

He had needed her daughter—*their* daughter—to bring his Jennifer back to him.

Any thoughts of maintaining his distance after today were gone. He hoped Lynn saw it the same way. He didn't want to hurt her; damn it, he saw a reflection of his own chaotic emotions in her eyes. Worse yet, he saw Rose in her.

But he couldn't let Shelly go, any more than he could let Rosebud go.

He was going to be Daddy to both girls, whatever it took.

"How about if we go get that hot dog you were promised?" he said easily, and, with only a small pang, took Rose's small hand and let Shelly go to her mother.

CHAPTER FIVE

HOW LONG HAD IT BEEN since she had sat beside the phone waiting for a man to call? Years. Eons, Lynn thought wryly.

And this was more like being a teenager, when she'd desperately wanted to pick up the phone and hear *his* voice, and yet was terrified every time it rang that he might be on the other end of the line. She'd never felt at ease socially, never known the right thing to say. If the boy she had a crush on called, she'd blow it, Lynn had been certain during those difficult years. Her mother had said comfortably that she'd learn.

Lynn scowled at the silent telephone on the wall. *Yeah, Mom?* she demanded. *Then how come I haven't?*

This was different, of course. She wasn't interested in *him.* It was Rose, sweet, shy Rose, whose voice Lynn hankered to hear. But she couldn't see Rose without going through her daddy, which Lynn fiercely resented even as she felt as protective about Shelly.

Seeing her natural daughter once had seemed as if it might be enough, back when they planned the one-day visit. Just knowing that she was healthy and loved...

She made a sound in her throat and prowled the kitchen. Silence from the bedroom, where Shelly napped.

Enough? Sure. Like that first piece of chocolate would be enough. Like you could eat three potato chips and then put the bag away.

A taste was worse than never having.

Feeling Rose's chubby arms around her neck and hearing her throaty giggle in Lynn's ears had been heaven. Rose and Shelly had taken to each other immediately, and yet they were so different. Lynn had applauded but never understood Shelly's boldness and flamboyance. In Rose she saw herself, not because of the freckles or the hair, but because Rose hung back when a braver soul forged forward, because Rose's hand clung to Daddy's instead of letting go, because Rose wanted oh so desperately to be sure she would be safe before she leaped.

Lynn understood all of that. She had been—was—afraid. Her own mother had had to boot her gently out of the nest. When the time came, Shelly would fly without hesitation. Rose would wobble, come back, flap her wings and try again.

Lynn wanted to be there to coax and urge and comfort, just as her mother had been for her.

It wasn't as if Rose had another mother, she thought defensively. Then she might have made herself let go, though it would have hurt terribly. But Rose needed her. She was certain of that.

Oh, why didn't the man call?

When he hadn't on Sunday, she had figured he wanted to wait until Rose wasn't around. Or perhaps he needed to think. But now it was Monday, and there wasn't a reason in the world that he couldn't phone from his office. Why wait? Why not settle this now?

Perhaps she should call him. The anxiety that immediately swelled at the very thought annoyed her terribly. There she was, frightened of doing something straightforward. She wanted to talk to him. Why *not* call?

She didn't reach for the phone. After buckling Rose into her car seat and circling the car to where Lynn and Shelly stood, Adam Landry had said, "I'll call." His eyes had met Lynn's; she had nodded. Of course they had to talk. More than ever, they had to talk.

I'll call.

Why should the ball be in his court? She had rights equal to his.

But, oh, she didn't want to pick up the phone. She didn't want to catch him at a bad moment, hear that brusque, impatient note in his voice. She wanted him to be the one calling, because he was eager. She imagined him conciliatory, agreeable.

Was he ever, except with his daughter?

Lynn sighed and considered making blueberry muffins as a surprise for Shelly when she woke from her nap. It would give her something to do.

The telephone rang.

Lynn stared at it, a lump clogging her throat. On the fourth ring, she snatched it up before her answering machine could do so.

"Hello?"

"Lynn, this is Adam."

"Oh." Brilliant. "Yes. Um, hello."

No "how are you?" Or "we had a great day, didn't we?"

Instead, he said straight out, "I want to see Shelly again. I'd like to keep seeing her."

Relief washed over her even as worry began its familiar niggle. To see Rose, she needed him to want to visit Shelly. But how far would he go? What if he went to court for custody, claimed he would be the best parent for both girls?

She'd borrow the money from her parents and fight him, of course. Tooth and nail.

"I'd like to keep seeing Rose, too," she said.

A pause ensued. She wondered if he had the same mixed feelings. Or was he so confident of his ability to win that he didn't consider her a threat?

"It was awkward, all of us together," he said at last. "Maintaining a pretense."

"Yes," she agreed, but with a thrum of hurt she chose not to examine. "Do you have another suggestion?"

"That's why I called. What if we were to take turns dropping one of the girls off for the day? Maybe work our way up to weekends? For now, surely you could spend a Saturday shopping or seeing a movie or something in Portland?" The last was thrown out carelessly; why should he care what she did? "When I drop Rose off, I could take a drive up the coast, have lunch in Cannon Beach, maybe. Just to give you time with her."

"Won't they think it odd, after we said we were friends?"

"We'll make excuses." A hint of impatience

sounded in his voice. Obstacles weren't to be considered.

"Yes. All right," Lynn said. "We might have to make the visits short at first. Shelly has never played at a friend's house for more than a couple of hours at a time."

"Rose is used to day care."

He spoke arrogantly, and yet she heard something. Uncertainty? Did he remember Rose's clinging hand? Her reluctance to climb onto the strange lady's back, even after several hours spent building a sand castle together?

"Does it have to be a weekend?" Lynn asked.

"Does it have to be?" The surprise in Adam's voice cleared. "I suppose leaving the bookstore is difficult on weekends."

"Saturday and Sunday are my busiest days. And I have to pay someone else to be there when I'm gone. The store is closed anyway on Monday and Tuesday. Later in the winter, on Wednesday, too."

"I suppose I could take some Mondays off," he said thoughtfully. "Sure, why not? Rose would be thrilled to stay home from day care."

Aha. So Rose might be "used" to day care, but was not necessarily enthusiastic.

"Shall we say next Monday?" he continued. "Can you bring Shelly here?"

"Certainly." They might have been arranging a transfer of funds or the repair of an appliance. She reached for a notepad. "Tell me how to find your place."

A moment later, she hung up, the plans firmed, a map drawn. She would take Shelly to play at Rose's house. Go shopping herself for a few hours. It would give her a chance to see Rose briefly, and in return Adam would bring Rose here the next Monday.

It sounded simple enough, but a gnawing hole in her stomach told her simple didn't mean easy. She was going to hate leaving Shelly with her father. Not being there to see what he said and did.

What if, after a few visits, Shelly wasn't happy to see her mom after the day spent with Daddy? What if she wanted to stay, and he encouraged her? What if Shelly always had to go there, because Rose was too shy to be left here?

Lynn squeezed her eyes shut on a burning sensation and thought, *what if I die of loneliness, on one of those Mondays?*

"ARE WE ALMOST THERE?" Shelly's neck stretched as she tried to peer ahead.

"I think so." Lynn glanced again at the directions and address that lay on the seat beside her. The neighborhood was reinforcing her worst fears. Adam Landry had money. Plenty of money.

What chance would she have if he took her on?

"There," she said, spotting the numbers on the mailbox. A paved driveway led onto wooded grounds. Rhododendrons grew under mature cedars and hemlocks and firs. She caught a glimpse of a tumbling stream and an arched stone bridge.

Money.

Ahead, the house seemed to grow out of the hillside and the forested land, the cedar siding and shake roof blending in, the several levels and the rock work around the foundation somehow disguising the sheer size of the structure. Lynn suddenly imagined Rose wandering in the middle of the night, lost and scared, trying to find her daddy's bedroom.

Don't be silly, she told herself sharply. Rose seemed loved and secure. Her bedroom would be near his. Surely.

Lynn admired the flower beds filled with shade-loving plants like hostas and Solomon's seal that flowed into the natural landscape as if God himself was the gardener. She couldn't quite see Adam Landry on his knees in the dirt pulling weeds. Even if he had built a sand castle with gusto. No, he'd have a gardener, as well as a housekeeper.

The car rolled to a stop. "Well," she said, trying to sound hearty. "We're here."

"Oh." Shelly's enthusiasm seemed to have dwindled. She stared at the house, her voice small. "I don't see Rose."

"She doesn't know we're here yet." Lynn attempted a cheerful smile. "Did you see the bridge? I'll bet Rose will show you around her woods."

"Like I showed her my beach."

"Right." Except, these woods really *were* Rose's.

Shelly unbuckled her own car seat and inched forward. "Can we go see Rose?"

"You betcha."

They didn't reach the front door before Adam came out with Rose holding his hand. Today he wore crisp khaki slacks and a polo shirt with a tiny—and probably expensive—emblem on the pocket. What he looked was handsome, unapproachable and not quite real: the wealthy professional pretending to relax.

Lynn had felt more comfortable with him when he wore jeans and a T-shirt.

The two girls murmured, "Hi," and hung their heads.

Adam's dark gaze met hers. "Come on in."

She wondered if he would have invited her at all if their daughters had gone racing right off to play.

Inside the carved-wood door, a slate entry led to a large living room with a wall of windows, pale nubby carpet and warm, comfortable leather furniture. A few antiques lent character to a room that might have been too colorless and modern for Lynn's tastes. She loved the wool tapestry that hung on one wall, a dark African mask on another.

The elegance of the room made her confidence plummet another inch.

"What a beautiful room."

"Thank you." He barely glanced at her. "How are you, Shelly?"

"Fine," she whispered.

"Rose has been excited about having you come."

Shelly peeked at her friend but said nothing. Rose hid behind Daddy's leg.

He tried again. "Would you like Rose to show you her room?"

Shelly didn't let go of Lynn's hand. In her piercing voice, she asked, "Mommy, are you gonna go?"

"That's the plan." She sounded as bright and fake as a dinner-plate dahlia, Lynn thought ruefully. "Remember? We talked about it. I'm going to do some mom things. Shop, and call a friend. I'll bet you won't miss me for a second."

"Yes, I will," Shelly said clearly.

"Not once you start to play—"

"*I* like to shop, too."

Out of the corner of her eye, Lynn saw Rose's face start to crumple. A crease deepened between Adam's brows.

"Honey," she said gently, "I know you'll have fun with Rose. We don't want to disappoint her."

Shelly held her hand in a death grip. This time she whispered, "Can't you stay, Mommy?"

God help her, she was pleased that Shelly *hadn't* dashed off without caring whether her mother left. How petty could you get? These visits *had* to work! Darn it. She was an adult. She owed it to both children to be selfless.

Crouching, Lynn looked her daughter in the eye. "Honey," she began.

Adam interrupted, "Maybe I can talk your mom into staying for a while. Rose and I planned a nice lunch. You'll join us, won't you, Lynn?"

Oh, right, she thought. *Now* be cordial. Pretend this "dumping her daughter for the day" thing was her idea. His easy, "of course you're welcome" voice made her the villain.

Torn between her daughter's pleading brown eyes and her own flash of anger, she couldn't speak for a moment. Just as well, because the pause gave her time to realize that he was right: they had to pretend. And, by God, she could do it as well as he could!

"I'd love to," she said, smiling. "Maybe first Rose would show me her bedroom."

Her gaze met his briefly, with a chill on both sides that neither of their voices revealed. *You don't want me in your house,* her eyes said, *but she's my child.*

I'll sit on her bed and admire her toys and coax her into friendship, whether you like it or not.

Sure you can, his said in return. *Today. Because the girls have left me no choice. But don't get your hopes up, lady. We're not setting a precedent here.*

"Good idea," he said with the same charm he'd show a new client. "Rosebud, I'll bet Lynn will enjoy seeing your dolls."

The floors were hardwood beyond the living room, the halls spacious. She caught glimpses into other rooms: one that held a dark big-screen television and a bank of stereo equipment, a formal dining room, an office with a huge leather chair and a state-of-the-art computer and a fax machine that hummed as it rolled out pages. Rose led the way, Shelly gaining enough confidence to peer through doorways and finally let go of her mom's hand when Rose said, "My bedroom is that one."

All the way, Lynn felt Adam behind her with a prickling, disquieting awareness. *In the presence of mine enemy.*

What she hated most was the knowledge that her reaction was partly sexual. Adam Landry would have been the kind of boy she'd watched from afar in middle school and high school and college. With that build, he must have been an athlete. With his confidence, he was probably the student body president. Petite, sparkly blondes would have hung on his arm, not quiet, shy girls with difficult hair.

This man was that boy all grown up, and she was no more capable of exchanging snappy repartee or sultry looks than she'd been then.

Worst of all, the man he'd grown into was obviously capable of kindness and restraint and intense love. *Then,* she had told herself the popular boys were shallow. Her mother had agreed, hugged her and told her to look for a late-bloomer, they were the best kind.

How disconcerting to discover that she still secretly wished he would notice her. Not as if she really truly wanted him, but because his attention would mean she had arrived. She could be one of those girls who casually slipped an arm around any boy's waist, who laughed with him and boldly asked him to dance and assumed she would have a date on Friday night.

No, it wasn't that she wanted Adam Landry to share her unnerving awareness. Heaven forbid. He was the enemy. He only represented something to her. He awakened inchoate girlish longings she'd thought long dead. He was a symbol.

She grimaced when the girls weren't looking her way and wondered for the forty-second time: Why couldn't Shelly's birth father have been a nice plumber with a tub of his own?

"See? This is my room," Rose said shyly.

"Ooh," Shelly breathed, and Lynn's heart sank anew.

Right behind her daughter, she stepped into a young girl's fantasy kingdom, all pink and purple, with shelves and shelves of dolls, some porcelain, some meant for play. And horses—Breyer's statues of the Black Stallion and Misty of Chincoteague and a unicorn with a glittering horn. The gleaming mahogany rocking horse was an objet d'art, not a child's plaything. Rose had her very own cushioned window seat heaped with stuffed animals, and a small Ferrari parked in front of a huge pink plastic Barbie house, completely furnished.

Lynn stood there with her mouth open. Her worst fear had come true. Rose would never want to visit her. Shelly would never want to come home.

He had bought his victory.

SHE'D TRIED. Adam had to give her that. She clearly didn't want to stay any more than he wanted her to.

Or so he told himself. If he were being brutally honest, he'd admit that he had sweated all week over this visit. He felt inadequate enough with Rose. What in hell would he do if Shelly skinned her knee and cried or got homesick and wanted her mommy?

His mother wasn't a feminine woman. A potter, she had most often worn denim overalls and rubber boots she could hose off. Barb Landry was a creative, passionate, intelligent woman, and not for a moment even in his childhood would he have traded her in for any of his friends' mothers, but she hadn't been terribly interested in her son's childish problems, either. She wanted nothing more than to be back in her studio, as if the spinning of her potter's wheel had mesmerized her so that she could never wander far from it. He'd always known, when she made him lunch or looked at his artwork or helped with homework, that she would have preferred to be footing a bowl or delicately incising a pattern in a vase or experimenting with firing temperatures.

From her he'd learned to focus with an intensity most people couldn't manage. A single-minded commitment to work brought success. He'd learned the power of words and books and ideas. He'd grown up to be self-sufficient.

He hadn't learned a damned thing about parenting. Especially, about parenting a little girl.

Adam envied and resented Lynn Chanak's ease with both Shelly and Rose. He doubted she ever wondered whether she was doing everything wrong. Her ability to talk warmly and directly to a child without patronizing was exactly why he didn't want her here. In comparison, he felt wooden, even less capable of appearing to be the perfect father-figure than usual.

Her same ability explained his relief when she'd graciously agreed to stay.

It didn't explain why he couldn't seem to take his gaze from her nicely rounded hips and tiny waist as he followed her down the hall. Today she wore a little black miniskirt that exposed plenty of leg and fit her bottom like…

He swallowed an expletive. The completion of that sentence was a figure of speech. His hands had no business on her butt.

When she paused in Rose's bedroom doorway, his gaze moved upward to the generous swell of breasts barely disguised by a plum-colored silky shirt loose over a white tank top. He wondered if she knew the lace of her bra showed through the thin ribbed knit tank.

Then there was her hair, gathered into a high ponytail that spilled thick auburn curls to the middle of her back. The wanton disorder of those curls was an intriguing contrast to her slender, pale neck and firm chin. Her hair would be glorious tumbled across a pillow.

Adam almost groaned at the lurch of sexual desire. Unlike many men, he didn't make a habit of seeing every woman as a sexual object. He couldn't remember the last time he'd pictured a woman in his bed.

This was sure as hell not the one to start with.

Think of Rose, he told himself. *Think of Shelly, and the god-awful mess all their lives already had become.*

His mouth twisted. Add even a flirtation, and he and Lynn wouldn't have a hope of achieving the friendly, flexible, rational relationship they would need to make this bizarre attempt to share their daughters work.

Through his preoccupation Adam finally became aware that Lynn had been silent for too long. Still on the threshold of Rose's bedroom, Lynn studied every shelf, every corner, with a care that made him nervous. What was wrong? Had he tried too hard?

"Does she know how lucky she is?" Lynn asked.

He plumbed her tone for sarcasm and came up with sadness. Because she'd never be able to buy as much for Shelly?

"I wanted everything to be perfect for her." He took a step closer, looking over her shoulder into his daughter's room, where both girls crouched in front of the Barbie house and talked animatedly. "I wasn't trying to spoil her."

"I didn't say you were."

"But you don't like her room."

She gave him an anguished look. "It's fairyland. What little girl wouldn't be thrilled?"

He still didn't get it. "You think Shelly will be jealous?"

Her smile trembled. "I think she won't want to come home."

Adam felt stupid for not understanding. "You can't buy love." Although Rose's room looked as if he'd tried, he saw suddenly.

The next instant, he squashed his chagrin. Damn it, he'd worked hard for his success! He sure as hell wasn't going to be ashamed of his ability to buy his daughter what she wanted.

"No. You can't buy love." But she didn't sound certain. "It's all so neat. Did you clean specially for Shelly's visit?"

His grunt held little amusement. Here was the kicker. "Rose doesn't play with most of this stuff. She doesn't want to be up here by herself. She has friends over once in a while, but otherwise…" He shrugged.

Rose still cried at night, too. A couple of times a week she crept down the hall, whimpering, and slipped into bed with him. The books he'd read said parents should never let their children sleep with them, but sometimes he weakened. He'd never been good at listening to his Rosebud cry herself to sleep.

One more thing he wished he could ask other parents, but didn't have the nerve. Did other three-year-olds need a diaper at night? Did they wake with nightmares, fear the shadows in the closet?

He had done everything he could to make Rose's bedroom beautiful and friendly. Obviously he lacked the knack. If Jennifer had been here…

But she wasn't. All he could do was his best.

"I'd better go work on lunch," he said abruptly.

Lynn gave him a distracted glance. "Can I help you?"

"It's a one-man job."

As he turned away, she went into Rose's bedroom. All the way back to the kitchen he could hear her voice, sweetly feminine and bubbling with delight, as she chattered with the girls. He had no doubt she would admire everything Rose most loved and succeed in entrancing his daughter. She would know exactly what to say, would feel perfectly comfortable sitting cross-legged on the floor joining in their games.

He'd expected Rose to talk about Shelly this past week, and she had. What he hadn't anticipated was that she'd also keep bringing up Lynn's name.

Tuesday, on the way home from day care, she had pulled her thumb from her mouth and said out of the blue, "Lynn is prettier than Amanda's mommy."

Amanda's mommy was sensational, all legs and cleavage and pouty mouth, but as it happened he agreed with Rose. Lynn was prettier.

Wednesday, in the middle of Ann's dinner, Rose had said shyly, "Lynn is funny, isn't she?"

Lynn had freckles, Rose had also told him another day, as if he hadn't noticed. And she ran fast, didn't she?

Lynn, it appeared, had acquired a fan club. And he was jealous. Adam swore under his breath and savagely chopped a green pepper, then scraped it into a bowl.

He'd moved on to whacking an onion when he realized he was no longer alone.

She stood hesitantly just inside the kitchen. "You could use help."

"I can chop. It's one of my few kitchen skills."

Her smile looked too damn much like Rose's. "Are you sure you have enough for me? Shelly is more comfortable now. I could probably get away."

"No. I should have suggested this in the first place."

She nodded seriously, her ponytail bobbing. "Why don't we do the same next week? You join us for lunch, then slip away for a bit. There's no reason not to take it slowly."

He resented her wisdom, as well as the implicit truth: they had years to get to know their respective daughters. This relationship was damn near as permanent as marriage.

"You're right," he said curtly.

She bit her lip. "I'm sorry."

"For what?" He looked up, jaw muscles locked.

Antagonism flared to life in Lynn's eyes. "No. I have nothing to be sorry for, except that this happened in the first place. I won't apologize again."

Adam swore and shoved the cutting board away, setting down the knife. "Well, I will. I'm being a jackass. I just… Oh, hell. I had visions of my two daughters and I having a carefree day. The truth is, I have no idea how to talk to Shelly. I'm not exactly a natural parent. Not the way you are."

Shock replaced the hostility. "But Rose obviously adores you. Why on earth would you think…"

He immediately regretted having opened his big mouth. "Forget it. I'm just not used to kids. You think when you have your first baby that the two of you will learn together.''

"Yes," Lynn said softly, that indefinable sadness creeping over her. "You do."

He wasn't the only one raising a daughter alone, he belatedly remembered. "How long ago were you divorced?"

"Six months after Shelly was born—" She stopped abruptly. Shelly, of course, was not the baby born to her that day. "Three years ago," Lynn amended.

"What happened?" None of his business, of course, but he found himself unexpectedly curious about her, not just Shelly.

"Oh, it was a mistake from the beginning," she said vaguely. "Having a baby didn't help. It wasn't his idea."

He made a sound and reached for the fresh mushrooms. "Jennifer wanted a baby so badly. She had a couple of miscarriages." Now why had he told her that? "When she got past four months with her pregnancy, she was so happy." His throat closed.

"And then she never knew…" Lynn pressed her lips together. "That must haunt you."

"You could say so." He cleared his throat. "I want you to understand why I need to be part of Shelly's life."

"I do," she said so quietly he just heard her. Lynn had bowed her head and was staring down at the pattern she was tracing on the tile counter. Her face was colorless and vulnerable when she looked up. "But I still won't let you have her."

Was that what he'd hoped? If so, he'd been a fool.

"We're stuck with each other," he said.

"It would seem so." She sounded as conflicted as he felt.

Adam set down the knife for the second time. He held out his hand across the kitchen island. "Well, Ms. Chanak, I suggest we make the best of it."

This smile, a twist of her lips, didn't produce dimples or the tiny crinkle of lines on the bridge of her nose. Her gray-green eyes remained grave as she took his hand, her own small and fragile in his stronger grip. "You have a deal."

Somehow her hand lingered in his; somehow he was reluctant to let her go. Solidarity, he told himself. Relief. Maybe they could be friends.

"Tell you what," he said. "Why don't you call the girls? This is a do-it-yourself pizza lunch, and I'm ready for everybody to make some hard decisions."

This smile was more natural, dimples and a curve of cheek as she started from the kitchen. "That kind of decision," she agreed, "I can make."

He didn't have to wonder what she meant.

CHAPTER SIX

DESPITE THEIR LITTLE TALK, the next couple of visits were no easier. Rose definitely didn't want Daddy to leave her, although she and Shelly had a grand time together so long as he stayed near. When he did leave, she cried inconsolably. Brave Shelly did somewhat better after that first time at the Landrys' house, but the third time Lynn came back, after an absence of five hours, only to be met at the door by a grim Adam.

His formerly pristine shirt was rumpled, rolled up at the sleeves and wet. His hair stood on end and an unpleasant odor wafted from him.

"Shelly's throwing up," he said bluntly. "I was about ready to call the doctor."

"Oh, Lord." Panic, well out of proportion, surged through her. Lynn whisked past him. "Where is she?"

"Lying down in Rose's bed." Although she moved fast, he was right behind her. "She has a big bowl next to her. For what good it does."

Lynn paused in the hall a few steps from Rose's open bedroom door. "She missed?"

He made a sound in his throat. "She's puked on the floor, Rose's bed and me. Rose is crying because she's scared. I think Shelly has a fever, but she doesn't want me taking her temperature. I couldn't give her anything to lower her temp anyway. It would just come right back up.''

The panic had begun to subside. Or, more accurately, she had recognized it for what it was: guilt. Her little girl had needed her, and she wasn't here.

''I wondered why she was so tired this morning,'' Lynn said, remembering. ''Her friend Laura has been sick.''

''Now you tell me,'' Adam muttered.

She ignored him and went in to see her daughter. The girls had done some damage, she saw on the way. Puzzle pieces were jumbled on the floor and unkempt Barbies strewn as if a tornado had swept through the room. It almost looked normal for a child's bedroom.

Rose curled, teary eyed, on the window seat. Face wan, Shelly lay in bed, looking so small and fragile and miserable that Lynn's own eyes burned.

''Oh, sweetie!'' She detoured to give Rose a quick kiss on the head and murmured, ''Shelly will be okay. Don't worry.'' Then she sat on the edge of the bed and laid the back of her hand on Shelly's forehead. ''You're toaster hot. Gracious, you've had an awful day, haven't you?''

Her daughter's face crumpled. ''Where were you?'' she wailed. ''I wanted you!''

Gathering Shelly into her arms, Lynn whispered, ''I know, I know. But Adam has taken good care of you, hasn't he?''

The three-year-old shook her head hard. ''I wanna go home!''

Lynn glanced toward the doorway and saw the

hurt in Adam's eyes before he shuttered his expression.

Hugging and swaying, Lynn said softly, "I don't know, sweet pea. The drive would be awful if you're throwing up."

"Don't go!" Her daughter latched convulsively onto her.

In a friendly voice that gave away nothing of what he must be feeling, Adam said, "Why don't you two spend the night? Your mom can have a room down the hall, and you can either stay here in Rose's bed, or share with Mom."

Lynn hated the alternatives. How could she say no and subject poor Shelly to the long, winding drive home over the Coast Range? But to stay, when she at least must be unwelcome…

Of course, she had no choice. As, she thought grimly, she so rarely did these days. Of course, it was unreasonable to blame Adam, who must be chafing as much as she was at losing control over such a hunk of his life.

As much? Who was she kidding? He was a man. Men wanted and expected to be in charge. Oh, yeah. If she resented him sometimes, he was probably angry enough to hire a hit man to rid himself of her.

"Thank you." She was just as capable as he was at putting on a good front. "I think we'd probably better stay."

She carried Shelly down the hall, helped her into a borrowed nightgown and bathed her forehead while he changed the bedding. Rose shyly came to visit Shelly while Daddy took a shower.

"Are you gonna pook again?" she asked.

Shelly nodded vigorously and shot to a half-sitting position. "Mama?" she begged in a strangled voice.

Lynn positioned the bowl in the nick of time. Rose watched wide-eyed. Heaven help them if this flu bug was a two-week affair instead of a twenty-four-hour quickie! Especially if—or should she say, when—Rose caught it.

Lynn was helping Shelly rinse out her mouth when Adam appeared in the doorway. In faded sweatpants and T-shirt, hair wet and finger-combed, he was breathtakingly sexy and a world more human than he usually seemed to Lynn.

"Do you want me to call the doctor?" he asked.

Lynn shook her head. "Not unless she keeps heaving once she's emptied her stomach. I take it they had lunch before she got sick?" Unfortunately, she could have itemized the menu.

"Yeah." His expression was sheepish. "They had macaroni and cheese, and hot dogs. Ice-cream bars. Oh, yeah. And Kool-Aid. Lots of lime Kool-Aid."

"I noticed," she said dryly.

Poor Shelly's face was flushed, but her eyes had become heavy. Lynn clicked on a bedside lamp at its lowest setting and motioned to him to switch off the overhead light. When she glanced back, he and Rose were gone.

She sang softly, smoothing Shelly's hair back from her hot forehead, until her daughter slept. Even then she sat there, just touched by lamplight in the dim room, thinking in despair, *How can we keep doing this?* What if she told him it just wasn't working?

Yes, but how could she? She saw Rose, scared and sad, hugging herself on the window seat in that gorgeous bedroom that was still strangely sterile. Her face, always so serious. Her need to hold on tight to Daddy, because who else did she have?

Me. She has me, Lynn's heart cried.

So, of course, she had no solution to the dilemma. They *had* to keep doing this. It was no worse, she told herself, than what many parents subjected their children to after a divorce. As long as those children grew up knowing they were loved, they forgot about the weekends when they didn't want to go to Daddy's, or the summers when they were packed off to Mom's. Love was what counted.

Lynn slipped out of the room, surprised, when she checked her watch, to find that it was seven-thirty. Shelly's usual bedtime was eight, so no wonder after her wretched and exhausting afternoon that she was already sound asleep! Muffled by a wall, Lynn heard splashes of water, a giggle followed by a deeper voice. Bath time. Maybe Rose had been ''pooked on,'' too.

She left the door open a crack. Two steps down the hall, Lynn turned back for another look. Shelly hadn't stirred. Fingers crossed that she stayed that way, Lynn went into Rose's room and sat cross-legged on the floor, putting puzzles back together. How helpful, she mocked herself, and felt like a thirteen-year-old girl who just happened to be hanging out in front of a cute boy's house. *Oh, do you live here?*

Well, damn it, she wanted just once to tuck her daughter into bed! She closed her eyes briefly, imagining herself smoothing back Rose's curls, kissing the freckles on her nose, whispering, ''Sleep tight, don't let the bedbugs bite,'' seeing a soft, sleepy smile light the face of this child she had carried for nine months.

Was that too much to ask?

Adam appeared with Rose in flowered flannel pajamas. For a moment, he hesitated, then nodded stiffly. ''Thank you.''

''No problem.'' Keeping her voice low, Lynn set the last completed puzzle on the pile.

''For some mysterious reason, Pansy here lost her appetite. She doesn't think she wants any dinner.''

A sleepy chuckle as Adam settled her into bed. ''Rose, Daddy! Not Pansy.''

Lynn made a face. ''I think I lost my appetite, too.''

''And you didn't eat the same things Shel—'' With a harrumph, he stopped. ''Never mind. Rosebud, I'll bet Lynn would like to say good-night, too.''

Oh, bless him! Instantly feeling kindlier, Lynn said, ''I'd love to.''

''Sleep well, honey.'' He kissed his daughter tenderly, carefully tucked blankets around her, and quietly left the room.

Lynn asked, ''Do you have a night-light?''

''Daddy forgot to turn it on.'' Rose sounded puzzled. ''Daddy never forgets.''

Daddy had left her something useful to do. Grateful, Lynn turned on the bright porcelain light and then sat on the edge of the bed. ''Sleep tight,'' she said softly. ''Don't let the bedbugs bite.''

A small giggle rewarded her. '''kay.''

Lynn let herself feel the intense pain and delight she usually denied, the bone-deep connection to *this* child. She hungrily looked, and saw herself as she never would in Shelly, who might be prettier and who she loved unshakably, but who did not look back sleepily with Brian's eyes, whose forehead didn't have a curve as familiar as the ache in her heart.

Oh, God, she wondered, *Am I as bad as Brian? Is passing on my genes so important to me?*

But, no, of course it wasn't. She felt the same as she ever had about Shelly. What she had to accept was that she could so quickly also love a child she hadn't known a month ago.

On a shaky breath, she bent and kissed her daughter's forehead.

Rose accepted the kiss with equanimity. "Are you gonna sleep with Shelly?"

"Yep."

"Sometimes I sleep with Daddy," Rose confided.

"When Shelly gets scared, she sneaks into bed with me, too."

"Oh." Rose pondered. "Daddy says big girls sleep in their own beds."

"Well, I guess big girls do, but you're not so big yet, are you? And even grown-ups get scared sometimes at night, if they hear a funny noise."

"Daddy doesn't get scared."

Lynn knew for a fact that wasn't true—the idea of losing his Rosebud was enough to scare Daddy to death. But she only smiled and said, "I wish I didn't." Then she kissed Rose again, this time on that small freckled nose. "Now, you go to sleep. Maybe Shelly will feel better in the morning and you two can play."

Rose smiled, sweet and shy. "'kay," she said again. "Night, Lynn."

Lynn's heart swelled and her sinuses burned with the effort not to cry, but she kept smiling through them. "Good night," she murmured.

She left the door open six inches and the hall light on. Thank God, Adam wasn't lurking outside the door. She needed a minute alone to wipe away the tears and convince herself that it could be worse: she might never have known, never have found Rose.

A peek in the guest room assured her that Shelly still slept, her face flushed but her breathing even. Then, nerving herself, Lynn went downstairs.

She found Adam in the kitchen. He glanced up, taking in far more than she wanted him to see with one sweep of his sharp gaze. But he only asked, "Shelly still asleep?"

She nodded.

"It's getting a little late to start the dinner I'd intended. How would French toast grab you? Or an omelette?"

"Either would be good."

His brows stayed up and he waited.

"French toast." She didn't care.

He'd already had the eggs out on the counter. She watched as he put a pan on to heat and started cracking eggs into a shallow bowl.

"Thank you for letting me tuck her in."

His jaw bunched. "Not much of a gift."

"You could have shooed me out."

"I hope I'm not that selfish."

He whisked the eggs efficiently but with latent violence. Wishing she could be whipped into an acceptable, smooth form as easily?

"Adam..."

"Do you like syrup?"

Frustration infused her voice. "Yes, but..."

"Let's eat and then talk. Okay?"

Lynn let out a gusty sigh. "Yes. Fine."

Not at all to her surprise, the French toast was thick, golden brown and crusty. Butter—real butter—pooled like sunlight. He'd even sprinkled the top with powdered sugar.

They took their plates to the kitchen table set in an alcove surrounded by windows that looked out at the dark garden. It must be a perfect spot in the morning.

She took her first bite. "This is wonderful! Do you buy your bread at a bakery?"

"Bread machine."

Lynn murmured with pleasure again. She must have been starved, she realized. She'd gone to a sandwich shop for lunch only to give herself something to do, one more way to kill the hours while she was exiled, but the sandwich had been dry and the turkey the kind that tasted fake. She'd had only a few bites.

"We hardly know each other," Adam said suddenly. "I think that's my fault."

Lynn set down her fork. "Yes. It is."

He acknowledged the hit with a grimace. "I'd like to change that. Tell me something about yourself. Where did you grow up? How'd you end up with a bookstore?"

"Eugene." She sounded rusty. She had the

sweaty-palmed feel of a fifth-grader standing up in front of the class to give a presentation. "I grew up in Eugene." That sounded bald all by itself, so words kept coming. "My mother was the secretary for the History department at the university. I never met my father. I think my mother had an affair, which isn't at all like her, but she wasn't married and didn't like to talk about him. 'It was just one of those things,' she always says."

Adam listened to her with the same concentration he probably gave to stock quotes on the Internet. He didn't interrupt, didn't look away, gave no sign of being bored. Lynn couldn't remember the last time anyone had really wanted to hear about *her*.

Which might have explained why even then she didn't shut up.

"I don't know. Maybe that's not the truth, either. Maybe Mom went to a sperm bank and just didn't want me to know my father was nothing but a few statistics in a catalog. You know—gray eyes, 130 IQ, five foot eleven, red hair." Oh, God, she thought belatedly. Why was she telling him this private suspicion?

"I do know my father," Adam said unexpectedly, "and I couldn't tell you a hell of a lot more than that about him. He and my mother suit each other, but he's not a warm man."

"What's he do?"

His grunt must have been a laugh. "He's a pathologist. Appropriate, isn't it? He's very, very smart, and cold as a morgue."

"But your mother…"

"Is an artist. A potter. She doesn't do dinner plates

or pitchers. These strange shapes connect..." His hands tried to form one of his mother's creations out of thin air, but he shrugged and gave up. "Ugly as hell, some of what she does, but the critics don't see it that way. It 'speaks to the heart.'" He fell silent.

Beginning to be puzzled, Lynn asked tentatively, "Are you proud of her?"

"Mmm?" He looked startled. "Sure. I have one of her pieces in the living room. Remind me to show you. The thing is...she's pretty distant, too. If I hadn't seen her working at her wheel, I'd have a hell of a time imagining her and Dad tangled in bed together."

Lynn blinked.

He closed his eyes briefly and rotated his neck. "I shouldn't have said that. Sorry."

"No. That's okay. I shouldn't have said what I did about the sperm bank, either." He'd offered her a trade, she realized. A glimpse into his privacy in exchange for one into hers. Whatever else Adam Landry might be, he wasn't selfish. His generosity compelled Lynn to continue, "But you're right, we should get to know each other. Warts and all."

Adam met her eyes, his breathtakingly intense. "What I'm trying to say is, ever since I brought Rose home I've been parenting by guess and by God. I'm the one browsing the parenting section in the bookstore. I can't call Mom and ask how to handle a two-year-old whose only word is 'no.'" Adam made another of those rough sounds meant to be a laugh. "Mom says, 'Why ask me?'"

"Why ask her?" Lynn echoed incredulously.

His mouth curved into something more closely approximating genuine amusement. "See, she handled it when she had to, but...absently. I guess that's the best way to put it. She was always focused on her art. I'll bet she doesn't remember me at two or three."

"But...that's appalling!" And terribly sad.

He ran a hand over a chin bristly with the day's growth of dark beard. "No, that's Mom. She's a cool lady in her own way. Brilliant, passionate about her art, smart about the business side of it. Just not all that interested in wiping snotty noses or leading pre-schoolers around the zoo."

Fascinated, Lynn pushed her plate back and crossed her forearms on the table. "Why did she have children, then?"

"An accident?" One cheek creased. "I've never had the guts to ask her."

Lynn sat there absorbing what he'd told her. Finally, she mused, "At least I had my mother. She might have been a little mysterious about my father, but, you know, I never really cared. She was always enough. Maybe that's why being a single parent hasn't been that hard for me." She smiled crookedly. "You might say, that's the pattern I know. But you..." She started to reach out to touch his hand, but stopped herself. "You've done an amazing job. Rose adores you."

"We've done okay," he said gruffly.

"Better than okay."

He shifted. "Maybe you'd better save the accolades for a few months. I screw up. Sometimes I think Rose is babyish for her age, and that's my fault."

"Babyish?" Why did she keep having this urge to take his hand, as if he needed comfort?

"Didn't you notice she went to bed with a diaper on? Three-and-a-half years old, and she still wets her bed."

"Lots of kids do," Lynn said, puzzled at his perturbation. "Maybe she's an extra sound sleeper. She seems to do fine during the day."

He shoved himself to his feet and grabbed their empty plates. "She has accidents."

"So does Shelly."

At the sink, Adam stood with his back to her. "Not when she's with me."

"Rose hasn't had one with me, either."

He stayed completely still for a moment. "I figured I was doing something wrong."

What could she say? Lynn fumbled for the right words. "Children, um, aren't like a product you assemble. They aren't perfect, any more than we are." Then she flushed. "I'm sorry. That was patronizing."

"I deserved it." When he turned, he was actually smiling. The fact that one corner of his mouth crooked higher than the other lent charm to a face that was usually too austere. "Anyway, funny thing. You've hit the nail on the head. *I* was expected to be perfect. I didn't want to lay that burden on Rose, but apparently my expectations weren't buried very far under. As you said, patterns."

Lynn didn't want to feel sympathy or liking or even understanding. She couldn't afford to. *Stop,* she told herself. *Now.*

"This isn't working," she said abruptly. "These visits. I hate them."

Between one blink and the next, he became a stranger again. "We agreed to take it slowly."

"I don't like to shop. The movies are all made for teenagers. I dread these days." She sounded peevish instead of firm. *Me, me, me.* "No," she argued with herself. "It's not me. If the girls were happy…but they're not. They're too young to be bounced back and forth like this."

"Then what do you suggest?" His voice was harsh. "Shall we just stay in touch? Send each other photos at Christmas?"

"No."

"Goddamn it!" he shouted. "Then what?"

"I don't know," she yelled back, suddenly furious. "But something different!"

"Different."

Lynn swallowed, moderated her tone. "Maybe… maybe less often. Maybe, for now, we need to put up with each other instead of pretending we can each have both of them."

Adam swore and massaged the back of his neck. "We are pretending, aren't we?"

"Yes." She pressed her hand to her chest, which inexplicably burned. "That's exactly what we're doing. Shelly and Rose don't understand."

"Today, all she wanted was you."

"Rose cries when you leave her."

"She cries at her day care, too. Sometimes I have to pry her hands off me."

Lynn hated that picture, but she couldn't blame

him. He was a good father; Rose loved him. He had to work.

"What shall we do?" she asked miserably.

"Maybe you're right. Maybe we went at this in too big a hurry."

She didn't want him to agree, Lynn was shocked to realize. She didn't want to go back to before, however serene it seemed in memory. To not see Rose as often. To not see him as often.

Now, what did *that* mean? she wondered, jarred. Had she come to have some kind of fellow feeling for Adam, because he was the only one who truly understood what she was going through? Was it self-defense, to bond with him?

Or—dear God—had she developed some kind of adolescent crush on the man? Was some of her Monday morning anticipation because she would see him, not just Rose? Did that explain some of the hurt and letdown, when he didn't invite her past the doorstep?

"Even the days I have both girls aren't that great, because Rose wants you. And because, oh, because it's like this special event. It's not *life*. I want Rose to feel at home with me," she struggled to explain.

He watched her with understanding that delved beneath her breastbone. "Question is, do you want Shelly to feel at home with me?"

Lynn gave a small, twisted smile. "Probably not. How do you feel about the idea of Rose happy with me?"

"Oh, I'm jealous as hell."

"I guess we can't help how we feel. Just what we do about it."

"You're not suggesting a change because you're jealous, too?"

He was asking for honesty. Lynn tried to give it. "I don't think so. I hope not. Tell me the truth. Do you look forward to Mondays?"

"No. Hell." He scrubbed a hand over his face. "The drive is getting damned old, and I don't like wasting a day over there any better than you do here. Okay. We can do better."

"How about fewer but longer visits? Overnight stays?"

"Rose has never even spent the night at her grand-parents'."

"Would you, um, consider staying over the first few times?"

The austerity was back as he frowned, and she quailed a little at her boldness.

"On your couch?"

"You can have my bed," she said, too quickly. *Why so eager to persuade him?* she asked herself. "I'm shorter. I'll take the couch."

"I do have the extra bedroom here." He was still thinking. "They have more fun when you're around, too."

"I know it's awkward."

"At first it was awkward." He contemplated her, but she couldn't tell what he was thinking. "I'm not so sure it is anymore."

"Maybe we could be friends." *Only friends?*

"All right." The lines between his dark brows cleared. "I'm game. How about if we make it the weekend after next? I'll come Sunday and Monday.

That way I can entertain the girls while your shop's open on Sunday.''

''It's not too long for you to take off?''

A shrug. ''I can bring my laptop. Put in a little time Monday. I can be flexible.''

''Okay.'' Two weeks. How would she wait two weeks to see them again? ''Um…'' she began apologetically. ''My place is pretty tiny. I've put my money into the business. Maybe we can eat out,'' she decided with quick relief. But, oh God, he'd still have to use her shabby bathroom, see the chips in the porcelain sink and tub, bump his head on the too-low lintel.

She had a suspicion he read her shame and anxiety as if her face were the open screen of his laptop.

''Real life, remember?''

''Yes. All right.'' She was taking a risk in baring her life for his scrutiny. In court, he could use her poverty against her. But he could have done that anyway, she reminded herself. It wasn't any secret.

And she was beginning to believe, to hope, that he wouldn't. If she was wrong, heaven help her.

''I'd better go check on Shelly.'' She picked up her silverware and glass. ''Unless you need help cleaning up…''

Adam crossed the kitchen and took them from her, his fingers bumping hers. ''Don't be ridiculous. Go.''

Foolish that her pulse bumped in sync.

''Thank you, Adam. For listening.''

His eyes softened. ''We should have talked sooner.''

''No one said this would be easy.''

''Has anyone else ever had to figure it out?'' He

released a breath. "Good night, Lynn. Make yourself at home if you wake up before I do in the morning."

She edged backward. "Right." At home. "Sure."

"I left Rose's shampoo in the shower. I'll put out clean towels."

"Thank you." Why was she still standing here? Why was she wondering, hoping, at the way his eyes seemed to darken, at the step he took forward?

"Rose needs a mother's touch."

Rose. Not him. Of course not him.

She was being foolish. He looked at her oddly sometimes because of her resemblance to his Rosebud. Not because she was a woman and he was a man.

This new plan wouldn't work, either, if she started suffering delusions. *So don't,* Lynn told herself sharply.

With a cool nod and another good-night, she went.

CHAPTER SEVEN

ADAM TRIED TO ROLL OVER and had to muffle a groan. The damned couch was not only a foot too short for his big frame, but it was about as comfortable as squatting against a driftwood log on a rocky beach: okay for a while when the sun was hot and the beat of the surf steady and lulling, but nowhere you'd want to snooze for eight hours.

Lynn had offered, four or five times, to sleep out here and let him have her bedroom. Offered, hell, she'd tried to insist. But, no, he was too chivalrous to accept.

He still didn't regret his refusal, and not just because he liked to think he was a gentleman. It would have made sense for her to sleep on the couch instead of him. She probably could have stretched out. She might have even rested more easily on the lumps and bumps. Along with being a good ten inches shorter than he was, she must weight fifty pounds less.

What Adam hadn't liked was the idea of invading her private space. Of being surrounded by her scent and her most intimate possessions. Oh, she'd have cleaned up for him. No sexy bras would be draped across the Lincoln rocker he'd glimpsed from the hall, and she wouldn't leave a diary open to yesterday's entry, but her makeup decorated a dresser, her books covered a bedside table, the prints on the walls were her favorites, the contents of her drawers…well, he'd bet homemade bags of dried lavender and rose petals perfumed her lingerie.

That one glimpse into her sanctum was enough, thank you. The bed was an old-fashioned double with a mahogany spooled head and footboard. It was heaped with pillows in lacy cases and covered by a fluffy chenille spread the color of butter. The makeup was arranged on embroidered linen darkened to old ivory. Late roses spilled languorously from a cream-colored stoneware pitcher.

The room was utterly feminine and graceful. Pretty, but in a womanly way rather than a girlish one. The fact that Lynn Chanak was a woman, and a sexy one at that, was something he tried hard not to think about.

He'd become good at blocking out that kind of awareness. Living like a monk, a man had to build some defenses.

Oh, he'd tried dating after the first year of mourning. Rhonda McIntyre, a commodities broker, had cornered him in the elevator and flirted with so little subtlety even he'd noticed. Why not? he'd figured.

The evening was a flop. She made plain her disinterest in children. They talked trading and the bull market for lack of any other topic. He kissed her on her doorstep and declined her invitation to go in.

A couple of months later, he'd dated another woman a few times—a single mother he'd met at the preschool. She was struggling to make ends meet as a secretary, and she had a hungry, desperate quality that scared him. She wanted marriage, and she wanted it soon.

Since then, he hadn't bothered. Now and again, a woman would turn his head on the street. Maybe her leggy stride, or the lush curve of a bottom in a tight miniskirt. A cleavage, or the smooth line of a stranger's throat as she laughed.

He was tempted sometimes to call Rhonda or another woman like her, just because his body ached for release. He'd never imagined being celibate for over three years. Nights, Adam stayed up later than he should, because climbing into bed alone was when he felt the loss. Jenny came to him most readily then, with an airy laugh or a teasing tickle of her fingers, and he would almost roll to gather her into his arms when he'd remember with a painful stab that she was gone for good.

Her death had come so damned fast. No time to prepare, to say goodbye.

The afternoon it happened, he'd talked to her quickly from the office, half his attention on the notes he'd been making on a new software company. He had dropped his car off for new brakes that morning, and the mechanic had let him know they had to wait for a part. "No problem," Jenny had declared. They chose one of their favorite restaurants in downtown Portland and arranged to meet there. He'd walk over, they'd go home together.

"If you're *sure* you don't mind being seen with a woman shaped like a gray whale," she'd said, so blithely he could smile into the telephone knowing she was only fishing for a compliment. She was well aware of her beauty, body swollen with his child, her breasts heavier in his hands at night, the mystery making her gaze remote often enough to tantalize any man. Jennifer had never lacked in confidence, during her pregnancy least of all.

Grinning, the last thing he said to her was, "Just make sure they seat you before I arrive," and she'd told him he was a rat.

Neither of them said goodbye or "I love you."

He was ten minutes late. Jenny wasn't there, hadn't been seated. He had a drink while he waited. Punctuality never had been one of her virtues. When she was half an hour late, he tried her at home. No answer. She had a way of forgetting to turn on her cell phone, but he tried it, too.

A police officer had answered, told him his wife had been hit head-on by a drunk driver. She had been transported to the hospital with a potential head injury.

She was already gone, his Jenny. Dead in every way that mattered, except that the beat of her heart and the soft machine-induced breaths sustained their baby. For lack of a brake cylinder in stock at the garage.

But cursing fate didn't change a thing.

From that day forward, he looked at other women, and he saw Jenny. He couldn't bed one and close his eyes. She would move wrong, sigh wrong, be too patient.

So he stayed celibate even when his body protested.

Like tonight.

Thinking about Lynn Chanak's bed had more to do with his restlessness than the lumpy cushions did.

Hell, maybe he'd have been better off between her sheets than imagining her there.

At bedtime she'd used the bathroom first. Thinking he'd heard her door shut, Adam went down the hall with his toothbrush just in time to meet her face-to-face outside the bathroom. Her faded flannel bathrobe gaped enough to expose a fine white cotton nightgown edged with lace as pretty as that on her sheets. Brushed until it crackled with energy, her hair tumbled over her shoulders and breasts. She smelled like soap and woman, her cheeks pink from scrubbing.

God help him, he'd looked down to see her bare feet peeking out beneath the ragged hem of her robe. Her toes, curled on the cold floorboards, were a hell of a lot sexier than Rhonda McIntyre's musk-scented cleavage as she deliberately bent to pick something up right in front of him.

Blushing, murmuring that the bathroom was all his, Lynn had fled, leaving him with an ache that kept him awake with a vengeance.

His sexual fantasies these days weren't specific. He imagined burying himself in a woman's body without thinking too much about her voice or her face or her cold feet sneaking to warm themselves against him in bed. Now, being tormented on Lynn Chanak's ancient couch, every time he closed his eyes, he saw himself tangling his fingers in that mass of glorious hair. He imagined her pretty, virginal nightgown. The smell of her soap and the lavender and roses drifting from her bureau.

She was the mother of his daughter. *Her* body had once swelled with another man's seed, but it was his

Rosebud she'd carried. Knowing that muddled his thoughts. When he tried to see his Jenny pregnant, he imagined Lynn instead.

It didn't help to tell himself that she'd be horrified if she knew he was lying out here on her couch lusting after her.

What if he acted on it? What if he kissed her? What if she didn't slap him?

Would he long for Jenny when he bedded Lynn?

Swearing, Adam rolled over again and stared up at the dark ceiling.

Even if he didn't think about Jenny, what he felt wasn't love. It was celibacy butting up against involuntary intimacy with a woman. It was encountering her barefooted in her nightie with her teeth freshly brushed and her cheeks rosy. It was seeing her as his child's mother.

And it could not be. The inevitable hurt feelings and anger would destroy any hope of sharing their daughters.

Grimly Adam tried to shut off the show his imagination was directing. Obviously, it was time—past time—he found a woman with whom he could laugh and enjoy sex, if nothing else.

Any woman but Lynn Chanak.

OF COURSE, BY MONDAY morning, rain dripped dismally from a gray sky, killing his hope of taking the girls to the beach. The kitchen table didn't seat four, so Adam sat wedged between Rose and Shelly while Lynn munched toast and served them.

"No movie theater in town," he remembered.

"Nope. Lincoln City is the closest. And I don't think anything is playing that they'd enjoy."

"Any ideas?" he asked without hope.

"We could hang around here." Whisking back and forth between stove and table, she barely glanced at him. "The girls'll be happy playing. You can do whatever it is brokers do. Use your laptop to check what prices are going up or down. That terrorist bombing in Rome probably panicked a few stock-holders."

He didn't give a damn whether Intel had dropped a point and a half because some zealot had blown up himself and half an office building just outside the Vatican. He didn't want to spend the day with her. But he'd had the girls yesterday. Today was, in a sense, her turn. He couldn't decide to leave until mid-afternoon at least.

"Sure," he said without enthusiasm. "Sounds good."

"You girls could dress up," Lynn suggested. "I'll get the box down if you want."

"Dress up?" Rose brightened. "We could have a parade. Like we do at preschool."

"Yeah!" Shelly bounced. "And maybe sing!"

"And dance."

"You could put on a performance for us." Lynn set more bacon on the table.

"Let's go practice." The girls were gone in a flurry, Lynn behind them to get down "the box."

Adam usually avoided cholesterol-laden foods like bacon, but he gloomily began crunching a strip. When Lynn reappeared, he asked, "What's in the box?"

"Oh…" She smiled and took a tea bag from a canister. "Dress-up clothes. I'm always adding new stuff from the thrift store. I have feather boas and gaudy jewelry and high heels and scarves. Lots of sequins. You'll see." Pouring hot water into her mug, she added over her shoulder, "But what makes it magic is, I only let Shelly into it every once in a while. On a day when she's really bored. Or like today, when she and a friend can put on a production."

Magic. Adam guessed he did okay as a parent, but he didn't know how to make magic. This woman did.

"What are you thinking about?" she asked.

Surprising himself, he told her.

"Nonsense." She joined him at the table. "A dress-up box is a girl thing. Why would you think of it?"

Jennifer would have, he knew.

"That doesn't mean you don't come up with your own ideas. Or at least provide Rose with the opportunity to find them elsewhere."

"Preschool."

"Sure. Why not?"

"If she loved it there, she wouldn't hate going."

Lynn lifted out the tea bag, squeezed it and set it on the edge of a breakfast plate. The rich scent of orange and cinnamon overrode the greasier flavor of bacon.

"I don't know about that," she said calmly. "Just because Rose cries when she has to say goodbye to you doesn't mean she has a terrible time. Doesn't she tell you about her day?"

"Sure she does." He ate another strip of bacon,

simply because it was there. "They're teaching the kids sign language. She shows me new signs every day. The goat tries to eat her hair, which means we have to wash it that night. I catch her sometimes giggling with a bunch of other girls when I get there early."

"I rest my case."

He took a last swallow of coffee and tried not to notice that her knees were bumping his under the small table. "Since you're so wise, tell me this— why do I worry constantly about whether I'm screwing up, while you know instinctively what to do? Is it the difference between a woman and a man?"

That difference was exactly what he *didn't* want to think about. So why throw it out on the table for discussion?

Because it was on his mind, he concluded.

"I know women who are terrible with their kids and men who are great. No." She shook her head, and her braid flopped over her shoulder. "I suspect it has more to do with the fact that my mother was an affectionate woman and yours wasn't. Parenting is a learned skill. Maybe it *is* easier to learn as a child, like a second language. You're having to work a little harder. That's all."

How simple. He felt like an idiot to be so comforted by an answer as obvious as this one.

"What would you normally do today?" he asked, more abruptly than was polite.

"Clean the kitchen." Lynn nodded toward the sink. "Do a little housework. Pay bills. Thumb through publishers' catalogs."

"Don't let me distract you."

Her clear-eyed gaze saw right through him. He wanted them not to spend the day together.

"Sure," she said agreeably. "The phone is here. Do you want to spread out on the table? I'll have it cleared in a minute."

"Let me help."

She'd already pushed back her chair. "This is a one-cook kitchen. We'd be tripping over each other."

Instead of going to the living room for his brief-case and laptop computer, Adam watched as she ran hot water into the sink. No dishwasher. He'd vaguely thought everybody had one.

In the past twenty-four hours, he had become shockingly aware of how near to the bone Lynn Chanak must live. The furniture was all secondhand. No, third- or fourth-hand. The linoleum in the bathroom and kitchen were both worn to the point where the pattern had become a memory and seams were peeling. She and Shelly had two bedrooms—if you could call Shelly's eight-by-eight feet with a slanting ceiling a room. Crummy bathroom. Creaky plumbing. A small eating space in the kitchen and a living room no bigger than his den. Woodwork and floors needed stripping or replacing, windows were single pane, and he wondered about the building's wiring.

It appalled him to think about the reaction of Jennifer's parents, if they could see where their grand-daughter was growing up.

Funny thing was, the only uncomfortable part of this apartment was the couch. The place was tiny, too small for two adults and two children, but probably fine for just a mom and toddler. With the same imagination she'd used in creating the dress-up box, Lynn had managed to give the old house charm on a shoestring.

She'd rag-rolled paint on plaster walls to subtle effect and used bright enamel on wood furniture. Posters of far-off places and wreaths of dried flowers brightened bare spots. The tiny hall was hung with family photos. He'd lingered that morning to study them. Bright pillows were probably hand-sewn rather than bought; he'd bet she had crocheted the afghan, as well. She had an eye for color, he thought, an ability to bring cheer to the drabbest room.

His own house could use a little.

"I'm done," she said briskly, whisking a dishcloth across the table. "It's all yours."

"Thanks."

He tried to concentrate after that, but it was hard when the girls kept popping out for an opinion on the latest ensemble or to ask the words to a song. And he remained conscious of Lynn, who murmured apologetically when she slipped into the kitchen for stamps or a cold drink, who eventually heated soup and made sandwiches for everyone. When the girls at last teetered through their dances in gowns worthy of Vanna White and heels high enough to do a swan dive from, it was Lynn he noticed most. Her delight was so genuine, her laughs in the right place, her clapping endearingly enthusiastic.

She had that magical ability to see through a child's eyes. In that, she reminded him of Jenny, who had never seemed quite grown-up to him.

But unlike Jenny, who had never worked, Lynn successfully ran a small business and coped with a

young child. On the way to the bathroom this morning, he'd seen her worry as she wrote checks, sighed,
laid an envelope aside, then changed her mind and
opened it again. She must have nothing put away.
What kind of health insurance did she carry? he wondered, when he should have been thinking about the
alarming, precipitate drop in the price per share of a
small software company that had recently gone public and which he'd recommended to his clients.

Did he have a right to ask Lynn about her finances? If she was anxious now, what would her
checking account look like in March after the winter
slowdown in the tourist trade? Would she take help
from him?

Instead of suggesting that he and Rose leave right
after lunch, Adam let Lynn put both girls down for
a nap. Maybe he'd take them all out to dinner.

Lynn came into the kitchen. "Well, they're giggling in there, so I can't guarantee they'll actually
get any sleep, but it seems worth a try."

"Rose can catch up on the way home," he said
indifferently.

"I'll leave you to work." She had some bright
catalogs in her hand.

"Publishers' lists?" he asked, nodding at them.

"Yeah. I enjoy choosing what books we'll carry
as much as I do selling them. Of course the reps try
to push certain ones, but a bookseller needs to know
her own market."

"What do you look for?" he asked with real curiosity.

"Um…" She was still hovering in the doorway.

"Why don't you sit down?"

"Can I get you something to drink?"

"I'll take a cup of coffee." He couldn't remember the last time he'd had instant, but it wasn't bad stuff. The caffeine kick was the same.

While she boiled water, he thumbed through spring catalogs from Little, Brown, Simon & Schuster and Scholastic. Every single book looked bright and appealing.

As they drank coffee, Lynn talked about what she found did well for her: local history and flora and fauna, of course, fiction set in the Northwest, a few paperback bestsellers, children's books. "When it rains," she said with a quick grin, "the kids suddenly need indoor entertainment." Gardening books, she continued; something about going on vacation in an ambience like Otter Beach inspired people to think they'd go home and transform their yards into cottage or Japanese gardens.

"I have some sidelines, too, including a few needlework and latch-hook rug kits. Vacation makes people dream."

"And you don't have to worry about a Barnes & Noble opening in the next block."

"Right." Her pretty, round face looked rueful. "Of course, the reason I don't have to worry is that there isn't enough volume of business here to attract one. Which also limits any possibility of expansion or growth for me, too."

"How about a second store? Say in Cannon Beach or Lincoln City?"

"I've thought about it. They each have independents now, and it doesn't make sense for two of us to compete. And with Shelly a preschooler, the travel and headaches don't seem very appealing. But maybe someday…'' She shrugged. ''If one of those stores should come up for sale…''

Adam drummed his fingers on his thigh. ''What do you do about health insurance?''

''I have coverage.'' Her formerly artless tone became wary. ''Were you worried about Shelly?''

''I want her well taken care of.'' Even he recognized how tactless that sounded, but too late.

Gentle green eyes became fiery. ''Are you suggesting I *don't* take adequate care of her?''

''No.'' He grimaced. ''I'm sorry. I don't always express myself well. I know you're doing the best you can. It's probably better than I do. I just got to worrying about whether you make enough to manage.''

''Well, don't,'' she said stiffly. ''I'll let you know before Shelly and I are out on the street.''

Irked, he said, ''I was trying to offer help.''

Brows lifted, she said coolly, ''Were you?''

''Clumsily.''

''Then thank you.'' She gathered up her catalogs. ''But we're doing just fine. I happen to believe that luxurious surroundings aren't essential to emotional well-being.''

''I won't argue.'' Although he'd never forgive himself if he left Shelly with her and they both died some night in a fire started by antique wiring.

She stood, tiny curls escaping the severe braid to frame her face. Instead of leaving the kitchen immediately, Lynn hesitated. ''I know today wasn't what you had in mind.''

"Actually," he said, "I didn't have anything in particular in mind."

"You would have preferred a movie or a day at the beach."

"I thought the girls might," he corrected her, knowing he was lying.

"Real life, remember?"

"What about you?" he challenged. "Was this a good visit?"

"Yes." She sounded surprised. "I'm not totally comfortable with you sometimes, but otherwise... yes."

"Will things get better between us?"

"I'm sure they will." But she wasn't meeting his eyes. "Once I'm sure you won't try to take Shelly from me."

Adam felt an instant of disappointment that irritated him like hell when he realized its source: he'd wanted her to admit she felt an attraction to him that was a problem. Either she was being less than honest, or she didn't feel any of that edgy awareness that had him concentrating on her face so he didn't stare at her breasts under a tight T-shirt or imagine wrapping his hands around her small waist.

"We have an agreement, don't we?" he said.

"We have nothing in writing. Nothing that will keep us out of court."

"Goodwill."

"I don't trust it. I want to trust you, but I don't completely. How can I?"

He did trust her, he realized somewhat to his shock. Lynn Chanak didn't have a deceitful bone in her body.

"We could do a written parenting plan."

She sighed. "No. I just need time. And…and a routine. I'm happiest when I know what's coming."

"Like a child."

"I suppose." She tried to smile. "Living on the edge is not for me."

"And yet," he said softly, "you must feel as if you are all the time."

"Financially, maybe."

"Is your ex-husband helping?"

"He was. Until this happened." She gestured toward the bedroom, where silence had finally settled.

Adam frowned. "He quit paying child support?"

"I'm okay without it."

"The bastard."

"Took the words out of my mouth." Another of her almost-smiles hid a world of hurt. "He figured you wouldn't want his child-support checks."

"I'd shove 'em down his throat," Adam growled.

"Obviously, I made a mistake there. Except…"

"For Rose."

"Yes. I wouldn't change things if I could."

"Do you have a picture of him?"

"Sure. There's one in the hall. After all, he's Shelly's dad. Or she thinks he is."

Adam wanted, violently, for his daughter to know *he* was Daddy. Always and forever. Patience, he counseled himself.

Lynn came back in a moment with a framed photograph of a handsome young man with a confident grin, Nordic blond hair and vivid blue eyes. Although he had noticed it earlier, Adam took it from her and studied it closely.

"Not much of him in Rose," he decided, glad.

"Except his eyes. No," Lynn agreed, "there's even less of his personality in her. I always thought Shelly took after him. He mountain climbs and does that dangerous freestyle skiing and rides motocross. Unlike me, he enjoys taking his life in his hands. Shelly can be so reckless. At eighteen months old, I heard her sobbing in her bedroom. When I raced in there, I found she'd managed to climb out of her crib and scale her dresser. She was perched on top, finally scared."

"Rose never did get out of her crib. After I bought her a twin bed, I had to sit next to her until she'd gone to sleep the first few nights, because she was sure she'd fall out." He had tried to hide his impatience, not understanding her timidity. He'd tried to justify it by the loss of her mother. She hadn't gotten it from either him or Jenny.

"She sounds so much like me," Lynn said quietly. "Finding our daughters the way we have, I keep being hit by how much is innate instead of environmental. Rose is mine and Shelly yours, no matter how much we want it otherwise."

A clamp squeezed his chest. He couldn't deny a word she'd said, however desperately he would have liked to. *Rose is mine and Shelly yours.* He adored his Rosebud. He wouldn't let her be someone else's.

"We'd better go as soon as Rose wakes up," he said with brusqueness calculated to hide his disquiet. Staying was no longer an option. He needed distance to think about this. To figure out whether he really did trust this woman.

"Sure," Lynn said, with a faint ironic smile. "I assumed you would."

"But you'll bring her over in two weeks? And stay?"

"Of course I will."

"We have each other over a barrel, don't we?"

Their eyes met, stark honesty between them for once. "You could say that." Was it bitterness or fright that made her voice momentarily tremulous. "You have Rose, and I have Shelly."

"A balance of power."

"I don't feel balanced." She pressed her lips together. "You and I both know, I could never come up with the money to fight you."

"But I'd never hurt Shelly by destroying you."

"I have to believe that. Don't I?" She backed away. "Now, I'll leave you to...to do whatever..." Whirling, she was gone, and Adam was left to wonder whether those were tears clogging her throat.

CHAPTER EIGHT

ALTHOUGH NOT MORE THAN a few months old, this library book was already well read, the pages opening easily to the beginning.

"Not all princesses are beautiful," Lynn read. "In fact, some are plain. A few are even ugly."

A child curled on each side of her. Rose sucked her thumb; Shelly held tight to her flannel blankie. Both were rapt on the simple watercolor drawing of a truly ugly princess whose tiara crowned a head of lank brown hair.

She read on, their small bodies warm, their giggles sweet to her ears. Both girls smelled of soap and minty toothpaste. They wore nighties and fluffy socks to keep their toes warm. When she finished and asked if they wanted another story, two vigorous nods were her answer.

Since they'd visited the library just that afternoon and chosen twenty books, she imagined story time would go on for a cozy half hour or more. It was her idea of bliss.

The only mildly discomfiting note was Adam's presence, and she didn't find it nearly as disturbing as she would have a month before. Familiarity bred...well, not indifference, unfortunately, but something almost as good: near trust. Even liking.

This was the fourth visit since they'd agreed on these overnight stays. Counting, Lynn realized in amazement that over three months had passed since that first time when Adam had walked into her bookstore with Rose holding his hand.

Tonight he was reading in what she'd learned was his favorite chair, brown distressed leather with wide arms and a big ottoman for his feet. The newspaper rustled as he turned pages. Once, when the girls got a good belly laugh from the story, Lynn glanced up and saw him smiling as he watched them over the paper. A month ago, his smile would have died. Now their gazes met in mutual understanding and even a degree of warmth before she turned the page and continued the story.

The third book told of a boy's relationship with a beloved uncle who was a navy captain. It was about the celebration of homecoming and the sadness of goodbyes. When Lynn closed the book, Rose took her thumb from her mouth.

"I don't want you to go tomorrow."

Lynn wrapped an arm around her and squeezed. "Oh, sweetie, I'm going to miss you, too."

"How come you have to go?"

The newspaper had quit rustling. Aware of Adam listening, Lynn said, "We live in Otter Beach. If I'm not there, who will open the bookstore?"

"Can't we stay longer, Mommy?" Shelly asked from her other side.

Lynn let the book slide to the floor and put her other arm around her daughter. "You know we can't, sweetie."

"But why?" Shelly pleaded.

"These are just visits. Rose and Adam will be coming to see us soon. Maybe we can all make a sand castle again. Remember the first time?"

"Can we go tomorrow, Daddy?" Rose begged.

Adam lowered the *Oregonian*. "No, Rosebud, we can't. You know I have to work. Grown-ups have responsibilities."

She cried passionately, "I hate 'sponsibil…bil…"

"Let's enjoy the visit while we can," he suggested. "We have fun when Lynn and Shelly come to stay. Don't spoil it by being sad. The boy in the story Lynn just read to you wasn't always sad when he was with his uncle, even though he knew he'd have to say goodbye, was he?"

She pouted, teardrops trembling on her lashes. "No," she finally whispered, tremulously.

The telephone rang and Adam groaned.

Picking it up, he said, "Yeah? Oh, Mom. Hi, how are you?" After a moment, he nodded. "I'll put Rose on for a second."

He crossed the room and handed Rose the cordless phone. "Say hi to Grandma McCloskey."

Not his mother, then, but Jennifer's.

Rose whispered a shy hello. After a moment she said, "I have a friend here. We're listening to stories."

Adam's hand shot out. "Okay, say bye now."

"Daddy says I gotta go. Bye," she managed to say, before he whipped the phone out of her hand.

Covering the mouthpiece, he said, "I'll go talk out in the kitchen."

"My grandma calls, too," Shelly told her friend. "She's comin' to see us."

"At Christmas," Lynn agreed. "In fact, she'll be here in only seven days."

"My grandma comes at Christmas, too. She says she's gonna bring lots of presents." Rose sounded satisfied if not excited.

"My grandma, too!"

From the kitchen, Adam's voice rose in an angry rumble. "What are you saying? Are you threatening me?"

To cover it, Lynn said brightly, "I'll tell you what. Why don't we take the books up and read some more stories in Rose's bed?"

"Okeydoke," Shelly said, hopping up with alacrity.

"But maybe Daddy wanted to listen," Rose said more doubtfully.

Lynn wrinkled her nose. "It sounds like your daddy is talking to someone else now. He's kind of mad, huh? Does business make him that way? He can come upstairs when he's done."

He did appear eventually, after ten or twelve more books. Both girls were getting sleepy, and when Lynn saw him in the doorway she set down the book. "Bedtime."

"Read another one!" Shelly protested, but the words slurred.

"Dream a story," Lynn murmured. "About an ugly princess and…"

"No, a beautiful one," Shelly interrupted. "'Cuz I'm beautiful, aren't I?"

Rose took her thumb from her mouth. "Me, too."

"You're both beautiful." She kissed them and stood up, passing Adam mid-room.

She went downstairs without pausing, leaving Adam to tuck their daughters in. *Trade about,* she thought, even as she missed the quiet ritual of turning on the night-light, smoothing the sheet over the blankets, breathing in the sleepy essence of two small girls as she touched her lips to smooth foreheads. She'd had all evening. From the rage she'd heard in his voice and the tension in the set of his shoulders, he needed any comfort they could give him.

They'd had dinner earlier with Rose and Shelly, but she poured two cups of coffee and helped herself to a second, sinful slice of lemon meringue pie from the bakery. When Adam came into the kitchen, she waved the knife at the pie. "Would you like a piece, too?"

"What? Oh. No."

She put the pie in the refrigerator. He was leaning against the island, frowning into space.

"Is something wrong?" Lynn asked.

His glower turned her way. "Wrong?"

"You were…um, yelling."

His eyes seemed to clear as if he were noticing her for the first time. "Oh, my God. Could you hear everything?"

"Just something about a threat. I don't think the girls did."

His head bowed suddenly and he pinched the bridge of his nose. "That was my mother-in-law. As you probably gathered. They figured out that Shelly must be visiting, and they wanted to come over. If not tonight, tomorrow."

"You said no."

Adam swore. "They'd swarm over her like yellow

jackets on jam. I can't make them understand why we should move slowly. They only know one thing—they want their granddaughter. Jenny is gone, and Shelly is all they have left, Angela keeps saying. She's like a goddamn broken record.'' He breathed out heavily.

Pie and coffee forgotten, apprehension rising, Lynn asked, ''What did you mean about her threatening?''

His gaze met hers, and she read in it both apology and anger. ''She says they're considering filing for a court order giving them visitation rights if not custody.''

''Custody?'' Lynn sagged back a step.

''They wouldn't get it.'' His face looked haggard, but his voice was strong. ''We're the parents. I'm behind you. Their lawyer will tell them to forget it.''

''But they might get visitation.''

''I don't know.'' He hammered his fist on the tile countertop. ''Damn them!''

''No. Don't say that.'' Perhaps the time was coming, Lynn thought, when they would have to tell Rose and Shelly the truth. Would it really be so hurtful now? If they were assured that nothing would change? ''I understand how they must feel. It's not so different than what we've both gone through.''

''They're a complication we don't need.''

''No.'' Lynn managed a smile of sorts. ''I poured you some coffee.''

She took her own to the table in the nook, and after a moment Adam followed her. This was only the third night she'd spent in this house, and yet these few minutes after the girls had gone to bed already felt familiar. They couldn't talk in front of Rose and Shelly. This was their time.

They sat in silence for a moment, Lynn making a production of stirring sugar into her coffee. Then unexpectedly, Adam said, "I wish you weren't going tomorrow, too."

She quashed a momentary thrill. He didn't mean her, he meant Shelly. "These visits have been nice, haven't they?"

"You're good with them."

She sneaked a look. The lines still between his brows, he was staring down into his coffee as if waiting for pictures of the future to form.

"Thank you."

"You ever considered opening a bookstore in Portland?"

"And competing with Powell's?" The famous bookstore filled a whole city block. "I don't think so."

He frowned at her. "If you lived closer, we could see our daughters more often."

"You could move to Otter Beach."

"You know that's impossible," Adam said impatiently.

What was this all about? "I have an established business," she said reasonably. "Moving wouldn't be any easier for me."

"What if you could find a bookstore for sale over here? Or a good location to start one up?"

She set down her fork. "You're serious."

"Damn straight." He took a swallow of coffee with the air of a man tossing back a shot of whiskey.

"Aren't you getting tired of these teary goodbyes, too?"

"Of course I am, but..."

"But what?" He leaned forward, his expression persuasive. "Think about it. Will you do that?"

"Do you have any idea how tough it was to start up a small business?"

Adam opened his mouth, but she overrode him.

"Without my parents' help, Shelly and I would have starved," Lynn said fiercely. "Ninety percent of small businesses don't make it. I did. And you want me to throw that away. Start all over. It's just not that easy!"

He wasn't ready to give up yet, she could see. He still leaned forward, intent on his perfect plan. "What if you found a going concern that's for sale? Portland has plenty of suburbs that support bookstores."

"Sure it does. Some of those stores are a lot bigger than mine. I couldn't afford them, even assuming I could conveniently find a buyer for my store at the snap of my fingers. Others...well, independents are being driven out of business by the hundreds. Thousands. On-line booksellers like Amazon.com are taking some business. That's bad enough, but as you pointed out yourself, in a metropolitan area like this I'd have to worry about a Barnes & Noble going in on the next block. Heck, B. Dalton and Waldenbooks are already at the mall. And you've got malls around here." She pushed away her half-eaten pie, her appetite gone. "Take a look. Either the independents are big enough to compete, and are therefore out of my league, or they're on the verge of bankruptcy. Trust me.''

Adam sat back, his dark eyes not wavering from her face. After a moment, he said, ''You could get a job.''

''Sure I could. Working for someone else. Hey, maybe if I was lucky B. Dalton would hire me to be a manager! Golly. That would be a thrill after owning my own store.''

His mouth twisted. ''All right. You've convinced me. Bad idea.''

''I *am* tired of saying goodbye. It'll get worse once Rose knows I'm really Mommy and Shelly thinks of you as Daddy. But what can we do?'' Now she was pleading with him. ''We do have responsibilities.''

''Sure we do,'' Adam said flatly. ''One of mine is going to be pacifying Jennifer's parents, convincing them to be patient.''

She'd almost forgotten. ''If you talked to them first, wouldn't they be satisfied just meeting Shelly? For now?''

He closed his eyes wearily. ''If only she didn't look so damned much like Jenny.''

''I'm sorry.'' She bit her lip. ''I forget.''

A razor edge of pain showed in his brown eyes. ''I don't.''

Had his wife known how much she was loved? Once upon a time, Lynn had fooled herself into believing she and Brian were in love, but even then she had known they weren't soul mates, meant for each other through the centuries. But he was handsome, and he wanted her, and he made her laugh. Love was supposed to grow, wasn't it? The grandest kind, she had always believed, was in the quiet clasp of gnarled hands that had known each other's touch for sixty years or more. Why couldn't she and Brian have that, if they worked at it?

Now she knew better. Perhaps the grandest love *was* the kind ripened by half a century or more together, but people couldn't endure each other that long, didn't care enough to hold on through hard times, if what they started with wasn't more heartfelt than "he wanted me" and "he was handsome."

Adam, she guessed, had been lucky enough to know real love.

"You still miss her." Lynn touched the back of his hand.

"When I let myself."

His hand turned over, slowly, giving her time to withdraw. She didn't. He gripped her hand gently, his so much larger, browner. Lynn lifted her gaze to see that he, too, was studying their hands.

"Tell me about your husband," Adam said unexpectedly. "Why did he think you'd been unfaithful?"

A sting of hurt cured her of any drift toward a romantic mood. She tried to yank her hand back, but he held on.

"I know you weren't," he said. "Even I can see that you're not the kind of woman who'd lie to her husband. So why couldn't he?"

You're not the kind of woman who would lie. A barrier of wariness inside her sagged and finally collapsed. Was it possible that her newfound trust was a two-way street? That they really could be friends?

"He never completely trusted me." Her fingers

curled into a fist and Adam let her go. She tucked her hand on her lap, under the table. It seemed to tingle, as if he were still touching her. "Brian would accuse me of not loving him." She made a face. "I'd feel so guilty. I couldn't figure out what I was doing wrong. My mother and I love each other, but we're not...not physically demonstrative. You know?"

Adam nodded.

"Maybe that was it, I'd think, and I'd force myself to hug and kiss even when it embarrassed me in public. But no matter how hard I tried, it was never enough. He'd come into the bookstore where I worked, and be mad because I was laughing with some customer. He'd decide we hadn't really been talking about books, and accuse me of sneaking around behind his back. It was a nightmare."

"Was he abusive?" Adam asked quietly, but with a flat, dangerous note in his voice.

"No. Oh, no." She sneaked a look at his face, set in hard lines. Her nails bit into her palms. "Brian's not that bad a guy. I just...lacked whatever it took to make him feel secure."

"*You* lacked?" Adam growled in the back of his throat. "Seems to me, he's the one with the problem."

"I tried to tell myself that. Our marriage got harder and harder, the more I had to think constantly about what I was really feeling and how he'd interpret the way I was acting. Only, then one day I realized—" here was the hard part "—he was right. I didn't really love him. Not heart and soul. The way he claimed to love me." Lynn shrugged with difficulty, the next words hurting her throat. "I shouldn't have married him. I remember getting cold feet the night before the wedding, but how could I tell him I'd made a mistake then? And my friends all laughed and said everyone chickens out at the last minute, so I decided it was normal. But I think I'd been pretending from the very beginning. He'd say, 'I can't live without you,' and I'd tell him the same, but because he expected me to, not because I had any understanding of what that meant. Until I had Shelly, I couldn't imagine how it would feel to fear losing the one person in the world who was essential to me.'' Lynn met Adam's gaze again in appeal. ''I should have felt that way about him, too, shouldn't I?''

''How old were you when you got married?''

Taken by surprise, she had to think. ''Um... twenty-two. It was the summer after I graduated from college.''

''That's pretty young,'' Adam said conversationally. ''Maybe too young to feel something so profound.''

Unwilling to grasp such an easy excuse, Lynn challenged, ''How old were you and Jennifer?''

''I was twenty-five, she was twenty-two like you.''

''Did you know, deep inside, that she was the one person for you?''

Adam moved in the obvious discomfiture of a man put on the spot. He rubbed his hands on his thighs, and the chair scraped on the vinyl floor. ''I'm not sure men put things in such poetic terms,'' he finally said. ''I wanted her to be my wife. To me, that was a commitment. Once you're in it, you make it work.''

Did that mean he disapproved of her because she was divorced? ''I thought that, too. Brian was the one who moved out. I wasn't giving him what he needed. I think,'' she said a little wryly, ''he'd found someone who could. Although he hasn't remarried.''

''The bastard.''

''But it was my fault.''

Adam uttered an obscenity that shocked her eyes wide-open. ''Get real,'' he said bluntly. ''If the jerk had really loved you, he'd have worked to earn your love, not tried to extract it by whining. He'd have been there with you through thick and thin, not hunting for what he 'needed' elsewhere. And he sure as hell wouldn't have abandoned you financially now, whatever came before. That's not love, even past tense.''

Lynn blinked, then smiled tentatively. ''Thank you. I think.''

''You're welcome.'' The frown that had begun to seem perpetual had returned to his brow. He stood. ''I'm going to call it a night.''

Her gaze found the copper wall clock. Barely nine? What he really meant was, he'd had enough of their tête à tête.

''Good idea.'' She sounded as repulsively chirpy as a morning talk show host. ''I'm in the middle of a book I'm enjoying. Here, just let me rinse this plate off…''

''I'll finish cleaning up.'' His tone allowed no argument. In the confines of the kitchen, his sheer size unnerved her. Except for the three years with Brian, she had never lived with a man, much less one as large and imposing as Adam Landry.

Murmuring disjointed thank-yous and good-nights, Lynn fled. Somehow, she feared, she'd blown this conversation, either disgusting him or boring him, she didn't know which. What had possessed her to go on and on about her marriage? Why not just say, *Brian was the jealous type and I could never satisfy him?* Why admit that her ex-husband's suspicions had been right? Why bare her soul and confess her sense of inadequacy? And this to a daunting man who held a power near to life and death over her?

She peeked in at the girls and saw that Rose had scooted over to cuddle with Shelly. Both heads shared a single pillow. Tears stung her eyes at the sight of her two daughters, as close as the sisters they weren't. Lynn went on to the bathroom and brushed her teeth with unnecessary force. In the guest room, she stripped quickly and pulled her nightgown over her head. Even between flannel sheets with a comforter pulled high, she felt cold.

And lonely, although she and Shelly wouldn't drive away until tomorrow afternoon.

"MERRY CHRISTMAS, HONEY." Lynn's mother heaped the last wrapped gift under the small Douglas fir that just fit in the corner by the window. Downstairs in the bookstore was another, more elegantly decorated tree, a Noble fir wrapped in gold and mauve. This one had tiny lights, a string of popcorn and handmade ornaments interspersed with a few red and green glass balls. Because Shelly had helped trim the tree, the ornaments were clustered where a three-year-old could most easily reach, but Lynn didn't care.

"I'm so glad you're here." She sat at one end of the couch and curled her feet under her, contentedly watching her mother. She began a wistful "I wish…" before thinking better of it.

But mothers had a way of finishing sentences. "Rose were here, too?"

Yes. Oh, yes, her heart cried. She said only, "I'd like you to meet her."

Irene Miller had her daughter's hair without the red highlights, in her case cut short into a curly cap shot with a few gray hairs she ignored. A little plump, she was a placid, quiet woman who had seemed satisfied with her life as a single mother and secretary when Lynn was growing up. Lynn didn't remember her ever even dating, so it had been a shock when she called, during Lynn's sophomore year at the University of Oregon, to announce that she was engaged to be married. Hal Miller had been a guest lecturer at the university where she was a departmental secretary.

"He absolutely insisted I have dinner with him," she had said with a breathless laugh, as though still surprised at either his determination or her own willingness to be swept away, Lynn never knew which. "We've seen each other often since then."

Lynn had grown very fond of her stepfather, who had insisted this afternoon that Shelly was going to take him to the beach. He had winked conspiratorially over her head; today was Christmas Eve, and Shelly was beside herself with excitement. Wasn't Grandma going to put presents under the tree? she'd asked twenty or thirty times. Mama had *promised* she could open one this evening. *When* could she open it? Now?

But she was young enough to be diverted, and the

two had gone off very happily into a misty, chilly day, both so bundled up they looked as if they were heading for the Arctic.

Hearing other mothers whining about how their husbands never took over the child care and gave them a break, Lynn usually wondered why they wanted one. She enjoyed Shelly's company. Shelly's naps gave her a little time to herself. When she absolutely had to run errands without her daughter, baby-sitting was available. But she had to admit, in the week since her mother and stepfather had arrived, she was discovering how nice it was to have someone else cheerfully offer to go to the grocery store, whip up dinner or take Shelly away for an hour here or there. She could get spoiled.

Her mother rose easily, smoothing her slacks as she admired the Christmas tree. Then she came and sat on the arm of the couch beside Lynn. Although Lynn had told Adam the truth—Irene Miller's warmth was in her smile and words more than in her rarely bestowed hugs—this time her mother put out a gentle hand and smoothed her daughter's hair from her face.

"You said he might bring her for a visit next week."

"Yes." Lynn smiled with difficulty. "Of course."

Her mother studied her worriedly. "Will you get used to seeing her only sometimes? Or are you always going to regret that you didn't share more of her life?"

"I don't know." Lynn had wondered the same thing, but it wasn't as if she had a choice. "What can we do?"

"You're lucky that he wants only the best for both girls, too."

"I know I am," Lynn said on a sigh. "I was so sure at first that he'd try to take Shelly from me. But he really does adore Rose. He calls her his Rosebud, did I tell you that?" Of course she had. She'd talked of little *but* her newly discovered daughter this past week. Her mother must be getting sick of hearing her go on and on! But she couldn't seem to help herself. "I think he really, truly does want the same thing as I do for the girls."

"Whatever that is," Mrs. Miller said softly.

Trust her mother to figure out how muddled Lynn's dreams still were. But what could she and Adam do other than experiment until one day the routine was right?

"Do you think Shelly is ready to find out Adam is her father?" Lynn asked, as much for reassurance as in the belief her mother really had the answers.

Mrs. Miller made a face. "Is anyone ever ready to find out something like that?"

"I wouldn't have been," Lynn admitted. "In fact…"

"In fact?"

She was sorry she'd begun. Or was she? Now that she had a child of her own, she wondered more than ever about her own father.

"Do you know, I used to imagine all kinds of things about who my father was."

Her mother stood and went to the tree, moving an ornament from one branch to another as if she'd suddenly noticed a lack of balance. Her back to Lynn, she said almost casually, "Oh? Who was he? A movie star?"

"That crossed my mind, along with a cowboy or a spy or Roberta's dad. Do you remember him? He was...oh, a TV repairman, I think."

Mrs. Miller didn't laugh at the very idea as Lynn had expected. In fact, she said nothing.

Twining her fingers on her lap, Lynn continued steadily, "But what I finally decided was that you'd gone to a sperm bank."

That one did get a reaction. Her mother spun around. "What?"

"Women do it." Lynn watched her carefully. "I thought maybe you were single and decided to have a baby. And that, well, you chose what qualities you wanted and didn't know anything else about the donor. Which is why you never talked about him. My father."

Her mother's laugh was semihysterical. "Oh, dear! Oh, I should have guessed that you might think of something like that." She seemed to sag, still standing there in the middle of Lynn's tiny living room. "Do you want to know the truth?"

"Yes," Lynn said quietly. "I always have, you know."

But never so much as lately, she realized. Ties of blood weren't necessary to love, she had discovered, but they did exert a pull she had never understood.

"He was a married man." Shame crept over Irene Miller's cheeks, although she met Lynn's gaze. "Not your friend Roberta's father, although he might as well have been. It was...it was something that should never have happened. I suppose I was lonely, and...if it had been just a one-night stand, a case of being swept away, I could excuse myself. But actually I...I slept with him several times.''

"Oh, Mom," Lynn whispered. "Things like that happen. *He* was the one who was married!"

Her mother's chin lifted with conscious dignity. "I can only be responsible for my own decisions, and I knew better. I despised myself, but I was lonely and he was such a kind man! I thought his marriage must be in trouble." Her smile was faint and tinged with remembered bitterness. "But after a couple of weeks, when he'd said nothing about leaving his wife or our future, I realized that he had no such thing in mind. I was the one with foolish dreams. I quit my job—he was my boss. He probably started a...a fling with the next secretary. Very likely he made a habit of them.''

"And you found out you were pregnant.''

A single woman with no great job skills and distant parents who were unlikely to help, she must have been terrified.

This smile was more genuine, but her mother's eyes were misty. "I never regretted what happened, not the way I should have, because out of it I had you. Please believe that.''

"Oh, Mom!" Lynn catapulted off the sofa and wrapped her arms around her mother, who hugged her back although such embraces weren't commonplace for them. "I do believe you, because I feel the same about Shelly. It scares me sometimes. I think that I should have realized I didn't love Brian enough. I shouldn't have married him. But if I hadn't…'' She shivered and pulled back a little. ''Then I wouldn't have Shelly.''

An odd thought sifted into her mind. No, *she* wouldn't have Shelly, but Adam would. The mix-up would never have happened that night at the hospital. *Rose* was the child who wouldn't have been born. Quiet, sweet-faced Rose.

The very idea was equally unendurable.

A thunder of feet on the stairs gave warning before the door burst open and Shelly called, ''Me and Grampa are home! Did Grandma…oooh,'' she breathed, when she saw the bright packages spilling out from under the tree. Puzzlement replaced the dazed joy in her eyes when she saw her mother's face. ''Why is Mommy crying?''

''Oh.'' Lynn dashed at her cheeks. ''Happiness. I'm just being silly, punkin.'' And feeling dizzily as if she had been remade in a new form. She had a father. She would never meet him, but now she knew, which seemed to matter.

Her daughter frowned. ''But Grandma's crying, too.''

Hal Miller laid hands on his small step-granddaughter's shoulders. ''I think she's crying from happiness, too.''

''But I cry when I'm hurt. Or scared. Not when I'm happy,'' Shelly objected.

''Grown-ups do sometimes,'' Irene said. She gave Lynn another quick, spontaneous hug. ''When they realize how lucky they are.''

''Right.'' Lynn blinked back more tears that threatened despite her smile. ''You know what, sweetheart? I think this might be a good time for you to open that present.''

Shelly squealed and flung herself to her knees in front of the tree. "I want the *best* present!"

Hal, gentle, balding man that he was, ignored the undercurrents of emotion and settled onto the sofa with a smile. Lynn's mother went down on her knees and joined her granddaughter in a colloquy about which present would be the most satisfying, considering she got only one tonight.

Lynn stood back and watched, fighting a strange desire to cry. She had a successful business, a home, her parents, and Shelly. It wasn't as if her real daughter was abandoned in an orphanage or lived in a home without warmth and love. There would be a beautiful tree in Rose's living room with ten times the presents under it that Shelly had. Her grandparents—perhaps both sets of grandparents—would be there tonight, and, best of all, her daddy would do everything in his power to insure that her Christmas was joyous.

Once upon a time, Lynn had only wanted to be certain her child was happy and loved. Why, oh why, was that knowledge no longer enough?

Why did grief swathe her in gray that took the glory out of the bright sparkling lights on the tree and the wondering "ooh" in her daughter's voice as the wrappings gave way to her still-clumsy fingers? Why did she mourn, only because Rose was not here?

CHAPTER NINE

ROSE'S SMALL HAND CREPT into Adam's. "Do you think Shelly got good presents, too?"

"I bet she did," Adam said heartily, although he felt sick looking at the torrent of ripped paper and bows and ribbon covering the floor. Toys and new clothes and books formed islands in the midst of the chaos. No, he knew damn well Shelly didn't get as much.

But then, Rose didn't need any of it. He'd bought less this Christmas and had made a point of taking Rose shopping to choose gifts for children whose parents couldn't. Somewhat to his surprise, given her egocentric age, she had helped him, earnestly debating which Barbie would be the most fun if you could only have one, which remote control car was the coolest. She'd learned that word lately from bigger kids at the preschool, piping up in her little girl voice, "Cool."

Adam's relative restraint in the gift department was meaningless, however. Her two sets of grandparents had come bearing carloads of goodies. On the one hand, he was glad: even Jennifer's parents weren't turning their backs on Rose. Although Angela had given him a couple of wrapped gifts to set aside for Shelly, she hadn't stinted where Rose was concerned.

On the other hand, he wished they had more time for Rose instead of so much money. Rose would have loved to go to their house one day a week instead of to preschool. But no, they were too busy. Visits instead were special occasions that usually cost a hell of a lot and took the place of something deeper.

He'd begun to realize that the McCloskeys must have raised their only child in much the same way. If Jenny had had a flaw, it was her liking for luxuries and for her own way. She pouted with such charm, somehow he'd never minded, but just lately he had begun to wonder whether that might not have changed. He felt disloyal that the thought had even edged into his mind but couldn't dislodge it.

Would Jenny have had the patience to be a good mother? Or had she looked forward to having a baby like a child wanting a doll? Of course she was going to do it all herself; she'd read a million books and planned every glorious moment. What she hadn't foreseen was that having a sobbing baby waking you every couple of hours all night long, night after exhausting night, was not glorious. Those parenting books hadn't showcased a photo of a three-year-old's stinky diaper. The whining of a tired child was mentioned, certainly, but the boy in the picture was so cute the reader couldn't imagine how explosively tired and angry and tense a parent could get.

Sometimes—God help him—his imagination balked at the idea of his Jenny coping. If she'd lived, by now they might have a nanny who would present a sweet-mannered, clean child for a good-night kiss.

He tried to convince himself he was doing Jenny an injustice.

Once again, he shoved the disloyal thoughts under a pile of mental garbage that he hoped would keep them from surfacing again.

"We'll see Shelly next week," he reminded Rose. "You can show each other your new stuff. And exchange presents."

Rosebud's fingers tightened and her eyes pleaded. "I wish we could see her today."

So did he.

He wanted to spend Christmas with both daughters. And with Lynn, who was inescapably part of their peculiar mixed family. The day stretched bleakly before Adam and Rose. Both sets of parents had come last night. He'd cooked a huge ham and all the trimmings then. The two mismatched couples had made polite conversation and avoided inflammatory subjects like politics. His parents had left as soon as possible with their usual excuses. He imagined that today his father had gone to the hospital and his mother was working at her wheel and keeping an eye on the red-hot kiln.

Angela and Rob had wanted him to bring Rose to their house today, but he'd demurred. The past week, they'd dropped talk of lawyers and court—the Christmas spirit must have gotten to them—but the threat wasn't removed, only in abeyance. It tainted his affection for them. Just lately he'd noticed, too, that Rose was nice to them, but not comfortable. She didn't run into their arms for a hug, or go to Grandma when she bumped herself on the coffee table, or confide in her shy voice to Grandpa.

Not the way she did with Lynn.

"Don't you want to play with your new toys?" he asked Rose now, as they stood looking at the aftermath of last night's and this morning's whirlwind of gift opening.

"Will you play with me?" she pleaded.

Not dolls. Please, not dolls. "Did you get any games?" he asked hopefully.

"Uh-huh." Her mood lifted. "Chutes 'n Ladders. I've played that one at school. And Grandma 'Closkey gave me a clown game. Only, I don't know where it is."

Oh, God. He supposed he should clean up. Where was *his* Christmas spirit?

In Otter Beach. The answer came swiftly, certainly.

"Lily," he said, "let me make a quick phone call."

"Okay." She didn't correct her name, a barometer of how spirited *she* was feeling. "Then can you help me find my new games?"

He crushed her into a hug. "You betcha, Violet."

A giggle rewarded him. "Daddy! I'm *Rose*."

In the kitchen, Adam dialed and drummed his fingers while the phone rang once, twice, four times. When someone picked it up, "Jingle Bells" was playing in the background. "Hello?" said an unfamiliar woman.

Rose's grandmother. "Uh...merry Christmas to you. May I speak to Lynn?"

"Of course." The voice was warm and friendly. "And the same to you."

Lynn came on a moment later, sounding breathless. "Adam!" she exclaimed, when he'd identified himself. "Did Santa visit?"

Thinking about his living room, he said ruefully, "Big time. Did he touch down there, too?"

"Oh, yeah. Did you want to talk to Shelly?"

"Actually…" Unconsciously he squared his shoulders. "I was wondering. Do you have anything special planned for today?"

Stupid question. It was *Christmas,* for Pete's sake. But he didn't retract it.

"No," Lynn said quietly. "Except, my parents are here."

"So you said. Um, what I was thinking is…" Damned good thing he didn't stumble and fumble like this all the time. He finished more strongly, "That maybe Rose and I could drive over today. She wants to play with Shelly, and your parents could meet her."

"Today." Lynn sounded dazed.

"If it's not convenient…"

"No," she said quickly. "No, I'd love to have you. I just thought…aren't you getting together with your parents? Or Jennifer's?"

"We did that last night."

"Oh." He could hear a dawning smile in her voice. "Please. Come. We'd love to have you. Can you stay the night?"

"Your parents…"

"Have a room at an inn." She laughed. "That sounds fitting, doesn't it?"

"Rose and I'll pack up and be on our way as soon as we can."

"I'm so glad you called."

He was, too. Suddenly Christmas Day had become joyous.

LYNN CHANAK'S HOME at Christmas was everything he'd imagined it would be. Everything, despite the poverty of her possessions, that his wasn't.

Her mother and stepfather were warm, uncritical and present not just in a corporeal way, like his own parents. The Millers seemed delighted to meet him and they swept Rose into an affectionate circle of games and stories that soon had her chattering as naturally as she did with him.

Carols played in the background, the delicious smell of turkey and stuffing in the oven drifted from the kitchen, the decorations were more affecting for being modest and homemade. If Shelly hadn't gotten as many gifts as Rose, she hadn't suffered. She and Rose would have plenty to do today.

A cold rain fell outside, but the early darkness pressing at the windows suited the season and made him all the gladder for the golden glow of life and liking in here. With four adults and two children, there were hardly enough places to sit; except for the girls and Grandma, who insisted on joining them at the kitchen table, they ate with plates on their laps and drinks carefully set on the floor at their feet. He and Hal Miller, Lynn's stepfather, talked about the economy and the stock market. Miller had enough investments to be interested and to have some intelligent questions and observations about the recent, unexpected drop in the prime rate. The feds had everyone puzzled.

"I've bought shares in several of the more solid Internet companies, even though they're not making much of a profit yet," he commented. "It's got to be the future."

Lynn made a face. "Don't tell me you've invested in my competition?"

"'fraid so." He grinned. "Figured we'd better have a cushion in case the independent book business crashes."

She rolled her eyes, but grinned. "Oh, thank you. I'll have you know we had a fabulous Christmas season!"

"Weather was good this fall," Adam said. "Did that keep tourists coming?"

"It didn't hurt, but tourism is booming over here no matter what the weather," she answered. "Off-season rates entice people to get away for a few days. I guess an ocean storm sounds exotic and wonderful compared to a Portland or Seattle drizzle. Everyone hopes to find a treasure washed up on the beach afterward. In the meantime, they get here and it's rainy and cold and they didn't bring enough to do in their hotel rooms." She sounded smug. "They come and see me."

"Ah." Her stepfather nodded seriously. "Not hard to find something to read in your place. I browsed yesterday." He glanced at Adam. "Good section on money and investing."

"I noticed." Adam had browsed, too. Wanting— *well, hell, admit it,* he thought—to find out how smart Lynn Chanak was.

Very, he had concluded. She knew her business, which a surprising number of people who hung out a shingle didn't.

Lynn excused herself to dish up apple pie, à la mode, for those who wanted it. The pie was warm and obviously homemade. Flaky crust, the apples spicy, tart and melt-on-the-tongue soft.

Taking a sip of coffee followed by a mouthful of pie, Adam almost groaned in pleasure. Without a drop of alcohol, he felt as if he'd imbibed a snifter of fine cognac, not enough to get fuzzy, just enough to make him relaxed, benevolent.

In one corner of the living room, Rosebud and Shelly squealed happily over a game that seemed to involve contorting their bodies into absurd positions to put hand or foot on big bright colored circles on a mat. Grandma Miller spun a dial and announced, "Right hand, blue!" and the girls both collapsed in an attempt to move their hands.

The next round, they spun the dial while Grandma and Mom played. Adam savored the sight of Lynn, her nicely rounded bottom sticking up in the air as she struggled to keep left foot on yellow, right on blue, and her hands on two different colors. Her legs, he couldn't help thinking, were deliciously long, her hair a glorious tousle that tumbled to the mat and exposed a pale, delicate nape. Her cheeks were flushed with laughter, her eyes bright, her groans throaty.

Damn it, he was *happy,* Adam realized in some astonishment. He and Rose had good times, but it wasn't the same. He *liked* being here, or having Lynn—and Shelly, of course—staying at his place.

He wished they could do it more often. He was amazingly comfortable with Lynn. As far as he was concerned, she could just move in with Shelly…

Bang. He might as well have walked into a sliding glass door. Dazed, head pounding, Adam saw the answer to everything through the clarity of the glass.

A marriage of convenience. Miraculous convenience. They could share the girls, each have a legal claim on the other one. The grandparent problem would be solved. He could help Shelly and Lynn financially. He didn't have to miss them. Rose and Shelly would be sisters in truth.

He hardly saw Lynn fall amid giggles, leaving Grandma triumphant but needing a hand to straighten up and unkink her back. Adam was too busy examining his incredible idea.

Yeah, okay, he argued with himself out of habit, he wasn't in love with her. Presumably she wasn't with him. But he wasn't seeing anyone else, and he hadn't heard even a hint that she was. He liked her. They could talk about things he usually stayed close-mouthed about, and he had an idea she felt the same about him. God knows, they had something profound in common: their daughters.

He wasn't looking for a love match. Once was enough. But he missed having a woman in his bed and at the breakfast table. He'd been disconcerted by his attraction to Lynn, but what had formerly been a problem now was a bonus. Despite the peculiar beginning, they might make a comfortable, affectionate marriage out of it. It didn't have to be temporary. He could see himself growing old with her.

Assuming she saw the logic of his proposal.

Damn, he thought in astonishment. Proposal? Did he mean it?

"Is something wrong?"

Adam swung his head around sharply enough to crack a vertebra. Lynn had sat down on the couch beside him and was gazing at him with soft concern.

"Wrong?" he croaked. "No. Nothing's wrong." It was right. He wanted to shout and seize her hand. Go to his knees.

Now? Her parents were making leaving motions. He could let her tuck the girls into bed, and then ask.

But he wasn't a man of impulse. No. Wait until the chill gray light of morning and see whether his idea seemed as brilliant. Maybe he'd be dying to escape back to his big solitary house after a look at Lynn Chanak in her bathrobe before a cup of coffee.

Of course, he'd seen her that way before, and she'd looked cute.

Wait. Don't be an idiot, he told himself. *Be sure before you jump.*

Morning was soon enough.

ADAM AWAKENED at the damned crack of dawn after another wretched, chivalrous night on Lynn's too-short couch. He felt as if he'd had more than a snifter or two of that nonexistent cognac. His head pounded, his mouth was dry, and his joints ached. He dreaded the drive home.

Christmas was gone, and with it his cheer.

He couldn't stand under the hot spray in a shower, because that might wake everyone else up. Disgruntled, he rooted in his overnight bag and got dressed in clean clothes. After gulping a couple of painkillers in the bathroom, Adam went to the kitchen, put water on to boil and dumped two teaspoons of instant coffee into a mug. Then he braced his hands on the edge of the counter and stared at the kettle, waiting for steam and gurgling.

What if she walked into the kitchen right now? Smiled shyly, offered to make breakfast? Adam asked himself. Would he wish her to Hades, or feel his mood lift?

The kettle stayed still. The force of his stare didn't heat the water.

His thoughts stumbled back into a rut worn by a night's worth of brooding.

Was he insane to think of marrying a woman he didn't love, didn't even know all that well except as the mother of his three-year-old daughter?

No.

The answer stayed the same. It made sense. So much sense, he couldn't believe he hadn't thought of the possibility before. He wondered if Lynn had.

Maybe it would have occurred to him before if he didn't find the idea of a temporary marriage abhorrent. He was old-fashioned in believing that a wedding vow should be kept. No matter how convenient it would be to take Lynn and Shelly into his household, he wouldn't have considered proposing if he didn't think they could make the marriage work for the long haul.

The teakettle whispered and gave a little hop.

He heard a footstep a second before Lynn said, "Good morning."

There she was in a new, nubby cotton bathrobe and fuzzy slippers, with her tousled hair, sleepy eyes and sweet smile reminding him sharply of his—no, *her*—daughter on early weekday mornings. Yet there was nothing childlike about her. The bathrobe sagged open above a loosely knotted tie, giving him a glimpse of flowery flannel and creamy throat and chest with a sprinkling of cinnamon freckles. He had to tear his gaze from the first swell of breasts beneath a lacy edging on her nightgown.

"Good morning." After hearing his scratchy voice, he cleared his throat. "Did I wake you?"

"No, I just didn't sleep well." Her gaze flew to his. "Oh, dear. There's no way you did, either. I wish you'd let me take the couch."

"Maybe next time."

"I'll hold you to that." Lynn advanced hesitantly into the kitchen. "Your water's boiling."

"It is?" The kettle was rattling on the burner, steam bursting out. "Oh. Right. Can I get you something?"

"I'll make a cup of tea." She stood on tiptoe and took down a copper canister that held tea bags.

Adam wanted to take a step across the tiny kitchen, wrap his hands around her waist and bury his face in her wild, soft curls.

Hands fisting, he managed to stay put as she murmured under her breath and got out a mug, adding sugar and one of those tea bags that brought the scent of oranges and spice into the kitchen. With an apology, she took the step to him, but reached past him for the kettle. Adam stood frozen as she poured boiling water into first her own cup and then his.

"Are you hungry yet?" she asked.

"Um? Oh." The grit was in his throat again.

"No." Still he didn't move, watching as she took her mug to the table. "Were the girls still asleep?"

Her smile was fond. "Rose was giving little snorts. Shelly has her head under her pillow."

She'd momentarily distracted him. "Rose sounds like a little pig when she's deep under. I've wondered if her tonsils will need taking out."

"Well, snoring is not hereditary," she said in amusement. "Brian didn't, and I'm pretty sure I don't."

So she slept quietly. Would she burrow like Rosebud did when she slept with him? Would she murmur under her breath, the way she did when she was puttering around the house? Would he wake to find her head on his shoulder?

He grabbed his mug and took a scalding gulp. The burst of caffeine failed to clear his head.

"I'm not looking forward to going home," he said abruptly. *Okay, it was a beginning.*

Lynn looked up in surprise. "You're welcome to stay another day if you'd like. I know Shelly would be pleased. In fact, stay as long as you'd like. Are you taking the week until New Year's off?"

"No, I wasn't planning to."

Actually, a generally disappointing Christmas retail season was playing hell with the stock market. Right now, he didn't give a flying you-know-what.

He took another gulp of coffee, then tried a new tack. "I was thinking."

"Yes?" Her eyes were wide and clear, a gray as luminous as the dawn sky.

"I've thought of a solution to this back-and-forth business."

Her lips parted and he imagined that her expression became wary, but she said nothing.

"Will you marry me?"

She stared at him for the longest time. Adam shifted uneasily.

"Say something." He sounded gruff. Defensive.

"I…" Lynn swallowed. "You mean as a…a sort of convenience?"

"At first." He rubbed his hands on his thighs. "For the girls. We can take it slowly." Dimly he realized that this wasn't coming out the way he'd intended it to. He sounded as though he was proposing a cold-blooded legal contract, not a flesh-and-blood marriage. "I'm not saying we'll get divorced. Down the line, I mean." Oh, yeah, that was coherent. "I thought maybe we could make it work," he stumbled on. "You and me."

He'd have sworn she hadn't blinked in two minutes. The owl-like stare had him twitching like a second-grader in trouble with Teacher.

"Is this another way of convincing me to sell the bookstore and move to Portland?" she finally asked.

"No." Yes. Of course he wanted her to. She'd no longer need the income.

No, he realized in confusion, he didn't want her to give up something she loved. Besides, he liked this house, its creaks, the sound of the ocean always throbbing in the background.

"I thought," he tried again, "that for now we could commute. I could come over here two or three days a week, and you could bring Shelly to Portland on the days when the bookstore is closed. We could be together most of the time without changing anything.''

Who was he kidding?

But she didn't call him on it. Instead she continued to study him with grave eyes. ''You're serious,'' she said at last.

''Damn straight I am.'' He was getting irritated. ''It would let you be Rose's mother, me be Shelly's father. It would solve all our problems.''

''But…marriage.''

She *hadn't* considered the possibility, he could see. She was too shocked.

''We get along well. We want the best for Shelly and Rose.'' They had to talk about sex. ''I won't push you into the marriage bed, but I thought, down the line…'' He'd said that already. Spit it out, he told himself. ''I find you attractive. I can wait, but I don't, uh, find the idea unappealing.'' The palms he rubbed on his thighs were sweaty now. ''If you do…''

''I…'' Suddenly she wasn't looking at him. ''No, I suppose not. I just hadn't…'' Her voice died away.

''I hadn't, either.''

''Marriage.''

He wished she'd quit saying the word in that incredulous way. ''I think we can pull it off.''

Her pretty greenish-gray eyes flashed with annoyance. ''Pull it off? We're not talking about a corporate merger. Or…or a buyout.''

He went to her at last, sitting across the tiny Formica table. ''Lynn, I won't pretend to be in love with you. I haven't thought of you that way. But I like you, and I do love my daughters. Both of them. I know you do, too. Can't we learn to love each other, too?''

Her soft exhalation sounded as if he'd landed a blow to her body. She seemed to sag inside that thick chenille robe. "I need to keep the bookstore."

"That's fine."

She looked fiercely at him. "It'll mean compromises for you, too."

Hardly daring to breath, he agreed, "Of course."

"Then—" her eyes closed briefly, and when she met his gaze again, hers was dazed "—yes. I'll marry you."

He was shaken by a surge of exhilaration out of proportion to the deal they'd just struck. Disquieted, he hid a response that was partly sexual. Instead, he stood, took a step and kissed her cheek.

"Good," he said inadequately. "When?"

"I...I suppose there's no reason to wait." She still sounded shell-shocked. "My parents are here."

He kept a tight rein on his gratification. "We can apply for a license today."

A tremor passed through her. "All right."

"You won't regret this," he said quietly.

This time she visibly shuddered. "I hope and pray you're right. But for Rose and Shelly..."

She'd do anything. He'd counted on it. And it scared the hell out of him to think of what they were going to do for the sake of two toddlers.

THEIR WEDDING DAY DAWNED clear and cold, with a wind that sliced through overcoats. Lynn's minister had agreed to marry them when he heard the details of their situation, although he had expressed reservations about marriage as a solution.

So there they were, gathered in the small white church two blocks from the oceanfront, a tiny cluster at the altar. Lynn's mother and stepfather had come, of course. A friend of Lynn's was maid of honor; likewise, Adam had asked Ron Chainey, his closest friend, who was also his business partner, to drive over from Portland to stand as best man. He told his own parents about the wedding but didn't expect them to come and wasn't surprised by their absence. Jennifer's parents he hadn't invited. Their shock was too evident, their fear that he would forget their Jenny.

Lynn wore a navy-blue sheath with creamy pearls, her hair in a loose roll. With him in a dark suit and white shirt, the two of them looked as ready to attend a funeral as a wedding.

The brightest note was provided by the two flower girls in matching white dresses with frothy full skirts—Grandma Miller had outfitted them. Each carried a small basket filled with dried rose petals that the girls scattered in front of the altar.

"Dearly beloved," began the minister, an older, balding man whose doubts were as plain as his kindness. He talked about duty and affection and "for better or worse." Standing beside his bride, Adam listened, but the words rolled over him. He'd never expected to hear them again as a participant.

Jenny, forgive me, he thought, but she wasn't real to him right now. Lynn was, although she felt more like a stranger than ever.

"To love and to cherish…"

Would love come? The very idea felt like a betrayal of the wedding vows he'd made long ago. But even they had said "till death do us part." Jenny was gone, Lynn here.

All he had to do was turn his head a fraction so that he could see the flower girls, both wide-eyed and radiant.

"You mean, Lynn will be my mommy?" Rose had asked, with such hope his heart had flipped over. "And she'll still be Shelly's mommy, too?"

"That's right," he'd said gravely. "And I'll be Shelly's daddy. You'll have to share me. Do you mind?"

She had shaken her head hard and squeezed him around the neck. "Shelly's my best friend," Rosebud whispered.

"Now she'll be your sister."

They held hands during the ceremony, looking enough alike in their white dresses, with their hair done the same and sprinkled with glitter, that he could see how they might have been mistaken for each other as infants. Closing his eyes, he could just summon the glimpse he'd had of his newborn daughter being handed to a nurse, body slick with blood and God knows what else, fuzz of brown hair damp against her head, eyes squeezed shut and mouth forming a circle as she drew air for a first sob.

If only they had banded her then...

"Do you, Lynn Marie Chanak, take this man, Adam Thomas Landry, to be your lawfully wedded husband..."

Jenny would still be dead. Was this so bad?

"I do," Lynn said clearly.

"Do you, Adam Thomas Landry, take this woman, Lynn Marie Chanak, to be your lawfully wedded wife, in sickness and in health…"

For better or worse.

He stole one last glance at his daughters and said, in a strong, confident voice, "I do."

CHAPTER TEN

LYNN STOLE A LOOK at the man sitting at the other end of the couch—the *new* couch, the one bought today, only hours after she'd let that same man slip a wedding ring onto her finger. He was her husband, she thought in disbelief that leaped to life every time she let herself realize what she'd done.

She was married.

She gave her head a small shake that failed to reorient her. This had been the strangest day of her entire life, which was saying quite a bit considering she'd also had the experience of discovering that her baby had been switched with another in the hospital. It was another strange day on top of a string of them. Her mother telling her about her father, then Adam asking her to marry him, totally out of the blue.

Her parents had urged them to take a short getaway by themselves. In a panic at the idea of being totally alone with her new husband, Lynn had made excuses. Adam had seemed relieved, which bothered her a little bit. Hadn't he been the one to talk about sex and how he wanted this marriage to last? Obviously, he wasn't consumed with lust for her.

Which should have left her feeling relieved and didn't. Lynn told herself it was natural to have her ego mildly bruised by his lack of enthusiasm. Déjà vu. She was back in the halls of her high school, invisible to popular boys.

Adam wouldn't have noticed her then, and didn't seem all that eager now to do more than legally claim his daughter.

The end result today was that instead of a romantic wedding getaway, wanted by neither party, Lynn and Adam had left the girls with Lynn's mom and step-dad and had driven to Lincoln City for lunch. Even that minor social step wasn't an overwhelming hit. Conversation was stilted. Mostly they discussed their future schedule, how to commute with the least fuss and make room in each other's homes. She felt as if she were discussing the logistics of a publisher's fall campaign with the rep.

Only, these logistics had to do with where Adam could keep his underwear and toothbrush and where she would sleep.

"Rose can have several drawers in Shelly's dresser," Lynn suggested, in her practical mode. "That way you won't have to pack each time for her. I have space in my closet for some of your things, too, if you'd like. Maybe we could add some wire shelves, or…" Momentarily she balked at picturing his shirts hanging next to hers, at the idea of him wandering bare chested into her room in the morning to search for clean clothes. Lamely she added, "Well, whatever you need."

She suspected he would look very nice bare chested. Although dark haired, he wasn't a hairy man as, strangely, her blond husband had been. She imagined smooth, tanned skin over supple muscles. Did

Adam work out regularly? There was so much she didn't know about him.

She tuned back in to see him pulling out his wallet. Lynn was embarrassed to realize she hadn't even noticed the waiter presenting the check. Had she been staring at him the entire while?

If so, Adam hadn't noticed. A slight frown suggested he was as pensive as she was. While counting out money, Adam looked at her. "There's going to be plenty to work out, isn't there?"

It boggled the mind. Astonishment washed over her with the cold force of an ocean wave. She'd never done anything so impetuous.

He cleared his throat. "I thought we could go shopping while we're here. If I'm going to be at your place half the week, we need a new sofa. It doesn't exactly count as a wedding present, considering I'm buying it for selfish reasons, but I want you to pick it out."

Selfish reasons. That meant he intended to continue sleeping in the living room. He'd give her time.

He didn't want her.

Of course, it was relief that had her nodding like an idiot. What else could it be? "I shouldn't let you spend the money, but...okay."

In the furniture store, she sucked in a breath at the first price tag she turned over.

Adam gripped her arm and moved her past a mini-showroom that featured chintz-covered furniture and an armoire so rustic you could get a splinter from opening a cabinet door.

"Don't worry about price. Let's get something decent. Preferably a sleeper."

Don't worry about price. Imagine being able to say something like that. Imagine meaning it! she marveled.

Somehow, he continued to grip her arm. Occasionally his hand moved to the small of her back as he steered her. At the hospital that first day, she'd resented his masterful attitude. Today, she was too numb. Too aware that she had just married this man. Someday, the big hand gripping her arm might unhook her bra, cup her breast, slide under the hem of her nightgown...

She gulped. He gave her an sidelong look but didn't comment.

They finally agreed on a brocade sofa that pulled out into a queen sleeper. Lynn didn't watch him write the check for such an unbelievable amount. When he joined her where she stood contemplating a cherry end table, Adam said, "I talked them into delivering it this afternoon."

And paid extra, she was willing to bet. She only nodded. "Do we need to get home, then?"

He glanced at his watch. "I suppose we should."

The salesman ushered them out the front door. "Mr. Landry, Mrs. Landry, I hope you'll come again."

Mrs. Landry. *I'm a married woman,* Lynn thought, stunned.

The couch arrived less than an hour after they got home. The two husky teenage boys carried her old one out with them.

Lynn still couldn't decide whether buying a sofa was symbolic of how far apart she and Adam were, how unreal their marriage, or whether it had been an act of intimacy: the first home furnishing they'd chosen together. Nesting.

Her discomfiture was increased when, presumably to be tactful, her mother and stepfather decided to drive up to Cannon Beach and go out to dinner, leaving Adam, Lynn and the girls to have their first evening as a family.

She had to keep telling herself nothing was different. Adam had spent the night before. She'd spent the night at his house. The only difference now was that they'd taken a legal step to clarify custody of the girls.

Annoyingly, her mind summoned words she didn't want to hear. *For better or worse. In sickness and in health. Do you take this man…*

She heard her own voice, soft and fervent, *I do.*

The traditional ceremony had not asked, *Do you take this man's daughter?*

She had known the promises she was making, as Adam had known the ones he made.

If only she'd had time to *think* before she committed herself to marriage. To forever.

But would I have refused him? she asked herself, and knew the answer. Of course not.

Silently calling herself a coward the whole time, Lynn dawdled over cleaning the kitchen after dinner, drawing out the girls' story time, the small evening rituals. She took forever to braid Rose's long curly hair, telling herself she had a right to indulge herself with the daughter whose first three years of life she'd missed. At last, even Rose began to wriggle and mumble, "Ouch."

Adam was the one who said firmly, "Bedtime, girls. Let's get those teeth brushed."

Lynn almost protested, but realized she was using their daughters as a barricade between herself and her new husband. Not fair, to them or her.

He supervised the toothbrushing and changing into nighties, Lynn tucked them into bed. When she reluctantly returned to the living room, Adam was watching CNN. She sat as far from him as she could get on the new sofa, sinking into its comfort with a sigh of involuntary bliss. She would never have spent so much for a piece of furniture, but she could enjoy it, couldn't she?

Adam snapped off the television. In the sudden silence, Lynn's heart took an uncomfortable leap. It was their wedding night. What did he have in mind?

"Your parents have been exceptionally understanding," he said.

Conversation. She could make conversation, she thought in giddy relief. "I suppose this seemed like a good solution to them, too."

"Does it to you?"

Lynn was startled into really looking at him. "I married you, didn't I?"

"Yeah, but I've been wondering if you're not belatedly getting cold feet." Tension in the set of his shoulders belied his calm tone. "Did I rush you into something you're regretting?"

"We did rush." She was still in shock; her feet were so cold she had to tuck them under her. But she couldn't let him take all the responsibility. "You're right, though. Look how happy the girls are. This really makes sense."

"Logic and emotions don't always take the same road."

"No." She struggled for honesty. "I may be sorry later. I hope not. I never thought I wanted to get married again. I wasn't very good at it the first time around." She shook her head when he started to say something. "I know you blame Brian, but I'm the one who wasn't ready to be married. I wasn't deeply in love. I guess I'm a little scared because I've just done the same thing again. But at least we're in the same boat. Our feelings aren't out of balance."

"No." His expression was odd. "Arranged marriages have worked in the past. I don't see why we can't make this one."

She wanted more than that, Lynn was astonished to realize. *Making it work* sounded so emotionless, so lacking in passion.

She forced herself to meet his eyes. "I'll try." Her voice cracked. "I can promise you that much."

Adam held out a hand to her. "I'm…not a casual man. You're my wife. That means something to me."

Yes, but what? her heart cried.

Hardly knowing what she did, Lynn laid her hand in his. His fingers tightened, and she felt his heat and strength. No, more than that: the determination and caring that made him the man he was.

It wouldn't be hard to love him, Lynn thought. She couldn't seem to look away from their hands, intertwined. The contrast made her intensely aware that they were not just parents. Not just two people dragged into a nightmare and making the best of it. They were a man and a woman.

Husband and wife.

Her heart seemed to be pounding so hard it deafened her. Slowly she dragged her gaze to meet Adam's, and saw a glint in his eyes that made her feel...peculiar. Excited, frightened, shaky.

It had been so long since she'd felt anything like this that she took a moment to realize her response was sexual. How weird that, just because he was now her husband, she felt things she hadn't yesterday or the day before.

Or had she? Lynn wondered with a fluttery sense of panic. She had always known what a sexy man he was. She'd simply figured he was out of her league. Now, all of a sudden, she owned the league.

For better or worse.

"Lynn..." His voice was rusty. "I'll give you time."

Because he didn't really want her? Or because he was a gentleman? She wished she were sure.

"I...thank you." Was that truly what she'd wanted to say?

He looked down at their hands but didn't release hers. "Your phone's ringing."

"It is?" She felt stupid the minute the words slipped out. How strange. She had once thought herself in love, but never with Brian had she felt as if everyone else in the world had faded away, like a photograph where the surroundings were misty, the focus on the two subjects. She swallowed. "I mean, I'd better answer it."

"Sure."

He was the one to release her hand. She wasn't

sure she'd have had the strength herself. How very strange.

Yet to someone else, Lynn thought, she would have looked perfectly normal as she stood and went to the kitchen. The answering machine had picked up; she heard her own voice, followed by Brian's. He hadn't called in months. Why now? Lynn hesitated with her hand just above the phone.

"Lynn? Are you there?" Pause. "Listen, I wanted to say…"

Belatedly it occurred to her that Adam might be able to hear him out in the living room.

She grabbed the receiver. "I'm here."

"Oh. Uh, hi."

"What do you want?" How cold she sounded!

The breath he drew was audible. "I've just been thinking…well, if you're really strapped for money, I mean, I could help out."

Her mouth actually dropped open. "You're offering to send me child support?"

"Well, I don't know about regular…" This awkwardness wasn't like him. "But I can send you some money when I've got extra. If you need it."

Of course she'd needed it! Her anger crystallized, and yet through it she realized that, in his own way, he was being generous.

"I miss Shelly. How's she doing?"

"She's fine." When had she last mentioned her daddy? Lynn couldn't remember. Before Adam, certainly.

"Mom and Dad were saying they'd like to see her, too."

Lynn closed her eyes. "I got married today."

"You got married?" he echoed incredulously.

"To Shelly's father."

Silence. Then he said at last, bitterness there but muted, "So everything's all wrapped up. You've got both kids and his money. You don't need me." He made a sound. "Hell, you never did."

A spark of anger incinerated her usual guilt. "That's a lucky thing, isn't it?" she flared. "You haven't exactly been here for your daughter lately, have you?"

"I said I missed her."

"Uh-huh. Well, she's probably forgotten you in all the months it took you to come to realize that. She's three-and-a-half years old, Brian. She needs parents who are here. Fortunately, she has them now."

She heard him breathing heavily. The old Brian would have had a comeback that would succeed in making her feel low. This one surprised her.

"Yeah. You're right," he said humbly. "Jeez, I'm sorry."

"Shelly loved you."

"She just never *felt* like she was mine," he explained in a tone of unwonted humility. "I guess that shouldn't have made any difference, but for me it did. But she's a great kid. And, um, I wouldn't mind meeting this Rose."

Lynn sighed. "We haven't told either of the girls what happened. That part scares me. I don't want them to feel insecure. Someday we'll have to. But in the meantime, it's awkward."

"Yeah. I understand. Maybe I could, like, just drop by and see both the girls."

"You have a legal right," she said stiffly.

"You know I wouldn't hold that over you. Just let me know when you think it might be a good time. Okay?"

"Yes, fine," Lynn said slowly.

She half expected there to be some catch, but apparently Brian had said what he intended to, and his goodbye was hasty. Bemused, she returned to the living room.

Adam hadn't turned the TV back on. His head was bent over a book she'd left sitting on the coffee table. It was an anthology of short stories and poetry about mothers and daughters.

"What do you think?" she asked, nodding at it as she sank onto the couch again.

"Jenny had cut this one out of a magazine, back when she was pregnant." His voice was strangled. "She was sure she was going to have a girl."

Lynn hesitated, not knowing what to say. What terrible luck, to have left something out that would remind him of his first wife!

At last she settled for, "I wish you'd show me more pictures of her."

"I have a photo album." Adam gently closed the book and set it on the coffee table. "Remind me. Sometime."

She sensed that the subject was closed with the same gentle finality as the book covers. *Please don't intrude, she heard in his tone.*

"Was that your mom?" Adam asked.

"On the phone? No. It was Brian. He's apparently been feeling guilty," she said dryly. "He says he misses Shelly. He was willing to send money if I needed it.''

"You told him we were married?'' Adam's gaze homed in on her face, its intensity unnerving.

"Uh-huh.'' She paused. "He'd still like to see Shelly sometime. And meet Rose.''

Adam shifted restlessly. "Life's getting complicated. Maybe we should tell the girls. They won't understand much of what happened anyway. I've read that adopted children are less likely to have problems later if they've always known, and the adoptive parents tell them as much as they can handle at any given age. I think we should do the same.''

Lynn nodded slowly. "We almost have to. So your parents and in-laws can meet Shelly, and Brian and his parents Rose.''

"I wouldn't suggest it if that were the only reason.''

Had she offended him? Meeting his gaze, Lynn said quietly, "I didn't think you had. I know how much you love Rose. And Shelly.''

"They're what matters,'' he said with intensity she took as a message.

Not you. Not us. Even if it is our wedding day.

The very thought felt selfish. She should be totally focused on the well-being of Shelly and Rose, grateful that Adam was doing the same. Not wishing he cared about her.

"Of course they are,'' she agreed.

Stroking the brocade fabric of the sofa, she closed her eyes momentarily. Thank heavens, Brian had called when he did! She had been on the verge of making herself look foolish.

Adam couldn't have made it clearer that he didn't want her, that he'd married her for her daughter. How else could she interpret the grief on his face when the poem Jennifer had loved brought back memories of her? The firm reminder that this wedding had taken place because of the girls?

"Do you know," Lynn said with what she hoped was a pleasantly apologetic smile, "I think I'll get ready for bed. If you don't mind my using the bathroom first?"

"No. Of course not," he said courteously. But when she stood and started past, his hand on her arm stopped her. His voice changed. Deepened. "Thank you. For today."

"For today?" she repeated stupidly.

"For agreeing to be my wife."

Was he flirting with her? Reassuring her? She had no idea.

This man she'd married confused her. But then, she thought, looking down at his big hand gripping her arm, they had given themselves plenty of time to untangle the mystery each represented to the other. They'd promised a lifetime. She didn't have to understand him today.

"I'm glad." She flushed. "I mean, that we did it. And that you're not sorry."

He smiled, his eyes a warm rich brown. "Good night, Lynn. Sleep well."

"Good night." Cheeks still glowing, new hope fizzing in her chest, Lynn went to peek in at their children and to brush her teeth.

TELLING THE GIRLS turned out to be absurdly easy. After lunch the next day, Adam took Rose for a walk when the rain let up. Lynn settled down on that sublimely cozy new sofa with Shelly on her lap, head against her shoulder.

They had fewer such moments these days. Having two children was a mixed blessing. Holding this child she'd loved from the first day, powerful emotion swelled in her chest, bringing a sting of tears to Lynn's eyes.

"I love you, punkin," she murmured against her daughter's silky head.

Shelly gave her a compulsive hug. "I love you," she whispered with unusual force.

Lynn bit her lip. "I have something I have to tell you."

Shelly didn't move for a moment. Finally she uncurled enough to look up with big, solemn eyes the exact shade of her daddy's. "Are Rose and Adam going home today?"

"Tomorrow." Lynn smiled, if shakily. "But Monday we'll go to their house. I guess it's our house now, too. Just like this is theirs."

Her forehead puckered. "Is Rose my sister, now?"

"Yes. That's kind of what I have to tell you about."

Shelly waited.

"A few months ago, Adam and I found out something. You and Rose were born the same night in the same hospital. Almost at the same time."

Her frown deepened.

"What we found out is, the hospital mixed you two up. The baby who came out of my tummy was

Rose, not you. You came out of Adam's wife, Jennifer.''

Alarm stirred. ''But *you're* my mommy.''

''I'll always be your mommy. I love you,'' Lynn said fiercely. ''But haven't you noticed that Rose looks kind of like me? We have the same impossible hair and—'' she wrinkled her nose ''—these freckles.''

After a long pause, Shelly nodded.

''And *you*,'' Lynn said, and gave her a squeeze, ''look just like Adam's wife. Except for the parts that look like him. Your eyes are the same color.''

''You said he could be my daddy now. Right?''

''Right.''

''But you're still my mommy.'' Only the barest hint of a question imbued her declaration.

''Always and forever.'' Choked with emotion, Lynn still hesitated. ''I just thought you should know,'' she explained carefully, ''because you have more grandparents who want to meet you. Adam's mommy and daddy, and his wife's. I mean, his first wife's.'' *Oh, forget it,* she decided. ''Rose's grandparents are yours now, and yours are hers.''

Shelly looked perplexed.

Metaphorically Lynn threw up her hands. Making a face, she said, ''I guess it's a good thing your dad and I got married, huh? We're one family, so we can share all those grandparents, right?''

Shelly's expression became crafty. ''If I have more grandparents, do I get more presents? When I turn four?''

''Probably,'' Lynn admitted. She tickled her daughter. ''You greedy little thing, you!''

Shelly giggled and then burrowed back into her arms. Around the thumb she'd popped into her mouth, she asked, "How come Rose and Adam went outside? Without us?"

"So he could tell her the same thing I just told you. That really I'm her mommy, and he's your daddy."

The thumb came out. "But you're still mine, too."

Lynn wanted to make very, very sure Shelly believed her. "Forever and ever," she said strongly. "And Adam's still her daddy, no matter what."

Shelly nodded. "That's okay," she said matter-of-factly. "We can be sisters, just like you said. I *like* Rose."

"I know." Lynn hugged her and rocked gently. Shelly's eyelids grew heavy and at last her thumb fell from her mouth. Smiling and crying, just a little, Lynn carried her to bed.

Not three minutes later, she heard footsteps on the stairs and Adam appeared with Rose in his arms. With swift intensity, his gaze took in Lynn's face, and she guessed that he saw the traces of tears. But she smiled.

"Hi. Did you guys have a good walk?"

Rose looked at her with vivid blue eyes. "Daddy says you're my mommy."

She smiled tremulously. "That's right."

"I never had a mommy before."

"I know."

"Can I call you Mommy?"

"You bet." Her heart sang.

"'kay." Rose wriggled. "I want down, Daddy."

He lowered her to the ground. She came to Lynn

and said sweetly, "Daddy says I should take a nap. Do I hafta?"

Laughing, Lynn went to one knee in front of her. "Yep. Moms and Dads usually agree."

"Poop," she said succinctly.

"Come on." Lynn held out her arms. Rose climbed trustingly into them. "Shelly's already asleep. Can you be really, really quiet, or would you rather nap in my bed?"

"Can I look at books if I nap in your bed?"

"Why not?" Lynn said recklessly, not checking to see what Adam thought of the plan.

"Your bed, please." Rose sounded prim.

"Sleep tight, Zinnia," Adam said above her.

"Daddy!"

"Yeah, yeah. Rose."

Her eyes misty, Lynn smiled at him over their daughter's head as she stood. His answering smile was wry. He knew what she felt, and felt the same. Today, they had gained something and lost something. Being an exclusive parent was heady. You were the whole world to your daughter. Now, suddenly, Rose and Shelly didn't have just a mommy or daddy. They had both. They had permission to love equally.

Now Lynn had Rose's soft arms around her neck, had her whisper, "I'm glad you're my mommy." In turn, she had to live with the small hurts inflicted when Shelly was fascinated by her real daddy, wanted him instead of Mommy.

But this was the way it should be, Lynn thought as she tucked Rose under the quilt on her bed, as she tiptoed into Shelly's rooms to snitch a stack of picture books for Rose to look at under the covers, as she kissed Rose's forehead and quietly slipped out of the room.

A family.

Anchored by a mommy and daddy who had never kissed, never shared a bed, didn't know each other's birthdays. Weren't in love, never had been.

Didn't know if they could be.

But Lynn trusted Adam enough to know that she wasn't alone in hoping they would find love, in *wanting* to find it.

Today, she chose to be an optimist and believe they would.

CHAPTER ELEVEN

LYNN'S FIRST OFFICIAL ACT as Adam's wife might be the most difficult. She had to play gracious hostess to his first wife's parents. Knowing they must resent her taking their daughter's place, she had to understand and respect their grief.

Or perhaps, she thought with a small sigh as she checked the lasagna in the oven, Angela and Rob McCloskey would know perfectly well that they had no reason to resent her. She might be Mrs. Adam Landry in their daughter's place, but she hadn't replaced Jennifer in his heart and probably never would.

The girls were playing in Rose's bedroom when the doorbell rang. Suddenly flustered, Lynn pulled off her apron and hurried to the front door, meeting Adam in the foyer. On a wash of greetings, Adam waved them in. The night was wet and chilly, and even the dash from the car had left water beading on their hair and coats.

Jovial and bluff, Rob McCloskey was clearly a man's man, who looked as if he belonged out on the golf course with a foursome. His elegant wife gave Lynn an immediate pang, because Shelly might look like this when she was in her fifties. Lynn could see her in the shape of Angela McCloskey's face, the set of her eyes. Lynn heard her daughter in this stranger's musical voice.

The resemblance confirmed a truth that her heart didn't want to accept: Shelly wasn't really hers. She came from these people. Lynn's claim was emotional.

The introductions were cordial. Adam hung wet coats in the closet and ushered the McCloskeys into the living room. Lynn smiled because she didn't know what else to do.

"What can I get you?" Adam asked.

"White wine," his mother-in-law said with a pat on his arm. She then turned to study Lynn with a thoroughness that might have seemed rude under other circumstances.

"I do see Rose. My dear, you have the same hair!"

"You mean, the same impossible hair?" Lynn laughed ruefully. "And I would have known you for Shelly's grandmother anywhere."

A crack in her smiling demeanor let pathetic eagerness show. "It's true, then? Adam said she looks like Jennifer."

The men were talking a few feet away. Lynn bit her lip and asked in a low voice, "He did warn you, then? From the pictures he's shown me of your daughter, the resemblance is uncanny. I didn't want you to be taken by surprise."

"He did, and we've been so excited about meeting Shelly. With our Jenny gone, you can't imagine how we felt when Adam told us Rose wasn't hers. Not that we don't love Rose. We do, of course. But Jennifer was our only child."

Hoping she sounded more comfortable than she felt, Lynn said, "Yes, Adam's told me. I know this must be very difficult for you."

Through a shimmer of tears, Angela McCloskey smiled radiantly. "Oh, it was! But now she's home. Oh! Not that you didn't give her a home. But, oh, you know what I mean."

Lynn knew exactly what she meant. She chose her next words carefully. "I love Shelly dearly, although I admit that sometimes she's a mystery to me. Finding out she didn't carry my genes explained a few things. She's so fearless! And a chatterbox."

"So was our Jenny. She was so sunny from the moment she was born. People adored her, you know!"

Lynn kept smiling, hard as it was. "I know Adam did."

Or should she say *does?*

"Well, where's our little girl?" Rob boomed.

"Why don't we go on up there?" Adam suggested, adding deliberately, "Rose is excited that you're coming."

"Rose is such a delight," Angela said confidingly, as Adam herded them toward the stairs. "What a gentle, sweet girl. Perhaps more like you."

Kindly phrased and meant, perhaps, but Lynn had the uneasy feeling she and her daughter both had just been damned with faint praise.

Lynn hung back as they neared the girls' open bedroom door. *Please, please,* she thought, *don't scare Shelly. Don't hurt Rose.*

"Girls," Adam said quietly, "your grandparents are here."

Drawn despite herself, a pedestrian to a car accident, Lynn followed the others into the bedroom, where the girls were plumbing the new dress-up box Lynn had begun here.

Rose tried to scramble to her feet but teetered on her high heels. "Grandma. Grandpa."

Shelly had wrapped a purple feather boa around her neck. A glittery tiara tilted rakishly in her hair. She looked like a tiny, garish elf queen.

Staring up, she asked boldly, "Are you my grandma and grandpa?"

Angela McCloskey choked. Lynn couldn't see her face, but she knew tears must be streaming down it.

Lynn was startled when Adam reached out and took her hand in a bruising grip as he watched the drama unfold. She hadn't even realized he'd dropped back to her side. Or had she come to his?

Rob McCloskey started to speak and had to clear his throat. "Yes," he said at last, thickly. "Yes, your mommy was our daughter."

"But *my* mommy's right there," Shelly began, but stopped as her forehead puckered. "Oh. You mean, the mommy who had me in her tummy."

"That's right," her grandfather said. "She was once our little girl. Our Jenny."

"Did she play dress-up, too?"

"Oh, yes." Angela knelt beside the trunk and reached in. Her voice was almost steady, but tears tracked mascara down her cheeks. "She was as pretty as you are."

"I'm a princess," Shelly said with satisfaction.

Angela lifted out a filmy white shawl. "A very beautiful princess."

Quiet Rose burst out, "*I'm* a princess, too, Grandma." Her voice went very quiet. "Me, too."

Angela McCloskey won Lynn's liking and respect forever when she smiled through her tears and held out the shawl for Rose, not Shelly. "Of course you are! Our princess. And this is just what you need to finish your outfit."

Adam's fingers laced with Lynn's and he drew her out into the hall. Gently he shut the bedroom door, leaving the McCloskeys alone with their granddaughters. Both their granddaughters.

And then he brushed his knuckles across his wife's cheek. They came away wet with her tears.

ADAM PULLED INTO his driveway, laptop and briefcase on the seat beside him, and felt like a Norman Rockwell man of the house: eager to throw open the front door to the delicious scent of dinner in the oven, hear the squeal of delight as his children raced to fling themselves at him, and kiss his wife's soft, demurely presented cheek.

He gave a grunt of amusement. The picture was surprisingly accurate except for the last part. So far, the only time he'd kissed his wife's cheek was at their wedding when the pastor said, "You may kiss the bride," and somehow she'd turned at just the right time so that their lips didn't meet.

But, damn, he looked forward to getting home anyway, a pleasant change from the last difficult years. Instead of Rosebud being with him, slumped wearily in her car seat, thumb in her mouth, she was at home ready to dash to meet him with Shelly, her eyes bright, her face animated, her giggle floating behind like a vapor cloud.

Why hadn't he realized how much easier life was when you were married?

Or would be, he reflected, if theirs wasn't a commuter marriage. Today was good; tomorrow would be, too. Then he and Rose would be alone for two days, after which they'd pack up and make the too-familiar trek across the rolling Coast Range to a first glimpse of the broad Pacific Ocean, the constant throb of the surf, and the tiny apartment above the bookstore.

But, hell, that wasn't so bad, either. The trip got old, sure. He wished the apartment was bigger. But even on rainy days, Adam liked to run on the beach in the early morning. In the short months he'd known Lynn, the bookstore had come to feel homey with its dark wood, bright book covers, playroom for children and the quiet talk in the background. He'd sit at a table with the *New York Times* spread in front of him while the girls disappeared into the castle. He enjoyed watching Lynn greet people with her warm, gentle smile, guide them to a shelf, chat with them as if the conversation was the most fascinating of her day. When someone loved a book on her list of favorites, her face lit up with the joy of finding a kindred spirit. Days when she seemed unusually quiet, he was almost tempted to draw a lone shopper aside and whisper, "Tell that woman your favorite writer is E.B. White."

He had been surreptitiously reading the man's essays and had discovered the charm. They were whimsical, sharp-witted, good-hearted: everything that Lynn was and valued.

Tonight, in his lonely bed, Adam intended to start her favorite fantasy novel by an author named Robin McKinley. Reading the books Lynn admired was a backdoor way to get to know her, but worth the effort. She was passionate about reading and her children.

Adam was beginning to wish she was passionate about him.

They had been married only a few weeks, and his good intentions and patience were eroding with stunning speed. Take tonight: he parked in the garage and went straight into the kitchen.

"I'm home," he said unnecessarily, because Lynn was already turning from the stove with a welcoming smile.

"Girls!" she called. "Dad's home!"

Feet thundered from the living room and he found himself enveloped in giggling little girls. He tossed them in turn into the air and rejoiced in the squealed "Daddy!" from both.

Such a small word, to mean so much.

Satisfied, they galloped away just as quickly, and he went toward his wife who was stirring something on the stove.

"Spaghetti," he said, seeing the bubbling sauce.

"Yes, I hope that's okay."

He didn't like it when she sounded anxious.

"I've told you. I'm not picky."

"That doesn't mean there aren't foods you hate," she said with some spirit.

The sauce smelled good, but he liked even better

the clean citrus scent of her hair, caught in a ponytail today. Gorgeous as it was tumbling around her shoulders, Adam found her most irresistible when her hair was up, tiny tendrils escaping to draw his gaze to her slender neck. He wanted to kiss her nape in the worst way.

She stole a shy look at him and then ducked to clatter in the pan cupboard. "Let me get the spaghetti on," she said in a muffled voice, "and we can eat in ten minutes."

What if he just kissed her? Was she shy because she wanted him to, or because she saw his intent in his eyes and it scared her?

Nothing in his experience told him how to handle this courtship. He knew how to romance a woman he was dating, although God knows it had been a long time since he'd done so seriously. But Lynn was his *wife*. They were getting to know each other, developing a degree of comfort. What if he made an unwelcome advance and blew what progress they'd made?

Another difficulty was that he didn't want to be dishonest with her. He liked her, he found her to be sexy as hell. But he hadn't let go of his feelings for Jenny, and he didn't know if he ever could or wanted to.

Tenderness, liking, sparks between the covers—he was hoping for all those this time around. But he was afraid that if he started bringing home roses, Lynn would get the wrong idea.

Adam wasn't sure why that bothered him. He'd *married* her, for God's sake. He took the vows seriously. He wouldn't be unfaithful.

But when he took to thinking about love, he started feeling edgy, uncomfortable. Disloyal. He didn't want to be a man who slipped on a new wife to replace the old as if they were nothing more than a succession of favorite shirts. He'd *loved* his Jenny, although already memories were slipping away. He wouldn't so quickly dishonor her or his feelings.

But, damn, he wanted to have hot sex with his second wife.

Celibacy had been no more than an occasional irritation until he had a woman in his house. Now it was more like a bad back, an ever-present ache that stabbed sharply when he moved wrong.

Proximity explained it, he kept telling himself. Lynn was a pretty, shapely woman, but would he especially have noticed her if he'd happened into her bookstore? No. Love was when you were struck by lightning, when you knew this was *it*.

This was just sex. Plain and simple.

But something told him putting it that way to her wouldn't lure her down the hall to his bedroom. *Lure.* See? Even his choice of words to himself implied a lie.

"Why don't you help the girls wash their hands?" She was bustling around him as if he were an inconvenient post holding up the kitchen ceiling. If he'd been staring lustfully, she hadn't noticed or was pretending not to.

A lot of pretence going on, Adam thought grimly.

But he was still glad to be home, glad that dinner was bubbling on the stove instead of sitting in the refrigerator with a sticky note from his housekeeper telling him how to cook it. He was glad Rose hadn't had to spend ten hours at preschool today, and that Shelly had been here to hug him when he walked in the door.

And he was glad that Lynn would be there after the girls went to bed tonight, quiet company if both read, good conversation if they chose not to.

He was glad not to be alone.

"Sure," he said, "if I can't do anything here."

She cast him a mildly amused look as she dumped spaghetti and boiling water into a colander. "Nope. Just get Rose and Shelly."

At the dinner table, she said grace, something he'd never done but which seemed, if nothing else, to introduce a different note to mealtimes for the two three-year-olds. At breakfast or lunch, they'd giggle, make messes, even occasionally start food fights. At dinner they were on their best manners. He liked the change, as he liked most that Lynn had brought with her.

Tonight the girls told him about the playground and how it had started to snow—slushy rain, Lynn interjected with crinkled nose—and they got all wet but they played anyway—did Daddy know your bottom stuck to a wet slide?—and Mommy made them take a hot bath when they got home.

"We were sea lions," Shelly told him. Bouncing in her chair, she barked like the ones on the rocks offshore from Otter Beach. "Like that."

"Yeah. We were *both* sea lions!" Rose said.

Lynn laughed. "Of course, most of the bathwater washed up on the beach."

"The beach!" They thought that was hysterically funny.

He grinned at her. "Sounds like fun. I hope you had some beach towels."

"I used half the contents of your linen closet," she said, a smile shimmering in her eyes. "Thank goodness for your little elf."

"Ann? You don't see much of her, huh?"

"She pleasantly made it known she'd just as soon not 'trip over us.' I try to either take the girls someplace, or at least keep them out of her hair. She's going to be glad when we're gone Thursday."

He wasn't. He hated Thursdays. Lynn and Shelly packed up at the crack of dawn and drove away so that Lynn could open the bookstore at ten. He had to drop a sleepy Rose off at day care, where she cried. Ditto Friday, except that instead of the two of them sharing a solitary dinner, they grabbed fast food and headed for the coast and their home away from home.

Where Rose got to sleep cuddled up to her new sister, while he got the couch.

After dinner, while he and Lynn companionably cleaned the kitchen, she told him that Brian's mother had called.

Brow crinkled, she said, "I think she was ashamed of herself. And maybe ashamed of Brian. She regretted not being more supportive—quote unquote. It was a strange conversation. I haven't heard from her in months."

His basic cynicism asserted itself. "What did she want? Rose?"

Lynn paused with her hands in a soapy pan, her lips pursed. "You know, I really think she was genuine. She said that, when we think the time's right, she and Walt would like to meet Rose and see Shelly again. She said as far as she was concerned, Shelly would always be her granddaughter. It sounded a little pointed, which is what made me think she was disillusioned about Brian.''

"Her contrition is a little late," Adam growled.

"Isn't it better late than never?" Lynn suggested gently.

He took one last swipe at the counter. "Yeah. Probably. Whatever you want to do about them is okay by me. I can be nice."

Her smile was quick, amused and approving. "I know you can."

Thanks to that smile, he was in a damned good mood when he started the dishwasher and watched Lynn pour two cups of coffee. He enjoyed their evening talks. To his surprise, she'd shown real interest from the beginning in what he did, how he made decisions on what companies were going to make money for his clients, what triggered his gut feelings. He'd noticed that she was reading a book on investments plucked from her bookstore shelf, which pleased him unreasonably.

Jenny had laughingly declared that his work was boring. "You don't even see real products or real money. It's all on paper. Numbers." She had delicately shuddered. "I don't know how you can make yourself care."

Adam remembered arguing. "It's real, all right. Think of the buying and selling of stocks as the blood running through the veins of the economy. That—" he'd melodramatically stabbed a finger at the open page of closing stock prices "—is the report from the lab technicians who just ran tests on the blood."

She pouted prettily. "Oh, fine, but we don't have to *talk* about it, do we?"

The subject had been turned that time, and Adam found that he rarely commented on work. Personalities in the brokerage firm where he was now a senior partner, sure. Jenny liked office parties and gossip. The guts of his work, she didn't want to hear about.

The memory bothered him, but he excused her. She'd been young, good Lord, probably no more than twenty-two. A kid, she would seem to him now. He probably had been prosing on as if some rise or fall in prices was the be-all and end-all of the universe. As if the stock market wouldn't plunge up and down as often as a frisky colt out to pasture. Of course, it was relatively new to him then. Hell, he hadn't been that much older than Jenny, twenty-five when they set up housekeeping. They were newlyweds, and other topics of conversation hadn't been hard to find.

Jenny would have matured if she'd had the chance. He didn't want to compare her to Lynn. It wasn't fair. If nothing else, circumstances had been different. Jenny hadn't needed to take a crash course in her husband's interests and character. She knew him. *Except,* a disquieting voice murmured in his ear, *for the facets of him that didn't interest her.*

She never suggested he change jobs, Adam argued with himself.

She liked the money.

She just didn't want to be bored by a blow-by-blow account of his day at the dinner table every evening. So what?

Shouldn't she have loved the whole man? whispered that insidious voice.

Maybe, Adam thought, beginning to be irritated. But he didn't love her any less because she was possibly a little self-absorbed. She'd been spoiled as a kid. When he met and married his Jenny, she was young, beautiful and sexy, the center of a crowd at every party. Motherhood would have changed and enriched her, just as loving Rose had irrevocably changed him.

He'd be willing to bet Lynn had been considerably more frivolous before she'd had a child, too.

Hard to picture.

Adam shut the door on any further debate.

It figured, however, that as if to make a point tonight Lynn brought the book on investing when he and she carried their cups of coffee into the living room.

Which meant only that she wanted to know who the hell she'd married, Adam countered the voice before it could break the silence. Just as he did.

"Learning anything?" he asked, nodding at the book.

Lynn wrinkled her nose. "I think I'm getting more confused. All these formulas. P/E ratios." Sounding honestly puzzled, she asked, "Why not just stick to investing in companies whose products you like? Or stores that are well run and clearly busy? Avoid the stores you hate because merchandise is cheap or clerks are always slow or that you hear people grumbling about? I mean, doesn't common sense work?"

"Yeah, to some extent," Adam agreed. "For the individual investor, that's exactly the advice I'd give."

She looked pleased.

"However," he continued, "remember how many of the corporations on the stock market make products that are invisible to the average consumer. Operating software for computers, or a circuit board in airplane navigation systems, or whatever. Also, because a local store is well run and popular doesn't always mean the whole chain is. Haven't you had a place you really liked suddenly go out of business? Maybe go bankrupt?"

Lynn nodded thoughtfully.

"Could be the problem wasn't even with that chain of appliance stores or whatever. They might be owned by a giant retailer who has been sucking them dry to plug a drain in another branch of their empire. Maybe this other branch makes jeans, and they haven't kept up with the youth market. How are you going to know this?"

"I'm not?"

"Probably not," Adam agreed. "Our job is to know well ahead of time when problems are going to cause a corporation to retrench or go belly-up. So our clients don't take a bath. It's no different than you making informed decisions on what books to carry. Sometimes I imagine you just flat out love a book. Mostly, you've learned what your customers will buy. Or won't buy. I'll bet you carry stuff you personally despise because you know it sells."

"Sure I do." She gave a gusty sigh and with an

air of dogged resolve flipped open the book. "You've convinced me."

"Are you planning to start investing?" he asked, trying to sound careless.

"Oh, sure. As soon as I franchise." Her cheeks turned a little pink. "I just thought it might be a good idea if I knew what you were talking about when you have a good day, or a bad one."

"Ah." A sense of warm satisfaction filled him. When she had said she would give this marriage her best, she'd meant it.

The evening was typical. They read, she asked questions that spurred brief, sometimes spirited, discussions, and finally she reached for her bookmark and said in that ultracasual way she had for this particular pronouncement, "I'm off to bed. If only the girls would sleep in."

Usually he didn't try to hold her, but tonight, for reasons obscure to him, he hated the idea of her disappearing upstairs.

He set down his newspaper. "Before you go. I've been thinking. When do you go back to having the store open more than four days a week?"

"Usually April." She closed her book and looked inquiring. "Why?"

"What the hell are we going to do then?"

"Go back to weekends?" Lynn said tentatively. "And Mondays and Tuesdays? I'm always closed on Mondays and can hire someone to cover the store on Tuesdays. Or stay closed."

Two days here. Two there. Three apart.

"We were unhappy when we were doing it, and we weren't married then." He didn't give her a chance to respond. "What about when the girls start school? Does Rose go here and Shelly in Otter Beach?"

"I don't know!" Her fingers clenched the book in her lap. "Is this where you suggest again that I sell the store?"

God. He hadn't meant to walk this road at all tonight, or any time in the near future, even if he could foresee the potholes ahead. He'd only wanted to keep her from going off to bed.

But maybe they should face the problems before they arose.

"I want you to start thinking about the future," he said evenly. "That's all."

"Keeping the bookstore and my own home was part of the deal." Her eyes were huge, beautiful and dark with apprehension. "You agreed."

He tossed the newspaper aside. "Maybe at the time, neither of us was thinking about this marriage as a long-term proposition. Now I am. And I'm asking that you do, too."

She sounded tart. "And why, all of a sudden, are you planning fifteen years ahead?"

Evade, or tell the truth?

Half the truth. "The kids are happy. Things are going well. Why not?"

"Because we're still strangers."

Why did that hurt? "I thought we were getting past that."

Her tongue touched her lips. "I feel as if I still know hardly anything about your past."

"You've met my parents. What else is there to say?"

"Your marriage…"

Wariness lent a hardness to his voice. "Jennifer has been dead for three-and-a-half years. She has nothing to do with us."

Lynn was silent for a long moment. He resisted the urge to shift under her probing gaze. At last she nodded. "Maybe you're right." Her tone was pleasant but distant. He'd lost her, somehow.

"I'm not trying to pressure you." Another lie.

"I will think about the possibility of selling the store," she said, as she set her book aside and stood. "I have been already, to tell you the truth. You know I love what I do, but I also recognize that you can't practically move to Otter Beach, and I could find work over here."

"You could not work at all for a few years. I make plenty."

"But then I'd feel like a kept woman," she said gently. "I know I shouldn't. We're married, after all, but…" An almost infinitesimal pause gave away what she was thinking: *but I don't feel married.* "No," she concluded, "I need to maintain some independence."

Adam wished he could be sure her fear was rooted in the failure of her first marriage, in the knowledge that sometimes a woman had to be able to take care of herself and her child, rather than in a lack of commitment to *this* marriage. He wanted to know she was in it for the long haul, too.

When she gave herself to him, when she shared her bed, he would know.

Until then, every waking moment would be uncertain.

Was that what he wanted? Not so much her body as reassurance?

Hell, no, he thought, letting his gaze sweep once over her, from that mane of unruly hair to slender bare feet. He wanted both. Her body beneath his, and her trust held out on an open palm.

Neither could be coerced.

"Okay." Adam made his voice deliberately soothing. "You need to feel as if you're earning your way. I don't have a problem with that. And I'm really not trying to push you into anything. Until Shelly and Rose start kindergarten, we can probably go on this way. I'm just, uh, not looking forward to you and Shelly packing up Thursday. We feel like a family when we're together."

Their eyes met and she smiled with dawning warmth, although her mouth was tremulous. "We do, don't we?"

Then come to me, he thought. *Blush. Say, "I think it's time we take the next step."*

"Good night, Adam," she murmured, and left the room.

He had to grit his teeth to keep from stumbling to his feet and begging, *Don't go.*

Maybe he would have noticed her, if under completely different circumstances he'd wandered into her bookstore. Heard her soft laugh and been tempted by her hair before she turned to face him. Seen a blush turn her cheeks to wild roses as her lovely, cool eyes met his.

Groaning, Adam tried to remember Jennifer, the way she'd looked up through her lashes, the coy tilt of her head, her throaty laugh, her sultry mouth, but it was all just words, fleeting impressions. Lynn was real, vivid, *here.*

Jennifer was a long-lost dream.

Even Shelly no longer reminded him of her mother. He knew objectively that they looked alike, but his little girl had so much personality of her own that only her cheerful, endless chatter and her boldness recalled Jennifer. Perhaps when Shelly was a teenager she would bat her eyes and smile with deliberate, mysterious purpose. But for now…hell, for now she had Lynn's directness and the sweetness of a much loved child.

Not Jennifer's hunger for attention.

Now, where had that idea come from? he wondered, frowning, but knowing it was true. His Jenny had wanted always to be the center of attention. Her own company was never enough.

Adam swore aloud. He'd loved his wife, and she was dead. Why all the analysis now?

So he could justify letting Lynn walk into Jennifer's place? Not just in his home and bed, but in his heart?

No! he thought, on a shattering wave of remembrance too vivid. Suddenly he did see his Jenny, still and warm, but gone, her life an illusion given by machines.

Adam buried his face in his hands and yanked at his hair. *Remember her alive!* he told himself fiercely. Remember her generous sensuality, her quirky sense of humor, her lively mind and effortless ability to make whatever she touched beautiful. Her flower arrangements—he seized on the memory. He used to think they were like her, careless and artful at the same time.

He couldn't let her go. Not so easily. Not so quickly.

He could give Lynn everything but his heart.

CHAPTER TWELVE

EVERY TIME SHE HEARD a car engine, Lynn went to the kitchen window. No Adam.

For the first time, she'd left Shelly with Adam and Rose, coming home to open the bookstore all by herself. The quiet drive had been an unexpected pleasure. She was so rarely alone to let her thoughts drift aimlessly, to listen to Bizet's *Carmen* instead of *Sesame Street* songs. But that was two days and a night ago. Now she missed her family terribly.

She glanced at the clock for the twentieth time. Dark had come hours ago. Front and back porch lights were beacons in the night—the strong beam of a lighthouse calling them home, Lynn thought fancifully.

Thursday evening she'd read a murder mystery, not had dinner until nine o'clock and then eaten an entire pint of mint-chocolate-chip ice cream, feeling decadent the whole time. Tonight she used her energy and anxiety to clean. Floors and sinks shone, and she'd moved every piece of furniture so that not even one dust bunny escaped her.

At eight-thirty, half an hour after his usual time, she heard the deep, throaty murmur of Adam's Lexus and the crunch of gravel under the tires.

With a rush of pleasure, Lynn dropped a handful

of forks—she'd been rearranging the silverware drawer—and hurried to the door. Footsteps clattered on the outside stairs. Little-girl voices called, "Mommy! We're home!"

Opening the door, Lynn scooped to snatch first Shelly, then Rose up into her arms for huge hugs. They felt so solid, smelled so sweet, and she didn't know how she had been able to endure two days without them.

Below, the car door slammed again in the darkness, and Adam came into the circle of porch light and started up the rickety staircase, burdened by a duffel bag and…was that a hula hoop? She hadn't seen one in years.

Shelly didn't like the fact that Mommy's attention had wandered for even a moment. Tugging on Lynn's hand, she did a little dance. "Mommy, I went to school with Rose! We learned to write letters! Didn't we, Rose? And how to count in…well, the way somebody else talks. I don't remember who. You wanna hear me? *Uno, dos, tres,*" she enunciated with earnest care. "Rose knows how, too. Don't you, Rose?"

"Course I do," Rose declared with the air of a big kid. "*Uno, dos, tres.* See? And Teacher said I know my colors. My shirt is orange. Isn't it, Mommy?"

"Mine is purple," Shelly said importantly. "I know my colors, too, Mommy."

"I know you do, sweetie. And very well, too."

The hula hoop slung over Adam's shoulder rolled off and bounced down the stairs. He mumbled something not meant for three-year-old ears, dropped the duffel bag on the landing and chased after the neon-green plastic hoop.

The girls turned to watch, giggling in merriment. "Grandma gave us one a' those," Shelly explained. "A hoo...hoo..." Her lips pursed in a perfect circle. "Hoo..."

"Hula hoop," Lynn supplied.

Grinning ruefully, Adam started back up the stairs.

"Hoo-hoop. She said she played with one when *she* was a girl. She wriggled. Like this." Shelly swiveled her hips so hard she fell down laughing.

Rose, of course, had to demonstrate and tumble theatrically amid more giggles.

"Grandma must have looked very funny," Lynn said, trying to imagine the petite, elegant woman waggling her hips like a Hawaiian dancer. Now, that she would have liked to see.

A small cloud stilled Shelly's laughter. "I can't make the hoo-hoop work."

"Daddy says we don't got no hips," Rose agreed.

"Have any," Lynn corrected automatically.

Daddy rolled the hula hoop into the house. "Here it stays," he said firmly.

Losing interest in it and Mom, Shelly popped to her feet. "Let's go play," she commanded.

"Okay," Rose said happily.

They raced down the hall, rattling pictures on the wall, and flung open the door to their bedroom.

Lynn frowned, a new worry niggling. "I hope Rose doesn't get too used to going along with Shelly. Does it seem to you as if...''

Flowers appeared under her nose. "Happy anniversary," Adam said huskily.

Her wondering eyes took in roses and huge fragrant lilies and a scattering of tiny white bridal wreath. She breathed in the glorious scent and then looked up in astonishment at her husband's face. "Anniversary?"

"One month," he said gravely. "Today."

The paper cone crackled as she took the bouquet from him and cradled it. "Thank you." She sounded—and felt—absurdly shy.

"A kiss might be appropriate." He wasn't smiling, to suggest that he was kidding; he just stood there squarely less than a foot away and waited.

Did he mean it? Heat blossomed in her cheeks and her pulse sprinted. She'd known this was coming. She'd seen in his eyes that he was thinking about her that way. As a woman. She wanted him to. She'd just had no idea in the world how to hint that she wouldn't mind if he did kiss her.

But did he have to leave it up to her?

Maybe he was trying to give her an out, if she really detested the idea. He was being a gentleman.

As stuffily as Miss Manners, Lynn admitted, "A kiss would be one polite way to thank you."

"Then?"

Taking a breath and hugging the flowers to her breast, she rose on tiptoe to give him a quick peck.

It didn't work that way. He bent his head to meet her halfway. Their mouths touched and a shiver skidded down her spine. Somehow he came to be gripping her upper arms. The heavy scent of lilies rose from between them, thickening the air. His lips teased hers apart, then hardened. She heard a groan and the kiss deepened, but...

"Mommy!" Feet thundered down the short hall behind her.

Lynn jerked away, her heart hammering and her face so hot it must be the color of a lobster. "Yes? What is it?"

"Mommy, where's flower blankie?" Shelly asked with a hint of anxiety.

The faded, warn flannel crib blanket was rarely far from Shelly.

Her mind cloudy, Lynn couldn't look at Adam. "Did you take it to Adam's house?"

Shelly's brown eyes widened and her mouth formed an O. "I forgot it," she whispered, and then her face scrunched miserably as tears formed. "I want my flower blankie!" she wailed.

Lynn crouched to hug her. "It's not in the bag?"

"This is all clothes," Adam said. "I'm sorry. It's my fault. I should have checked."

"You know, your blanket is fine in your bedroom at Adam's house. It'll be waiting for you Sunday night."

"I want it now!" Shelly screamed. "Daddy can go get my blankie."

"Honey, it would take him all night." Lynn knew darn well that reason wouldn't forestall what was coming. But she had to try, didn't she? "You can do without it for three days."

Sobbing, the three-year-old flung herself onto the floor and drummed her heels. Lynn sighed, remembering last night's peace and quiet. Ah, well. She was glad Shelly was home, even if she was screaming and turning purple.

Rose never threw temper tantrums. She stood now

halfway down the hall, her thumb in her mouth and her face a study in worry and perplexity.

It took Lynn half an hour to calm her distraught daughter. Adam and Rose settled in as Shelly sobbed, hiccuped, and finally burrowed in her mother's arms for a few minutes of comfort and resignation.

"Do you feel better now?" Lynn asked. They were alone in the living room, cuddled in the depths of the new sofa.

Shelly nodded against her breast.

"Do you want to get ready for bed now?"

A sniff, and Shelly's head bumped Lynn's chest as she nodded again.

"Okay. Up we go."

On the way down the hall Lynn caught a glimpse of Adam and Rose sitting at the kitchen table sipping from mugs of cocoa with marshmallows floating atop. Fortunately, Shelly didn't see.

Teeth brushed, in her nightgown, Shelly finally remembered that she shouldn't be the only one who had to go to bed. "Where's Rose?" she demanded.

"She'll be along in a few minutes." Lynn ran the brush through her small daughter's thick mink-brown hair, so unlike her own. "I bet she took a longer nap than you did today, huh?"

"*She* slept on the way. I wasn't sleepy."

"I think she'll be ready for bed pretty soon. Now, let's tuck you in." She plopped Shelly down on the bed and kissed her. "I missed you, punkin."

Shelly's eyes watered again. "I missed you, too. I wanted *you* to kiss me g'night. Only you weren't there," she accused.

"No, but your daddy was." Lynn kissed the snub

nose. "And it sounds as if you mostly had fun staying with Rose and Daddy."

They chatted about preschool, and Lynn felt an easing inside of some tension she hardly knew had been there. The possibility of losing Shelly terrified her still. What if she hadn't been missed at all?

At Shelly's sleepy request Lynn left on the lamp beside the bed and slipped quietly out. In the kitchen, Adam smiled at her.

"Want some cocoa?"

Her gaze shied away from his. She hadn't yet let herself think about what had happened, but she'd have to soon. It changed everything. Unless he'd hated it, he would want to kiss her again.

She wanted him to.

"Please." Another blush fired her cheeks at the double meaning.

A glint in Adam's eyes told her he'd guessed at some of her thoughts, or at least that the kiss was in the forefront of his.

"You c'n have a marshmallow, too, if you want," Rose told her generously.

"Thank you. I'd like one."

"How come Shelly cried like that?"

"I think she was tired," Lynn explained. "Have you ever felt really sad, mostly because you were tired?"

Rose nodded, but doubtfully.

The kettle sang, and a moment later Adam's big hand set the mug of cocoa in front of her at the kitchen table.

"Thank you." Lynn sent a smile his way without quite meeting his eyes.

"I like cocoa." Rose sounded quietly satisfied. Perhaps she also liked having Mommy and Daddy all to herself. Neither girl was used to sharing. It was a wonder they got along so beautifully.

Lynn suggested a game, which they played. Then she ran a bath for Rose and stayed with her. Braiding her hair took time.

But bedtime couldn't be put off forever. Adam did the honors and tucked Rose in. Lynn washed mugs and wiped the table and arranged the flowers more carefully in the stoneware jar Adam had put them in. They were glorious, too fancy for anything but crystal, she thought, tilting her head, but she would enjoy them anyway.

Was it possible she and Adam had been married for a month already?

Every nerve strained for the sound of his footsteps in the hall. He would come looking for her, she knew. To take up where they'd left off?

Or would he give her breathing space by asking how business had been for her, by telling her what the market had done this week, how Shelly had liked staying over with Rose?

She felt jumpy. Where was he?

"Shelly's sound asleep."

Lynn gasped and whirled. He blocked the kitchen doorway, his expression inscrutable.

"You scared me!"

"I'm sorry." He didn't sound sorry, but rather… pleased. As if he was glad she'd been affected enough to be jumpy. "What were you thinking about?"

"I…the flowers are gorgeous."

"I'm glad you like them." He strolled toward her.

Her back to the kitchen counter, Lynn had nowhere to go. Did she want to flee? All she had to do was say, *You're crowding me. I need time.* Was he? Did she? It was hard to think with her heartbeats pounding in her ears and her knees wanting to buckle.

He stopped inches away. Lynn swallowed and stared fixedly at the buttons on his white shirt. The tie that he must have worn today was long gone, probably slung over the seat of the Lexus along with the suit jacket. He was dauntingly handsome in charcoal slacks and a dress shirt, his face dark and saturnine in contrast to the white. Several of the top buttons were undone, exposing a tanned throat. All she had to do was reach for the next button.

"I enjoyed kissing you." His voice was a soft rumble.

Lynn sneaked a peak upward, expecting to see the gleam in his eyes, but a frown was gathering on his brows. He wasn't sure of her, she realized suddenly. Did he share her same apprehensions? The possibility stunned her. He was a confident, handsome, wealthy man.

Stuck with her by circumstances. He probably didn't know what to make of her. She wasn't his usual kind of woman.

She was nothing like his beautiful, charming wife, Lynn thought, with a sinking feeling.

Okay, she argued with herself, maybe she wasn't anything like his Jennifer, but he'd kissed her. He wanted her. He seemed to like her. That was enough to build on, wasn't it?

"I enjoyed it, too," she admitted shyly, eyes still downcast. "I mean, the kiss."

"Good." He reached for her hand and placed it on his chest.

Slowly she splayed her fingers, flattening her palm. Wonderingly, she felt his heart beat, as hard and fast as hers. The knowledge that he was as affected by her as she was by him allowed her to look up.

Muttering something she couldn't make out, Adam bent his head and kissed her again. The first kiss had been the kind a man might give a woman on her doorstep before he said good-night. This one was between two lovers: urgent, needy, a promise and a demand. He drank in her breath, his tongue stroked hers. His fingers dove into her hair and cupped the back of her head.

I'm your husband, he said without words. *Our bed is right down the hall.*

It scared her, the demand, but the urgency awakened her own and the promise enticed her. *We're husband and wife. We have children and a life together.* Lovemaking would seal the bond, make Adam hers.

She uttered a soft moan and slipped her arms around his neck, rising on tiptoe so that she could be closer to him.

He strung heady kisses across her cheek, nibbled at her earlobe, tasted her throat. When he lifted his head, she saw the hot light in his eyes.

"Is this an invitation, Lynn?"

She'd hoped he would just sweep her into his arms and carry her down the hall, making a decision, not asking for one. Trust Adam to need the words. He wouldn't let her be a coward.

But she wasn't quite brave enough to say *Yes. Please.* She had to hope he would understand that her confession was also tacit permission. "I'm not very experienced. Brian was the only man..."

Adam laughed huskily. "Sweetheart, this isn't a job interview. Experience is not required."

Lynn had seen only two photos of his wife: a smiling one of her pregnant that hung in a silver frame beside Rose's bed, and the one Adam carried in his wallet and had shown her that first day at the hospital. It was that one she saw now, in a too-vivid flash—the sultry eyes and full, sexy mouth, sleek hair and confident tilt to her head. She would have known how to seduce her husband, how to please him.

Lynn wished desperately that she hadn't thought of Jennifer.

Maybe experience wasn't required, but she'd feel more sure of herself if she had it. "No, but..." she began.

Adam didn't let her finish. "What experience could prepare us for each other? We have to learn as we go. Together."

She had the dreadful feeling she was being conned, that he was too slick, too quick with his answers, but she kept coming back to the fact that he was her husband. Sooner or later, he would join her in her bed down the hall. Why not sooner?

Sooner, Lynn thought hazily, was good. Deep in her belly, desire cramped. Oh, yes. She was ready. As ready as she would ever be, considering what a failure she was with men, how little she understood her own heart.

But her heart had nothing to do with this. This was an old-fashioned marriage of convenience, and she didn't have to worry about love, did she?

"Yes," she murmured. "You're right. I just don't want you to be disappointed."

"Disappointed?" His mouth had a tender twist. "What if I disappoint you? Would you hold it against me so soon? If tonight isn't perfect, we'll get it right another time. You have to tell me what pleases you."

Brian had never asked, but she knew the lack of pleasure she'd had with him was as much her fault. It had never occurred to her to say aloud, *This pleases me. That doesn't.* She'd tried with body language to tell him, but in the midst of passion silence was what he heard.

Silence was always easier for her.

"You...you'll tell me, too?" she asked breathlessly.

"You'll please me," he said in a rough voice unlike his own. "I've wanted to touch your hair since that day at the hospital. I've been dying to see if you have freckles anywhere but here." He kissed her nose. "To hear you say my name as if you mean it."

Excitement flowed through her like a drug in her bloodstream. Every hammering beat of her heart sent a tingling thrill farther toward her fingertips and toes.

"Adam," she whispered.

"Yes." His eyes smouldered. "Like that."

She let her head fall back as he kissed the hollow at the base of her throat. A whimper escaped her when he touched her breasts, cupping, weighing, teasing.

"I think," he said hoarsely, "it's time for me to invade your bedroom."

She'd felt the same about his, as if when she explored his house an invisible force field had kept her from stepping through the doorway. This one room was a part of him too private for her to know.

"We'd better check that the girls are asleep." Her voice came out as a mere thread of its normal self.

"Mmm." He kissed her, slow, deep and hot.

Melting, she hardly knew when he flicked off the kitchen light and steered her down the hall, pausing briefly in front of the girls' room.

"Sound asleep," he murmured, and swung her into his arms.

With a muffled squeak, she stiffened and clutched at his shoulders. "What are you doing?"

"Shh. Don't want to wake the girls." With his shoulder, he turned off the hall light and carried her into her dark bedroom. "Symbolism is important. We skipped this part on our wedding day. Seems like the thing to do now."

He was carrying her across the threshold. A shiver passed through her. *My woman to carry home,* the gesture seemed to say. Their marriage wasn't that kind.

Think about it tomorrow, she decided. Worry then. Now she could be grateful he was choosing to romanticize their lovemaking.

Beside the bed, he lowered her with the care and finesse of a man with plenty of practice. He kissed her even as he reached for the lamp on her bedside table. A part of her was shy and wished he hadn't turned on a light, but she also liked the idea of being able to see him. How terribly unreal it would seem tomorrow, if they grappled in the dark, if she couldn't see his expressions, his body. She might wonder if she'd dreamed the whole thing.

Adam undressed her slowly, telling her how beautiful she was as he tossed aside her shirt, her bra, her jeans and socks. His own shirt joined hers on the floor, so that Lynn could flatten her hands on his chest as she'd imagined doing. His body heat almost burned her fingers. He had a vee of fine dark hair, and otherwise his skin was smooth over well-developed muscles. She liked the way he sucked in a breath when she grazed his nipple or when her hands ventured lower.

In the end, she was too shy to make the move. He did it for her, grasping her hands and placing them on his belt.

"You undress me," he said rawly.

She trembled as she undid his belt, unbuttoned the waistband of his trousers, inched the zipper down over the long, thick bulge. Brian's penis had rather repulsed her; she didn't like to see it, and couldn't account for why she did very much want to see Adam's.

It was smooth, hard and large, and she was dying for the moment when he would push it inside her. Lynn moaned and then was shocked that such a wanton sound had come from her.

Adam shucked the rest of his clothes in a few

quick movements. Deafened by the thunder of her own heartbeat, Lynn stared as she'd never done before. He was beautiful, and *hers*. Tall and powerful, sleekly muscled, his skin a golden hue. Her own freckled, pale skin looked so pallid in comparison, as if she lived under a rock.

But he was finding those freckles and kissing them. First her chest, then he turned her gently and trailed his lips along her spine. She quivered when he slipped her panties down, caressing her thighs and calves with long strokes of his hands.

"Beautiful," he murmured, and turned her to face him.

She tried to cover herself, an arm across her breasts—though he had already seen them—and the other hand hiding the curls as wild as those on her head.

Adam lifted her onto the bed and followed her down in a tangle of limbs.

"Your hair on my pillow," he said thickly. At least, that's what she thought he said. A dark flush ran across his cheekbones and his skin seemed taut over the angles of his face. Braced on his elbows above her, he finger-combed her hair until it was spread in every direction on the lacy white pillowcase. "Just like this."

"It's awful hair. Always in knots."

He seemed fascinated by every wild strand. "It's glorious."

"Poor Rose had to get it from me."

"Poor Rose will be driving the boys crazy in ten years or so."

"Shelly will be prettier." What an absurd conversation to be having with a man whose weight was bearing her down.

She'd distracted him and he looked surprised. "Will she? I'm not so sure."

But Rose looked so much like her, and Shelly so much like his first wife. Did that mean—could it mean?—that he really thought she, Lynn, was as pretty as his beloved Jenny?

Heartened by the very idea—at least he was letting her pretend—Lynn tugged his head down to hers. The kiss started slow and sensual, but couldn't stay that way. His thigh was between hers, and she could feel his erection butting against her belly. She wanted more than kisses, she wanted...

"Ooh," she breathed, when his hand flattened on her belly and then stole lower, exploring, teasing, stroking. "Oh!" she cried, and clutched at his hand. "Now. Please."

"Wait," he said in that voice so unlike his own. "I have something here." Leaning off the bed, he grabbed his pants and took a packet from his pocket. Adam ripped it open and, swearing at hands that had become clumsy, put on the condom.

She watched in fascination and something like disappointment. She'd wanted him, just him, inside her. She should feel lucky that he'd come prepared. It had never occurred to her that if they took this next step, birth control would have to be part of it, or else they might have another child before they knew it. Then they would be tied together forever.

She wasn't so certain she minded the idea. A child,

with Adam…little shivers rippled in her center, sexual pleasure simply because she imagined being pregnant with his child.

He might have claimed they had to learn together, but she felt as if she was in the hands of a master. He knew what to do to give her pleasure. He had her arching like a cat and whispering urgent pleas. "Do you like that?" he'd murmur, and, "Oh, yes," she would sigh.

But she explored as well, if timidly. When he groaned or she felt his muscles jerk, her own excitement escalated. He wanted her; she hadn't been wanted so often in her life.

He was the one who couldn't wait at the end, who with sudden stark need parted her thighs and pressed inside her. She felt his shuddering restraint, knew he was holding back so that he didn't hurt or frighten her.

Lynn's heart gave a squeeze. As he gritted his teeth and eased the last inches inside her, she had a fluttering moment of panic. She'd lied to herself.

Her heart *did* have something to do with this. Even if he didn't feel the same.

Adam spoke, his voice so guttural she couldn't make it out. *I love you,* she imagined, knowing she would despise herself later for the pretence but holding it to herself nonetheless. As Adam began to move steadily, surely, she clutched at him with frantic hands and let her last protective walls fall.

The cramping, exultant wave came then, tumbling her head over heels in the tsunami. She could not fall in love, she thought desperately, and was so terribly afraid she already had.

ADAM HELD HIS WIFE until her racing pulse quieted, her breathing slowed, until he felt her boneless relaxation against him. Only then did he ease away, tuck the covers around her, and sit on the edge of the bed.

He buried his face in his hands and thought, *It couldn't have been that good. I couldn't have felt so much.* The explanation was much simpler. He hadn't had sex in over three years. The triumph at claiming her, the raw, primitive exhilaration because she was his, those were natural emotions. Lynn was his wife, and he'd been driven lately by the need to make their relationship fact. Any man would have felt the same.

And, hell, he wouldn't like himself if a certain amount of tenderness wasn't added to the brew, if he hadn't given a damn whether she was pleased or not.

Anything else was in his imagination.

Swearing under his breath, Adam rose to his feet and then froze when Lynn made a soft sound and burrowed deeper in the pillow and quilts. When she settled down, he went quietly to the window.

Jennifer, forgive me.

No! There was nothing to forgive. He'd married for Rose's sake, for Shelly's, and he owed it to them, to himself, to Lynn, to make this marriage real and lasting. Jennifer would understand.

He wouldn't let himself think even for a moment that this lovemaking had been more honest than anything he'd ever shared with Jennifer.

Lynn's shyness, her obvious astonishment at her effect on him and even at her own physical response, had touched him. He was flattered, maybe, by the implication that she'd never found such pleasure with her worthless husband, that only he, Adam, had the power to awaken her sexuality.

Jennifer and he had been good in bed together. Brazen, she'd loved to flaunt her delicate, perfect body. *Shy* was a foreign word to his Jenny. That didn't make her response to him any less meaningful.

Staring out at the soft yellow glow of street lamps, able to hear the muffled beat of the surf though the window was shut, Adam wished like hell that he could be as casual about sex as men he overheard talking in the locker room of his health club. Half of them were getting it on the side even though they were married, he'd learned. It meant nothing—a little fun, an itch scratched.

Adam didn't want to have an affair. All he asked was that he be able to make love to his wife without feeling as if he was cheating on Jennifer, without this constant, tearing remembrance that she'd lost everything, that all he could do in return was prove that his love was enduring.

Maybe he hadn't been ready to test himself by bedding Lynn.

Flattening his hands on the cold glass, Adam grimaced. Too late, he reminded himself. There was no way in hell he could tell her in the morning that this had been a mistake, that maybe they should keep their relationship platonic. He owed her better than that kind of hurt.

And the truth was, he didn't want to go back. He wanted to see Lynn's eyes flutter open in the morning, see the dawning awareness, the pretty pink blush. He wanted to kiss her and make love to her in the soft light, taste her sweetness before breakfast.

He wanted to make a habit of sleeping with his wife, in every sense of the word.

Forgive me, Jenny.

CHAPTER THIRTEEN

"WHY IS DADDY SMILING at you like that?" Rose whispered loudly. She stared at her father with deep suspicion.

As a family, they were strolling the beach for goodies tossed up by this week's storm. High tide had left a string of slippery, stinking seaweed and a long curving line of smooth small stones and broken shells, among which treasures might be found. Walking ahead with Shelly, Adam was relaxed and handsome in jeans and a cream-colored Irish fisherman's sweater that added bulk to his shoulders. A breeze off the ocean ruffled his dark hair.

They were all supposed to have their heads bowed as they searched for bright bits of agate or perfect shells, although heaven knows, after living here for three years, Lynn didn't need even one more sand dollar or stone, however pretty. Adam couldn't be too serious about the hunt, either, because when Shelly crouched to poke at wet stones, he had directed a wicked and very sexy grin at Lynn.

Little girls weren't supposed to understand that the kind of smile he'd just given Mommy was something to make every smart woman wary. Rose's knowledge was apparently instinctive.

Adam and Lynn had been married for six weeks

now. The girls were only beginning to notice that something was different between their parents. Rose had looked thoughtful a few times, but was easily distracted.

Lynn figured she'd try again. "Maybe Shelly found something good," she suggested, knowing perfectly well, and with secret pleasure, that he wasn't nearly as interested in a polished agate as he was in stealing a kiss when Rose and Shelly became preoccupied.

Bouncing back up, Shelly skipped beside Adam. Her small hand was in his; every so often he swung her over a log or rock protruding from the gravelly beach, to her delight. "Daddy is *strong,*" she had declared happily, preferring him as a companion on this walk.

Her eagerness to walk with Daddy would have hurt, if immediately afterward Rose hadn't slipped her hand confidingly into Lynn's and said softly, "I don't like it when Daddy swings me like that."

Rose had a gift for such moments. Lynn couldn't quite decide whether Rose really was afraid when Daddy swung her, or whether her empathy was already developed to the point where she sensed her new mommy's distress. Surely at only three, she couldn't be mature enough to understand other people's feelings! Yet she seemed extraordinarily sensitive to mood, and despite the fact that she'd been given almost anything material she'd ever wanted, Rose was shyly grateful for small things that Shelly would have taken for granted.

Perhaps she wasn't as smart as Shelly and would never be the leader, but she knew instinctively how to be a friend. Lynn worried only that, growing up, she might hide feelings or depression or anger because she didn't want to upset anyone else. As the two girls became old enough to understand, what effect would the switch in the hospital have on them? Lynn had read about one of the best-known cases, where the child had ended up with big problems. Would the same thing happen with Shelly or Rose? Feelings of resentment or insecurity would be natural, surely.

Of course, she thought in rueful amusement, Shelly wouldn't be able to keep them to herself. Already, she talked through everything. She was utterly incapable of keeping a secret.

Rose, however, was another matter.

Lynn breathed in the salt-laden air and gazed out at the broken surf and the curve of the earth far beyond.

When she glanced back, she found Rose's gaze wide and inquiring. "How come Daddy went to bed with you last night?" she asked innocently.

Lynn gulped. Oh, dear. The kids hadn't actually caught them in bed together yet, and she hadn't been able to think of a way to casually say, *Your daddy and I are going to sleep together from now on.*

"I saw him come out in his 'jamas," Rose continued. "He only wears his bottoms, you know."

Lynn knew.

"He says the top wraps him up like a mummy 'cuz he rolls and rolls and rolls when he sleeps."

Lynn smiled down at her daughter. "That happens to my nightie sometimes, too."

Rose's forehead crinkled. "What's a mummy? Is it like you? Only, you're not all wrapped up."

Lynn explained that a long, long time ago, before her grandparents' grandparents' grandparents were born, Egyptians had wrapped dead people in linen bandages before putting them in a tomb.

Rose's face brightened. "I 'member this boy at my school! He came to the Halloween party with toilet paper around him." She gestured. "Like that. He was a big kid. Was he a mummy?"

"Well, pretending to be one," Lynn conceded. "He probably thought it would be a scary costume."

"He wasn't dead," Rose said earnestly. "Kids kept ripping his toilet paper. He got raggedy."

"That's what happens to costumes at a party, if you're having enough fun." Lynn glimpsed something bright ahead, just poking out of the sand. She steered Rose toward it.

Rose pounced. "Mommy, look!"

It was a whole bottle that Rose pried out of dried seaweed. Probably a beer bottle, but the shape was unusual, the glass roughened by sand and salt water.

Lynn squatted beside Rose, who was wiping sand and crusty seaweed from her find. "What do you think, is there a genie in it?"

Aladdin was one of Rose's favorite movies.

"No." With one eye, Rose peered inside. "It's empty. The top must've fallen off, and he got out. Maybe he doesn't have to give wishes no more."

"No more wishes?" Lynn's gaze went to her husband's broad back and dark head, bent as he listened to Shelly chatter. "What a terrible thought!"

"Genies get tired of doing wishes, you know,"

Rose continued importantly. "Sometimes they need a 'cation."

"A vacation?" Lynn pretended to think. "I suppose they do."

"Daddy said maybe we could all go on 'cation sometime. He said maybe Hawaii. It's got beaches, he says. But you got beaches here, too."

"The ones in Hawaii are made of silky, golden sand instead of rocks. And the sun shines there lots more than it does here. Everywhere there are big colorful flowers and waterfalls tumbling into pools, and whales right offshore."

And Adam wanted to take her? It could be a sort of honeymoon, to make up for the one they hadn't had.

Shelly suddenly crowed in delight. Face alight, she pointed into the foamy fingers of the waves. "Lookit! There's one a' those glass balls!" Hopping up and down with excitement, she exclaimed, "An' it's a big one!"

"Don't you have sharp eyes." Adam lifted her onto his shoulders. "Okay, punkin, let's go get it."

Rose and Lynn followed them across the wet gravel left by a receding tide. Sure enough, the Japanese float bobbed into sight and then vanished as a wave broke over it.

"Shoot, it's getting away," Adam said, pausing at the water's edge.

"Catch it, Daddy!" His daughter bounced even harder and grabbed his hair. "Don't let it get away!"

He looked ruefully down at his running shoes and jeans, then plunged into the ankle-deep foam. "Ah! It's freezing!"

Knee-deep before he could get his hands on the glass fisherman's float, Adam grabbed it, swore and dropped it back into the water.

A mother's anxiety seized Lynn, who watched with an eagle eye. He should have left Shelly behind. What if she fell off? What if an extra big breaker should knock him down?

A wave did surge in, soaking him to his thighs. Shelly seemed to have a grip on his hair as she kept bouncing and cheering him on.

"It's going away again, Daddy! Those ol' crabs won't hurt you. You better get it, 'cuz it's mine and I saw it first."

Gingerly he picked it up again and waded toward shore. One more cold wave washed up to his knees, and then he was squelching triumphantly up above the foaming edge of the surf, his teeth a flash of white as he grinned like a conqueror mounting the ramparts.

"What is it?" Rose asked dubiously, as he set it down and they all hunkered in for a look.

A foot in diameter, the green glass fisherman's float still had the twine net encasing it. Tiny pale crabs scuttled all over it.

Lynn explained that it had floated all the way from Japan, where fishermen used glass floats still instead of plastic ones to anchor their nets. She helped evict the crabs.

"I bet somebody'd buy it, huh, Mom?" Shelly asked.

"I'm sure they would, but maybe you'd like to keep it." Two months ago, she'd have been grateful for the extra cash it would have brought, Lynn thought wryly. "To remember today by."

"Can I?"

"Yep." Adam smiled at her. "If not for your sharp eyes, we never would have seen it." His gaze touched Rose as if by accident, and then he lifted a brow at Lynn. "Do you find these often?"

"Hardly ever anymore," she admitted. "But see what Rose found?" She pulled the bottle from her coat pocket. "It's empty, so we figure the genie must be taking a vacation. In Hawaii."

Shelly stared covetously at the bottle. "I bet a genie *did* live in it. Do you think he'll come back?"

"Who knows?" Lynn let it slip back into her pocket. "You both found treasures today, didn't you?"

On the way home Shelly and Rose ran ahead. Adam had to lug the big glass float. He paused once, when the girls found a tidal pool, to snatch a quick kiss, his lips cold but stirring warmth in her.

Shelly's piercing voice penetrated Lynn's euphoria. "Daddy's kissin' Mommy! Look, Rose. How come he's kissin' Mommy?"

Adam drew back. "It would seem I'm making a public demonstration of my affections."

"He kisses *me*," Rose declared.

"Not like that," Shelly said in a tone of horrified fascination. "Not on the lips!"

Facing the girls, his free arm looped around Lynn's waist, Adam said, "I like kissing Mommy, too. Mommies and Daddies do kiss on the lips."

"Eew." Shelly made a troll face.

"Trust me," Adam said with amusement, "you'll understand someday."

"What if a boy at preschool wants to kiss me on the lips?" Rose asked seriously.

"You pop him in the nose," he suggested.

The girls burst into giggles and scrambled onto a long log washed in by the sea and half-buried on the beach so that it made a perfect balance beam for three-year-olds. They could fall without hurting themselves.

"Rose already asked why you were sleeping with me," Lynn said, as she and Adam paralleled the girls' path.

"What did you say?"

"Nothing. She got distracted. You told her you don't wear pajama tops because they end up wound around you like a mummy's wrapping, and so I had to explain that a mummy is *not* like me."

He laughed, creasing his cheeks and warming the cool planes of his face. The fluttering in her chest Lynn felt at the sight of him was becoming familiar. She'd married this man in cold blood, and now she was feeling everything she had when she'd imagined herself in love with Brian.

Everything, she admitted silently, and more.

In comparison, what she'd felt for Brian had been…a crush. A girlish stage that would have passed if they hadn't rushed into marriage. If only she hadn't been so inexperienced, so socially inept, she would have known whether her feelings for him were special or not.

Was she fooling herself again, just because…well, because she so enjoyed making love with Adam?

Lynn stole a sidelong glance at the man striding beside her, looking astonishingly carefree for the buttoned-down, austere stockbroker he was. She had fallen in love awfully fast, hadn't she?

But in her heart she knew better. She had begun the tumble a long time ago. That day in the hospital, probably, when she'd seen how much he adored his Rosebud. When she realized he felt all the same conflicts she did. Every kindness he'd given her since, every smile at the girls, every willing boost onto a kitchen chair, every game played, every grave answer to a silly question, had polished the slide down which she rocketed. How could she help it? Despite his doubts, Adam was a wonderful father. Beneath his usual rigid courtesy and occasional bluntness, he was a marshmallow. Nothing was too good for Shelly and Rose. Or her, now that he felt an obligation to her. He was chivalrous, sexy and determined to do the right thing.

What's not to love? she asked herself frivolously.

Her feelings were anything but. She knew how lucky she was. Adam would be a good husband if it killed him. His moral standards wouldn't let him look at another woman, even if he didn't love his wife. But it wasn't just that. They could be happy together; these past two weeks demonstrated that. She was sure he was contented, at least.

All she had to do was keep her mouth shut. He must never, never know that this marriage was no longer one of convenience and friendship for her. He'd only feel uncomfortable, perhaps even obliged to make up some pretty lies to reciprocate. She couldn't bear that.

Be grateful for what you have, Lynn told herself. Why spoil it by wishing for more? If Adam came to love her in return, well, it would happen. Perhaps slowly, but heartfelt emotions couldn't be forced, shouldn't be pretended. She would never want that.

She had lived her entire life appreciating what she had and not hoping for too much. She could go on that way.

What she wasn't sure she could do was bear the regular separation from Adam. Although she hadn't yet said aloud, *I will sell the bookstore,* the idea had taken root and was settling in. Owning her own bookstore had been a lifelong dream, and she loved every moment of it. Working for someone else, even in a wonderful store like Powell's in Portland, would never bring her the same joy.

And oh, how she'd miss Otter Beach! The sound of the surf and the bark of sea lions out on the stack, the tangy air, the fresh breeze and the fog that rolled in off the ocean on hot days. *How shall I list the ways!* she thought. The crunch and slide of walking on the gravelly beach and the shoot of spray through the blowhole. The vendors along the boardwalk, the tourists and even the traffic on the brick streets. To her mental list she hastened to add her garden, and her new refrigerator and her rickety back steps she would decorate with potted geraniums come summer.

This was home, the first and only home she'd ever made for herself. But today was…she mentally ticked off days on her fingers…the tenth of February. Always, by the middle of April, she had gone back to her summer schedule, having the store open Tuesday through Sunday. Just over two months away.

That would mean two more days a week when she had to be here, and Adam had to be in Portland. Could she afford to hire someone to cover at least one day? Would she and Adam split the girls up? Or alternate who got to keep them? After only two weeks, she'd become accustomed to sleeping with him: to being able to tuck her cold feet beneath his calf, to the sound of him breathing beside her at night, to that exhilarating, sexy glint in his eyes when he wanted her.

Before Adam and Rose, she had loved her life here. Shelly and the bookstore were enough. Now they weren't. It was that simple.

Soon, she told herself, she had to start looking for a buyer.

Lynn wasn't quite sure why she hadn't told Adam about her plans. Some residual caution held her back. *Be sure,* her fearful inner self whispered.

But she was sure. Not that he would ever love her, but that she did love him. And both her daughters. She was spread too thin. She had a family now, a real family, and they had to come first.

She would definitely look for a buyer. But when Adam wrapped an arm around her and steered her away from the breaking surf and toward the stairs that led up to the boardwalk and the town, she didn't say, "Adam, I have something to tell you."

He was the one to speak instead, calling to the girls, "Come on, munchkins. We need to get you cleaned up, so we can head out for Portland. Daddy's got to go to work tomorrow."

As usual, they had to take two cars, one of the drawbacks of their commuter marriage. Today, the girls rode with him. She followed his Lexus all the way to Portland. When he got too far ahead, he slowed; when she missed a light, he waited on the shoulder of the road. She pulled into his driveway right behind him and helped him unbuckle the girls from their car seats and carry them, both sound asleep, into the house that was now her home, too.

Although the subject had been on her mind, she still didn't tell him while they put together a quick dinner and ate it, or even later when, without a second thought, she passed the spare bedroom that had once been hers and joined Adam in his spare, masculine bedroom dominated by a king-size bed.

In the master bathroom, she brushed her teeth at her own sink—this bathroom alone was bigger than her kitchen above the bookstore—and slipped on her nightgown. She came out to find Adam waiting, wearing only pajama bottoms that hung low on his hips. He drew her into his arms for a tender kiss that quickly became more intense.

"You won't need this," he murmured against her cheek, as his fingers gathered her nightgown at each hip preparatory to shimmying it over her head.

Purring like a contented cat, she hooked her thumbs inside the waistband of his pajamas. "Mmm. You won't need these, either."

He sucked on her earlobe, an oddly delicious sensation. "When the girls are grown—" he nipped instead, his low voice husky "—we'll sleep naked. Let's make a pact."

A thrill swelled in her chest, out of proportion to his idle words. He must be happy with her, or he wouldn't be thinking about such a distant future.

Would he? Was it possible that he was starting to feel something special, too?

Lynn couldn't have spoken to save her life. She only sighed and let her head fall back as his mouth moved softly along her throat, pausing to trace her collarbone, before continuing down to her breast.

Why couldn't he love her? she asked a nameless somebody, in hope and defiance. Was it so impossible? Was she unlovable?

Pleasure shivered through her as he suckled her breast, stroked her hips with his large hands, cupped her bottom and lifted her up so that she cradled his erection and had to wrap her legs around his waist.

"I want you," he growled, that hot light in his eyes.

Foolish words trembled on her tongue, but she swallowed them. She could not tell him. She couldn't ruin everything.

"I'm all yours," she whispered instead, and hoped he didn't know how completely that was true.

ALMOST THE BEST PART of being married was having somebody to talk to. Lynn loved the evenings, after the girls had gone to bed. She and Adam invariably cleaned the kitchen together and then took herbal tea or coffee to the living room, where they read some of the time in companionable silence, but most often talked. "Of shoes—and ships—and sealing wax—Of cabbages—and kings," to quote Lewis Carroll.

Not so far off, either. She and Adam hadn't yet discussed sealing wax, but she thought they'd covered cabbages—she detested them, he loved even such horrors as corned beef and cabbage—and kings, in the form of royal weddings. They had taken the girls shoe shopping one day, and gone to a park overlooking the Columbia River where they could see huge freighters unloading cargo from foreign climes.

She had missed such conversation dreadfully. Lynn and her mother had been good friends. Until Adam, Lynn had never been able to talk to anyone the way she could to her mother. In college, she'd had friends and roommates, of course, but all of them were so busy with finals and labs and boyfriends, and really everyone at that age was so self-centered, she realized now, that nobody listened very well. Probably including her.

Brian was a natural storyteller, but the stories were all about himself. His prowess as a high school and college sports star, his adventures mountain climbing and skiing, his starring role in campus theater productions. She had been fascinated and awestruck and grateful that he wanted to be with her, but after the first year she began to notice that he wasn't very interested in *her* dreams or successes, and he'd cut off her attempts to discuss politics or philosophy or a book she had read by reaching for the remote control or grabbing his jacket and saying casually over his shoulder, ''I promised Cranston I'd whip his butt at one-on-one. You were just going to read or something anyway, weren't you?'' He always said it that way: *just.* You're going to do something unimportant, dull.

Adam enjoyed reading as much as she did. Lynn was flattered when she discovered him reading a book she'd mentioned loving. Since then, he had read several based on her recommendations. He didn't always feel about them the same way she did, which she didn't mind. They'd had some rousing arguments.

The television was rarely on here, she'd discovered. The girls watched a couple of favorite shows and, naturally, Rose had a huge collection of videos mostly bought by Grandma McCloskey, but Adam limited how much Rose could watch a day, as Lynn had always done with Shelly. He religiously watched the news, primarily because world events had such a bearing on the next day's stock market. A revolution in some tiny country half a world away would impact the U.S. economy because a raw material for manufacturing came from there. She was impressed by Adam's instant grasp of the import of such news. Obscure political events took on meaning for her, too. She found that she read the newspapers and watched the television news with more interest now.

Only occasionally did she bump against a closed gate beyond which she wasn't welcome. A very few topics brought stinging reminders that their closeness was illusion.

Tonight, for example, Lynn curled her legs under her at one end of the sofa and said, "I forgot to tell you that your mother called today."

Adam laid down his book willingly. "What did she want?"

"Nothing special. I think she just wanted to chat." Lynn frowned, trying to remember. "She didn't leave a message."

"What did you 'chat' about?" He looked unwillingly fascinated. "I didn't know my mother knew how."

"Oh, she has an opening in a San Francisco art gallery next weekend. She asked if I'd like to come over and use her potter's wheel and kiln." As explanation, Lynn added, "I'd told her I took a couple of years of ceramics in college. I loved using a wheel."

"Ah." He sounded amused and a little bitter. "The way to her heart."

"Did you learn?"

"She tried," Adam said shortly.

"Did you?"

"Probably not." He laughed without much humor. "I felt about her studio like most kids do about a baby brother. It was my competitor for her attention, and it always won." This smile, though crooked, became more relaxed, more genuine. "Besides, I have not a grain of artistic ability. I made the ugliest damn pots you've ever seen."

"It's odd that we were both only children. I felt a little more secure than you did, though."

"Were you lonely?" He looked as if he really wanted to know.

"No." Why hadn't she been? "We were such good friends. Mom didn't seem lonely, so how could I be?" Lynn had never told this to anyone, but now she admitted, "I was terribly shocked when Mom got married. It made me wonder—oh, this sounds terrible..."

Adam finished for her, "You wondered if she'd ever really been as happy as you thought she was."

"Yes." Lynn made a face. "I suppose everyone grows up and looks at their parents and one day realizes maybe they weren't quite who you thought they were. If that isn't too muddled a sentence."

"Clear as Perrier," Adam assured her with a grin. "Except 'everyone' doesn't have to reevaluate a parent, because some of us knew ours. Mine are just who I concluded they were."

"Are they?"

He went still. "What's that mean?"

"Just that…" She hesitated. "I had the impression your mother was probing to find out whether I'd be a suitably loving wife for you. She seemed concerned."

"Concerned," he repeated flatly.

"Some people aren't very demonstrative."

He gave a short, hard laugh. "My mother is not demonstrative."

"You think she doesn't love you?" But he was so quick to hug Rose, to smooth away a tear or tickle her into laughter! He couldn't possibly have learned that from books!

"I think she feels an obligation."

"Well, I think you're wrong," Lynn said stoutly. "She was definitely suspicious of me." She thought for a moment. "I guess that's natural since she knows why we got married."

"Then she doesn't have any reason to worry about you breaking my heart, does she?"

"No." She spoke quietly, not letting him see that he had hurt her. "You're right. Maybe I misunderstood."

Say, *You* could *break my heart,* she begged him without words, her gaze lowered to the pale amber of her cinnamon apple tea. Say…

Gentler, his voice broke her pitiful thoughts. "You're not unhappy, are you?"

"Me?" Lynn made herself look up with wide eyes, as if astonished at the question. "Why would I be unhappy?" *Because I love you, and you don't love me,* she answered her own question.

"Some women are romantics." His tone was odd.

She would have sworn she wasn't one of them. *She* had never intended to remarry; *she* was incapable of the depth of passion and commitment a man would want in a wife.

She was an idiot, Lynn thought, and fully deserved the fix she'd gotten herself into.

"Not me," she claimed, and took a calm sip of her tea.

She felt his gaze resting on her and would have given almost anything to know what he was thinking. But for some peculiar reason her emotions seemed close to the surface. If she had met his eyes just then, she might not have been able to keep her secrets.

And she must. She must! She was so lucky, had so much, she wouldn't be foolish enough to let herself ache for the little that Adam couldn't give her.

"Did I tell you what Rose said today?" she asked with a smile so bright it felt brittle.

Without moving a muscle, Adam relaxed. Lynn sensed it with every fiber of her being. He had feared she would ask him something he couldn't answer, or didn't want to answer. Like, *Can I break your heart?* Or even, *Are* you *happy?*

Instead she was deliberately reminding him of what they had in common: their children.

He laughed in the right places at her story, told one of his own, then commented on the book he was reading. The evening was ordinary, pleasant; out-wardly both were comfortable.

After turning off the lights and going upstairs, they even made love. No, Lynn reminded herself, tears burning her eyes as she lay sprawled atop him in the aftermath, her face hidden against his chest, not love, *they had sex.*

There was a difference, and she had been pretending there wasn't. A mistake she would try very hard not to make in the future.

Adam rolled, settling her against him, and she sighed and turned away as if already half-asleep.

They could be content, even happy, without both being deeply, passionately in love. And so she reminded herself again: enjoy what you have, be grateful for Shelly and Rose's sake, and don't grieve for what you can't have.

Hot tears, falling silently, wet her pillowcase.

CHAPTER FOURTEEN

"COFFEE, SIR?" The waiter accepted Adam's nod and refilled his cup. "Our cheesecake is excellent."

Adam skipped the dessert; Lynn decided to indulge. The three partners in Adam's firm were having dinner with their wives at a Portland restaurant. This was throwing Lynn in with a vengeance. She had never met these friends and colleagues, and both they and their wives had known Jennifer.

Now, amid general chatter as the others debated dessert, she touched Adam's thigh and murmured, "I'm going to the rest room. Will you ask if they have herbal tea? I forgot."

"Anything but peppermint." He knew her tastes.

When she rose, Jillian, another of the wives, stood as well. "I'll join you."

As Jillian passed Adam to follow Lynn, she leaned down and murmured in his ear, "I like her. You're a lucky guy."

Erica, sitting on Adam's other side, had overheard. With the other two women wending their way between tables toward the back of the elegant restaurant, she said, "I'm so glad this marriage has worked out for you, Adam. Ron told me the circumstances, I hope you don't mind. It sounded like a prescription for disaster, and instead the two of you are a pair of lovebirds!''

Lovebirds? Adam thought incredulously. Where the hell had she gotten that idea?

"You do look happy," agreed her husband, who had been Adam's best friend since university days. Ron Chainey was the only one here who'd met Lynn, as he'd been the best man at the wedding. "You've been keeping Lynn tucked away." His grin was wicked. "Now we know why."

Erica, a buxom redhead who was unapologetically plump, patted his hand. "I'm so glad, after Jennifer, that you've found someone."

"He always was a lucky son of a gun." Ron aimed a mock punch at his shoulder.

When Adam failed to volunteer details about his married life, conversation drifted again. Eugene Warren, the third partner in their brokerage, wanted to complain about his clients' demands for Internet stocks, an old refrain.

"HiTech is the latest." He rubbed the top of his head, already balding though he was only in his mid-thirties. "The P/E stinks!"

The price to earning ratio, a standard for judging whether a stock was overvalued, was lousy for most Internet stocks. Amazon.com stock sold for as much as companies with solid earnings, even though the Internet book mart still wasn't posting a profit.

"You know that's true of all Internet stocks," Ron said mildly.

Warren stuck like a tick to his grievances. "They're going to crash one of these days. A company like Amazon.com or HiTech has no real assets.

Hell, a few phones and a warehouse are all that's behind the fancy graphics. What are we valuing?''

"Potential?" Adam suggested.

"All in the eye of the beholder. The projections are pie in the sky! If it looks too good to be true, it is. You know that. Let's have a little healthy cynicism here, can we?''

Desserts arrived, and Ron picked up his fork. "Gene, we've talked about this before. We can't use the same standards for judging these companies. They represent something completely new, a different way of making money. They're breaking ground. Sure, prices will probably shake out at some point. But in the foreseeable future? I don't think so. HiTech has a great website, they're delivering the product fast, and customers are flocking to them. I think their market will grow.''

Gene Warren continued, his thesis something to the effect that shopping on the Internet was a novelty. People would get tired of waiting for their computers to load web pages, tired of having to return items that didn't look anything like they did in the tiny grainy picture on the computer screen.

Waiting for his wife to return, Adam couldn't keep his mind on an old discussion about business. He hadn't seen Lynn in a dress more than a time or two. She was beautiful tonight, in a simple teal-colored sheath of rough silk. That glorious hair was anchored in a French roll on the back of her head, the tiny runaway tendrils appearing intentional.

When she'd twirled for his approval, she'd smiled impishly. "This dress is courtesy of your credit card, I must warn you.''

"It's stunning." Her legs went on forever. No, not forever, as her deliciously rounded bottom suggested. "*You're* stunning," he amended, probably sounding as dazed as he felt. "Worth every penny, and a hell of a lot more."

"Why, thank you."

She sounded the tiniest bit breathless, which made him wonder whether it was so obvious that he would have liked to whip that zipper back down and strip the simple little dress right off. Or maybe just hitch it up to her waist…

Damn. Sitting here at the table, he was hardening at the idea. Whatever else you could say about their marriage, the sex was good. Better than good. Incredible. No wonder they looked happy.

They *were* happy. He was reasonably sure she felt the same.

Eugene Warren's axiom echoed in his ears. *If it looks too good to be true, it is.*

Damn Eugene Warren and his perennially pessimistic outlook, Adam thought in irritation. Just because life was good didn't mean something had to go wrong. His arrangement with Lynn was giving them both what they wanted. How could that go sour?

Sure, you're getting what you want, an inner voice jeered. *You're getting everything: a willing, passionate sexual partner, both daughters, all the trappings of a happy marriage. In return you're giving…what?*

Knowing he was being defensive, still he fired back, *The same.* Lynn wasn't suffering here.

He wasn't the only one who thought she was happy. Even these old friends had a similar impression. He and Lynn had everything going for them. The only part of a conventional marriage they'd skipped were the words *I love you,* and neither he nor Lynn needed them.

Deep in his brooding, he didn't hear her footsteps. She was already pulling out her chair and saying, "Ooh. Look at that cheesecake," when he caught her scent. Adam stood and pushed in the chair after she'd sat.

"Thank you," she murmured, and began talking to Jillian across the table. Something about an art fair for children that was being held at a school.

"Face painting," Jillian was saying, "you know the girls would love that! Oh, and there's always sand art and finger painting for the little ones, and origami. And swirl art!" She laughed. "Now, there's a mess to clean up! But the kids have a great time. Do bring Shelly and Rose."

Adam wanted to kiss Lynn's neck, right where those tiny wisps of auburn hair curled like miniature tumbleweeds. She had incredible skin, milky pale with just a hint of peach, like the redhead she wasn't quite. He'd pull out the pins securing her hair one at a time, until the thick mass of curls tumbled into his hands and over her bare shoulders. Slither that silk sheath down her slender arms, exposing the lacy bra he'd caught a glimpse of as he zipped up the dress for her. Why, he wondered idly, was undressing a woman such a turn-on, even when a man knew what he'd find under the silk?

Because he liked what he would find, he answered himself. From an erotic cloud of hair to her generous breasts, he loved her body. And it wasn't just that.

Her kisses were shy, not provocative. Sweet, as if they meant something beyond the moment. The sounds Lynn made he found especially endearing. It was as if she couldn't help herself. He liked that: knowing she was shy, and probably blushed the next day at the memory of herself sobbing with pleasure or whimpering at the touch of his hand, but that he moved her beyond inhibitions.

One of the men asked him something about the Trailblazers, Portland's pro basketball team, and Adam answered, but as briefly as possible. Impatience barely in check, he waited for Lynn to finish her cheesecake.

As she swallowed the last bite, he tossed some bills onto the table and said abruptly, "We need to get home. Grandma is baby-sitting, you know, and it's after her bedtime."

A wide, devilish smile spread across his buddy Ron's face. "Uh-huh. Sure. It's Grandma's bedtime you're worrying about."

"Shut up," Adam said amiably. He took Lynn's hand and tugged her to her feet. "We're newlyweds, aren't we? We're entitled."

They escaped only after a couple more minutes of razzing. In the lobby, Lynn shrugged into her coat when he held it for her. Neither talking, they went out into Portland's usual chilly, damp night.

"*Are* you concerned about Angela baby-sitting?" she asked, as he unlocked the passenger car door for her.

He pulled her to him for a quick, hard kiss. "Nope. I got to imagining how much I was going to enjoy unzipping your dress."

"Oh." He could hear her blush, if such a thing were possible.

On the drive home, Lynn agreed that she liked his friends, liked their wives, had indeed made plans to take Rose and Shelly to the art fair at the elementary school where Jillian served as PTA president. Yes, she thought she could be friends with Jillian in particular; did Adam know that she'd written a children's book and was seeking a publisher?

Despite her willingness to answer direct questions, Lynn was rather quiet. It seemed to Adam that her voice was constrained. Maybe she was tired, he decided. Could be she'd been nervous about meeting his friends and was relieved it was over. Or she was anxious about leaving the girls with Angela. There were any number of reasons she might be a little distracted.

But on top of his earlier brooding, it bothered him that she wasn't as open as usual, that she seemed to be doing some brooding of her own.

If it looks too good to be true... The wail of a distant siren seemed to whisper just to him.

He had too many moments like this, when he felt as if he were balancing a dozen wineglasses on his nose like the Chinese acrobats he'd taken Rose to see last fall. Any misstep and he'd see them teeter, arc in slow motion through the air, shatter on the floor. Maybe it was losing Jennifer the way he had. He knew how quickly the rug could be yanked out from under you.

Especially when the only promises given were "I'll try my best," and a more formal "I do."

At home her smile seemed forced, too, when An-

gela jabbered about the cute things Shelly said and
how smart she was and wasn't it nice that the girls
loved each other like sisters?

"Thanks for baby-sitting, Mom." Adam kissed
her cheek and managed to get her heading toward
the front door. He walked her out to her car, thanked
her ten more times, and stood with hands in pockets
watching until the brake lights winked once and her
BMW disappeared into the trees. Asking her to baby-
sit had been Lynn's idea; he had always waited in
vain for her to volunteer. She'd agreed with such
alacrity, he guessed she had *wanted* to be asked. Apparently he and she were two of a kind. Thanks to
Lynn, his relationship with Angela and Rob was the
best it had ever been.

More surprisingly, he'd realized recently that he
was seeing more of his own parents, too. Just today,
his mother had called to chat. She'd asked a few
probing questions about his marriage, which made
Adam wonder if Lynn hadn't been right after all. His
mother might care more than he'd suspected. These
past weeks, they'd come to dinner several times and
had Lynn, Adam and the girls over to their place.
Hell, his mother had even given Shelly and Rose a
tour of her studio! Adam was coming to the unwelcome conclusion that he had shut his parents out, not
the other way around. He was lucky that Lynn was
around to mend fences he'd evidently damaged in
his clumsiness.

Lynn. He locked the front door behind him, anticipation quickening in him. He could take his wife to
bed. At last. There, at least, they were close, their

moods invariably in sync. She wanted him, he had no doubt about that much.

She'd left lights on downstairs but had apparently already gone up. Disquiet touched him. Was something wrong? Had somebody said something tonight that upset her? Damn it, why wasn't she talking to him?

Irritably he asked himself why he was jumping to conclusions. Maybe she'd slipped upstairs to get ready for him. He might find her lounging in a sexy pose on the bed. He just hoped she hadn't taken the dress off. He wanted to save that pleasure for himself.

Flipping off lights as he went, Adam paused in the upstairs hall, as he knew Lynn would have done a few minutes before, to step into the girls' bedroom and assure himself they were both safely tucked into bed, healthy, their sleep untroubled. As he stood beside the bed, Rose's eyes opened and she gazed sleepily up at him.

"Daddy," she whispered.

He bent down, cupped her face and kissed her forehead. "Mommy and I are home. You sleep tight, sweetheart."

"'kay, Daddy," she murmured even as her heavy lids sank closed. After a moment of stillness, a small snore escaped her parted lips and she rolled away, nestling closer to Shelly.

Adam's smile died when he reached his bedroom and saw Lynn. Her back was to him. She'd already shinnied out of her panty hose, unclipped her earrings and let down her hair. As he watched, she massaged her scalp, then ran her fingers through the curls and shook them out. At last, she groped behind her neck for the zipper on her silk dress.

He stepped silently behind her and eased the zipper down. She started, then bowed her head to let him work. As the dress parted, he brushed his lips along her nape. The skin was so soft here. With his fingertips Adam traced her spine, ignoring the catch of her bra, slipping inside her panties. She moaned.

"Are you tired?" he asked. "You didn't wait for me."

"I am tired," Lynn admitted.

"If you want to go right to sleep…" Hoping like hell she'd say no, Adam nuzzled the curve between neck and shoulder.

She sucked in a breath. "I thought I would." Her voice was throaty, not much above a whisper.

Disappointment smacked him in the face, fear in the gut. She might just be tired. But what if it was more?

He straightened away from her. With determined civility, Adam said, "Then you'd better get right to bed. Would you rather I read downstairs for a while?"

"No." Lynn turned suddenly and wrapped her arms around his neck. "No, don't go. I'm not that tired."

"If you want to sleep, it might be best…" The translation, he thought grimly, was, *I need to put some distance between us if I can't have you.*

Her eyes were huge and dark, and he felt tension quivering through her. "You've changed my mind. If…if you're still in the mood."

The disappointment evaporated like a cold sweat;

the fear lingered. She tugged his head down to hers with a hint of desperation. Her mouth was needy, her fingers on his tie and shirt buttons clumsy. She seemed suddenly frantic for him.

He shrugged out of his shirt as she swept it from his shoulders. Her dress pooled at her feet. As he flicked the catch of her bra, she was already unbuckling his belt and unzipping his fly, taking him in her hands. She made mewling sounds as he reached inside her panties and found her hot and damp.

"Yes. Right now," she whispered, an ache in her voice. "I want you."

He stripped the panties from her as he laid her on the bed. The ceiling light was still on. There seemed nothing romantic about what they were doing right now, but he was past caring or remembering the slow seduction he'd planned.

Her urgency had communicated itself to him. He didn't even get his pants off before she tugged him down. Thrusting inside her, he drank in her cries with his mouth. She whimpered when normally she would have sighed softly. Clutching desperately at his back and shoulders, her nails bit into his flesh. When his mouth left hers, she pleaded with him.

"Harder. Faster. Oh, yes. Now! Oh, please, now!"

Ripples traveled through her belly and she cried his name. "Adam!"

Groaning, teeth gritted, he finished with a triumphant shout, emptying himself inside her. He collapsed on top of her, his mind eddying in a dark whirlpool. What in hell had happened here? Why had she been too tired one second, then too impatient to wait for him to kick off his trousers the next?

He liked being wanted. He didn't like the fact that she had seemed to need the physical release more than the intimacy of their lovemaking.

He must be crushing her, he realized. It seemed a superhuman effort to roll to one side, but he managed. When he tried to take Lynn with him, keep her wrapped in his arms, she stiffened.

"I'm cold," she said in a small voice. "I think I'll take a shower. If you don't mind."

That brought his eyes open. "Why would I mind?"

"I'll be back to bed in a few minutes." She was definitely beating a retreat. She slipped off the bed and scooped up her dress, holding it in front of her as if to hide her nakedness. A second later the bathroom door shut and he heard the shower start.

He usually felt good in the aftermath of sex. This time he felt…obscene. Sprawled on his back on the bed, ankles cuffed by his trousers.

Swearing, Adam sat up and finished undressing. He hung up his slacks and tie, draped the shirt over a chair, and pulled on his pajama bottoms. He brushed his teeth and splashed water on his face at one of the two sinks outside the bathroom. Leaving on the lamp at Lynn's side of the bed, he switched off the overhead light and climbed into bed.

Her shower wasn't a quickie. It ran and ran, as if she felt the need to scrub every inch of her body, or simply to let the hot water unknot the tension he'd felt. Guessing that she'd prefer it, Adam pretended to be asleep when she finally, quietly, came out. Water ran briefly in the sink as she too brushed her teeth. A moment later the mattress gave as she sat. The lamp went out, and she slipped in on her side of the bed, seemingly careful not to touch him.

Wide-awake, Adam wondered how Lynn really felt about him. She had entered willingly into their bargain, but he knew damn well that was for the sake of the girls. When he screwed her tonight—there was no other way to put it—did she pretend he was someone else? When she'd pulled his mouth down to his, changing her mind with such odd abruptness, did she hunger for the physical connection without it mattering who held her?

Did she think about him during the day, or in the night when they were separated? Had her feelings for him grown, or were they still two strangers who happened to share a bed?

Adam hadn't expected to feel so insecure. Not daring to move, he stared into the darkness and knew that something was missing for him in this marriage. He didn't like discovering that he wanted her to love him. She said, "I want you," and it wasn't good enough. The words and everything that went with them counted after all.

What kind of jerk did that make him, considering he didn't, couldn't, return her love?

Did she wonder if he closed his eyes and imagined he was making love to Jennifer? The idea unexpectedly jolted him. Was that what was wrong?

The possibility was particularly ironic considering his own guilt because he so seldom did think about Jennifer anymore. She was slipping away from him, Lynn's vivid presence routing the ghost. He had trouble seeing Jenny's face anymore, hearing her laugh; she no longer visited his dreams. He sure as hell didn't imagine her when he was making love to Lynn.

That guilt crushed him suddenly in its grip. He'd lied to himself, he thought in despair. He'd never intended to hold Jennifer close to his heart once he had remarried. His promises on their wedding day, the vows he'd sworn to God beside her deathbed, all meant nothing. Out of sight, out of mind.

Muscles rigid, Adam wasn't sure he could keep lying here in this bed next to his too-still wife. He needed to be away from her. Able to pace. Bang his head against a wall. He needed to find Jennifer again, if she was here at all.

Or maybe, just maybe, he needed to find a way to say goodbye. Lynn deserved better than their farce of a marriage. Could he give it to this shy, gentle woman with guts, brains and a heart?

Before he lost her?

Her breathing was regular, soft. His gaze sought the light numbers on the clock. He'd been lying here for twenty minutes now. She must be asleep.

Making slow movements only, he edged his legs over the side of the bed and sat up, then, careful not to tug at the covers, stood. He kept a bathrobe on a hook inside the bathroom door. He'd earlier turned down the thermostat, so he shrugged into the bathrobe. Lynn hadn't moved. She had to be asleep. She wouldn't even notice he was gone.

He didn't turn on a light until he reached his home office downstairs. There, Adam ignored the computer and fax machine. It was the large leather album he reached for, the one he kept on a low shelf so Rose could look at photos of her mother whenever she chose.

He sat in the large leather armchair and opened the album in his lap. On the first page were pictures taken while they were engaged. God, she looked young, was his first thought. Not so different from Shelly. A girl. She sparkled, Jenny did, even in a photograph. He traced the lines of her pixie face, alight with laughter, and remembered the first time they met, when she'd chattered so fast he didn't know half of what she said. She was beautiful, but in a different way with her eyes slanted like a cat's, her high cheekbones and pointy chin. She'd worn her brown hair short, increasing the elfin effect. Next to her, he had always felt stolid, slow moving. Even his thoughts couldn't jump from idea to idea with the lightning speed of hers. He had fallen in love with Jenny McCloskey immediately, and loved her until the day she died. Loved her even afterward, when he had been left to raise their daughter alone.

Slowly he turned the pages and watched her mature from that laughing girl to a stylish, sophisticated woman who never quite lost the mischief in her eyes. In the last photos, Jenny was pregnant, her face slightly rounder, her stomach ripe with their child. Not Rose, but Shelly.

Ah, Jenny, Adam thought, *are you really gone? Is it time to say goodbye?*

"You still miss her."

His head shot up so fast he bit his tongue. *Damn.* Lynn had sneaked up on him. She stood in the doorway, looking small and vulnerable in the thick chenille robe that had been a Christmas gift from her mother. Her eyes were fixed not on him, but on the open album.

Adam resisted the temptation to close it. He swallowed. "No. Most of the time, I don't think about her." *Because of you.* But he didn't say that. It sounded too much like an accusation.

"May I see?"

Wordlessly he turned the photo album and held it out. Lynn took it from him and gazed down at his first wife, pregnant with the child she had raised as her own.

With shock he saw her eyes brim with tears. She touched the photo, too. "She—your Jennifer—would have adored Shelly."

Adam opened his mouth to say *and Rose,* but he couldn't. Jenny had been so quick, so impatient, he thought Rose might have driven her crazy.

Lynn swiped at her tears with the back of her hand. Her voice sounded just a little hoarse. "Why tonight?"

"What?"

Now she did look at him, her gaze bravely holding his. "Why did you come down to look at her pictures tonight?"

God. He wanted to evade, but he could see that she wouldn't let him.

"I'm forgetting her. I swore I wouldn't do that."

"She's dead."

Anger flashed through him. "Do you think I don't know that?"

Her eyes were too clear, too all-seeing. "Sometimes, I'm not sure."

"What the hell does that mean?"

"She's been dead for almost four years. Shelly's lifetime. And you're still grieving as though it was only four months ago."

"Would you want to be forgotten that quickly?"

Lynn answered without hesitation. "I would not want to linger here, if some wisp of my presence crippled the people I'd loved."

He got to his feet, dumping the photo album, not looking at where it lay sprawled on the hardwood floor. "Crippled? Rose didn't know her to mourn. And look at me. I've remarried, I make love to my wife. Hell, I was so damned eager tonight, I didn't get my pants off! How is that crippled?"

Unblinking, she stared at him for the longest time. Anxiety clenched his stomach and knotted his hands at his side.

Whatever he expected, it wasn't what came.

"I love you," she said quietly.

He expelled all the air in his lungs as if a fist had driven it out.

"You love me," he said stupidly.

She loved him, Adam exulted. Her strange mood tonight meant nothing.

"Do you love me?" she asked, equally quietly.

He hadn't caught his breath yet. Not a single word presented itself. *She loves me,* tangled in his mind with one last seeking cry, *Jenny.*

Jenny was gone. Lynn was here, and his heart swelled with the startling awareness that he wouldn't want it any other way.

"See?" Lynn spoke gently. "You can't say it, can you? Or anything close."

His mouth worked.

She laughed, but sadly. "I shouldn't have even put you on the spot, should I? Love wasn't part of our deal. You warned me. I thought that wouldn't matter. I just didn't know that I was already falling in love with you."

"I...care." *God.* Even he knew that was inadequate.

"I know you do," she said with that same terrifying gentleness. "You're such a good, loving father, and you've been so kind to me. So...caring. Reading books I liked. And listening to me. I appreciate that. Really I do."

He had never felt so lumpish, even with Jennifer. He knew he needed to find the right thing to say, but he kept shying away from the obvious—*I love you.* Did he love her? Was that what he'd been feeling? Was that why he needed the words from her, the reassurance? Why he wanted her, thought about her constantly, missed her when she was on the coast? Why he'd begun imagining what a child who was his and hers together would be like?

Panic made his heart pound so hard he could hear the beats. *Think!* he told himself, his customary caution coming to his rescue. *Be sure. Don't spout off at the mouth and then be sorry.*

Lynn squeezed her hands together in front of her, looking uncomfortably as if she were praying. "I thought I could live with you and be your wife, even if you were still mourning for Jennifer. But I can't. No." She stopped him before he could speak. "It's not her. It's the fact that you don't love me. Someday you'll get over her, and you'll be ready to love again. You won't want to be married to me."

"I will never not want to be married to you." This much he knew, with unshakable certainty.

Her tiny, grateful smile ripped at his heart. "You say things like that, and it weakens my resolve. But the truth is, we're married only because I wouldn't move from Otter Beach. Well, I've decided. I'll sell the store and get a job and an apartment in this area. We can do some kind of joint custody thing. Maybe they can spend a week with me and then a week with you. Or if I can get days off during the week, I can have them then and you can have them on weekends. Or something. We'll make it work. But we will not be married just because it's the most convenient way to each have both girls."

"We *are* married."

Tears sprang into her eyes again. "It's not necessary anymore."

Anguish made his voice raw. "I don't want to lose you."

Tears ran down her cheeks now. "I'm not going far. Maybe…maybe we can be friends."

"Friends?" Adam repeated incredulously. "Goddamn it, I don't want to be friends!"

Lynn's face crumpled like a small child's. She whispered, "I'm sorry," and fled.

Adam's mouth formed the words *I love you*.

Too late.

CHAPTER FIFTEEN

EYES BLINDED BY TEARS, Lynn stumbled up the stairs. At the top she waited, listening, for a moment that stretched until a sob tore its way from her chest.

He wasn't coming after her.

She ached to crawl into bed with the girls and hold their small warm selves close, but waking them would be selfish. Instead she slipped as quietly as she could into the spare bedroom. She wanted to disappear; she wanted him not to find her, if he decided from guilt to offer awkward apologies and excuses. Closing the door behind her, she leaned back against it and let her legs collapse.

In a small ball on the floor, she cried silently so that Adam wouldn't hear her if he passed in the hall. His pity she couldn't bear. Anything but that.

I...care. She heard his stiff voice again, the faint hesitation, as if even such a tepid word required thought.

When had she decided she couldn't bear to go on living with a man who only "cared" for her, when she loved him desperately? The knowledge had crept up on her, though it terrified her. What would it mean to her daughters, who were so happy in a real family?

But they would be unhappy if their parents were,

she convinced herself. Mommy and Daddy didn't have to be married for them to feel secure and loved.

Tonight Lynn had looked around at Adam's friends and their wives, heard mention of Jennifer, and thought, *They all know he doesn't love me. They know he married me for his daughter. They feel sorry for us. Perhaps for him especially.*

She would have felt pity for someone in the same situation, once upon a time. Imagine, being married to a man you didn't love! Putting up with his foibles, sharing housekeeping and memories, friends and family. Worse yet, accepting him into your bed.

Lynn remembered the years of rooming with other women, the small irritations that added up to resentment despite an initial spirit of cooperation and friendship. How would she feel when she first saw Adam hide exasperation? When she first heard suppressed annoyance in his voice? When he didn't reach for her at night? It was all inevitable. Even desire didn't last, when it wasn't founded in true emotion.

She had been determined not to make love with him tonight. Not when during dinner she had realized she would have to suggest a separation, have to let him out of a bargain he couldn't have wanted to make. But she hadn't been able to help herself. His fingers sliding down her spine had offered unbearable temptation. Just once more didn't seem like too much to ask, did it? She wouldn't let herself think about later, about morning, about never feeling his mouth against hers again, his big warm hands on her breasts, his body filling hers. Just once more, they could come together and she could know they were a whole.

A last memory. It would be her consolation. That, and the knowledge that at least she would never have to hide her tears when he didn't want her anymore.

Now, curled on the floor, Lynn wiped at her wet cheeks and longed for a tissue to blow her nose. Bed, she thought. She would crawl into bed, and maybe find the oblivion of sleep.

She did creep between the crisp, cold sheets of the guest bed. As the night inched on, what fitful sleep she found came with dreams of grief and loss. The gray light of a rainy dawn awakened her to a pounding headache and a yawning chasm where her heart should be. Shivering, she wished for another blanket but made no move to get up and find one. Any other morning, she could have scooted closer to Adam, borrowed his warmth. But he was alone in their bed, and she was alone here, down the hall, all because she had followed him downstairs in the middle of the night and found him poring over photographs of his first wife.

Her shivers spreading, Lynn gazed sightlessly at the rain droplets running down the window. Had she made a terrible mistake? He did care, she knew he did. They *were* friends, closer all the time.

But not so close, she realized with a wrench of sadness, that he would talk about his Jenny with her. Oh, no. That part of his life stayed behind a barred door. She was not a real wife, who was entitled to admittance. They had a deal, and it didn't include letting her know the real woman he had loved.

Lynn's teeth chattered, but still she didn't move.

He had wanted her, she thought, but the comfort was too cold to help. He was a man, she was available. He found her "attractive," he had said once. "Attractive" was as chilling as the knowledge that he "cared."

She should go home, she thought. Take both girls, if Adam would let her, and heal in a place where she belonged. There she could plan the future. Advertise for a buyer, put out feelers for a job, talk to Shelly and Rose and hope she could make them understand. She needed some time before she could face Adam again.

Eventually she heard the shower down the hall. After the water stopped, she imagined him dressing. She had loved to watch the muscles in his broad, bare back flex as he bent to put on socks and shoes, as he rifled the contents of his closet in search of a favorite shirt. Then he would look so serious as he bent over to use the mirror to adjust his tie and impatiently rake a comb through his hair.

Had he slept easily? she wondered. Lynn tensed as the soft sound of his bedroom door closing came to her. Footsteps approached down the hall, paused outside her room, and finally continued downstairs. She lay shivering in the cold bed she'd made for herself until she heard the purr of his car pulling out of the driveway.

At last she dragged herself out of bed and went to their—no, *his* bedroom—where she grabbed clothes and toiletries before returning to the guest bath. His presence wasn't as strong here.

Warmer on the outside after a shower, she began

packing as she waited for Shelly and Rose to wake up.

She was making breakfast for them an hour later when she found the note Adam had left propped against the counter backsplash.

Lynn, I meant what I said last night. I don't want to lose you. We need to talk, but maybe we both have some thinking to do first. I assume you're planning to go home this morning. Take Shelly and Rose if you'd like, or drop them at preschool. Let me know. I'll be in touch.

Adam

To the point, offering her room to hope, if she'd been so inclined, and gracious. Typical of the man she loved.

Lynn crumpled the note in her hand, fought back tears, and turned to face their children.

"Girls, we're going to Otter Beach today."

How could he not have known he was in love with his wife?

Feeling like death after a sleepless night, Adam asked himself the same question over and over without getting a complete answer. Yeah, he felt guilty because Jennifer was dead and he wasn't. He'd felt like a scumbag because his love wasn't going to last for all eternity, because he could apparently transfer his affections in the blink of an eye. Maybe he'd been bothered because loving Lynn was so damned convenient he didn't believe his own feelings.

And maybe, it had just happened so gradually, he

hadn't noticed the moment he slipped from liking and lust to love and a deeper kind of passion.

Midmorning, he checked his voice mail and heard Lynn's voice say unemotionally, "Adam, I'm taking both girls with me. I guess we do need to discuss a visitation schedule, but they'll be fine with me until this weekend. I'll call then."

Click.

He stabbed number one on his phone and listened again. She didn't sound distressed, sad, angry, hurt. Nothing. Back to square one. He'd pick up the girls, drop them off. Lynn would be pleasant, remote, well organized. He and she would have a relationship as cozy as the one he had with Ann. Post-it notes passing in the night.

"No!" The sound of his own voice, feral, hoarse, shocked him. He shot to his feet and paced.

He wouldn't have it.

She loved him. He'd heard her say the words *I love you*.

No, Adam had no intention of letting his wife get away. He'd go after her.

As soon as he could figure out why he had been so slow on the uptake, and why she was so ready and eager to run.

Had his determination to give her and Shelly everything left Lynn feeling bought and paid for? He tried to remember the expression on her face when she told him the silk dress had gone on his credit card, but all he could see was how glorious she looked. Hell, maybe she'd sounded a little rueful, but not resentful. He'd swear she hadn't.

Was it because he'd pressured her to sell the store

and move to Portland? But if that was the problem, why was she now agreeing to do just that? No. It didn't equate.

He stared out the window at the rhododendrons budding for spring and swore under his breath.

Who was he kidding? He'd made passionate love to Lynn and then sneaked downstairs to moon over photos of his first wife. What woman wouldn't be deeply hurt? If he'd said his goodbyes to Jennifer, not left his loss festering, Lynn wouldn't have walked out.

He hoped.

"Mr. Landry..." his secretary said behind him.

"What?" he snapped as he turned, then scrubbed a hand over his face and said repentantly, "Sorry, Lydia. I'm running on empty today."

"Your three-o'clock appointment canceled." His middle-aged secretary eyed him warily. "I could re-schedule the four-o'clock appointment. I thought perhaps..."

"That the office would be better off without me?"

She smiled faintly. "That you might like to leave early."

"Yeah." Damn, his eyes felt dry and gritty. "I would. Thanks."

When she left and quietly shut the door behind her, Adam tugged his tie loose. He had the afternoon free. He could head for Otter Beach.

And what? Hand Lynn a dozen roses, say, "Gosh, the words just wouldn't come fast enough last night, but I do love you?" and expect her to invite him in?

He was still incredulous at the discovery he had made last night, long after Lynn gave him a last look so full of hurt he'd never forget it and walked out of the room with dignity.

His lips had formed the words *I love you* before his brain caught up. He *loved* her? This pretty, quiet woman he had once believed he would never have noticed if they met casually? The woman who frowned in fierce concentration as she read about investing money she didn't have, who asked earnest questions so she would be able to understand his life? The woman who loved both girls effortlessly, had endless patience with them, who could play dress-up as if she were still three years old herself?

The woman who kissed him with incredible innocence and sweetness, who could still blush though she'd been married and divorced, who made love generously and lovingly?

He groaned and squeezed his eyes shut. How could he not have known?

He left the office without any desire to go home. An hour of aimless driving brought him where he'd probably intended to go in the first place: the cemetery where Jennifer had been buried in a gleaming mahogany casket. He shuddered at the memory of the casket. He would rather be cremated, himself, than be shut into a satin-lined box for eternity, but he'd let Jennifer's parents make the decisions. They were the ones having trouble dealing with their daughter's death, he had thought. *He* knew she was gone.

Now he laughed hollowly. None of them had known she was gone. He least of all.

It was the way of her going, Adam thought, that had made goodbyes hard. Jennifer was dead, they told him, but she lay there in that hospital bed for another four weeks looking as if she'd open her eyes any moment and smile. Dead, but she was breathing, her heart beating, a life growing in her womb. He still had trouble understanding: how could she give life, when she was dead? So when had she died? When was he supposed to understand and accept that his wife was gone?

He parked on the shoulder of the asphalt drive that wound through the cemetery, and walked across the springy grass to the flat marker with Jennifer's name and dates of birth and death. He was ashamed to have to hunt. The fragrant paperwhites in a pot must have been left here by her parents. Gestures like that would be important to them. Adam didn't often come. His laughing Jenny wasn't here, only the casket that held her earthly remains.

Perhaps, Adam thought slowly, he had known she was dead. The only place she still lived was in his memory. Those memories he had edited, he saw now. His young wife was charming, funny, sexy, good-hearted, but also spoiled and a little selfish. He had made her a saint and dared anyone—Lynn—to touch her place in his heart.

He finally let himself admit what part of him had known for a long time. The truth was, his feelings for Lynn went deeper, were based on more than youthful sexual attraction. Lynn was shy but gutsy. He admired her brains, her warmth, her taste. He loved her as a mother, a woman, a friend and a lover.

Maybe what he and Jennifer felt for each other would have matured into something similar.

Maybe not. Maybe they'd be divorced, like some

of his friends. Maybe they would live in brittle silence, because she wasn't really interested in him.

He would never know. She was gone, and he would always remember her with love and sadness for what she'd lost. Not what he had lost.

"Goodbye, Jenny," he said softly, but she was no more here to answer than she had ever been.

Adam turned and strode across the grass with new energy and purpose. He had to see his wife. This time, he'd find the right words.

If only she would listen.

SHE HAD EXPECTED HOME to be a haven. Lynn walked through the dark bookstore, finding her way between tall bookshelves and the dark bulk of chairs and tables by familiarity and with the help of the night-light left on in back.

She'd tucked the girls into bed an hour ago. Their whispers and giggles didn't last long. Impulse had drawn her down here, where her dream had come to life. The dream she was about to give up.

Tonight, she found only wood furniture and books without color and life. A business. Not very important, compared to the people she loved.

In the grip of a terrible restlessness, she gave in to another impulse and picked up the phone behind the counter.

"Hi, Frances," she greeted her teenage babysitter's mother. "Any chance Alicia could come over for an hour or two? Rose and Shelly are asleep. I'm desperate to go out for a little while. Maybe just for a walk."

"Of course she can come. All she's doing is

watching *Titanic* for the thirtieth time. Just a moment.'' Lynn heard her muffled voice; she must have covered the phone. Then, ''She's finding her shoes. She'll be over in a minute. Are you okay, Lynn? Is something wrong?''

''No, I…it's just been one of those days.''

''I can remember a few when I thought I'd scream if I didn't get away from the kids, and I had a husband to take over once in a while,'' her friend said indulgently. ''Alicia can stay all night, if you need her. But, if you're going out by yourself, be careful, won't you?''

The teenager lived only a block away. Lynn met her at the top of the back staircase. Hearing the TV go on quietly behind her, she pulled on a heavy wool sweater that had been Brian's—she would have been lost inside it if she hadn't rolled the sleeves up several times—and hurried down the stairs and across the street, toward the rhythmic boom of the sea.

She'd left the rain behind in Portland, an unusual circumstance. Here at the edge of the Pacific Ocean, torn bits of cloud drifted across the face of the full moon and a wind with the bite of winter whipped her hair back from her face.

The boardwalk was deserted, the stores dark and closed. Laughter and voices drifted from a restaurant, but nobody sat outside the way they did in midsummer. She took the concrete stairs two at a time, wanting to lose herself on the dark beach, with only the moon and the surf for company.

She wished Adam had never been part of her life here. That they hadn't raced across the beach with the girls shrieking in delight. That he hadn't gotten wet rescuing the Japanese float for Shelly. Sat at the table every Saturday in her bookstore, reading contentedly. Bought her a new couch, taught her the loneliness of her bed and the pleasures of sharing it. Cooked in her tiny kitchen, hung his toothbrush in the equally small bathroom.

Absorbed in memories, Lynn stubbed her toe on a half-buried boulder and fell painfully to her knees. Tears sprang into her eyes, but she shook them away, angry at herself.

I…care.

Couldn't he have tried? she thought pitifully. Pretended, just a little bit?

Lied? she asked herself harshly. Was that what she wanted? Give him credit. At least he was too honest for that.

She pulled herself to her feet and kept walking. White fingers of foam led her to the water's edge. Lynn walked parallel to the crashing surf, her way better lit now by moonlight. The wind bit through her wool sweater, stung her eyes, tangled her hair, but she reveled in the solitude and the cold, the white feathers and the steady throb of the surf.

Hugging herself, Lynn kept thinking, *I could be home in Portland. Debating with Adam, laughing with him, savoring the delicious anticipation of bedtime. Is this really better?*

Couldn't she have loved him in silence? He might have come to love her in turn, mightn't he? Why had she given up hope that he would?

I…care.

Couldn't that be enough? she begged herself. Was that so terrible? Didn't the greatest of passions often age into something no more exciting? So what if he still thought about Jennifer. She was gone, and Lynn was here. With time, he would think about his first wife less.

She stopped and faced the breakers as wisps of cloud raced in front of the moon. *Why wasn't I patient?* she thought miserably. *Why couldn't I...settle?*

Wasn't having something better than nothing?

How could she convince Rose and Shelly that she'd made the right choice if she didn't even believe it herself?

Lynn found a boulder to provide a windbreak and backrest. Huddled against the night and her own unhappiness, she remembered every moment of her married life, every word Adam had spoken, every touch. She tortured herself with full knowledge of what she had thrown away, and began to see that she was a coward.

She had been so terrified of losing Adam slowly, she had brought on a quick, clean break. She knew she'd be okay on her own. She'd done this before. What she had no idea how to do was coax a man into loving her, or how to endure his indifference when he made it plain.

Burying her cold face in the scratchy wool of the sweater sleeves, Lynn heard herself as clearly as if she'd spoken aloud. She'd be okay on her own. She'd done this before.

Oh, God. She had told Adam once that being a single mother came naturally to her, that it was the pattern she knew. She was comfortable as a mother, but not as a wife.

In her fear, she had made no effort to fight for Adam. Being a wife was too scary. Run and hide.

Her tears soaked the sweater sleeves, her nose dripped. If only she hadn't told him she loved him! Lynn thought wretchedly. Bitter, angry words could be taken back, but not her naked declaration.

I don't want to lose you, he'd said, but how could they go on as they had before, when neither of them would be able to forget that one of them loved and one didn't?

For the girls' sake, would he agree to live that way? Was she brave enough to try, if he would give her the chance?

The rags of clouds were knitting together into dark masses and the wind smelled of rain. Chilled to the bone, Lynn started back along the beach, the wind shoving her from behind. She was so cold! Her feet were numb and blockish in thin sneakers. Dressed so inadequately, she shouldn't have stayed as long as she had.

The first icy shards of rain came as she turned her back on the ocean and picked her way carefully between rough rocks and piles of driftwood toward the steps up to street level.

She was almost there when she saw that a man leaned against the railing only feet from the opening to the beach. With the lamplight behind him, he was dark, anonymous and imposing. She hesitated. Probably he only wanted his solitude, as she had, but it was awfully lonely out here if he were to threaten her. Still, there was no other easy way up the concrete and granite bulkhead, and she was very cold.

Taking a breath for courage, she bent her head and

hurried toward the stairs. She had set foot on the bottom one when he spoke.

"Lynn?"

"Adam?" she whispered. The wind whipped his name away, unheard.

"I've been waiting for you." He didn't move.

Slowly she climbed the few stairs. Hip against the railing, he faced her. His expression changed when he got a good look at her in the yellowish light from a sodium lamp.

"You've been crying." He sounded angry. Gruff.

"My eyes watered. The wind..." Why was he here?

He swore and stepped forward. The relief was overwhelming. Right this second, it hardly mattered why he'd come. Oh, how easy it was to let herself be enveloped in his warmth and strength.

"I'm sorry," she tried to tell him, but had no idea if he heard her.

He was swearing still, growling something against her hair. It seemed to be an echo. "God, I'm sorry. You've got to forgive me, Lynn."

"Forgive you?" What was he talking about? She tried to pull back, but his arms tightened, binding her to him.

"How did you find me?"

"The baby-sitter." At last his grip relaxed. "Can we go home, Lynn?" His hand, cold enough, caressed her frozen cheek. "You need a hot bath."

"Yes. Okay."

I...care. Of course he did. That had to be enough.

Her legs were reluctant to move. Adam had to steer her along the sidewalk, stop her with one hand from stepping out into the street in front of a lone car passing through town. Even her thoughts were sluggish now.

His Lexus was in its usual spot in the gravel lot. *Adam is here,* she thought, amazed.

The staircase seemed to go on forever. At the top, Adam bundled her inside. She stood in the kitchen, beginning to shake, and was distantly aware that he was paying Alicia and seeing her out.

When she heard water running into the tub, she shuffled down the hall to the bathroom. Still in his own heavy sweater, he was on his knees, testing the water temperature. When he saw her, his expression brought to life an ember of warmth inside her.

His jaw muscles flexed. "Shall I help you get undressed?"

The glow spread. "No. I'm okay. Just chilly."

"Damn it, Lynn—" He bit off whatever he'd been going to say. "I'll boil water for tea. I'll get you something to put on."

He started to brush by her, but paused, his body touching hers from thigh to chest. She felt the vibration when he spoke. "I hope you did all the thinking you intend to do."

She nodded dumbly.

"Good." He touched her cold cheek again, then left the bathroom, returning a moment later with her ugliest, most voluminous flannel nightgown and her old wool bathrobe.

He was obviously not setting the stage for seduction.

Lynn had plenty of time in the bath to worry anew as she thawed. Why was he sorry? What did she have to forgive him for? If anyone needed forgiving, it was her!

When she'd quit shivering and her skin glowed pink, she got out, toweled herself dry and put on her old gown and robe. Her hair. Lynn groaned, glimpsing the tangles in the mirror. If only she'd corralled her curls instead of letting the wind whip them into a frenzy. She took ten minutes to bring her recalcitrant hair to reasonable order and assemble it in a simple braid down her back.

Hope had thawed along with her flesh, but so had old fears. Adam might be here to talk about a divorce. Or to ask her to stay in their arrangement, while explaining gently how much he had loved his Jenny and why he would never be able to love her the same way. He might even be angry and planning to fight her for custody of the girls.

No, even terrified, she knew better. He would never do that. Not to her, not to Shelly or Rose.

He waited in the living room, sitting with his elbows resting on his knees, holding a steaming mug in one hand. Although she had made no sound, he looked up the moment Lynn appeared in the doorway. His gaze not leaving hers, he stood. "Here's your tea."

"Thank you." She held her head high as she ventured into the living room and took the mug from him. "I was cold."

"You're lucky you didn't die of hypothermia." He sounded angry again.

"I was on my way home."

"Were you trying to commit suicide?"

"I was walking on a cold night!" she fired back.

"I wanted to think! You told me to. I had to be alone."

He rotated his shoulders as if they ached. His tone was almost conversational. "What did you think about?"

Her tongue touched her lips. "You. Us," she admitted huskily.

"Your conclusion?"

She wrapped both hands around the mug, willing its heat to give her courage. "I was wrong. I…"

His expression was shuttered, just like that. "You don't love me."

"I shouldn't have told you I do," Lynn corrected him. "I was pressuring you. We had an arrangement, and it was working fine. I…" She bowed her head. "I got scared."

"Scared of what?" Adam asked, voice gritty.

"I know you like me and…and want me. At least I assume…" She stole a look at him and hurried on. "I was afraid after a while you wouldn't. That I wouldn't be able to stand it."

"You must have known I was falling in love with you," he shocked her by saying.

Afraid to grasp the hope that she had been nursing all along, Lynn looked up. "No," she said just above a whisper. "No, I had no idea." She squeezed her eyes shut. "But you don't. You couldn't make yourself say the words. 'I care.' That was the best you could get out."

He touched her at last, his hand cupping her chin. In a slow, deep voice, he said, "I love you desperately and passionately. I was just idiot enough not to know it."

"Not to know…" This felt surreal. A too-easy ending to a daydream. She didn't dare believe him.

Adam's mouth twisted. "Sit down. I need to tell you about Jennifer."

She obeyed, watching the expressions on his face, the anguish, the regret, the rueful awareness of how blind he'd been, as he talked about his young wife and their brief marriage.

"They kept saying she was dead. Wanting me to sign papers so that her organs could be harvested." He swore. "What a word. Harvested. I signed, but deep inside I didn't believe she was dead. She'd open her eyes suddenly and smile. Only she didn't. They cut Rose—no, Shelly—out of her, and then the surgeons took Jenny away. I didn't see her after they pulled the plug. I didn't want to at the funeral home. I always thought an open casket was macabre."

"You never said goodbye," she said, understanding.

"I thought I had. But I dreamed about her. I missed her like hell," he said simply. "I felt guilty when I met you and stopped missing her."

Somehow Lynn had set down the mug and was gripping Adam's hand in hers. He held on so tightly her bones ached.

"I started falling in love with you that first time we met, at the hospital. I wanted to touch your hair." With his free hand he stroked it now, and she felt as if each strand was an exquisitely sensitive nerve. "When we made love last night, you said, 'I want you,' and it wasn't enough. I felt like a bastard, but I needed you to say, 'I love you.' What didn't occur to me was *why* I needed to hear those words."

"But when I did say them…"

Their grip shifted; their fingers curled together. "Do you know what I felt?" he asked. "Triumph. Exhilaration. *She loves me,* I thought. It took me five minutes too long to realize that I love you back."

"You didn't come after me," she said painfully.

He made a sound that hurt to hear. "I had to…adjust. I'm a deliberate man. I like to be sure."

"But you are?"

"Jennifer," he said, "was my first real love. I want to believe we'd still be happily married if she had lived. But I've changed in these three, almost four, years. When I try to see her being the mother you are, I wonder. Jenny was used to having her way. A baby was a grand new toy to her, I'm afraid."

"I think," Lynn said carefully, "all women feel that way when they're pregnant for the first time. The baby seems so unreal! Of course, everything will go the way the books say it will. You don't really understand how unrelenting having a baby is until you're on your own and it's too late to chicken out. I saw that picture of her. Pregnant, I mean. She looked so proud and so happy. I can't imagine that she wouldn't have loved Rose as much as you do."

His mouth tilted into a crooked smile. "Maybe so. But she's dead. Part of me will always regret she didn't have a chance to be a mother. We had such dreams. Reality is, I'm the lucky one. I have Rose and Shelly and you. I wouldn't go back if I could. I want to wake up next to you every morning for the rest of my life, make love to you every night, use our vacations to go to Disneyland with the kids. I want to argue with you, clean the kitchen with you, and grow old with you. If—'' he swallowed ''—you can forgive me for hurting you like that.''

Lynn tumbled into his arms. ''Oh, Adam,'' she mumbled against his neck, ''I'm the one who almost messed everything up. I think it was just like with Brian. I wasn't comfortable. I like…controlling everything. Always knowing where I stand. I got a little panicky, and I convinced myself I'd be better off the way I was before.''

''Were you?'' He held her away from him, his eyes dark, turbulent.

She laughed and cried at the same time. ''These last months have been the best time in my life. Knowing you love me, too, is like…like…''

''Buying a thousand shares of Microsoft when it went public?''

The laughter won, though her cheeks were wet. ''Something like that. I was thinking more of fireworks and Christmas in July and all those clichés.''

''Fireworks,'' he said, his thumb teasing her lower lip, ''we can manage.''

His kiss proved the point. Giddy from relief and love and the onslaught of desire, Lynn whispered, ''Let's go to bed.''

''Mmm.'' Adam gripped her shoulders and set her away from him. ''One last thing. I'd like to wake up next to you every morning, but I'll settle for four mornings a week if you want to keep the store here. You need to know that.''

''Thank you.'' She pecked him on the lips. ''But I hate the drive, and I want to be with you. I might take a while off and think about what to do next. Or, hey, I might decide to take on Powell's Books after all! In my own small way, of course.''

''Uh-huh. And now—'' he stood and held out a hand for hers ''—your offer is sounding better and better.''

They did, of course, pause partway down the hall to watch thankfully as their daughters slept.

''Right now,'' Adam said softly, his words tickling Lynn's ear, ''I feel blessed.''

''Triply blessed,'' she agreed, and blinked away tears that were too joyful to shed.

Adam scooped her into his arms. ''Let's go make some fireworks!''

They did that, too, neither forgetting the words that counted, after all.

Mr Family

MARGOT EARLY

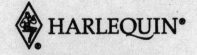

HARLEQUIN®

TORONTO • NEW YORK • LONDON
AMSTERDAM • PARIS • SYDNEY • HAMBURG
STOCKHOLM • ATHENS • TOKYO • MILAN • MADRID
PRAGUE • WARSAW • BUDAPEST • AUCKLAND

For my *ohana*

ACKNOWLEDGEMENTS

I would like to thank the following people, each of whom helped in some way with this book:

For enriching my appreciation and understanding of art, I'm grateful to Elaine Barnhart, Jan Carlile and Alan Fine.

To all my *ohana* who helped in large and small ways during the writing of this book, thank you.

Laura and Cecilia, your friendship and wisdom brighten my days.

And most of all, I thank the two closest to me, my husband and son, for your patience and love.

CHAPTER ONE

Santa Barbara, California
January

> WANTED: Woman to enter celibate marriage and be stepmother to four-year-old girl. Send child-rearing philosophies to Mr. Ohana, Box J, Haena, Kauai, HI.

"THAT'S THE WRONG page." Impatiently Adele reached over the butter plate with a long-nailed hand that seemed dwarfed by rings, onyx and jade in hand-crafted gold settings. She gestured for Erika to turn the magazine pages. "It's in the middle."

"Wait, wait. Look at this." Strangely excited—in the same way she became excited when a painting was going well—Erika Blade handed Adele the copy of *Island Voice,* open to the ad for a celibate marriage. In the last few months she had begun to pay attention to personal ads, to flyers for computer dating services, to bulletins for singles'-club activities. She never acted on any of them. Only desperate people did things like that, and she wasn't really even looking for a mate. Not exactly. She was simply...curious.

Celibate marriage. Send child-rearing philosophies...

If she was ever to answer a personal ad, this would be the one.

Erika and Adele sat at an ocean-view table in the Surf

Room, the grand glass-enclosed breakfast room of the famed Montecito Palms Resort Hotel. The glass-topped table was graced with potted violets, fine bone china, heavy English silver, the remains of breakfast, and transparencies of several of Erika's latest watercolors of women by the sea. Momoy Publishing, owned by Adele and her husband Kurt, had published many of Erika's paintings as limited-edition prints. In fact, Adele had brought the copy of *Island Voice* because she'd purchased an ad in it for Erika's recent serigraphs. Her work sold well in Hawaiian galleries.

But Erika was less interested in the prints Adele had already published than in her verdict on the work shown in the transparencies. Nervous, she'd flipped past her publisher's advertisement, lost her place and stumbled upon the personal from Mr. Ohana.

As Adele squinted at the ad, Erika took stock of the changes in her publisher's appearance. Though Adele was only five foot three and tipped the scales at 140, she'd never let that turn her from the world of haute couture—an attitude Erika admired. She loved color, and Adele was an ever-changing palette. Her hair was cut in a severe bob that slanted from ear level on the left to chin level on the right. Its present hue was eggplant— Cobalt Violet, Payne's Gray and just a touch of Cadmium Orange, if Erika had wanted to mix it from paint—and her dangling purple-and-sapphire earrings matched. During their eight-year professional relationship, Erika had come to anticipate meetings with Adele as a time to vicariously enjoy nail polish, chic hairstyles and makeup.

And at fifty-one, fifteen years older than Erika, Adele was one of the very few people in the world with whom Erika felt comfortable exposing something of who she really was. Adele was her judge, support and promoter of the thing most intimate to her—her art.

"Tell me you're kidding," Adele said. "Not the personals, Erika."

Erika suddenly realized that she'd been injudiciously enthusiastic about the ad. Even Adele would think she was crazy.

"God, is it the biological clock?" exclaimed her publisher. "If it is, I've got a fifteen-year-old son you can *have.*"

Erika laughed, glancing nervously out the window at the sun-soaked Santa Barbara Channel and the islands beyond. Because it was Adele, she said, "Oh, I don't know. Having a kid underfoot doesn't sound half-bad." After this too-truthful admission, she rushed on, "I'm trying to picture this Mr. Ohana."

"Well, I doubt it's his real name. *Ohana* is the Hawaiian word for family. Actually it implies extended family," explained Adele, whose second passion, after art, was Hawaiiana. "A feeling of helping one another, of loyalty."

Erika leaned over the table to stare at the upside-down personal ad. "Mr. Family?" The pseudonym seemed tinged with self-mockery.

"Yeah. He's got a real sense of humor. 'Send childrearing philosophies'?" Adele rolled her eyes, then gave Erika a dubious look plain as words. *Celibate? Surely it's not that bad.* Rather than dwelling on her artist's unnatural whims, she flipped through the magazine until she came to the advertisement for Erika's prints.

Erika took the magazine again and smiled at the ad for *Sand Castles.* "Can I take this?" Erika held Adele's copy of *Island Voice* questioningly above the straw carryall slung over the back of her chair.

"Sure. I brought it for you."

Erika slipped the magazine into her bag and met Adele's black-rimmed eyes.

Her publisher sighed. She gathered the transparencies,

glanced at one of them under the light and put them in
their envelope to return to Erika.

Erika's heart fell. But somehow she'd already known
Adele wouldn't take a chance on them.

"Erika, these paintings just don't have your usual
vigor—or depth. And they're very similar to things
you've done before."

It was true. "Is it because I used Jean for a model in
several of them? She's so gorgeous...." Her sister-in-law
had posed for some of Erika's best work, including *Sand
Castles.* "I'm having trouble making people look real."

"Well, in *Sand Castles* you certainly managed it."

Sand Castles was a watercolor of Jean with Erika's
eight-year-old nephew, Christian. Erika knew her feelings
for Chris had translated in paint. She had perceived and
understood Jean's nurturing of her stepson. Because, of
course, she'd played that role herself. It was Erika's best
piece ever. But in her publisher's candid response, she
saw the truth—that it was rare for her to capture so much
feeling in her art.

She counted on that honesty from Adele, who went on,
"No, I don't think Jean's the problem. I think you're
afraid to take risks, and you're trying to stay on familiar
ground."

The words tolled inside Erika like the bell of truth.
Afraid to take risks... Erika had her reaction, which was
emotional. Visceral.It was hard to get up after a fall.
Adele had watched; she should know.

"Look," said Adele. "I don't want you to feel bad
about this. I know what you've been going through this
past year. A lot of change. I think *Sand Castles* is going
to sell very well, and if it does maybe we'll do a second
series. In the meantime, you can work on some new proj-
ects." Scraping back her chair from the table, Adele drew
an enameled cigarette case and matching lighter from her
handbag.

Erika frowned. With soaring cholesterol and blood-pressure, her friend was a walking time bomb. "You know, I want to have you around for a few years, Adele."

"Trust me. I'm prolonging my life—using techniques from the Adele Henry school of stress reduction."

Cigarettes, cognac and French cuisine…

Adele changed the subject. "Speaking of Jean, did you say you're without her as a model for a while?"

Erika took the hint; she couldn't force Adele to take care of herself. "They're in Greenland. Studying walruses." Erika's father, Christopher Blade, had been a renowned undersea explorer, and her brother, David, had followed in his footsteps after his death. Now, David and his second wife, Jean, and his son were in the Arctic for a year. The expedition had followed closely on the heels of an overfishing study in Japan. In fact, they'd spent little time in Santa Barbara since David had married Jean a year before. The sea was their home. It had always been Erika's, too.

Adele contemplated the burning end of her cigarette. "Kurt and I are leaving for Hilo next week. Why don't you join us? Make it a painting trip?"

Erika smiled, shaking her head. She loved Hawaii; when she was nineteen, she'd spent three months there with her parents and David studying sharks. But she wouldn't intrude on her publisher's vacation time with her husband in their getaway on the Big Island. It occurred to her that Adele felt sorry for her. That was the last thing she wanted—from anyone. "Don't worry." She laughed. "I don't plan to answer any personal ads while you're gone." *Afraid to take risks.* She'd just confirmed it.

Adele drew on her cigarette with a wry smile. "Hawaii can be tough on *malihinis*—newcomers. Especially *haoles* like us."

Caucasians. Erika remembered the word.

"But, hey," said Adele, "Haena's a beautiful place. And all he wants is to know if you follow Dr. Spock or James Dobson." She rolled her eyes again. "Take my advice. Get a dog."

Erika's present living situation didn't allow for a dog. In fact, she'd never lived anywhere she could have one. Dogs were for people with homes. They implied permanence. Erika *wanted* permanence—if she could get it without more change. She'd known too much of that.

She contemplated the personal ad in *Island Voice*. Celibate marriage. She was probably one of the few people in the world who could see the appeal of that.

Mr. Family, she thought. Mr. Family.

Minutes later Adele paid the check with her gold card, and they stepped outside into a crisp winter breeze that made the palms chatter. Her faded carryall slung over her shoulder, her silk dress from Pier 1 Imports swishing against her legs, Erika accompanied Adele to her black Saab.

Erika walked with the slight limp that had become natural to her. Two years of rehab had made her strong and lean, but her legs would never be as they once were. She felt Adele's appraising glance.

"You look great," said Adele. "Really."

"Thanks." Adele had known her in the periods Erika thought of as Before, During and After. The present was After.

Something to remember, to be thankful for.

They paused beside the driver's door of the Saab and embraced. "Now take care," Adele told her, "and remember, the invitation to Hilo is open. Kurt would love to have you, too."

"Thank you, Adele." Erika released her. "Drive safely."

After Adele had backed the Saab out of its space and driven off, headed for an appointment with an artist in

Solvang, Erika made her way under the palms to her own car, the sun-bleached, sea-foam green Karmann Ghia she had bought eleven months before, when she began driving again.

Sliding behind the wheel, she set her carryall on the passenger seat. The copy of *Island Voice* showed from the top, and Erika drew out the magazine, thumbing through, looking for the ad for *Sand Castles,* to convince herself that she really could paint.

But she couldn't find the right page, and instead, she turned to the classifieds in the back. Mr. Ohana...

Haena's a beautiful place. And all he wants is to know if you follow Dr. Spock or James Dobson.

Nothing else.

Not even sex.

Erika shut the magazine and started her car. *Afraid to take risks.*

No pain, no gain; no guts, no glory?

No risk...no fulfillment.

Ever since David had met Jean, ever since Erika had begun to feel superfluous to her brother and his son, she'd been lonely. She missed Chris.

She wanted a family of her own.

But the usual route to that place was not for her. She always met the same obstacle in the road. *No, really, it's not you. It's me. I'm just not ready for this.* Trying to sound normal, blaming it on her accident.

Yes, Adele, I'm afraid. You would be, too.

Mr. Ohana's personal ad, however...maybe this was a risk she could take. A child. A celibate marriage. Yes, she liked the idea.

But why did *he* want it?

What's wrong with you, Mr. Ohana? she wondered. *What's your story?*

Pepeluali: February
Haena: the heat
On the island of Kauai...

THE RAIN SHATTERED through the Java plum trees and
the ironwoods, drumming on the roof of the bungalow
hidden in the foliage. Wet tropical blossoms gave off a
heady aroma scarcely noticed by the occupants of the
house. On the porch, Hiialo was catching rainfall in a
plastic cup to measure—a "science experiment," she had
told Kalahiki.

Kal was glad she was busy—and happy. Everyone
knew when she wasn't. He turned from the envelopes
littering the throw rug to the open front door and the
barefoot little girl beyond. He could hear her voice under
the rain, talking to a lizard out on the porch.

"Aloha, Mr. Skink. My name is Hiialo. This is Eduardo…"

Eduardo was an imaginary friend of Hiialo's, a thirty-
foot *mo'o,* or magical black lizard. A fearsome sight for
Mr. Skink, thought Kal.

"Oh, don't run away," said Hiialo. "Eduardo won't
hurt you. He only eats shave ice."

Danny's voice drew Kal's eyes toward the floor where
he sat. "Spark dis." Pidgin for "Check this out."

Running a negligent hand through his short-cropped
hair, Kal moved to stand over the muscular brown shoulders of his Hawaiian brother-in-law. On the floor in front
of Danny lay a photo of a bottled blonde whose curves
belonged on a beer poster. She stood beside a sailboard,
smiling brightly at the camera.

Well, sort of brightly. Kal was choosy about smiles. A
smile wasn't a matter of orthodontic work or a pretty
mouth. A smile came from the soul and shone through
the whole being. A good smile was contagious.

There was a sound from Kal's bedroom, the amplifier
going on. Jakka, Danny's cousin, six foot four and 240

pounds, emerged from the hallway, carrying Kal's Fender Stratocaster guitar. He played a riff, and Kal's own fingers itched for the strings. They'd planned to practice today.

Besides being part of his *ohana,* Danny and Jakka were members of his old band, the three-man band they'd called Kai Nui—high tide. And his former band mates haunted Kal's house as though waiting for something to change, for that tide to come back in. But today's jam session had never gotten off the ground. Danny, the percussionist, had seen Kal's mail and wanted to read the replies to his ad. Now he was perusing the letter from the blonde with the sailboard. He grimaced. "She's from the mainland."

Jakka, whose fingers were master of the bass, slowly attempted the lead-guitar melody to "Pau Hana," the song that had helped make Kai Nui the favorite band on the Garden Island. Long time ago…

Playing the right chords at the right tempo in his mind, Kal tried to lose the nervousness that had been with him ever since he'd visited his post-office box that day. Seeing the letters filling the box—and the larger stack he'd had to stand in line at the counter to collect—had made it real. He *hadn't* been serious when he sent the ad to *Island Voice.* He wasn't that desperate. It had been Danny's idea. Nonetheless, Kal had written the ad. It had seemed barely possible to him that somehow it would all work out. He might find someone he could get along with, someone who would love Hiialo. Hiialo would have two parents again, instead of just a never-there father—him.

And he…well, maybe things would be better for him, as well.

He hadn't expected many answers. At most, two or three. But now he was getting replies from not just Hawaii but the mainland. There were dozens of envelopes on the floor.

Danny pored over another letter. "Did you really say a *celibate* marriage?"

"Yes."

Jakka stopped playing and frowned at the letters on the floor. "*Nobody* wants that." A line divided his brow from top to bottom.

Kal said nothing. His stomach hurt. Work tomorrow. *On your left is Kauai's stunning Na Pali Coast. "Pali" means cliff, and...* He reached into his shirt pocket and surreptitiously popped an antacid.

"You know," remarked Jakka, "if you marry some rich woman, you could quit baby-sitting tourists and play with us again."

Danny said, "That's the whole idea."

"No, it's not," said Kal, with a fighting-dog stare no one challenged.

Maybe someday he'd play professionally again, but that hadn't been the point of the ad. Hiialo was.

Smiling, bemused, Jakka toyed with the guitar strings again.

Kal wandered to the front door. Hiialo had filled two cups with rainwater and was busily filling a third. Her hair, a sun-lightened shade of brown that seemed the consummate mingling of his own genes with her mother's, swung lank around her face and bare shoulders as she moved about the porch, wearing only a pair of boy's surfing trunks.

She was just four, so Kal didn't mind her playing at being a boy, going without a shirt as he often did. Still, it nagged at him. *He* shouldn't be her role model. He wouldn't be, if only...

Scarcely aware of the leaden pall on his heart, the dead feeling, he turned back to the room. To the letters on the floor. It wasn't going to work. No way could he invite a stranger into his life or his home—or within a thousand miles of his daughter.

Danny tossed his wavy shoulder-length hair back from his face and sat up straight as he read the message inside one note card. "Hey, Kal. This one's not so bad."

Kal stepped over the stack of opened letters and crouched beside Danny, who handed him the card.

Danny glanced at his watch and began to stand. "Gotta work, brah. Good luck finding your picture bride."

Picture bride. At the turn of the century, most immigrant plantation workers in Hawaii were poor single men. A man who wished to find a mate from his own culture had one option—to choose a woman from a photograph sent by family members or a marriage broker in his homeland. Then the picture bride came to Hawaii....

Kal groaned as Danny used his shoulder for support to push himself to his feet, feigning aching bones. Danny was on his way to meet his hula group. Besides playing drums, he was a dancer, like—

"Hey, wait for me!" Jakka unplugged the Stratocaster, then hurried back to Kal's room.

Danny swept up his car keys. Nabbing Hiialo as she came inside, he swooped her up in his arms. "Gotcha. And Eduardo's not stopping me." Danny was always willing to enter Hiialo's make-believe world, to accept the existence of her imaginary giant lizard friend.

As Hiialo squealed in delight, presaging her uncle's turning her upside down, Kal examined the card Danny had handed him. On the front was a watercolor of a woman with long curly gold hair swimming underwater with a dolphin. Ordinarily Kal didn't care for sentimental artwork—and he'd been around enough art to form an opinion. But something about this image struck him as realistic, natural, as though the woman and dolphin *were* actually swimming together. He studied the watercolor for a moment before he opened the card and read the writing inside.

The script was small and lightly etched, the letters running almost straight up and down.

Dear Mr. Ohana,
As Kurt Vonnegut says, ''There's only one rule that I know of—'' It applies to child rearing as to anything. ''Damn it, you've got to be kind.''

Sincerely,
Ms. Aloha

''So what do you think?''

Kal hadn't known Danny was paying attention. Even now, he was swinging Hiialo back to an upright position, his eyes on his niece.

Kal stuffed the card back into its envelope—another mainland address—tossed it on the stack with the rest and stood up. Taking Hiialo from Danny and feeling the comfort of her small slender arms circling his neck, Kal told his brother-in-law, ''I think this was a stupid idea.''

''What was stupid?'' asked Hiialo. Then, seeing Jakka emerge from the hallway, she said, ''What was that song you were playing, Jakka?''

Danny burst out laughing, and Jakka approached Hiialo, threatening to tickle. ''You didn't like my song?''

Hiialo grinned, and Jakka ruffled her hair affectionately. He met Kal's eyes, his own apologizing for his earlier remark. ''I miss our band.''

Kal thought, *I miss her.* He'd lost all his music in one bad night.

''Laydahs, yeah?'' Jakka squeezed Kal's shoulder briefly, then wandered out onto the lanai, down the steps and into the rain.

As Jakka crossed the tiny lawn to stand beside the zebra-striped door of his cousin's lavender-and-green

VW bus, Danny lingered on the porch. "You got to be kind," he mused. Swiftly he executed a *ka hola,* four bent-legged steps to one side and back to the other, his hands and muscular arms saying aloha. "I like Ms. Aloha." With a last tug on Hiialo's hair, he turned and leapt down off the porch and into the rain.

"Danny!" In Kal's arms, Hiialo perfectly and gracefully imitated her uncle's aloha, eliciting approving laughter from Danny and Jakka. Stirring useless pangs in Kal's heart.

Wish you could see her, Maka....

As his friends climbed into the Volkswagen and the bus backed out and disappeared down the wet driveway, Hiialo pulled the sleeve of Kal's T-shirt. "Can we go to the gas station and get shave ice? Eduardo's hungry."

"That *mo'o* is going to eat up my last dollar on shave ice."

"Please?" Hiialo smiled at him from her eyes, from ear to ear, from her heart. "And can we stop and see Grandma and Grandpa at the gallery? I have a picture for them."

Her grin made him grin, too. So much like someone else's smile.... Kal asked, "You know who has the best smile on this whole island?"

Hiialo kissed him. "My daddy." She slid down, starting for her bedroom, knowing they would go get shave ice.

"Put on a shirt," he called after her.

"I know," she said, as though he were so tiresome. "I have to dress like a girl."

DAMN IT, YOU'VE GOT to be kind.

Kal turned again on his mattress, trying to quiet his mind—and ease the burning in his gut. But the moon outside was too bright, and tonight he couldn't make his breath match the rhythm of the waves hitting the shore just two hundred yards away. He shifted his chest against the bottom sheet, wishing he could sleep. His fingers spread on the mattress, and he remembered touching something more.

But this bed, the captain's bed he'd built of koa just to fit his small room, this bed was only wide enough for him and then some—Hiialo when she bounced up beside him with a book in the mornings, wanting him to read to her.

Hiialo… Shave ice… His eyes closed, and his mind, drifting off, played music. His own. Chords. Finger-picking…

He opened his eyes and stared without focus at a groove in the paneling beside his bed. Sitting up, Kal grabbed a pair of loose cotton drawstring shorts beside the bed and pulled them on.

He put his bare feet on the floor and reached past his two packed bookshelves, filled with humidity-warped paperbacks, music books, lives of musicians. His fingers grasped the neck of the Gibson L-50, familiar as the limb of a lover, and he pulled it from its hanger on the wall. As he slipped out of the room, he passed the other instrument still hanging, the shiny chrome National etched with palms and plumeria, and those in cases on the floor, the Stratocaster and the Les Paul. The guitars saved him each night. Companions in the emptiness of forever. Loyal as dogs.

In the dark, he went into the narrow front room and pushed aside the hanging curtain to look in on Hiialo. She slept in one of his *puka* T-shirts—full of holes. Her mouth was open, her legs uncovered. Kal drew the quilt back over her.

"Thank you, Daddy," she murmured in her sleep.

"I love you, *keiki*." She made no response, and Kal headed out onto the lanai through the open front door.

He inhaled the ocean and the flowers, the jasmine

crawling up the wood rails, and as he sank down on the tired porch swing and stared at the plants in the moonlight, he felt the water hanging everywhere in the air.

A sprawling blue house with an oriental roof, a vacation rental owned by his parents, stood between the bungalow and the beach. No view from his place, but Kal could hear the ocean and the insects, the bugs of the wet season. He saw the gray shape of a gecko doing pushups on the porch. Watching it, he reached for the unseen with his mind and his soul.

Nothing.

Where are you? he thought. *I need you.*

It was one of those nights.

She was dead.

He strummed his guitar, tuned up in the moonlight. A flat, F minor, B flat seven… ''The Giant was sleeping by the highway/winds called pangs of love brewed on the sea…'' The words were symbols of Kauai and of his life—with her and without her. ''Why didn't you wake up, Giant?/Why didn't you wake up and save me?''

He sang into the night, the act of singing easing tension in his abdomen, and he didn't hear the sound of feet. But he noticed the small body climbing up onto the swing beside him.

Fingers still, he stopped singing. ''I'm sorry, Hiialo. Did I wake you?''

She shook her head, her lips closed tight, middle-of-the-night tears-for-no-reason nearby.

Kal rested the old archtop in the swing, the neck cradled in a scooped-out place in the arm. It was a system he often used—for holding a guitar so that he could hold Hiialo at the same time. He lifted her into his lap and cuddled her against him.

''I don't like that song,'' she said. ''It's sad.''

That was true. And the song was true. Mountains

didn't rise up to stop fate. Kal hadn't been able to, either. Not the accident. Or Iniki, the hurricane.

It wasn't a truth for children.

"Want to hear 'Puff'?" Kal had played "Puff the Magic Dragon" too many times in bars in Hanalei to consider it anything but agonizing. Still, it was Hiialo's favorite, and maybe Puff could wipe that teary sound out of her voice.

But Hiialo shook her head, snuggling closer against his chest.

Five seconds, and she'd say, *Wait here,* and dash off to get her blanket and a stuffed thing called Pincushion that Kal couldn't remember where or when she'd gotten. Whenever she tried that trick, he'd get her back into bed, instead. If allowed, she would stay up all night.

Like him.

Hiialo whispered, "I wish you weren't sad."

Something shook in Kal's chest. He opened his mouth to say, *I'm not sad.* But he never lied to her.

He hadn't known he seemed sad.

"You make me happy, Hiialo. The best part of my day is seeing you after work and finding out what you've been doing."

Hiialo's little fingers touched the few dark golden hairs on his chest. "Will you tell me a story about my mommy?"

Kal winced.

"Tell me about when you were in the band in Waikiki and Mommy—"

"How about not?" He kept his voice light. "But I'll play 'Puff.'"

She shook her head. He took a breath and watched the trade winds make some nearby heliconia, silver under the full moon, wave back and forth like dancers. Maka had moved like that.

Gone.

In a weary tone of resignation, Hiialo said, "I'll hear 'Puff.'"

"What an enthusiastic audience we have tonight." Kal set her on the swing beside him, then picked up his guitar. As he started to play and sing about the dragon, he thought, *I'm not the only one who's sad.*

Hiialo couldn't remember. But she felt the void.

Later, after he'd tucked her in with Pincushion and the invisible Eduardo, Kal went to get his guitar and hang it up in his room, and on the way he noticed the paper grocery bag into which he'd stuffed the letters to Mr. Ohana.

Damn it, you've got to be kind.

Yes, he thought. Be kind to my daughter.

He put away the Gibson, and then returned to the front room that was kitchen and dining room and living room crammed into a hundred square feet. He grabbed the grocery sack, took it to the boat-size chamber where he slept, turned on his reading light and dumped out the letters on his bed.

He had to push them into a heap to make a place to sit, and then he read them and dropped them, one by one, back into the paper bag on the floor. He'd work up a form reply to the letters. *Thank you for responding to my ad in Island Voice…Good luck in life and love. Sincerely, Mr. Ohana.*

Only one note he laid aside, without taking the card from the envelope. He could cut out the picture of the girl and the dolphin and give it to Hiialo to tack on the wall of her room.

Damn it, you've got to be kind.

Finally he took an old spiral notebook and a pen from his desk drawer, and he lay on his bed and wrote a letter he didn't intend to send to a woman he'd never met. The bag of letters on the floor seemed pathetic—answers from a sad but hopeful world to an even more pitiable plea.

But their collective refusal to despair gave *him* a fleeting, moonlight-made hope. And after he signed the letter, "Sincerely, Kalahiki Johnson," he got up and pulled open another drawer, the big bottom drawer, and drew out the shoe box full of photos.

Pushing aside the cassette case that lay on top, cached among things he loved, he flipped through the snapshots, careful of fingerprints. Careful of his own eyes. Pictures still hurt.

The photo Christmas card showing the three of them was near the top. It seemed right. Stealthily, not wanting to wake Hiialo, not wanting his actions to be known in the light of day, he went out to the kitchen to find scissors and finally picked up Hiialo's green-handled little-kid scissors from the floor by the couch. Biting closed his lips, his eyes blurring in the ghostly gray dark, he cut apart the photo.

Maka's arm still showed, stretched across his waist as she touched Hiialo, and for a moment Kal pondered how to remove it. But at last he left it, because then Ms. Aloha would understand what he'd tried to say with words.

CHAPTER TWO

Santa Barbara

ERIKA COMMITTED HERSELF to overcoming fear of risk. In the days after she answered Mr. Ohana's ad, she photographed scenes on the streets of Santa Barbara. A pink poodle outside Neiman-Marcus. Children giving away kittens in front of the supermarket. She spent as much time petting the poor dyed dog as photographing it, and she wanted to adopt a kitten. Instead, she developed the pictures and painted from them, telling herself this was the kind of gamble she'd promised to take. These were not women by the sea.

But what would Adele say? Would she say that Erika might lose her following? If her art stopped selling, if she had to get another job, she would die. Flower without water. Painting was all she had.

Erika's reaction to the possibility was detachment; she tried to feel equally aloof about the other risk she'd taken. Answering a personal ad.

So when she pulled bills and catalogs out of her post-office box and saw a number 10 envelope hand-addressed to Ms. Aloha, she muted her feelings. The response had come from K. Johnson, Box J, Haena, Kauai.

K. Johnson.

Mr. Ohana.

She didn't open the letter in the post office or when she reached the Karmann Ghia parked at the curb. Instead, she set her mail in the seat beside her and drove down State Street toward the harbor. She parked in the marina lot, in Jake Donahue's space. Jake was her brother's business partner and sometimes first mate on his ship. Jake was going to be in Greenland with David until June, and Erika was boat-sitting his Chinese junk, the *Lien Hua*. It was a usual sort of living arrangement for her.

Temporary.

Erika collected the mail and her shoulder bag and crossed the boardwalk, pausing at a gate in the twenty-foot chain link fence outside Marina C. She used Jake's key card to open the lock and made her way down the creaking dock. Erika was painfully familiar with the harbor. It was where she had lived with her brother and his son on David's old ship, the *Skye*. It was where she had lived During.

That was over, she reminded herself again. This was After.

Memories of that earlier time would always be with her. Some things shouldn't be forgotten. Some things couldn't be.

She reached the *Lien Hua*'s berth. Walking alongside the junk to its stern, she caught her muted grayish reflection in the dingy glass windows. Tall. Rayon import dress. Hair that fell several inches below her shoulders, neither smooth nor curly, brown nor blond, but simply nondescript.

Erika unlocked the cabin of the junk and ducked through the hatch, descending into the two-room space that contained all her worldly goods and most of Jake Donahue's. Her art supplies lay on the fold-out kitchenette table. Unfinished watercolors covered the meager wall space in places where the sunlight wouldn't fade them.

She tossed her mail on the narrow bunk where she slept. K. Johnson's letter was on top, but Erika resisted picking it up, tearing it open. Restraint was possible through routine.

She opened the overhead hatch, then dropped down a companionway to the unlit galley. In the gloom, the light on Jake's answering machine glowed steadily. No messages. From the small icebox run on dockside electricity, she took a bottle of fresh carrot juice. Erika removed the lid and sipped at it.

Suddenly she could wait no longer. She capped the juice, put it back in the refrigerator and returned to the salon and her mail.

She took K. Johnson's letter topside, where the air smelled of beach tar, and settled in a wooden deck chair in the shade of the mast. The closest sailboats were deserted, covered. Opening the letter, Erika was glad of the solitude, glad her brother was faraway across a continent and an ocean, glad Adele was across another, glad no one could know that she'd done this insane thing. That she, a thirty-six-year-old woman, had answered a personal ad involving a celibate marriage.

And a four-year-old girl.

As she withdrew the letter and unfolded it, something dropped into her lap. A photo, upside down. Erika didn't look. She put her hand against it, protecting it from the breeze, and turned to the page. The letter was written in black ballpoint pen on warped paper torn from a spiral note-book. Neat male handwriting.

Dear Ms. Aloha,
My name is Kalahiki Johnson, though you know me as Mr. Ohana, who placed a personal ad in *Island Voice.* I am thirty years old, and I was born and raised on the island of Kauai, where my father's family has lived for six generations and where I work as a tour guide on the Na Pali Coast.

My four-year-old daughter is named Hiialo, pronounced Hee-AH-lo, which means "a beloved child borne in the arms." Soon Hiialo will be too big to carry, but she will always be the most precious thing in my life.

Hiialo's mother was my wife, Maka. Maka was a hula dancer and chanter who won competitions in *hula kahiko,* traditional hula, and also in *hula auana,* modern hula, both of which tell stories. She was a kind and graceful human being in every way, and we loved each other deeply. Three years ago, driving back from a hotel where she'd been dancing, she was killed in a head-on collision.

Erika set down the letter, biting her lip, unable to read on.

She'd thought that he was some yogi who'd taken a vow of abstinence. Or maybe that he was impotent or burned out on relationships. She'd wondered about Mr. Ohana's reasons for wanting a celibate marriage, but she hadn't expected anything like this. Though she should have.

Why was it affecting her this way? And she *was* affected, her eyes hot and blurry, her heart racing with horror, as though she'd just learned of the death of someone *she* loved.

And he was only thirty.

Since then I have raised Hiialo alone, but I work long hours, and it's hard on her. I wish there was someone who could do what Maka would have done for our daughter and who would love Hiialo as she did.

If you are still interested in Hiialo and me, please write back. But understand that even if a permanent domestic arrangement is possible, your relationship with me would be platonic. Maka and I were married for seven years, and no one can replace her in my heart. I want no other lover, and I would prefer to live alone, if not for Hiialo. Please understand this, because, as you said, we all need to be kind.

Sincerely,

Kalahiki Johnson

Erika put the heel of her hand against her mouth, pressed her lips together. In her mind, she heard an echo of the past, and she couldn't shut it out. One word repeated itself.

David.

Her brother.

For the three years after his first wife's death, Erika had lived with him. For three years, she had been a mother figure to his son, Christian. That had been the best experience of her life, though it had begun out of duty. There had been much entangled pain—David's and her own, both caused by the same woman.

But this situation was different. So different.

Talk about risk.

The winter breeze pushed at her hair, and Erika reached for the photo in her lap, so that it wouldn't blow away. She turned it over, and her breath caught when she saw him.

He was a beautiful man.

Light brown hair, still damp from a swim, stood out in short uncombed spikes, as though he'd just come out of the water and shaken it. His lean muscular chest and arms were tanned the color of oak. The child's skin, the skin of the almost-toddler in his arms, was a shade darker. And darker yet was the rounded well-toned female arm brushing his body, the hand touching the baby.

Maka. He'd cropped her from the shot, all but her arm.

Erika absorbed every detail of the picture. The sea. The man's smile. His grin came from sensuous lips and slitted dark-lashed eyes of uncertain color and, clearly, from his heart. Anyone could see he held the baby often. Erika saw gentleness and love between the child in her green swimsuit and the man who held her in front of him, feet out to face the camera. Somehow the baby had been coaxed into a dimply laugh, and Erika wondered if her father's fingers cupped under one small bare foot were responsible.

The picture was like a book, and when she read it she cried.

Erika heard the dock creak and saw a couple who owned a sloop two berths down approaching. Not wanting to talk, she stood up and limped to the cabin door, slipped inside. The junk rocked gently. She listened to the lapping of water, to some wind chimes outside. The monotonous music of solitude.

Her heart felt simultaneously fearful and excited.

He had answered her letter. From however many replies he'd received, Kalahiki Johnson had chosen hers. His answer had contained no proposal of marriage, no promises. Just an invitation to write back.

She lay down on her bunk and read it again.

Twice.

Three times.

The light faded outside, and she turned on the lamp over the bunk and studied the photograph and the letter, memorizing the words, especially the last paragraph.

A sensible part of her, the part that was the older sister of a man who'd lost his wife, wanted to step back and say, "Oh, Kalahiki, you're young. You'll fall in love again."

But the photograph won a debate words would have lost. And Erika resisted admitting even to herself that he did not seem a man destined to live out his life in celibacy.

I have to tell him.

She would have to tell him about herself. Reveal her past to a stranger and hazard rejection because of it. It would be unconscionable not to tell him, but the prospect was horrible.

Erika found comfort where she could.

I don't have to tell him everything.

Haena, Kauai

KAL PEDALED HARD through the rain to the post office to collect his mail. The transmission on his car had given out, so that morning he'd cycled to the office of Na Pali Sea

Adventures in Hanalei in the rain. He would get home the same way, in the dark, on one-lane roads and bridges, veering into the brush and mud when headlights approached. Raindrops clattered against the wide green leaves all around him as he pulled up outside the small building of the Haena post office. It was after five, so the counter was closed, but Kal could still go inside and open box J.

"Please, Mr. Postman..." He thought in music all his waking hours. He dreamed music in his sleep.

Rain dripped from him onto the stack of bills and flyers he drew from the box. The letter from Santa Barbara was on top. The return address sticker read "Erika Blade" and had a logo of an artist's palette beside it. Alone in the office, he tossed the rest of his mail on a bench, sat down and opened the envelope, his curiosity stronger than his embarrassment over the letter he should never have mailed.

To Ms. Aloha.

Erika Blade.

She had sent another card. Same artist, different picture. A very old woman sitting in the sand, gazing out to sea. The ocean really looked like the ocean.

As Kal opened the card, the photo dropped out faceup.

A good-looking brunette in cutoffs and a faded T-shirt sat against the side of a weathered wooden building with a drawing board against her knees and a paintbrush in her hand. She had long muscular legs and a laughing smile.

A good smile.

But sunglasses hid her eyes.

Reflexively fishing for an antacid from a bottle in his pack, Kal studied every detail, down to the shape of her toes, before he turned to her small delicate handwriting, which covered the whole inside of the card and continued on the back. She had a lot to say, and as he chewed on a tablet, he read with curiosity, not with hope.

Dear Kalahiki,

Thank you for answering my note. Reading of your terrible loss made my heart ache. I am so sorry about your wife's death, and I wish there were something I could do to ease your grief.

My conscience dictates that I precede this whole reply with the advice that you not marry anyone at this time. Despite the things you said in your letter, I believe there is more love in store for you. You should find it before marrying again—for your daughter's sake and your own.

This is what I believe, but I can't know your heart. Leaving your choices to you, I'll introduce myself.

My name is Erika Blade. I am thirty-six years old and a watercolor artist. But probably, if my last name is familiar, it's because my father was the undersea explorer Christopher Blade. My brother, David, and I grew up on his ship, the *Siren,* and accompanied him and my mother all over the world on scientific expeditions until I entered art school in Australia and began to make art my career. While I was at school, the *Siren* sank and my parents were killed. My brother continued my father's work, and I have helped him some.

About five years ago, I was seriously injured in an automobile accident. Though luckier than your Maka, I was temporarily paralyzed.

During the three years I spent in a wheelchair, I lived on my brother's ship with him and his son, Christian. Chris was three at the time of my accident; he lost his mother soon afterward. For three years, I helped my brother look after him, and this experience shaped who I am today. I love children.

Eventually I decided to move off David's ship and into a place of my own. Shortly afterward, I regained feeling in my legs. With the help of therapy, I have been walking for about eighteen months, but because of knee injuries in the accident I still walk with a limp.

Because my parents are dead, my family consists of my brother, his wife, Jean, and my nephew, Chris. However, they are seldom in Santa Barbara anymore; David's work takes them all over the world. In any case, I want a family of my own. And, like you, I prefer celibacy. The arrangement you have suggested appeals to me very much. I think it would be good for me. I'm less sure it would be best for you and your daughter.

So, Kalahiki, I leave you to your thoughts. I would always be glad to hear from you again.

In friendship,
Erika Blade

The last line was her phone number.

On the front of the card, Kal found her name. No wonder she could paint the sea. Christopher Blade's daughter.

Did his parents have her prints in their gallery?

Erika…

When he'd placed the ad, it was with the hope that there was someone like her out there. Someone who wasn't interested in sex—but who still seemed capable of a meaningful relationship. Someone who loved children and would love Hiialo.

But Erika Blade didn't know Hiialo. And he didn't know Erika.

Can't do this.

Kal replaced the photo and the card in the envelope, put them in his day pack with the other mail and stood up. Pushing open the glass door of the post office, he went out into the rain and the scent of wetness and grabbed his ancient three-speed Indian Scout from where he'd leaned it against the siding.

The downpour pelting him, Kal flicked on the headlight on the handlebars and pedaled out to the road, his T-shirt and shorts immediately drenched anew. He crossed a long stone bridge, riding as though he could escape the rain, and his heart raced. His mind replayed the contents of the letter, and he knew he would read it again that night when Hiialo was in bed.

Christopher Blade's daughter. Three years in a wheel-chair.

He could hear his tires on the wet pavement and the sound of the violent winter surf just a block away, a sound that once would have called him to the breaks at Hanalei Point, to Waikoko or Hideaways. Freedom...

Don't even think about bringing her here, Kal. You never really planned to do it. It just seemed better than having your daughter in day care.

To temper tantrums and moodiness.

To trying to do it alone.

To messing up.

But he couldn't go through with this. It wouldn't be right.

Why not? Riding through the rain, Kal tried to remember exactly what Erika Blade had said about sex. Hardly anything.

Painful thoughts came.

Loneliness.

The glow of headlights cast a long shadow of his body and bicycle ahead of him on the water-running pavement. Kal steered into a roadside ditch, springing off his bike when the front wheel stuck in the mud. As rain streamed down his face, a red 1996 Land Rover whipped past. Kal recognized the vehicle. It belonged to a movie star who used his fifth home, in Haena, two weekends of every year.

Reminding himself to buy a helmet, Kal yanked his bike out of the mud and back to the road before he realized the front wheel wouldn't turn and the forks were bent. He stood in the rain, and it drowned his voice as he yelled after the long-vanished car, "I hate your guts, *malihini!* You killed my wife!" He knew it wasn't really the driver of this car who'd hit Maka—just someone like him. Someone who would never belong.

Kal leaned his arms on the handlebars, his head in his hands.

Erika Blade would be a *malihini,* a newcomer, too.

He wouldn't write to her again. He'd said personal things to her. She'd said personal things to him. They were even.

And her advice was sane. Wait for love.

Wait...

He'd waited three years, dated women. They'd made him miss Maka even more.

Kal picked up his bike, slung it over his shoulder and began walking home through the rain. There was nothing to wait for.

She would never come back.

THE OKIKA GALLERY in Hanalei was a renovated plantation-style house with white porch posts and verandas. Next door, separated from the gallery by a wide walk bordered with heliconia, anthurium, spider lilies and ginger, a similar building housed the office of Na Pali Sea Adventures, the outfitter for whom Kal worked. The two buildings shared a courtyard away from the street.

The morning after he received Erika's letter, there were no Zodiac trips going out, so Kal's job was to shuttle sea kayaks to the Hanalei River for the tourists who had rented them. At ten-thirty, when he returned from that errand, he slipped out for his break.

It was raining, but the espresso stand in the courtyard was still doing business as he dashed through the downpour to the steps of the gallery. He entered through the open French doors, and Jin, his mother's champion Akita bitch, stood up and came over to greet him.

"Hi, Jin. Hi, girl." Kal crouched to pet the dog's thick red-and-white coat, to rub her back and behind her ears, to look into her eyes in the black-masked face. As Jin licked his cheek, Mary Helen, his mother, abandoned a mat-cutting project at the counter to join him.

Kal had gotten his height from his father. With her neat tennis-player's body and no-nonsense short blond hair, Mary Helen stood barely five foot two. She always looked at home in shorts, polo shirts and slippers—elsewhere known as thongs—the footwear of the islands. Born and raised in Kansas City, Missouri, Mary Helen had first visited Oahu in 1960 and met King Johnson at a dog show, where their Akitas had fallen in love and played matchmakers like something out of *One Hundred and One Dalmatians.* Or so Kal had been told. His mother had left the Midwest and moved to Hawaii to marry King. Gamely she'd faced the challenges of island life, slowly exploring her new world, learning the social subtleties and embracing the cultural richness of Hawaii. Hawaiian quilting, Japanese *bon* dancing, foods as unfamiliar as *poi* and *kim chee*— Mary Helen loved them all. When she and King had children, they had given them Hawaiian names. Now, in the critical eyes of the locals, Kal's mother was considered a *kamaaina,* a child of the land.

Could Erika Blade do that?

"Hi, sweetheart," said Mary Helen. "No trips today?"

"No. I'm going to go get Hiialo in a minute." When Kal had no trips to guide, his boss, Kroner, let Hiialo work with him at the Sea Adventures office, doing small tasks her four-year-old hands could manage. Despite her tantrums, Hiialo had a knack for winning friends.

"She can come over here," his mother said. "I'll be here all day. I'm changing some prints on the wall."

Kal had come to look at prints, but his taking a sudden interest in the family obsession—art—would make his mother suspicious. "I'll bring her over to say hi. I'm going to clean the equipment room next door, so I thought she could help." His parents gave enough to Hiialo; she spent every Tuesday with them at the gallery.

"Oh, that's good for her." His mother smiled approvingly. "And she'll have fun."

Kal straightened up from petting Jin, who walked away to keep watch out the front door. Why had he placed that ad, anyhow? It wasn't as though Hiialo had no female influence in her life. She had his mother and his sister, Niau.

"Your dad took Kumi to the vet," his mother told him. "And Niau went to Honolulu. She took Leo some prints. Did you know he's remodeling? He wanted you to help."

"I know. He called me."

Kal's oldest brother—Lay-oh, not Lee-oh—ran a gallery on Oahu. Keale, the next oldest, was a park ranger on the Big Island. Uncles and aunts. What didn't Hiialo have? If he wanted, they could even get a dog, one of his folks' Akita puppies. Though he wasn't home enough…

He wasn't home enough.

He needed a partner.

Kal sensed his mother looking him over, and he knew she was wondering if he'd wind up in the hospital again, receiving a blood transfusion. Apparently deciding he was going to make it, she smiled and said, "Come tell me what you think of this oil painting. A man from Kapaa painted it, and I think he's good."

Where usually he would have begged off, Kal followed her to the counter, surreptitiously scanning the walls. He didn't need to look that far. When he reached the counter, he saw that one of the prints his mother was putting up or taking down was by Erika Blade.

He tried not to stare, but he recognized the model as the same woman in the dolphin card Erika had sent. In this print, the woman was building a sand castle with a boy.

It was the best of her work he'd seen. The interaction between the woman and child, their absorption in their construction project, conveyed a lot. Motherhood. Happiness. Friendship. Nurturing. Fun.

If Erika Blade had a lot of prints out, she was probably doing well. What Jakka had said weeks before needled him. *Marry a rich woman.*

Not a pretty notion, but practical. Kal *wasn't* looking for a woman to support him so he could play professionally again. But he worked six days a week. Needed to. *At least she can support herself.*

He dutifully assessed the oil landscape by the Kapaa artist. "It's nice." But his eyes drifted back to the print.

Jin left the door, wandered over to them and sat down by the counter. The Akita looked at Kal and so did his mother.

"Isn't that lovely?" Mary Helen asked, noticing his interest in Erika's print.

"Yes." Kal turned away, chewing on unasked questions.

"That's hers, too, up there," said his mother. "The girl sailing. We sell a lot of her work actually. Her name is Erika Blade. I think she's disabled."

"Oh."

Mary Helen's head was tilted sideways, as though she was listening for the *akua,* the island spirits, to give up secrets. She was staring curiously at Kal, picking up on the anomaly of his looking twice at a piece of art.

"Well, I'm going to get Hiialo," he said. "I'll see you later."

Then he left, before the *akua* could tell their tales.

CHAPTER THREE

Malaki: March

TO ERIKA'S DISAPPOINTMENT, Adele expressed misgivings about *Poofie* and *Free Kittens*. Good work, she said gently, but not enough universal appeal for a print series. How about something with *people* in it?

Erika was painting people now, but nothing she could sell: Six similar paintings, not just in watercolor but also in acrylic and oil. Two of the subjects had come from an incomplete photograph. The third eluded her and stood ghostlike on the side.

Maka, she thought, *who are you?*

She had shaped each different Maka using pictures of hula dancers from Hawaiian travel magazines, which now lay all about her studio. She had used no one model but had combined different characteristics.

What had Maka been doing? Was her other arm behind Kalahiki, holding him? Was her face turned up to his? What was she wearing? How tall was she? Her right arm was medium-size and well-toned—

The phone rang.

Erika had trained her heart not to leap at that sound, and now she debated letting the machine pick it up to prove her self-control. Ever since she'd received Kalahiki's letter—and answered it—she'd been unsteady. She shouldn't care so much. But she did. About a broken-hearted man she didn't know. Twenty times a day, Erika laid those feelings aside, put them in the place where she put her reaction to his picture, a reaction that was all wrong.

Kal's grief was his business, not hers.

That he looked like an engraved invitation to come to Hawaii and fall in love was irrelevant.

A celibate marriage was exactly what she wanted. A husband. A child. And no physical complications, no difficult intimacy.

She could keep her head, not get involved. It was easy when she remembered what doing otherwise could mean. Sex.

Yuck.

So he was hung up on his dead wife. Good. He could have his hang-ups; she'd keep hers.

The telephone rang again. She should answer. Adele was back from Hawaii. This might be something about work. *Like what? She's already rejected all my paintings.*

The phone rang a third time. Erika set down her brush, dropped down to the shadows of the galley and picked up the receiver. "Hello?"

There was a silence, like a punctuation mark. Then, "Hello. This is Kal Johnson calling. Is Erika there?"

She sank down on the steps of the companionway. With a slight breeze from the open hatches blowing her oversize T-shirt against her back, she clutched the receiver. His voice was low and resonant. Masculine. Unique.

God help her.

Sexy.

"This is Erika." She was in a vacuum and her insides were being sucked out of her. She heard the engine of a cabin cruiser crawling past in the harbor, and a slow wake rocked the junk at its berth.

"I'm not sure if you know who I am, but—"

"I know who you are. You're Kalahiki."

Across the Pacific, in the sun-dappled morning shadows inside the bungalow, Kal heard her say his name for the first time. At the same moment he saw Hiialo outside beating Pincushion against the porch. "Bad Pincushion! Bad! No talk stink!"

What had Pincushion said?

"I thought we should talk on the phone." *Brilliant, brilliant, keep it up, Kal.*

Erika bit her lip. There was a bellows stuck in her throat, and it was opening and closing with each beat of her heart. *Talk,* she thought. *Say something that will make him...*

Oh, she wanted it. They could settle into permanence—permanent celibacy, permanent family—and her life would not change again. Safe.

"Your daughter's beautiful." The ensuing pause was so long that at last she asked, "Are you still there?"

"Yeah. I... Erika..."

Silence surrounded her name. Silence...and feeling. It was so dark in the galley she didn't know why her eyes burned that way, why she felt so—

"I just wanted to tell you some things," he said. "I've thought a lot since I got your letter. Are you serious about this?"

Erika swallowed. *This.* As though he couldn't say it himself.

"Yes."

"My house is small. It's a bungalow. I could fix it so we'd have our own rooms, but it's still cozy. It's not right on the beach, either. Close, though."

Erika tightened her fingers on the phone. *Was he saying he wanted her to come?*

"I don't make a lot of money. I'm buying the house from my folks. They have a gallery, by the way. Actually they have three. I went into the one in Hanalei and looked for your prints. They have some."

Parents. Did his parents live near him? The thought was reassuring. *Mr. Family*.

She asked, "What's the name of their gallery?"

"The Okika. It means 'orchid.'"

His voice was both warm and sandpaper rough. It made her want to hear him talk more.

But he was quiet.

Erika asked, "What does Hiialo do while you work?"

"Um…she goes to a day-care center." Actually, she'd been to a few. One in a church basement with forty other kids. One with an elderly woman who had made the mistake of saying Hiialo needed a firm hand. The latest situation was a home with an unhappy dog tied up outside.

"My nephew used to be with me while I worked, when he was Hiialo's age." As soon as she'd said it, Erika wished she hadn't. She sounded too eager. *Desperate*.

But an opportunity like this wouldn't come again. Normal people wanted sex. Kal and his grief were her only hope.

"Hiialo is…" His voice startled her. "Well, she's moody. In fact, she can be a bugger sometimes."

"All kids can." The dock made its endless aching cries.

"I'd like to…" On the lanai, Hiialo was making Pincushion and her stuffed lion, Purr, shake hands. Kal remembered proposing to Maka. At Waimea Beach. Kissing. *I love you…*. "You could come over here," he said. "I'll buy your ticket. If it doesn't work out, I'll buy you a ticket home, too."

"I'll buy my own ticket." *Somehow*. Her hand was deep in her hair, tearing at it. She felt like crying. What if he didn't like her? What if he didn't think she'd be a good stepmother for Hiialo? What if… "When do you want me to come?"

"Not right away. I have to figure out some things. About the house." About how to tell his parents.

How to tell Hiialo.

"I'll call you again, yeah?" he said. "And I'll send pictures of the house. Maybe you could come in June?"

"That sounds great. I'm boat-sitting for my brother's business partner. He'll be back in June." Oh, she sounded flaky. Practically homeless.

"Good," said Kal.

Her worries evaporated. She was wanted—by a stranger. *Why was he doing this?*

He said, "Let's get off the phone for now. I'll call you again soon. Do you have any questions before we hang up?"

"Yes." With a presence of mind that astonished her, she asked, "What's your phone number?"

Moments later she set the receiver back in its cradle. Still sitting weakly on the steps, she leaned against the side of the counter and wept.

"DADDY, PINCUSHION'S stuffing is falling out." As Kal hung up the phone, Hiialo appeared before him, bringing everything into immediate and demanding focus.

"You beat the stuffing out of him. That's why it's falling out."

Hiialo started to look tearful, and Kal reached for Pincushion, who was made from a faded gray-blue sock and wore a turban. In addition to a split seam on the side, one of his felt eyes was coming off. Repair time.

"I'll fix him." Sewing up Pincushion would calm him.

A picture bride. Danny's analogy was accurate, and since the night he'd said it, Kal had stumbled upon two accounts of Japanese picture brides from the turn of the century. One was in the newspaper, the other in a book sold in the office of Na Pali Sea Adventures. And he'd remembered that his parents' next-door neighbor, June Akana, who had taught Japanese *bon* dances to him and his sister and brothers when they were kids, had been a

picture bride, too. She and her husband were in their
nineties, still going strong. Best friends. People could be
happy.

But the picture brides of old hadn't come to Hawaii
for celibate marriage.

Oh, shit, what were his friends going to say? They all
knew what he'd advertised for. He'd told them why, because of Hiialo, because he was never home and she
needed someone who could be. *He* needed someone who
would be. He killed a useless yearning. Not for love—
for life. His own.

The Stratocaster in his hands. Playing...

But he was doing this for Hiialo.

"You'll be all right, Pincushion," said Hiialo, patting
the toy in Kal's hand. She trailed after him as he went
to the kitchen drawer where he kept needles, thread, extra
guitar picks, junk. The scissors were missing, as usual.

"Hiialo, I need your scissors. Could you please get
them for me?"

"Yes, Daddy. Thank you for fixing Pincushion." She
went over to the couch and looked underneath it, then
went to her room to find the scissors.

Sunshine. Hiialo was like sunshine now, but she was
changeable as the north-shore weather. And sometimes
as wild.

Would Erika Blade, a thirty-six-year-old childless
woman, really be able to handle it?

Dear Erika,
I'm glad you're coming to Hawaii. I'll try to call
you once a week. Here are the pictures I promised
you of my house. You can see what Hiialo looks
like now. She is holding Pincushion, who is her favorite toy....

I mentioned my family on the phone. My folks
live in Haena, and my sister, Niau, lives in Poipu,
on the south side of the island. My brother Leo...

MIDAFTERNOON sunlight shone through the open hatch and the windows of the *Lien Hua*. Lying in her berth, Erika read Kal's second letter and studied the photographs he'd sent. At four, Hiialo was sturdy, with thick, wavy, medium brown hair cut in a pageboy. Even in the photograph, in which she was crouched on the lanai of the green bungalow with the thing called Pincushion, she seemed full of energy, ready to leap to her feet and race away. Not like Chris...

That's okay, thought Erika. *I know I can love her.*

If she was certain of anything, it was her ability to love and care for children. Chris had been exceptionally good, exceptionally bright. Exceptionally quiet. But she could love Hiialo. It would be easy.

Another photo showed Kal with his brothers and sister and parents and their three dogs, all Akitas. His father—King, said the corresponding name on the back of the photo—was tall and white-haired. His mother, Mary Helen, seemed compact and athletic. And Kal and his siblings all had a look of radiant good health and of energy and power—not unlike the dogs. One brother was bearded, the other clean-shaven. His sister had shoulder-length light brown hair. They were a handsome family. Kal was the youngest.

The photo and letter, the proof that he really was a family man in every sense, reassured Erika. Since his phone call, she'd had doubts. Kal was a stranger. With David so far away, no one would really know if she got into trouble.

She ought to write to him, tell him.

She ought to tell *someone* what she was doing.

But she knew what her brother would say: *Kal will get over Maka's death.*

For the hundredth time, Erika tried to quiet her qualms

about that. She *had* advised him to wait—for someone else, someone he could love.

She should send him photos of her and David and Chris and Jean to give him the same kind of reassurance he'd given her. But she had no photos of herself with them, only with Chris, when she was in a wheelchair.

Not an option.

She looked back to the letter.

…I haven't told anyone our plans. June is a long way off. Before you come, I'll explain to my folks and Hiialo. Also, my in-laws. Maka's folks live on Molokai, but her brother and her cousin live in Hanalei and they're like family. In Hawaii, *ohana*, or family, means more than just your immediate relatives. It can extend to all your loved ones—

The telephone rang, and she went down into the galley to answer. It was Adele, calling to ask how the painting was going. Did she have anything else yet? Had she tried placing those "other pieces" in a gallery?

"Ah…I'm just experimenting right now." Erika thought it through at light speed. "Actually a friend has invited me to Hawaii in June. I'm going to do some work there."

"Oh, great! Which island?"

"Kauai." Belatedly Erika recalled that Adele had seen Kal's ad. But surely it wouldn't occur to her that Erika had *answered* the ad.

It didn't. "Wonderful. I think it's recovered a lot since Iniki. The hurricane in '92? Try to get up to the north shore.…"

Erika listened to Adele's suggestions and chewed on her bottom lip.

Yes, it was good that David was in Greenland and no one really had to know what she was doing. She would write to her brother and tell him who she was staying with and where. But why say more? If it turned out that Kal didn't like her, no one would have to know the truth.

"Erika? Are you there?"

"Oh, yes, I'm sorry. I'm spaced out today, Adele. What is it?"

"There are some galleries on Kauai that carry your prints. I'll send you their names. I know they'd love it if you stopped in."

The Okika Gallery, Erika remembered. Kal's parents owned three galleries. It seemed like destiny. She longed to tell Adele everything. But if she did, Adele would worry. Anyone would worry, would question her judgment. Erika hated that. Better to say nothing, just leave Adele her new address and stick to her story. "All right."

After they'd hung up, Erika climbed back up to the main cabin, where the paintings of Kal and Hiialo and Maka confronted her. She *needed* someone to ease her anxiety, to believe with her in this risk she was taking, believe that it would work out.

There was really only one person who could help with that, and Erika wished the phone would ring again.

He had promised to call.

Apelila: April

Dear Kal,

Thanks for your letter and the photographs and your phone calls. I painted the enclosed picture for Hiialo. I did it using the photos you sent. I hope she can recognize who it's supposed to be....

The watercolor was of Pincushion. Kal loved it, had wanted to keep it himself. He'd considered taking it down to the gallery to get it framed, but then... Questions. How come he had an Erika Blade original. Of Pincushion.

I stole it, Mom.

Instead, he'd put the watercolor in a cheap document
frame, replacing a photo of the great blues guitarist Robert Johnson, and he'd given it to Hiialo, as Erika had
wanted, saying it was from a pen pal. After explaining
what a pen pal was, he'd added, "Sometimes I talk to
her on the phone, too."

Soon he'd have to explain more. To everyone. Erika
was coming to live in his house, maybe for good.

Sitting on the porch swing while Hiialo played in her
room, Kal remembered his phone conversation with Erika
just that morning. He had asked if she'd told her brother
what they were doing. "I wrote to him," she'd said, and
Kal had wondered if she knew she wasn't answering the
question. He was pretty sure she did.

He was pretty sure she'd told her brother almost nothing.

Kal talked to her once a week, always calling Thursday
at seven in the morning. It was his day off, Hiialo usually
wasn't up by then, and it was around ten in Santa Barbara. Making the call was agonizing every time. The cultural gap between them was bigger than Waimea Canyon.
But Kal wanted to know all he could about Erika Blade
before she arrived, before he brought her into Hiialo's
life.

She was hard to know. She turned conversations away
from herself and tuned into him, perceiving his difficul-
ties as a single father almost as though she'd been one
herself. Or had known one, which she had.

Her brother.

He left the swing and went inside. It was already one
o'clock, and he had things to do. He'd recently enclosed
the back lanai, creating a new room—for Erika. It still
needed finishing touches. But Danny and Jakka had
stopped by that morning, and a jam session had eaten

half the day. "Hiialo, let's go to Hanalei. I need something from the hardware store."

Kal heard a rustling from his room and took a step down the hallway, pushed aside the beads in his doorway and looked in. Hiialo peered up from where she crouched beside his open desk drawer, photos spread out around her. The portrait of a naughty girl.

Kal saw a photograph of Maka under the leg of his folding metal desk chair. Entering the room, he picked up the chair. The surface of the photo was marred, across Maka's face.

"What are you doing, Hiialo? Those aren't yours."

She began a cry he knew would rise to a full-throated wail. She looked at a photograph in her hands, a snapshot of her mother, and ripped it in half.

"Hiialo." Kal scooped her up, and she hit him with her fists and kicked him, screaming. "Don't hit. I don't hit you."

Her small arms and legs struck a few more times, to prove that she didn't care what he said, before she subsided to screams. He carried her through the beads and out into the main room and then through the curtain door of her room. Her voice had reached a high continuous sob, and she cried, "It's your day off! You're supposed to spend it with me! You're supposed to spend Thursday with me!"

Kal couldn't speak. Even as he left her on her bed, kicking the wall and crying, he wondered what he'd done that had made her that way.

Not enough time at home.

He should have skipped the music, told Danny and Jakka it was his day with Hiialo.

Listening to her shrieking, he wondered if all parents felt trapped. Guilty for wanting their own time. For wanting…

Music spun inside him, trying to soothe. *"Rock Me on the Water…"*

He went back into his room and saw the photos scattered on the floor, including the one that had been ripped in half. In the next room, Hiialo's cries reached a crescendo, and Kal crouched down to pick up all the Makas from the throw rug.

HIS FATHER CAME BY late that afternoon to look at some bad siding on his rental property, the blue oriental house in front of the bungalow. Kal was caretaker of the vacation home. He cut the grass and cared for the plants and cleaned after tenants left. The blue house had been rebuilt after Iniki; he'd just discovered that the siding was poorly installed.

Leading Raiden, one of the Akitas, up to the porch, King asked Kal, "Where's the *keiki?*"

"Taking a nap." They stood together under the porch awning with the rain pounding the roof and the garden, and at last Kal said, "Yeah, it's been a great day." He told his father about the photos.

King shook his head. He'd seen Hiialo in a temper, too. They all accepted her moods as part of her nature, but everyone hated the sulks and the screaming.

Together the two men toured the back-porch room, scrutinizing the construction. King had never asked the reason for the project; the house was small. When they'd examined the new room, Kal offered him some juice—he seldom bought beer, which he liked but which made him sick—and they sat on the veranda with Raiden exploring the yard nearby.

The Akita had a pure white coat and double-curled tail, and Kal studied the dog with admiration and envy. His parents' stud was immaculately bred, intensively trained, utterly trustworthy. Kal knew the time that went into raising an animal like that.

He didn't even have time for his daughter.

Watching Raiden lift his leg against the heliconia, Kal said, "I've made friends with an artist in Santa Barbara. Erika Blade. We write letters. Talk on the phone."

His father tipped back his cup of guava juice. "She's a big artist. How'd you meet her?"

"I placed a personal ad. She's coming to Kauai this summer. She's going to stay here."

Lazily King stretched out his legs and rocked the porch swing. "With you?"

On the top porch step, Kal shrugged. "Here." His house, not his bed.

The rain drizzled, creating waterfall sounds all around the lanai, and Raiden came over to lie at his master's feet.

"Is this romance?"

No, thought Kal. *It's practical.* "Something like that."

The rain poured from the gutter and splattered on the ground at the corner of the house. As Kal stared out at it, his father said at last, "Well, we'll look forward to meeting her." He stood up and so did Raiden. "I'm going to take a look at that siding."

Kal glanced toward his own house. All was quiet indoors, Hurricane Hiialo sleeping. Watching the Akita follow his father down the steps into the rain, he drew a quiet breath. King hadn't criticized, hadn't shown any disapproval at all. Kal knew that when his father had said they'd look forward to meeting Erika, he meant it.

His parents always kept things in perspective. They'd survived Hurricanes Iwa and Iniki.

And Kal had cried in his dad's arms after Maka died.

CHAPTER FOUR

Iune: June

HIIALO KICKED HER SEAT in the Datsun. Thud, thud, thud, in a mindless rhythm. Her lips were tightly sealed, her eyes nervous. In her lap was a plastic bag containing a braided *lei hala lei,* made of flowers of the pandanus tree, and a second *lei* made of braided red ti leaves.

"Stop kicking the seat, Hiialo." He ate a Tums. "You okay?"

She nodded.

She'd been up half the night, coming out of her room every five minutes for another drink of water. Must have picked up on his mood. All he'd told Hiialo was that he'd placed a want ad to meet a woman; he was lonely without her mom. His daughter had reacted as though what he'd done was sensible. But did she suspect the truth about Erika? That if all went well she would stay for good, as Hiialo's stepmother?

Kal saw the sign for the airport and manually worked the Datsun's broken turn indicator, flipping it back and forth as an Aloha Airlines plane flew in over the sea, descending to the terminal.

"Is your pen pal on that plane?" asked Hiialo.

"I think so."

Her lips clamped shut again.

Kal parked in the visitors' lot and came around to Hiialo's side of the car to lift her into his arms. "I love you, Ti-leaf.'' It was his special name for her. Ti leaves were a symbol of luck; she was all of his. Everything he had.

Hiialo kissed his face and rested her head against his shoulder. "I love you, Daddy."

Kal carried her toward the terminal, thinking, *Hiialo B. Goode...*

LOW GREEN SHRUBS—Hooker's Green Dark, thought Erika—lined the shore, and white caps dotted the ocean beyond. Her carryall was tucked under the seat in front of her, and she resisted reaching for it to open her compact. She looked fine—especially for a woman who hadn't slept in a week. She'd been too excited to sleep.

Absently Erika touched her hair. Days earlier she'd gone to the beauty college in Santa Barbara for a free haircut. The result was that her hair hung at one length, just brushing her shoulders. Nothing dramatic, but she was glad she'd done *something*. She wore a silk sheath of aquamarine—shin-length, with slits partway up both sides. Sandals, no stockings.

She hoped Hiialo would think she was pretty, would like her. That was everything. Meeting Kal was just...

Well, okay, it was natural to want him to like her, too. In fact, it was necessary. She couldn't afford to go back to the mainland. Adele hadn't wanted to publish prints from any of her recent watercolors. Erika didn't know what she was doing wrong, but it was months since she'd sold anything. Until she received royalties from *Sand Castles,* she had four hundred and fifty dollars to her name, not even enough for a ticket home. She was going to have to get a job.

But if she had a job, she couldn't watch Hiialo during the day.

I have to sell some art.

As the plane touched down, the captain welcomed everyone to Kauai. "The temperature in Lihue is eighty-five degrees…"

The plane taxied interminably before it stopped and the seat-belt signs went off with a quiet *ding*. Erika remained in her seat, letting the other passengers go first. She'd be slow on the stairs. Beside her was a diminutive local beauty in a beach cover-up and flip-flops. She jostled Erika with her bag, then turned and said in charming apology, "Oh, I'm so sorry!" Her voice was musical, her manner sweet. Had Maka been like that?

A graceful human being in every way…

Suddenly Erika felt about a hundred years old.

When the other passengers had passed, she stood up, ducked under the overhead and limped to the door. Slowly, holding the railings, she descended the stairs to the humid airfield and made her way to the small utilitarian terminal. As soon as she stepped inside, she smelled flowers.

He was there, conspicuous for his height and his looks and the little girl beside him, who wore turquoise shorts and a tank top silk-screened with the image of a surfer and the slogan "Breaks to da max!" She was peering intently into a nearby planter bigger than herself.

Kal spotted her and waved, and Erika walked toward him, conscious of her limp, of him watching her. Three yards away, she thought, *Your eyes are blue.*

Teal, so fine a shade that Erika was surprised she hadn't always known the color. A teal she could mix from Turquoise and Hooker's Green Dark. He wore off-white, slightly wrinkled cotton pants and an aloha shirt in navy blue, black and yellow, covered with trumpet vines and ukuleles. Despite the flip-flops on his feet, Erika knew he had dressed up for her coming, but in contrast to the men she knew in Santa Barbara, he seemed casual. Unpretentious. No designer labels, no cologne. Yes, red meat, yes, domestic beer. *Shaka.* Hang loose.

Mr. Family?

Like a daddy wolf. His wolf's expression was on her, assessing her, sniffing the air. Alert.

Mutely Erika submitted to the examination.

It was brief, though Kal found her face hard to absorb in one take. Brown eyes. Olive complexion. Smooth skin. She was tall and slender, with the honed limbs of an athlete.

And a slight limp.

He draped the *lei hala lei* around her neck, and her thick hair reached out and wisped against his fingers, clinging to them with static electricity. "Aloha," he said and touched his lips to her cool cheek. Strands of hair seemed to leap against his face, and he drew back.

Still feeling the kiss and his hands brushing her as he'd put the *lei* around her neck, Erika recalled the word for thank you. "*Mahalo*. What a beautiful *lei*."

Well, she'd figured out that *mahalo* wasn't Hawaiian for airport trash can, reflected Kal. When she clued into the fact that the word was used mostly by poolside entertainers and interisland flight attendants, she'd be all right.

She was fingering the *lei,* examining it as though she found it wondrous, which he had to admit it was.

In truth, the *lei* gave Erika an excuse not to look at Kal. A slanted half-inch white scar crossed the indentation above his upper lip. Its effect was to make her want to stare at his mouth, at his straight white teeth and the faintest gap between the front two.

Instinct distracted her from the flowers, made her glance down, and there was Hiialo, her arms reaching up with another *lei*. Erika crouched in front of her, and the little girl put the braid of reddish leaves around her neck.

"Aloha, Erika. I'm Hiialo."

"Aloha to you, Hiialo."

"My uncle Danny's hula group made these for you."

Had that been Maka's hula group, too? No wonder the *leis* seemed so intricate, so special. An unexpected welcome from people she had never met. People who loved Kal and

Hiialo enough to reach out to her, too. The depth of generosity, the level of hospitality and courtesy, seemed foreign—and beautiful.

No wonder Adele's so crazy about Hawaii, thought Erika, looking forward to sharing stories about her trip. Then she remembered it wasn't just a vacation. She might stay here.

Kal said, "Let's go get your bags."

As THEY DROVE NORTH, Erika tried to adjust to riding in a car with two strangers who might become the most important part of her life. Luckily there was a lot on the road to occupy her. Sugarcane grew in fields between the road and the sea. Outside a shopping mall, men harvested coconuts from royal palms that reached skyward like Jack's beanstalk.

When the businesses and houses of Wailua were behind them, Kal nodded toward the inland hills. "That's Nounou Ridge. We call it the Sleeping Giant. Can you see him lying on his back?"

"Yes." Erika knew from studying a map that they were on Kauai's main highway. It almost circled the island, stopping only for the impassable mountains of the Na Pali Coast. *Was Maka killed on this road?* How did it happen? Who was at fault?

Kal was thinking of Maka, too. The road was narrowing. They drove past the place where her heart had stopped beating. If Hiialo hadn't been in the back seat, he would have shown Erika where the cars collided.

He ran out of words until they neared the next town. "This is Kapaa. My folks have a gallery here. It's right there." He pointed out the Kapaa Okika Gallery.

Beyond the reflections in the windows, Erika caught a glimpse of paintings hanging against a light background. Then the gallery was out of sight, and the car trawled past shops full of tropical-print silks, colorful beach totes, surfboards and various trinkets. In a blink they left Kapaa, and the highway opened out with a view of the sea.

Miles farther on, as the road curved around the north shore, Kal indicated a lighthouse on a promontory. "Kilauea Lighthouse. You surf?"

"Not anymore." Not well enough for Hawaii's waves. Erika stole a glance at Kal. She'd seen in his photographs that he was attractive. But a photo couldn't carry a man's smell or his voice. She'd thought she was used to the low warm gravelly quality of the latter from talking to him on the phone. But hearing him speak and seeing his face, his body, all at once was a different matter.

The Pacific shifted colors under her eyes, like a quilt being shaken out.

We'll be fine, she told herself. *I'll get used to him, and he won't seem so sexy.*

The countryside became lush, and Erika could feel the dampness in the air as the Datsun passed valleys planted in taro. Blossoms spilled from tree branches, and the roadside flowers held as many shades as her paint box. In a tree whose limbs stretched out on sweeping horizontal planes, like a bonsai, sat dozens of white birds with exotic plumage on their heads. They reminded Erika of tropical ports of her childhood, and she thought of her parents, especially her mother, who had loved flowers.

What a place to paint.

She subdued the now familiar doubts… that she'd never sell another watercolor.

"Daddy, Eduardo's hungry."

Erika glanced into the back seat. Hiialo had one toy with her in the car, the thing Erika had thought was called Pincushion. A watercolor subject. But she must have been mistaken about its name. "Is that Eduardo?"

"No," said Hiialo. "This is Pincushion." She frowned, as though puzzled that Erika had asked. "Eduardo is a *mo'o.*"

"What's that?"

Hiialo seemed at a loss. "Daddy…"

"Mo'os," said Kal, "are giant magical black lizards of Hawaiian legend."

"Giant?"

"Thirty feet long." The topic was a good icebreaker. "The ancient Hawaiians worshiped their ancestors, who they believed could be powerful allies after death. Actually some people still depend on their *aumakua,* deified ancestral spirits, to help them out of trouble. In the old days, a *kahuna,* an expert in magic, would help people transform their deceased relatives into sharks or *mo'os* or whatever. *Mo'os* lived in ponds and were supposed to be fierce fighters, protective of their families."

"Except Eduardo lives in our house," said Hiialo.

Erika briefly entertained the notion that Maka had become a *mo'o* after death. It was a silly idea, but it seemed less cruel than death's stealing her, leaving her husband and baby alone.

There was only a shade of humor in her next thought: *I should make friends with Eduardo.*

With Maka's memory.

"We're coming up on Princeville," Kal said. "In a minute you can see Hanalei Bay."

The terrain was changing again. The green hillocks inland had become mountains, rich forested green and draped in billowing shifting mist. Banyan trees grew alongside the road, their roots stretching twenty feet down the earthen embankment to the asphalt. Erika understood why Kauai was called the Garden Island. Everywhere, everything was verdant; plants with sprawling leaves caught the mist and the first raindrops.

A moment later a shower came in a clattering torrent. Through the rain streaming down the windshield, Erika caught her first glimpse of Hanalei Bay. A Zodiac motored across the water, and then the bay was obscured again by a tangle of foliage, trumpet vines, bottlebrush trees, amaryllis blossoms.

In another few minutes they reached Hanalei.

"That's the gallery," said Kal, identifying a white building with a wraparound porch.

Hanalei was not the tourist trap Erika had half expected. Despite its galleries and T-shirt shops, surf shops and boutiques, the community had an unpolished small-town atmosphere. Leaving the shopping area, they passed a soccer field set against the backdrop of mist-cloaked mountains. Beside the field was a green clapboard church with dramatic Gothic stained glass, a bell on the roof peak and a side tower with a pointed pagoda roof. In the doorway two women in identical *holoku* gowns and *leis* corralled some small children. Other people emerged, and Erika realized it was a wedding.

Somberly she looked away.

Kal was silent.

As they left Hanalei and continued driving west, the road narrowed. Vines and blooms overhung the road, which was broken by one-lane stone bridges. To Erika, it seemed a fairy-tale place—enchanted. They passed the sign for Haena, and soon Kal turned right, toward the ocean, on a gravel road. At its end, amid a jungle of flora—plants with pointed Cadmium Red leaves resembling lobster claws, trees with frilled and lacy hanging blossoms—stood a Private Property sign. Kal turned down the dirt drive.

A stand of mixed tropical trees to the left hid a tiny one-story green house. The dwelling would have blended in with its background if not for its white porch pillars and railing, a faded wind sock hanging from the roof of the lanai and a child's bright plastic tricycle in the road. Erika recognized the bungalow from the photos Kal had sent.

But he didn't stop there.

"Where are you going, Daddy?" asked Hiialo.

The Datsun continued down the gravel drive. "I thought Erika would like to see the beach."

Separated from the bungalow by a forest of trees and shrubs was a vast lawn and a low slate blue house with an oriental roof. Palm trees shaded the beach. The calm summer sea was every shade of blue and green. It took Erika's breath. When Kal parked beside the beachfront house and she got out, she could only stand and hold her arms about herself as the trade winds cooled her body.

"This house is a rental property owned by my parents," said Kal, as Hiialo climbed between the seats and out his door. "It's occupied off and on. When my aunt and uncle from the mainland visit, they stay here. I take care of the place."

Erika stared at the sea. "I didn't imagine you were this close to the ocean."

No longer having to concentrate on driving, Kal studied her face. Prominent bones, smooth planes, a straight nose. He'd already noticed that with different expressions the whole arrangement of her features seemed to change—and that she had a way of looking at things with deep concentration, as though planning to paint them someday. Erika's was not a boring face.

"Daddy , I want to go home."

"*Bumbye,* Hiialo." In a while.

"We can go," said Erika. "I can walk back here anytime. This is just beautiful." *I want to stay....* She spotted a boat covered by a canvas tarp, lying on some vines under what seemed to be a pine tree. "Is that yours?"

"That's the outrigger," said Hiialo. "It was my dad's wedding present from my mom. She and Uncle Danny made it."

Maka. "It must be a very special boat," Erika said. Hiialo was sweet. This would be easy.

Kal moved toward the car. Erika would have preferred to walk to the bungalow, but they all climbed into the Datsun, instead, and he backed up the driveway, spun the wheel and reversed into a gravel space beside a wobbly green gardening shed.

He parked, switched off the ignition and stared straight

ahead, out the windshield. Then he looked at Erika. "We're here." He lifted his eyebrows slightly, then turned away, reached for the door handle and got out.

He and Erika carried her belongings up to the lanai. Seeing Kal and Hiialo kick off their flip-flops beside the door, Erika bent down to remove her sandals. When she straightened, she saw a gentle smiling expression in Kal's eyes. He held open the screen door. "*E komo mai.* Welcome."

Stepping into the shadows, onto a warped hardwood floor covered with irregular remnants of gold-and-green carpet, Erika surveyed the small front room. The walls were cheap paneling. On the right side was the kitchen, on the left a couch, an old end table and a throw rug. Over the couch hung a framed print of a schooner, a Hawaiian chief in the bow. A hanging lamp with a plastic tiffany shade advertising Coca-Cola dangled above the coffee table, and two pieces of batiked cloth blocked a doorway opposite the porch.

Erika peered down a hall and spotted a threshold obscured by bamboo beads. At the hallway's end was a real door, a solid door.

She glanced at the kitchen, the sink, the gas stove. Crayon drawings on the refrigerator. The baseboards looked streaky—perhaps hurriedly swept after a long dust buildup. For some reason, the sight touched her.

This place might become her home. Kal might become her husband—though not her lover—and Hiialo her child. It seemed hard to imagine, but she said sincerely, "I like this."

Kal swallowed, relieved. Surprised. "Thanks." He set down her duffel, garment bag and a blue suitcase she'd said contained art supplies and ankle weights. "Let me give you a tour."

"I want to show you my room," said Hiialo.

"Okay."

Hiialo went to the batiked curtains and pushed them apart. Ducking between them, Erika found herself in a tiny chamber with a single koa captain's bed. The wood was familiar; there had been a lot of koa on the *Skye*. Hiialo's closet was built into one wall, and a window looked out on a yellow-blossomed tree beside the driveway.

The watercolor of Pincushion hung over the nightstand, in a plastic frame, no mat. The cheap frame affected Erika much as the hastily dusted baseboards had. "This is a wonderful room, Hiialo."

Hiialo pointed to a turquoise-and-green ginger pattern quilt on her bed. "This is the quilt Tutu made for me. She gave it to me when I was born." Her gaze drifted up to Kal, behind Erika in the doorway.

Turning, Erika caught him with a finger to his lips. He and Hiialo must have a secret.

Tutu. "Is that your grandmother?" Maka's mother?

Hiialo nodded. "My *tutu* on Molokai. Not Grandma." She sat on her bed and turned on a lamp with a friendly-looking dragon at its base. "Would you like to see my Barbie dolls? I have Cinderella, too."

Kal tried to remember the last time Hiialo had shown an interest in dolls. The change seemed to confirm everything he'd suspected: a woman in the house could make all the difference.

But he said, "Let's let Erika settle in first, Hiialo." He stepped around the bed and opened the door to the remodeled porch. "This is your room."

Erika followed him. The narrow room ran two-thirds the length of the house. Windows stretched along two sides, bamboo blinds rolled near the tops of the frames. The sashes were raised, bringing in heady floral scents, and by the window nearest the driveway, new track lights shone down on an art table.

When Erika saw, her eyes felt hot. He didn't even know her, and he had done all this. He'd made a place for her to work.

What if I can't sell another painting?

She had to. She'd lower her prices. She'd paint women by the sea again.

Then she remembered something else—the things she hadn't told him. About her accident and her paralysis. It wasn't his business, but the untold facts made her feel sneaky.

Kal flicked the light switch. "It's hard to get natural light in this house. Too many trees. Tell me if you need more light for your work. The table's an old one my folks had in their Poipu gallery."

It was hard to get out the words. "Thank you."

"You're welcome."

Erika crossed the koa floor to the captain's bed. It was wider than Hiialo's—full-size—and covered with a slightly faded yellow-and-red handmade quilt. The pattern was tropical, Hawaiian, with vines and blossoms radiating out from the center. Where had it come from?

"Do you like it?" burst out Hiialo. "My great-grandmother made it for my daddy for when he was born. And my daddy built your bed."

She had to stop this feeling—like she was going to cry. He'd made everything so homey. He must want her to stay. Of course he did. He'd invested a lot in her coming.

Kal's bare feet moved over the polished hardwood until he stood beside her. He, too, examined the quilt, which his mother had brought over. It had been packed away in a box during the remodeling of his parents' home twenty years before, and he'd forgotten it existed. His mother hadn't. *You know, I looked and looked for this when you and Maka were married. You know where I found it? In the shed behind the kennels. Your dad and I were clearing it out the other day to make the new whelping room....*

Erika studied the quilt, wanting to soak up its history— and Kal's. "Which of your grandmothers?"

"My dad's mom. She grew up here. Hiialo is the sixth

generation of my dad's family to be born and raised in Hawaii."

"I remember."

There were four doors in the room, one that opened to the outside, toward the mountains. Kal opened the nearest, the original door to the porch, and went into his room.

Hiialo scooted in front of Erika into her father's bedroom, then huddled close to Kal. Erika followed more slowly.

Inside, her eyes were drawn toward the light from the open window. The quilt on his bed was purple and lavender and well-worn. It was folded over double, and it took a moment for Erika to realize why.

He slept in a single bed.

Erika looked away from the piece of furniture, as though she'd caught him there naked. He really *didn't* want a lover.

On one wall was a stereo and a rack of tapes and CDs that stretched to the ceiling. Bookshelves and two guitars hung nearby. One instrument was chrome, etched with Hawaiian designs, the other an old archtop. On the floor beneath them were an amplifier and two cases Erika suspected held electric guitars.

She was startled. Kal had never mentioned music to her. "You play?"

He nodded, without humble disclaimers.

"You never said anything."

Kal touched the Gibson, drawing sound from the strings. "No."

Erika decided he wasn't as simple an equation as she'd first thought.

The bathroom was across the hall. Thin strips of black mold grew on the tub caulking—difficult to prevent in watery climates. For a single father who worked six days a week and cared for a rental property as well, he kept a clean house. *You do good, Kal,* she thought.

"There's a gecko, Daddy," said Hiialo.

An orange lizard scaled the wall above the towel rack.

"Oh, cool!" Erika peered closer.

The lizard scurried away.

"They eat cockroaches," Hiialo told her.

Erika glanced at Kal.

He shrugged. "It's Hawaii. We get some." He stepped out into the hall, Hiialo one pace behind him. "You probably want to unpack, relax."

"Actually I brought some gifts for you."

Hiialo's eyes grew large.

In her own room, Erika crouched beside the bed, opened her tote and removed a gift bag. "This is for you, Hiialo."

As Kal entered the room, bearing Erika's other luggage and a large flat box containing watercolor paper, Hiialo peeked in the bag. "Oh, look! Oh, Daddy, he's cute! He looks like an Akita puppy."

Erika's gift was a small stuffed roly-poly dog. It was cinnamon-colored with a black muzzle and fluffy curled-up tail.

Smiling, Kal squatted beside Hiialo to look at the stuffed animal. "Sure does. Hiialo—"

Erika watched him mouth, *What do you say?*

"Thank you, Erika." Her grin was toothy, dimply.

Erika said, "There's something else in the bag."

Hiialo reached down to the bottom and pulled out a tin of felt-tip pens. Her face fell. She met Erika's eyes. "I already have these."

A blush burned Kal's face. "But some of yours are drying out."

Erika wished she'd chosen something Hiialo didn't have.

Hiialo put the pens back in the gift bag and hugged her stuffed puppy. "Thank you, anyhow, Erika."

"You're welcome, sweetie. I hope you enjoy them."

"I'm going to go make a little bed for my dog." A moment later she disappeared into her room.

Kal shrugged, an apology. "She's only four."

"She's darling," Erika replied politely. She lifted out another gift sack, this one heavier and decorated with suns and moons, and handed it to Kal. When he took it, she saw the veins in his sun-browned forearms and the calluses on his hands. He had nice hands.

Kal opened the bag and pulled out a thick navy blue T-shirt with a primitive design in black, white and rust on the front. The figure of a whale was circled by a field of white dots.

"It's a design of the Chumash Indians of Santa Barbara," said Erika.

"Thanks. I'll wear it now."

He set the bag, not yet empty, on the bed and started to unbutton his aloha shirt with the eagerness of a man who hated to dress up.

As he took it off, Erika had an impression of a lean muscular chest and roped abdominal muscles. Trying to ignore him, she memorized the colors in the flowers outside the window. When she sensed that he'd put on the new shirt, she glanced back at him.

He was holding out the hem, checking the fit, which was good. "Thanks," he said again.

"There's more."

Kal picked up the sack and withdrew a quart of beer from a micro-brewery in Santa Barbara. She saw him hesitate before he said, "Thank you. We'll have to share it tonight."

"Thank *you*, Kal. This bed…" It was bigger than his.

Wide enough for two.

"The drawers came off an old dresser. The rest was easy." He edged toward the window, touching the frame.

His legs, Erika noticed, were long. Even covered by the loose twill of his drawstring-waist pants, they suggested muscle. Though his skin was golden brown from the sun, it was also smooth, the kind of skin that made her want to touch the area around his lips and his mouth, touch that tiny scar. And the bare abdomen, the chest, the shoulders she had glimpsed when he changed his shirt. He was powerfully built. *Six years younger than me.*

The thought was not unappealing. He was certainly a grown man.

But her observation was distant. Uninvolved. She assessed him as she thought another woman might.

When he turned from the window, Kal found her staring. Shot by a feeling he hadn't expected—something sexual— he hurried to end the moment. "You probably want to rest. Are you hungry?"

"The food on the plane was good. I'd just as soon spend some time with Hiialo."

"Look, I don't expect you to baby-sit. That wasn't the idea." Not exactly.

Good. Maybe he wouldn't mind if she had to get a job. "Well, she's why I came," she said, suddenly needing to make that clear. *He could have changed his shirt in the other room.*

"Mmm," Kal agreed. Hiialo's door was opened just a crack, but he could hear her playing in her room, talking make-believe with her stuffed friends. He leaned against the wall he had framed. "So…you probably want to make sure you like us before we go any further with this."

Erika felt the quilt beneath her—and the bed. Things had gone pretty far. "I don't see anything likely to make me run away."

You haven't seen my daughter throw a tantrum.

But Erika Blade struck him as a woman who wouldn't flee difficulty.

"We can give ourselves as much time as we need," he said. "I was thinking of about six weeks."

Panic stricken, Erika thought she might break into hysterical laughter. *Six weeks* to decide if she wanted to spend the rest of her life in a celibate marriage to a man with more sex appeal than Brad Pitt?

But even making contributions to household expenses, she should be able to make her money last six weeks. And surely she could produce some marketable art in that length of time. "Six weeks sounds reasonable."

Kal nodded. The air in the room felt oppressive, stuffy, and he knew it was because of the topic, the future he'd planned, the prison of a marriage without touch, a marriage to a stranger.

He said, "I'll leave you alone. Maybe we can go swimming later."

She nodded and so did he. Kal hurried out of the room, then the house. Moments later as he stood on the lanai quaffing the air, he realized he hadn't been fleeing the awkwardness. He'd been getting away from Erika Blade's tawny arms and legs, her narrow bare feet, her brown hair and eyes. He was fleeing the woman herself.

Because he found her very beautiful, which was the last thing he'd expected.

CHAPTER FIVE

THEY AGREED ON A SWIM before dinner.

At five Kal threw on some faded red surfing trunks and went into Hiialo's room to tell her to put on her swimsuit. She was playing with her new stuffed puppy, whom she'd named Fluff. Kal wondered if Erika liked dogs.

"Hiialo, want to go swimming?"

"Yes! Hooray!" She tucked Fluff in a shoe box she'd lined with doll blankets, and then hurried to her closet, which looked about like his, a pit, and began throwing her clothes around, looking for a swimsuit.

Kal went out into the front room.

Erika was on the lanai, dressed in a coral swimsuit, a sarong around her waist. He could see the muscles in her suntanned back. *Strong.* Unaware of him, she crouched to touch a Mexican creeper growing beside the veranda. She studied it with the intense concentration he'd noticed before, as though she had to take a test on it later. He saw her eyes drop slightly, her lids brush her cheeks, and she swallowed.

Emotional... Whatever she felt, Kal understood. She'd just moved in with a stranger she'd met through a want ad.

He walked out onto the lanai and Erika straightened. He said, "You've got a towel. I was going to ask if you needed one."

"No, I—I brought everything."

"Literally?"

Erika met his eyes, and her heart moved from her chest to her throat. "Yes." She'd even sold the Karmann Ghia. "I don't own much. I've always lived on boats."

The way she said it made him wonder. She must have traveled all the time as a kid. No neighborhood. No best friend, unless it was her brother. Kal had never known anyone who could put all her worldly goods in four pieces of luggage and a cardboard box. "This house is kind of like a boat," he said, "that stays in one place."

His half smile, combined with the sober look in his eyes, made Erika feel he knew things she'd never told him.

Hiialo bounded out of the house, clutching her Pocahontas beach towel. "Let's go. Come on, Eduardo." She shouted, "Can we go in the outrigger, Daddy?"

Erika made the kind of involuntary wince someone does when the music comes on too loud. *Because of Hiialo?* Kal wondered. That would be bad. If his daughter was an amplifier, she would go up to eleven. Higher than high, louder than loud. "Not today."

Barefoot, Erika stepped down to the soft green lawn. The thatch was short and dense, different grass than she knew on the mainland. The warm earth invited her to sink in roots. She wanted to. She could be happy surrounded by so much color.

As Kal grabbed a faded towel from the clothesline, Hiialo bounded ahead toward the drive. Erika peered after her, then back at Kal. Her eyes were caught by a tree with white flowers and round waxy leaves. On one of the leaves, someone had etched a picture, a childish drawing of a girl in a dress.

Erika touched the leaf.

"That's an autograph tree," said Kal. "You can scratch something on the leaves when they're young, and the image grows with the leaves. Here." He picked up a twig from the ground and pulled an autograph leaf toward him. With the twig he wrote, "ALOHA, ERIKA," then let the leaf spring away.

Erika had been watching his hands. "Thanks."

They both turned toward the sea.

As they followed Hiialo down the drive, Erika again noticed the evergreens shading the beach. "Are those pine trees?"

"They're ironwoods. Some people call them Australian pines, but they're not true pines. They were introduced as windbreaks."

"Oh."

By the time the adults reached the beach, Hiialo had splashed into the surf. Erika glanced at Kal, but he seemed unconcerned.

He shouldn't let her go in alone like that. A seadweller all her life, Erika had strong feelings about children and water.

She dropped her towel in the sand near the high-tide line, and so did Kal. Casting her a quick smile, he turned toward the ocean and was soon wading after Hiialo. He dove into the breakers and came up with his skin glistening wet, his hair suddenly darker, yet still tinseled with blondish highlights.

Hiialo swam to him. "Let me dive off your shoulders!"

Erika limped into the foam. Small fish darted about on a reef under the surface. She waded over the wet rocks, then lowered her body into the sea and swam away from the shore, away from the reef. The water was cellophane clear. From the surface, she spotted a stingray and a dogfish. Unafraid of the ocean or its inhabitants, she swam out to Kal and Hiialo as Hiialo dove off his shoulders, then emerged, sputtering and small. Wiping hair from her eyes, she dog-paddled to her father's waiting arms.

As Hiialo wrapped herself around him like a koala on

a eucalyptus branch, Erika watched Kal's face. His eye-lashes were thick dark triangles, drawn to points by the salt water, and his eyebrows were black against his skin and his fairer hair. His face was not so much rugged and craggy as sensual, his lips one commanding feature, his eyes another. A straight well-shaped nose. The muscles in his arms and back shifted in the reflected light from the water as he lifted Hiialo, helping her stand on his shoulders again.

Her throat closing, Erika gave herself some quick advice.

Whatever happened, she mustn't fall in love with Kal.

KAL HAD SPENT a year as prep cook at the Hanalei Grind and watched the chef every chance he had. In honor of Erika's arrival, he prepared shrimp with a spicy Cajun sauce. He'd been surprised months before to learn that red peppers and garlic wouldn't irritate his stomach, could in fact be beneficial. Which was good. Giving up beer was hard enough.

While he cooked, with Nirvana playing from the front room speakers wired to the stereo in his room, Hiialo showed Erika her Barbie collection. Leaving the sauce simmering, Kal went into the bathroom, and before he turned on the shower he heard them talking.

"Oh, can I put that dress on her, Hiialo?"

Kal turned on the water, drowning the voice that, until today, he'd heard only on the phone—the voice that now had become one of the sounds of his house. He rinsed off the salt, soaped down, squirted shampoo on his hair. He was out in three minutes, and he shaved, then slipped into his room and pulled on a pair of baggy cotton shorts and the new shirt Erika had given him. After checking on dinner, he moved toward Hiialo's room. As he started to part the curtains and look in, he heard Erika say, "Who's this?"

"That's my mother and me."

Kal closed his eyes, listening.

"She's pretty, Hiialo."

"Daddy says I look like her. But mostly like me."

Erika had a low rich laugh. A kind laugh.

Kal stood in the shadows of the front room, not noticing that the sun was down and he hadn't yet turned on a lamp.

Sitting on the edge of Hiialo's bed, Erika examined the face in the photograph, the woman whose image was missing from the first photo Kal had mailed her. The woman he'd loved so much.

Maka was strongly built, with long wavy black hair and an infectious grin somehow made more attractive by the fact that her small teeth were fairly crooked. She looked like...fun. Clearly she was enjoying the baby she bounced in her lap. *A hula dancer...*

Erika remembered Kal's single bed and felt something too much like jealousy. But that was ridiculous.

The curtain on the door moved and he stuck his head in. "Dinner's ready."

Erika stood up while Hiialo turned off the dragon lamp, leaving her Barbies on the bed.

In the other room Kal switched on a light over the stove. "Hiialo and I usually sit out on the porch when the weather's nice." Taking plates from the cabinet, he started as Erika came up beside him.

"Oh, sorry. Let me help." She took the plates from him. "Silverware?"

"I'll get it!" Hiialo sprinted across the room and opened the drawer. It came out, and all the jar lids and silverware and knives with chipped blades crashed to the floor.

There was a silence. Seeing Hiialo's face begin to fall, Kal said, "It's okay."

But she was going to cry. *No. Don't, Hiialo.*

Erika set the plates on the counter and stooped to help gather the utensils.

Hiialo bit her lip, tears brimming, and Kal didn't breathe. Erika helped her pick up the things from the drawer, and he could see she was trying not to look at his daughter, not to make the four-year-old cry. It made him like her.

Kal scooped up Hiialo, held her against him, kissed her. "Find us some napkins, Ti-leaf, yeah?"

She nodded, blinking back her tears, and then she shimmied down out of his arms. "I'll pick up everything, Erika. You just relax on the porch."

Kal bit down a smile. She sounded like her grandmother. On the *haole* side, the Caucasian side. His mom.

Erika lifted her eyes and smiled at Hiialo. "Are you sure I can't help?"

Hiialo worked her mouth as she did when she was thinking. At last she said, "Okay." She squatted in her bare feet and bare legs beside Erika and collected some silverware. "Should we wash it, Daddy?"

"Yes."

Kal watched Erika's hair tumble in front of her, showing her bare shoulders. She was wearing a plain pale yellow dress with narrow straps, and as she bent over he could see the tops of her breasts, high smallish breasts he had noticed in her wet swimsuit.

He turned back to the food, trying to remember what had been happening before Hiialo pulled out the drawer.

The phone rang.

Erika tensed.

The telephone hung on the wall next to the refrigerator, beside the hallway. Kal lifted the receiver. "Hello?"

Erika thought she heard a woman's voice on the line.

"Hi, Mom.... Yes.... Yes." He pressed the mute button and addressed Erika, who was taking silverware to the sink. Her dress brushed his leg. "Want to have dinner at my parents' house Wednesday? It's my birthday."

A birthday. He'd be thirty-one. When she was thirty-one, she'd been in a car accident. And after that... Thirty-one had been a bad year. "Sure. If you do," she added, taking more silverware from Hiialo's small hands.

Kal put the phone to his ear again. "Okay. Thank you. We'll come. What should we bring?"

"Can we see the puppies?" demanded Hiialo.

Kal ignored her.

Erika whispered, "Do your grandparents have puppies?"

"They have two litters," said Hiialo. "I can't play with the new puppies yet, but the other ones might be big enough. They look just like my puppy you gave me. But we can't have a dog," she added, sounding resigned. "Daddy has to work too much. So I have Eduardo."

The *mo'o*. Erika found Hiialo's attitude surprisingly mature—and a little sad. Children should be able to have pets, but she knew Kal was being responsible. He didn't have time for a dog. If she was there...

But how likely was that—really?

Ten minutes later Kal sat on the porch steps while Hiialo and Erika shared the swing. The shrimp was messy, and they needed the dish towels Hiialo had brought from the linen cupboard—makeshift napkins.

Hiialo talked, and Kal hardly had to think, only eat and stare across the dark yard at the rusted white Datsun, which burned a quart of oil a week and needed new tires. New everything. The night was damp and fragrant.

"My uncle Danny—I just call him Danny, but he's my uncle," said Hiialo. "He's a hula dancer, and he teaches me hula sometimes...."

Kal picked up another shrimp.

"This is great, Kal."

Erika had spoken, and he glanced up in surprise. "Thanks."

"My dad is a mugician, too," said Hiialo. "He plays the guitar."

In the glow from the light at the end of the porch, Erika smiled. "I know. Will you play something for us, Kal?"

Hiialo set aside her plate and jumped down from the porch swing, knocking her fork to the ground. "I'll get his guitar."

"Hiialo."

She stopped.

Kal raised his eyebrows at the fork, then at her plate. "Grandma made chocolate-chip macadamia-nut cookies. Don't you want some?"

"Cookies!" she exclaimed.

He wondered how she'd planned to get down a guitar. They both hung high on the wall, and the National was too heavy for her to lift.

Hiialo took her plate inside, ending conversation on the lanai.

The tension eased from Erika's body.

The trade winds breathed on them.

By and by Kal said, "I've arranged to take an extra day off tomorrow. I thought you and Hiialo and I could do something together. Picnic. Sight-seeing. Also, you may as well know, my mom's not going to be satisfied to wait until Wednesday night to get a look at you."

Erika didn't smile. "How are your parents reacting to this?"

He was bringing a piece of shrimp to his mouth. He put it back on his plate. "Um...they know I..." He slowed down. There was no reason to tell her that his parents knew how much he missed Maka. "It's okay with them. They don't know... I don't talk to them about my sex life." Taking a breath, he retreated to a point of safety. "Anyhow, you're an artist. Art is their main thing, besides their dogs. They're prepared for the best."

That thought made Erika more nervous than if he'd said his parents were disapproving.

Kal stood up, picked up his own plate, then reached for hers. "Let's have some cookies."

Inside, Hiialo was standing on a chair washing her plate at the sink. He said, "You're a good girl, Hiialo. You want to wash these plates too?"

"Okay."

Twenty minutes later, they had finished the cookies, and he brought out the chrome resonator guitar. When she saw the instrument, Erika exclaimed, "How beautiful! Do you play Hawaiian music? What do you call it—slack-key?"

"Sure." He played everything. He sat down on the steps.

On the swing beside Erika, Hiialo looked sleepy and dissatisfied. The other guitar, the Gibson, was the guitar for playing "Puff." But she liked Hawaiian music, too, and when he began to play "Ua Kea O Hana," she made no complaint.

Even the opening notes were magical popular Hawaii. But when Kal began to sing, Erika's body hummed in response. His voice was powerful, rough and earthy, raking her heart.

When the song ended, she said, "You're great."

"My dad has perfect pitch," Hiialo informed her.

"I believe it." Such a voice. And he was good with that guitar. "Play something else."

"Puff," said Hiialo, not quite under her breath.

It was almost her bedtime. Kal told her, "Brush your teeth while I play another for Erika. After that I'll play 'Puff.'"

Once Hiialo had gone inside, he tuned the guitar to open G and played blues—Robert Johnson's "Come on in My Kitchen.'' Then he went inside for the Gibson, played ''Puff the Magic Dragon'' for Hiialo, and afterward he put her to bed.

Erika went into Hiialo's room to say good-night to her. It felt a little like baby-sitting, and it made her think of Chris, her nephew. Of three dark and difficult years. During. Maneuvering her wheelchair in the narrow confines of the *Skye*. Accidents and private struggles. Emotional exchanges between her and David. *Look, if you fall, don't just lie there. Call for me.* Silent nights full of taunting ghosts.

''Good night, Hiialo.''

''Good night, Erika.'' Hiialo hugged her new puppy. ''I love Fluff.''

Erika hoped Hiialo would love her as easily—and that Kal would accept her. She slipped past his tall body, unable to escape brushing his warmth, and pushed between the curtains in the doorway. Behind her, she heard the soft tones of him saying good-night to Hiialo and imagined him hugging her, tucking her in.

When he emerged, he went to the refrigerator and took out the bottle of beer Erika had brought from the mainland. ''Want some?''

''Sure.''

His back to her, he grabbed a plastic bottle from the counter, shook out a couple of tablets and popped them in his mouth. He noticed Erika watching. ''Ulcer.''

You're pretty young to have an ulcer. But what did she know about it?

He divided the bottle of beer between two mugs, and they went outside. There was room for three or four people on the porch swing, but he let Erika have it to herself and sank down on the steps against a post.

They tried the beer before she asked, ''Have you ever played professionally?''

''Oh…sure.'' He didn't want to get into it. It could

make him bitter in a hurry. He watched the night, the leaves lifting with a breath of wind. He heard the ocean, saw the quality of light change as the high beam of a full moon rose in the trees on the other side of the driveway.

On the swing, she waited.

Music. "Before Hiialo was born, Maka and I lived in Honolulu. We actually worked together for a while. I was in a *hapa haole* band. We played Waikiki hotels. Maka's hula group danced with us."

Erika had leaned forward. Her chin was in her hand. Listening.

"Then I had another band, Kai Nui. We're...we were kind of...I guess now they'd call us 'alternative.' We played a lot of rock and roll, but a little bit of everything. Our own songs were hard to classify, I guess." Hard to classify, but good enough to win the favor of the biggest island label—and the attention of the biggest of the late-night talk-show hosts. Later that hadn't mattered. Except to rub him raw inside. "We moved back here when Maka got pregnant. To be near our families. We had a place down in Waimea. Then Maka died, and Iniki leveled our house." And changed his plans. Bad luck. He changed the subject. "Are you afraid of hurricanes?"

Erika considered. When she was a child, the *Siren*, her father's ship, had been near hurricanes, but they'd never been caught in one. "Not especially."

"These houses—" his glance included the stretch to the beach, the whole neighborhood "—they've all been rebuilt in the last three years."

"Were you here during the hurricane?"

"Yeah." Living in a daze without Maka. Drinking rum every night after Hiialo was in bed. Staying up for hours trying to get her to drink goat's milk and formula from a bottle. Crying while she cried—and not just for Maka. "When we knew it was going to hit, I took Hiialo and came up here to be with my folks and my sister. It was pretty bad. The waves were coming up over the telephone poles. My folks' house is *mauka*.'' The inclination of his head indicated the direction inland. ''But they lost their roof, too.''

''*Mauka?*''

''Inland, toward the mountains. *Makai* is toward the sea. Forget compass points.'' Kal remembered his fears that having a *malihini* in the house would be annoying. What he felt now was different. He wanted to help her, so that she wouldn't say something wrong and be hurt by people reacting the way they could.

He returned to the weather. ''It's hurricane season now. A few times a year they say there's one headed this way. It can get to you.''

''You love this place.'' To have stayed through such mayhem.

''It's my home.''

She saw the bright white in the trees. ''There's the moon. I forgot it was full.''

Kal looked over his shoulder.

''I guess it comes from living on ships,'' said Erika. ''I always think home is where the people I love are.''

''Yeah, well, mine—they're here.'' Kal took a drink. In the moonlight, he surveyed the garden, remembering devastation. Wondering why Erika wasn't with the people she loved.

But her brother had remarried. The child she'd helped raise had a new stepmother. Kal wanted to ask her if she missed the kid, but he thought he knew the answer. He thought it had been there, in her letter. Unsaid.

The beer didn't last long.

They went inside, and Erika washed the pots and pans while he put the food away and wiped off the chipped Formica counter. When the last pot was in the drying rack, she said, ''I think I'll turn in.''

''Sure.'' Kal was squeezing out the sponge, wondering

how long he could keep the house clean. He glanced at Erika. "Good night."

"Good night."

Erika knew she shouldn't feel deflated when he turned his back.

In her room, by the full-moon glow that stole through the windows, she found the wall lamp above her bed and switched it on. She shut the blinds and checked that the outside door was locked. Then she undressed, donned an oversize Blade Institute T-shirt and folded back the covers of the bed.

The sheets were soft, clean, new. The mattress was firm. Turning out the light and pulling the covers over her, she felt alone and faraway from anyone who really cared about her. *And low on money...*

Her fingers clutched the edge of the quilt, Kal's birth quilt made by his grandmother, and she tried not to think about his face or the scar above his lip or his shoulders wet in the ocean.

Why had he never said the word "music" to her?

Closing her eyes, she saw him in her mind and wondered things she knew she shouldn't, things that could hurt her in the end. What it would be like to be wanted by him. To be touched by him.

To be loved by him.

CHAPTER SIX

IN THE MORNING, his mother called and invited them over for breakfast.

Kal didn't answer at once.

He'd awoken in the middle of the night, and like always, Maka was dead. But knowing Erika was in the room next door had made it worse. More real. Another sign that he had to go on without his wife. *I can't do this.*

"Kal?" said his mother. "If you have other plans, it's okay."

Erika came down the hall in cutoffs and a white crop top. There were surgical scars on her left knee. Kal had glimpsed them the day before, when they went swimming. Now he wanted to take a good look, but instead, he met her eyes. Remembered her face, so new to him that he'd lost the recollection in sleep.

The future that had seemed gruesome by night suddenly looked salvageable. Erika was a project, someone to learn about. The decision he'd made, asking her to come, was good.

Good to have someone for Hiialo.

He told his mother they'd be over at nine, and he got off the phone and asked Erika if she drank coffee and how she wanted it.

KAL'S PARENTS LIVED in a two-story plantation home set on a hillside above Haena. As Kal reached the foot of their drive, he spotted an elderly Japanese-American couple walking out of the driveway next door. He waved to them, and they waved back, smiling.

"That's Mr. and Mrs. Akana. She was a picture bride, too."

"Picture bride?" asked Erika.

Turning up the driveway, a narrow corridor of green, he smiled a little. "This is actually a very Hawaiian thing we're doing." He explained about picture brides.

Erika thought, *How silly I was last night, feeling alone.* What if she had never been anywhere before in her life and she had come to Hawaii from Japan to meet her new husband? What if she'd never spoken with him on the phone first? What if all she'd had, all he'd had, was a picture? She twisted around in her seat, trying to see the older couple, but the vegetation hid them from sight. After a moment Erika said, "It does sound a little like us." Though surely the Akanas shared a bed.

The wide second-floor veranda of the Johnsons' house appeared through the foliage. At the end of the drive was a patio with a red Subaru station wagon and a white-and-red Ford Ranger parked nearby. On the *mauka* side of the house, a volleyball net divided a lawn ringed with tropical flowers. On the *makai* side, facing the sea a half mile away, were the kennel runs.

As Erika got out of the car, carrying two jars of Java plum jam that Kal had handed to her before they left the bungalow, she heard dogs barking, and a giant with a fluffy white coat came snuffling up to her side.

"Raiden," Kal said, a hint of sternness in his voice. The Akita took his wagging tail toward him. "Good boy."

Hiialo clambered out of the car on Erika's side just as the front door opened and a woman came out. Erika recognized Mary Helen Johnson from the pictures Kal had sent. She tried to quiet her nerves as the woman moved toward them, her eyes on Erika with an expression of pleasure.

Kal abandoned Raiden and joined Erika. He couldn't remember the first time his folks had met Maka. Now he was introducing them to Erika, who might become his wife but would never be what Maka had been to him. "Mom, this is Erika Blade. Erika, Mary Helen Johnson, my mom."

"Hi, Erika. I'm so glad you're here." Mary Helen tossed highlighted blond bangs back from her eyes. "Oh, look, you brought us some jam! Kal buys this at the Haena Store. There's an old man who sells it outside. Come on in." She peered about the gardens and kennels. "I thought your dad was out here somewhere, Kal."

As they stepped through a generous foyer into a spacious family room, King Johnson came through the sliding glass doors, his white hair damp with sweat from some exertion. He shut the screen before he turned to face the others.

Mary Helen was saying to Erika and Kal, "You have to see the puppies."

"I want to see them now," said Hiialo.

King caught her up. "Even before you say hello to your old Grandpa?"

"Hi, Grandpa." Hiialo hugged him. Grinning in his arms, she said, "Can I see the puppies? Erika brought me a stuffed puppy, and it looks just like an Akita."

"Well, did she now. Hello, Erika. I'm King."

"It's nice to meet you." It *was* nice. She hadn't counted on their being so ready to welcome her, to like her.

But then she thought of Kal's single bed.

Erika felt like a fraud. She hoped they weren't anticipating more grandchildren.

Mary Helen showed them into a living room with a ceramic-tile floor. Erika sat with Kal on a blue-and-white plaid sofa while King brought one of the Akita puppies inside for Hiialo to play with.

It was cute, a deep rust fluff-ball with a black muzzle, and resembled nothing so much as a teddy bear—or the stuffed animal she'd given Hiialo.

"This is one of Kumi's puppies," King told Kal.

"How old is he?" asked Erika.

"Six weeks. We have another litter outside that's just a week old."

Kal watched Hiialo take the puppy in her lap. A moment later Erika left the couch and knelt beside her. She stroked the dog with her graceful artist's hands. Long fingers, practical nails with no polish. They showed her age. Her hair fell in front of her as she and Hiialo petted the Akita.

King brought in another puppy and set it down in front of Erika. This one had a much paler coat. "Want one?"

She said with appreciation and, Kal thought, tact, "Who wouldn't want one?"

"Daddy, can we get one this time?" asked Hiialo. *"Please."*

Kal shook his head.

Her mouth twisted, but for once she didn't beg.

Erika stroked the lighter-colored puppy. "Hi, you." The puppy licked her hands, and she made up her mind that if she did return to the mainland, she would find a place to live that allowed pets. But the thought reminded her of her financial situation, and she grew worried. What was she going to do? David would help her, of course, but she would never ask. He'd done enough for her.

Kal left the couch and sat down on the floor beside her, and Erika handed him the puppy. "Here."

Accepting the ball of fur, Kal lay back on the tile floor. "Hey, you little monster." As the puppy crawled on him, he felt Erika watching. But when he looked at her, her color deepened and she turned away.

Hiialo abandoned her puppy and came and sat on his stomach.

Kal groaned.

King corralled the deserted puppy and took him outside, and Kal let the other puppy lick his neck while Hiialo tried to grab the animal. Then Raiden's big head appeared above him, and a full-grown Akita-size tongue slurped across his face.

Kal sat up, not wanting to be belly-up to anything that big.

His father scooped up the remaining puppy, six hundred dollars' worth of purebred dog. "Raiden. Go lie down."

The giant obeyed.

Erika kept her eyes away from Kal. She should have guessed that he was a man who would lie on the floor and let children and dogs climb all over him. She liked men like that. And she already liked Kal too much.

Not that she'd want to have sex with him or anything. *Yuck,* she reminded herself.

She stood up, and Kal, beside her, wondered how she'd respond if he began nibbling on her calf. Or licking her. He restrained the uncivilized urge. She didn't seem like she was even used to being around dogs, let alone people who sometimes forgot they weren't dogs themselves. She jumped whenever Hiialo talked loudly or ran in the house.

When King had taken both puppies outside, Mary Helen offered everyone passion fruit or guava juice, kona coffee, bagels, mangoes and mango bread. "Mango season," explained Kal.

They ate in the living room. Hiialo knelt on the tile floor beside the coffee table, and no one bothered her about crumbs or dripping mangoes. Mary Helen turned the conversation to art and suggested places Erika might enjoy painting. "The Hanalei Bridge is a great landscape scene. Of course, I know you have your niche."

"Actually," said Erika, "I'm trying to go a little broader. I want to try something new in Hawaii." *Like selling something.* Kal's parents seemed interested, but Erika again felt her fraudulence. She had to talk to Kal about money. She'd try to paint again first, but—

"Do you have any new prints coming out?" asked Mary Helen.

"Just *Sand Castles.*" Erika looked at Kal. *Change the subject.*

Kal saw the silent plea in her eyes, but he wasn't sure what she wanted. Finally he put his arm around her and drew her against his side.

Erika shuddered.

Kal's stomach went warm. When his penis stirred, he shifted slightly. Less surprised than disturbed.

Mary Helen broke the silence. "You know, Erika, it would be fun if we could talk you into coming in and working at the gallery someday. Just sitting in a corner painting. An artist in residence." She added, "We sell mainly prints, but we do have some original pieces, as well."

Erika could feel Kal's heartbeat. His hand was stroking her arm, almost absently. "I'd love to." Her voice cracked. "Let me know what day." *Work at the gallery. Maybe Mary Helen and King would give her a job. Oh, no, she couldn't ask. They were absolutely the last people who should know she was destitute.*

"Can I come?" asked Hiialo, settling onto the couch beside her and spilling crumbs between the cushions.

Erika hesitated, turning to Kal. He was oblivious. Taking his arm from around her, he picked up an embroidered pillow. He set it in his lap and explored the floral design with his fingers.

"Hiialo spends each Tuesday at the gallery with us, anyway," said King. "It's up to Erika, Hiialo."

"Of course you can come," Erika told her.

The teakettle whistled in the kitchen, and King and Mary Helen both leapt up. Erika wondered if they were going to talk about her over the stove. Leaning forward, she reached for a glass of passion-fruit juice on the glass-topped coffee table. When she sat back, Kal's hand came up to touch the side of her mouth. His thumb wiped something away.

"Mango pulp," he said.

Erika sank deeper into the cushions. The right side of her body pressed against his left, but neither of them moved. When she dared a glance at him, he was watching her with his lips slightly parted, his eyes sweeping over her.

Her own face got hot, and she drank her juice, trying not to think.

THEY STAYED at his parents' house for an hour, and before they left they went out to the kennel runs to see the younger puppies. King slipped into the whelping shed with Jin, the mother, and he held the puppies up one by one so that Erika and Hiialo and Kal could see them.

One of the pups had markings almost identical to his mother's. A sharply defined white patch began midway on his chest and stretched down his legs and all along his belly. The rest of him was rust-colored except for his black ears and mask. He didn't protest being picked up by King, and Jin allowed it with the calm of a madonna.

"You've got an all-white one, Dad." Kal peered over the waist-high door of the shed.

"She's sold."

Erika was smiling at the puppy he held. "I like that one."

"Yeah. He looks like Jin." Jin was Kal's favorite of his parents' dogs, in looks, temperament and brains.

Hiialo lost interest in the puppies. Squatting in the gravel, she began to draw a picture with a stick.

"I've always thought of Akitas as aggressive," Erika said. "Your dogs are so nice."

"Well, all the spitz breeds are independent," admitted King, returning the puppy to its mother and letting himself out of the shed. "But you won't find a more loyal animal. You probably haven't heard the story of Hachiko."

"I'll tell her in the car, Dad," said Kal. "We've got to go." The day off was rare, and he and Erika and Hiialo had a lot of getting to know one another to do.

They said goodbye to Kal's mother, who surprised Erika with a quick embrace.

When they were buckled into the Datsun again, Kal reversed the car and started down the driveway.

Erika said, "So…the dog story."

"Oh, yeah." Kal was grateful to his father for giving them something to talk about. He wouldn't have to examine what had happened during breakfast. "Okay. Hachiko was born in Akita, Japan, in 1923."

"You're good with dates," said Erika.

"Tour guide."

"Tell about the train station!" Hiialo shouted.

Erika wanted to tell her to keep her voice down, but Kal obviously didn't care. She wondered if he was a little deaf. Sometimes musicians were.

"Okay," he was saying, "so Hachiko lived in Tokyo with a Mr. Uyeno, who was his owner. Every day Hachiko accompanied him to the train station and waited there for him to come home in the afternoon. Then, one day, Mr. Uyeno became ill at work and died before he could get home. Hachiko was only sixteen months old, but he never forgot his master. He went to the station every day

to look for Mr. Uyeno, and sometimes he would stay
there several days without returning home.''

Erika felt warmth behind her nose and eyes and wished
she had a tissue.

"He did that for nine years, and as people saw the dog
waiting and growing old, they were so moved that when
he died they decided to erect a statue in his memory.
There's still a statue of Hachiko at that train station.''

"No wonder your folks love that breed,'' Erika said,
blinking hard.

"Loyalty is a good trait. Hey, you're crying.''

Loyalty. Erika thought how loyal he was—to Maka's
memory. That single bed. Would never sleep with another woman.

They had turned onto the main road. "Are we going
back to the house?'' she asked.

"I thought we'd do some sight-seeing. A couple of
waterfalls. The Hanalei pier. We'll go down Waimea side
another day. You have to visit Barking Sands Beach. The
sand barks when you walk on it.''

"Let's take Erika to the *heiau,*'' said Hiialo from the
back seat.

She meant the old hula platform near Keʻe Beach, on
the north shore at the end of the Kuhio Highway, the
main road, the only road. There were actually two sites
of interest there, a *heiau* and a *halau hula,* the site of an
old hula school dedicated to the hula goddess, Laka. It
was a place no visitor should miss, but Kal didn't want
to go there with Erika. For him, it was Maka's place.

"What's a *heiau?*'' asked Erika.

"A temple ruin. After Kamehameha the Great died in
1819, Kamehameha II, who was a Christian, ordered all
the temple buildings and altars destroyed. Only the rock
platforms are left. Hiialo's talking about a place near
Keʻe Beach. There will be a lot of tourists there today. I

thought this evening we'd go to Ke'e in the outrigger, though.''

''And visit the *heiau?*'' asked Hiialo.

''No.''

They drove to a waterfall, walked through a wildlife refuge, then went into Hanalei and ate at a deli there and bought ice-cream cones for dessert. On the way home, Kal saw some little kids with a flower stand beside the old Hanalei Bridge. He pulled over and got out in the liquid sunshine, rain under the sun. Minutes later he was back with two floral bouquets that would have cost a mint on the mainland.

He handed one between the seats to Hiialo, the other to Erika. In the sun, her eyes were the color of mahogany. ''Aloha. Don't cry, eh?''

She smiled. *Good* smile.

''These are beautiful. Do you know the names, Kal?'' She touched a waxy red heart-shaped flower with a long yellow spadix.

''That's an anthurium. I forget the Hawaiian name.'' His suntanned callused hand fingered another with red bracts reaching upward in a pinecone shape. ''This is red ginger, *awapuhi.* This big pointy thing is heliconia. It comes from Mount Helicon in Greece. We've got some at home with more pink in them. Also, red lobsters and hanging heliconia. And these are *okikas.*'' Beneath the bouquet, her nearest thigh was thick with muscle and, at the knee, crisscrossed with surgical scars. The woman who'd survived a car crash.

He wished Maka had.

Easing away from Erika, he started the Datsun and drove home to the drenched garden outside the bungalow.

Before they could get out of the car, Hiialo asked, ''Erika, will you paint with me?''

''Erika might want some time to herself, Hiialo.'' *Or time with me.*

Erika turned around in the car. "Do you like to paint?" Her knee brushed the warmth of Kal's thigh, and she moved it abruptly. *Too much touching...*

"I'm going to be an artist when I grow up," said Hiialo. "Or maybe a hula dancer."

Erika didn't look at Kal, but she wanted to. A hula dancer...

They got out of the car. Hiialo ran through the rain to the porch and kicked off her shoes, but Kal walked more slowly, with Erika. Holding her flowers against her small body, Hiialo opened the door they had left unlocked and padded barefoot into the house. "I'll get you a vase, too, Erika. We use juice pitchers."

Erika climbed to the porch, two steps for each stair. Climb, pull the other leg up.

"Do these steps bother you?" asked Kal. "I could make a ramp."

Erika hugged the flowers in her arms. Her thick rain-dampened hair hung loose around her brandy-colored eyes. "No. I'm fine."

No ramps, she thought.

Kal wished he could read her mind. She'd survived a major accident. Had her injuries affected her sexuality? Why *did* she want a celibate marriage? On the porch beside her, he said, "You and I need to talk story."

"Talk story?" Why was she breathless?

"Shoot the breeze. Get to know each other."

Erika felt she had to sit down.

Hiialo came out to the porch carrying a cumbersome pitcher filled with water. A welcome third party.

Kal took both the pitcher and Erika's flowers. "*Mahalo,* Hiialo." Father and daughter grinned at each other at the rhyme. Kal put the bouquet in the vase, spilling water as the stems displaced it, and handed the pitcher back to Hiialo. "Can you take that to Erika's room?"

"Yes, Daddy."

"Thank you, Hiialo," said Erika.

"You're welcome." She marched back into the house.

Erika sank on the porch swing, and so did Kal. Draping his arms across the back, one hand almost touching Erika's hair, he gently rocked the glider.

His body, Erika estimated, was eighteen inches from hers, and his arm and his hand were behind her. The swing's slow rhythm reminded her of the gentle movement of a boat in its berth. Water splattered from the eaves.

Kal said, "You like to go hiking?"

"Yes."

He nodded slowly, staring out at the rain, his legs stretched out before him. Big. Relaxed.

"I'll have to take you to Waikapalae Cave sometime. You'll like it. You can swim down this tunnel and when you get to the end there's a place called the Blue Room. The light's all blue."

"I'd like that. I need to go painting, too." And how.

She felt something on the ends of her hair and realized Kal was touching her. The moment she discovered it, he stopped.

"Erika, how much of your body was paralyzed?"

Her breath froze. The question was intimate, like his hand on her hair. "Below the waist."

Where sex happens. Kal withdrew his arm from behind her. He couldn't keep his fingers out of her hair. Leaning forward, he tried to see her face. Her head was bowed, hiding her expression. But after a moment she lifted it and met his eyes.

His heart beat off time, and he felt the earth move....

It was just the swing, that he, with his feet on the ground, was rocking. He stilled it. "So...you couldn't feel anything?"

Better explain. But she couldn't; she barely knew him. "Right."

"Did you have someone to help you?"

"At first. Later I learned to do almost everything alone." What she could not do alone she hadn't done.

Kal sensed her withdrawing, shrinking like some kinds of insects did when touched by people. He didn't want to do that to her.

He stood up. "I think I'll play guitar for a while."

"Okay."

He left, and soon Erika heard him turn on the amp. She sat silent, keeping her eyes shut, recovering from his questions, revisiting the past. Wishing she could hide.

You should have told him.

The sounds of the electric guitar filled the house, and she heard running feet inside, Hiialo yelling, "Daddy, play 'Pau Hana'!"

How was she ever going to paint?

But if Kal was playing his guitar, maybe she could go down to the beach. As she got up to walk inside, she heard the guitar break into a beautiful melody with a joyous rock-and-roll tempo. In the hallway Hiialo was dancing. "C'mon, Erika. It's 'Pau Hana.' Let's dance!"

Erika limped over to the refrigerator. "I'd rather watch you." She didn't dance. Would Kal be offended if she asked him to turn down the amp? It couldn't be good for Hiialo's ears—or his. Maybe they were both going deaf.

But then the music paused, and the amp went off. Kal stepped through the beads in the doorway of his room. "Are we kind of loud for you?"

Erika teethed her bottom lip. "I'm not used to an amplifier. But the music's good. I've never heard that song."

"My dad wrote it!"

"Hiialo," said Kal. She was really wound up.

Erika said, "I thought I'd go down to the beach and sketch."

"Can I come?" exclaimed Hiialo.

Erika remembered telling Kal that Chris had come with her when she painted. Oh, what an ill-advised remark. She'd forgotten the fundamental way Chris had been different from other children. For three years after he'd seen his mother fall from the bow of the *Skye,* he had not spoken.

"Maybe Erika would like some space, Hiialo."

She did want space, but this would be a chance to spend time with Hiialo alone. "Hiialo, I'd love for you to come, but I have to explain something. When I draw or paint, I use the same side of my brain that works for language and talking. I can't have a conversation and paint at the same time. Can you bring some toys to the beach and play quietly while I paint?"

Her lips sealed shut, as though no word would escape them, Hiialo nodded.

"Then you may come."

"HOORAY!" She shot off toward her room, muttering to herself, "Whoops, not supposed to talk."

In the unlit hallway Kal asked Erika, "Want me to come, too?"

She shook her head. "We should give this a try alone."

"Good luck." He sounded as though he meant it.

ERIKA ACCOMPLISHED nothing at the beach—nothing worth keeping. Hiialo wasn't the problem; *she* was. She couldn't draw. She couldn't see a picture in her mind.

She had lost her confidence.

After about fifteen minutes Hiialo appeared beside her and said, "I'm going home."

Erika glanced toward the private road. It seemed a long walk for a four-year-old. She gathered her sketch pad, pencil and eraser and stood.

Hiialo said, "Why do you walk that way?"

"Oh." Erika managed a smile. "I was in a car accident. It hurt my knee."

"My mommy died in a car accident."

"I know." Erika wanted to pick her up, but she had too much to carry, so she began trudging through the deep sand up to the drive.

Hiialo, who had demonstrated that she could run like a greyhound, slowed her steps and walked beside her. And after they had gone a few steps, Erika felt a small hand slide into hers.

Immediately she felt the change in perspective a child could bring, the perspective that Chris had given her, that had helped change her from the self-involved person she'd been before her accident. In the past year, she'd lost that perspective, that appreciation for innocence and trust and a child's love. In the past year, she'd become self-centered again.

Her heart solemn, she held tightly to Hiialo's little hand and the comfort it brought.

THEY HAD DINNER early—stir-fry and rice with blackened tofu. While Kal cooked, Erika swept out the front room. Hiialo played make-believe with her stuffed friends on the couch. She was pretending to be Cinderella, being kind to the animals. A few minutes later she asked Erika if she could sweep, and Erika surrendered the broom.

Kal knew the serenity was temporary. Erika had been in his house for twenty-four hours, and Hiialo had been good the whole time. How long could it last?

After dinner on the porch they left the dishes, put on their swimsuits and walked back down to the beach to take a ride in the outrigger. At the edge of Kal's garden, Erika pointed to a tree with hundreds of slender aerial roots and fronds that formed one great pompom. "What's that called?"

"*Lauhala.* We call them walking trees, too. It's an

ancient tree. People used the leaves for sandals and bas-
kets and mats.''

Hiialo skipped ahead, the skirt of her neon green swimsuit bouncing with each step.

"I like learning the names of plants."

"Yeah?" Kal paused, ignoring the fact that his daugh-
ter had gone around the blue house and out of sight.
"Okay, this one's a tropical almond, a *kamani haole*.
You know *'haole'*?"

Erika peered down the driveway toward the crashing
breakers. Where was Hiialo?

"You and I are *haoles*. Hiialo is *hapa haole,* part
white. What's wrong?"

"We should catch up with Hiialo."

"She's all right." Kal crossed the driveway to touch
a cluster of orange hibiscuslike blossoms. "This is a *hou*
tree, not to be confused with the *hau* tree outside Hiialo's
window."

"Kal, is that a private beach?" She was still staring
after Hiialo.

Kal ran his tongue over his teeth. Mainland parenting.
He saw it all the time on tours. "Okay, we'll go." He
smiled and headed toward the sea, and soon they saw
Hiialo crouched on the beach near the high-tide line, poking something with a stick.

She saw Kal and Erika and stood up. To the blob on
the beach, she said, "Aloha, jellyfish."

Reaching her with Kal, Erika saw the blue bubble, the
twenty-foot tentacles stretching down into the water, then
swishing up with the incoming tide. Instinctively she
grasped Hiialo's nearest shoulder, pulling her back.
"That's a Portuguese man-of-war."

"Yeah," Kal agreed. "You usually see them over on
the windward side, east side." He scanned the beach to
make sure it wasn't a jellyfish invasion.

Erika said, "Those tentacles sting, Hiialo."

"I know." Hiialo lifted her face. "My daddy's been stung by one."

"You get box jellyfish here, too, don't you?" Erika asked Kal. Box jellyfish were related to the deadly sea wasp of Australia. Like the man-of-war, they presented a more serious danger to children than adults.

Kal kept his tongue in his cheek and his mouth shut. A week or two, and Erika would relax. Peaceably he said, "Let's take our canoe ride."

As Hiialo had told Erika, the outrigger had been his wedding present from Maka. Danny had found her a deal on the fiberglass canoe, and Maka herself had sanded and varnished the koa arms that attached the outrigger. With bicycle inner tubes, Danny had lashed the arms to the hull.

On the beach Kal uncovered the boat and dragged it down to the water. As he held it in the shallows, Hiialo scrambled in.

"Should I get in, too?" asked Erika.

He nodded. In the deep red glow of the sinking sun, her thighs shone amber against her coral tank suit. When she turned to climb into the canoe, Kal couldn't avert his eyes from the muscular backs of her legs, from the edges of her suit curving over her bottom. He wondered where her tan lines ended. He wondered...a lot of things. Why she'd answered his letter.

Why she wanted a celibate marriage.

If she liked sex.

He pushed the outrigger out into the sea and climbed aboard.

There were two paddles, and Erika took one. Kal divided his attention between speculative admiration of her body and the water turning purple and orange with the sunset. God, the spray felt good. The sea felt good, and the emerald cliffs rising beyond Ke'e Beach were steaming with mist. "Hiialo, what are you doing?"

"There's a crab in the canoe," she answered. "He's alive, but he's afraid of Eduardo."

Kal stopped paddling and bent forward, peering under the seats. Hermit crab. Hiialo was trying to catch him with a bailing cup.

"Kal, do you see that wave? Hiialo, sit down. You'll fall out." Erika had already figured out how she was going to grab her by her life vest if she went in. She was relieved when they reached Ke'e Beach.

As Erika helped Kal pull the canoe up on the sand, he saw a woman walking down the hiking trail that led to the *heiau*. A family was finishing a picnic at the far end of the beach, and a couple lay on towels under the iron-wood trees drinking beer.

Hiialo stripped off her life vest and ran toward the water, yelling, "Watch me bodysurf!"

Erika called, "Hiialo, wait!"

"She's all right," said Kal. "Relax."

Erika held her breath as Hiialo caught a wave and surfed into the beach on her stomach. Standing up in the wet sand, she looked for Kal, who came to join her in the low foam.

"Good ride, Ti-leaf."

"I'm going to build a sand castle, Daddy."

Erika watched her sprint across the sand to the outrigger, her feet slipping, to get her toys. Kal wasn't cautious with her. Someone should tell him—

Just go in the water. It's his kid.

Her conscience preaching a different message, Erika waded into the ocean and swam out over the first low breakers, then turned to look back at the beach. Kal was behind her, coming up for air, sparkling wet.

Erika searched until she found Hiialo alone on the shore over by the outrigger. "Are you sure you should let her bodysurf?"

Kal blinked, stood up, tossed water from his hair. "What?"

Hiialo pulled a green bucket and a blue cup out of the canoe and hurried purposefully down to the water. She was so small. "There are a lot of spinal injuries associated with bodysurfing."

As they floated over a wave together, he threw her a look. "So, you worry a lot, yeah?"

A remarkable comment from a man with an ulcer. "No, I don't." She hesitated only a moment, recalling Hiialo running down to the beach ahead of them—and out of sight. Then that jellyfish. "It's just that accidents are the greatest danger children face. I mean, literally, the leading cause of death to children." Time to stop. She'd said plenty.

Kal stared *mauka* at his daughter. Erika was afraid she'd made him angry. But all he said was, "You can't stop accidents."

Erika knew where that had come from. She couldn't let it go unchallenged. "Sometimes you can."

Kal swallowed. He'd had enough of the topic. "I have to work tomorrow." His stomach burned.

Erika took the hint. "Do you want me to watch Hiialo?"

"I'd like it." Kal tried to forget her ominous warnings. Jellyfish, bodysurfing… He couldn't stand the thought of something happening to Hiialo. Why did people do that to themselves, worry like that?

The frightening possibilities at which Erika had hinted had the power to make him cry, and he ducked under the water, clearing his eyes. When he came up, she was still there, vigilantly eyeing the shore. Her beautiful profile was in shadow. It made him angry that she'd upset him— and that she could excite him, too.

Disliking the combination, he turned away and looked for a wave to ride in to his daughter.

CHAPTER SEVEN

HE SHOULD HAVE GOTTEN Hiialo to bed sooner.

"I ruined it," she was saying now.

Kal stopped playing, his fingers poised on the guitar strings. He was sitting on the bed in Erika's room while she and Hiialo painted at the art table. Hiialo sat on books stacked on a chair to reach the table. For the past hour, she had been working on a picture of a whale and Kal's outrigger.

"You can fix that," said Erika. "Here, let me show you how."

"No."

Kal laid down the Gibson as he saw Hiialo's lower lip go out. Kilauea preparing to erupt.

She reached for a new piece of the inexpensive art paper Erika had provided.

"No, Hiialo," Erika said. "Would you like to fix your mistake?"

"No!"

Kal stood up.

Hiialo snatched up her painting and ripped it in two, then crumpled the pieces.

Kal breathed her name. "Hiialo—"

"Why did you do that, Hiialo?" asked Erika. "It was just a little mistake. You put a lot of time into that."

Starting to cry, Hiialo turned away from the table and lifted her arms to Kal.

He didn't pick her up, but the anger he felt was at

Erika. Would it have killed her to let Hiialo have another piece of paper?

Hiialo rubbed her eyes, sobbing. Tired. Kal glanced toward the window, then at the digital clock beside Erika's bed. Nine-fifteen. Forty-five minutes past bedtime. "Hiialo, why don't you say good-night to Erika and thank her for the painting lesson?"

Hiialo slid down off the books, and Kal caught her as she stumbled in her bare feet. She was wiping her eyes, still crying. "Good night, Erika. Thank you."

"You're welcome, sweetheart." Erika kept her own feelings inside. Kids acted out sometimes. And Hiialo was probably up too late. Ripping up the painting had been a bratty move, but it was her own picture, after all.

Chris would never have done anything like that, though.

Chagrined, Erika recalled her own certainty that she could be a good mother, that she could love Hiialo. And she remembered Hiialo's hand in hers on the beach.

"Daddy, pick me up."

"Please."

"Please," whimpered Hiialo.

Kal lifted her and pushed open the door to her room.

"Shall I run a bath for her?" asked Erika. Hiialo had already smudged her dad's shirt with blue paint.

Kal shook his head. "In the morning." He'd have to get her up early—or let Erika do it. He could feel Hiialo's sleepy head on his shoulder. She sniffled, her tears abating. For the moment.

As she cleaned up the paints and gathered the brushes, Erika heard Kal in Hiialo's room. "No. You have to brush your teeth."

"I'm too tired."

"In the bathroom."

"I'm too tired!" Hiialo screamed.

Erika took the brushes to the kitchen to wash them. As

Hiialo's screams echoed through the bungalow, two figures appeared behind the screen door. "Aloha!"

Danny. Kal was carrying Hiialo into the bathroom. Though her cries mellowed, she barely looked toward the door. Very tired, thought Kal, if she wasn't wriggling out of his arms to run and greet her uncle.

Danny and Jakka pushed open the screen door and stepped inside, holding two six-packs.

"Whaddascoops, Hiialo?" said Danny.

She turned her head away.

Kal gestured toward the bathroom. "*Pau.* Bedtime. This is Erika. Erika, Danny Kekahuna. Jakka Bennee. They're cousins." He grinned and reminded her of the Hawaiian concept of *ohana.* "We're all cousins." He shrugged at Danny. "Brothers."

Maka's brother. Erika wiped her hands. "Hi, Danny. Hi, Jakka." Her nerves were raw, her thoughts uncharitable. *If Hiialo was an angel, Kal wouldn't have had to advertise…*

Getting a handle on her emotions, Erika focused on Kal's friends. Danny was a handsome Hawaiian, not quite as tall as Kal but probably about his age. Long-haired, strong. Jakka was large, amiable, friendly.

Hiialo's bedtime dragged. Fussing about brushing her teeth. Then wanting to learn hula from Danny. Erika's annoyance grew. Chris had never thrown tantrums, and David would never have stood for it the way Kal did. In a tone without conviction, he said, "No hula. Get in bed."

Erika could see the child collecting about twenty stuffed animals from the floor while Kal lounged in the doorway, on Hawaiian time.

His friends put the beer in the refrigerator and wandered into his room. One of them plugged in his guitar and amplifier, turned it up, turned it down and began playing something that sounded like "White Rabbit."

The noise and the late hour shifted Erika's sympathies to Hiialo. A child needed peace at night. And a regular bedtime. The night before, she'd gotten the impression Hiialo at least had that.

When Kal emerged from Hiialo's room after kissing her good-night, he glanced at Erika, then went to his own room to join his friends. She couldn't make out what they said, only a warm sound of shared laughter. The amplifier went off, the latches on the guitar case snapped closed, the beads rustled.

The men returned to the front room. With a smile at Erika, Danny opened the refrigerator and took out a beer. He held it up, offering it to her. She shook her head, and Kal didn't take one, either.

Ulcer. Yes, she could see it.

Danny and Jakka sat down near the coffee table, Danny in the torn overstuffed brown chair, Jakka on the couch.

Kal lingered in the kitchen. Erika was washing a couple of glasses.

He said, "Why don't you leave those?"

She didn't stop. "I grew up on boats. It's habit—the way I do things."

"Want to sit down with us?"

Erika turned off the water and followed him to the couch.

Danny said, "So your name is Blade, like the undersea explorer? Christopher Blade! I used to watch him all the time on TV."

"He was my dad."

Danny grinned, his teeth lighting up his face. "You're famous. So wait. That means your brother's the guy who—" He stopped, then waved his hand, brushing away his blunder. "Forget it."

Erika tried. But she could tell that Danny's unfinished remark had made Kal curious. He was glancing between the two of them. *You knew it would come up, Erika.* Skye's death had made national news.

Dammit. The guilt came, and she knew it would spend the night. Along with what-ifs she sometimes thought were behind her.

Danny drained his beer, changed the subject. "So, Kal, your folks have Akita puppies. I'm going to get one this time, already told them. Your dad, he's the best. He promised me a deal."

"We saw them today. Both litters." Kal remembered the puppy who looked like Jin, the puppy Erika had liked. It would be gone in a week. Sold. Unless he said something to his dad.

Jakka intruded on Erika's thoughts. "So now that you're here, Kal can play music again, yeah?"

Play music again? Her heart beat hard. She'd missed something.

Like maybe the reason he'd advertised for a wife? Someone to watch his daughter while he stayed out till two in the morning, playing in nightclubs? Erika didn't want to believe it. From what she knew of his schedule, he didn't see enough of Hiialo as it was. Then again, Hiialo wasn't awake at two in the morning.

Yes, in that context, a celibate marriage made perfect sense.

Erika suddenly felt hollow inside.

Kal stared at the coffee table as though lost in thought.

Danny said, "Hey, Kal, I got a new CD player."

The conversation turned, and after a few minutes Erika excused herself to go to bed.

Kal waited until he'd heard all the end-of-the-day sounds—water running in the bathroom, bedroom door shutting—before he asked Danny, "What were you saying about her brother?"

"Oh!" Danny slapped his forehead. "Didn't mean to

embarrass her.'' He looked from Jakka to Kal and whispered, ''I think he killed his wife.''

''Honest kine?'' Incredulous, Jakka leaned forward, listening.

''She was rich. He got *twenty million dollars,* maybe more.''

Kal's head was spinning.

Danny saw his dismay. He tipped back his beer. ''You got to read the paper.''

Jakka said, ''We should get some gigs again.''

Talk switched to pidgin, the language of locals, and for a while Kal let himself dream with his friends. The way it used to be. Playing wherever they wanted, recording... His stomach hurt. He didn't have time for music. Anyhow, if they were going to play for money again...

He eyed his brother-in-law. Ever since Kai Nui had nominally disbanded, Danny had been devoting his energy to hula. Kal knew everything that meant, and ulcer pain made him want to pick a fight.

Jakka and Danny were talking about a new club in Hanalei, the Hunakai, which in the past two years had become the music hub of the north shore. The others were daydreaming about playing there, but Kal, feeling trapped and mean, said, ''We can't have a band again.''

Both friends sat back. Blinked at him.

Jakka cracked a smile. ''We still got a band, Kal. We got a tape out there.''

It was four years old, like Hiialo. People had forgotten Kai Nui. Kal said, ''Danny has too many obligations to his *halau.*'' He knew from living with Maka the allegiance a dancer felt to his or her school. Danny had moved on from the band, placed his loyalties elsewhere.

Danny's face seemed to pale slightly, the muscles to become rock-like. His stare was as unwavering as Kal's. But he said nothing.

That's what I thought. They couldn't go back to the

way things had been. Kal knew he should go to sleep—
before his bitterness found more words.

Jakka turned to Danny. ''So, yeah, how is it, brah?
Say, we get the band together again. Are you a drummer
or a hula dancer?''

Kal felt sick. Suddenly afraid of the loss of friendship—more than friendship, because Danny was family—he said, ''We're not getting the band together. Just
drop it.'' He stood up and went to the sink for some
water, wishing they would leave. He couldn't stand thinking about Kai Nui. Or about driving into Hanalei to work
the next day.

The others stood up, too, and followed. Kal felt Danny
beside him. His brother-in-law said in a mock-British ac-
cent, '''Where are we going, fellas?'''

Kal smiled, the pangs inside him intensifying at the
familiar quote. Beatles trivia. They used to do this a lot,
though in the past he'd been the one leading them. '''To
the top, Johnny!''' Pretending he still believed it.

Leaning against the counter on his other side, Jakka
said, '''Where's that, fellas?'''

Kal forced a smile, not wanting to make his friends
feel as shitty as he did. He and Danny said in unison,
'''To the toppermost of the poppermost!'''

They all stood there together in reverent silence for a
moment. Then Kal looked at Jakka and at his brother-in-
law, and Danny's brown eyes were looking right back at
him. Yes, if Kai Nui became a band again, Danny would
be with him all the way. Danny was not Maka, and for
him hula was an expression of his fealty to rhythm. And
to music.

Standing between his two best friends, Kal tried to ease
the tension in his abdomen, tried not to think of the weeks
and months and years ahead, guiding Zodiac trips. Nor
of Erika Blade and what Jakka had said she could do for

him. For all of them.

Allow them to play again.

HE KNOCKED ON HER DOOR in the morning, and after a few seconds she answered, wearing gym shorts and a white men's tank top. Face flushed, breathing hard. Her ankle weights lay on the floor.

Kal curbed his curiosity. "I'm going to work. Hiialo needs a bath."

"Okay."

"You want the car? I can hitch a ride."

As in hitchhike? The day before, she'd been shocked to see boys hitchhiking in Hanalei. "I don't need the car."

When Hiialo woke up, she wanted mangoes for breakfast. All those in the house and on the tree in the yard were green, but Hiialo said they should cut them up and dip the slices in shoyu—which Erika learned was soy sauce—and vinegar. The result was edible.

After breakfast, Hiialo took a bath, playing with toys in the tub, and then she asked to paint again.

Erika asked, "Are you going to be good?"

"Yes."

"Then, okay. That would be fun."

Hiialo painted a scene of palm trees and an outrigger and herself on the beach. It was, she said, for her dad's birthday. As Erika sketched her and wondered what *she* could give Kal—and also how she was ever going to get some painting done with Hiialo around—Hiialo stopped painting and stared at Erika's art supplies, on another part of the table.

She reached for a bottle. "What's this paint?"

"Oh, honey, that's masking fluid. Actually it's pretty cool. You want to see?" Erika set aside her sketch pad and picked up an old brush she used for masking fluid. She grabbed a test strip of paper, opened the small jar and dabbed the brush in. Hiialo watched her paint it on the paper. "Okay, then we let it dry, and we paint over it."

When the paint was dry, Erika let Hiialo peel off the dried mask, revealing the white beneath.

"I want to try it! I want white space on my picture!" said Hiialo.

"Okay, but I only use this special old brush, because masking fluid can wreck the other brushes." Some of the brushes she'd given Hiialo were old, also, but too fine to be ruined with the fluid. "If we put a little soap on the brush first, it keeps it even nicer. I should have done that this time."

Hiialo masked a sun for her picture's blue sky. When she'd finished her painting, they let it dry, then hid it in one of the drawers in Erika's bed. After that, Erika insisted they clean Hiialo's closet. They played Mary Poppins while they did it, and when Kal came home that night, smelling of gasoline and salt water and sweat, she told him the day had gone well.

Kal showered first thing and shaved and was glad Erika had offered to make dinner. They put Hiialo to bed on time, and he took the Gibson and went out on the lanai.

Erika followed with her sketch pad. The lamp shining from inside the windows and the early-rising moon would provide enough light for her to do a rough drawing.

Kal was tuning up when she joined him. He saw her sketch pad. "I can turn on the porch light, but it'll draw bugs."

"I don't need it." Erika sat on the top step, using a post for a backrest.

He began to play and soon seemed oblivious to her presence, though Erika could hardly take her eyes off him to track her pencil on the page. He started with a song she'd never heard, a beautiful pop melody with Hawaiian overtones, and his voice was a soft rough serenade, a melodious crawl along the scales. Had he written the song? The lyrics were poignant, reflecting the intensity of youth. It made her think about what Jakka had said the night before. Danny and Jakka had been Kal's band mates. Strange that after so many years they wanted to get together again....

But the music drifted away from her ears, leaving just the man, who became sketched lines on the paper. She'd drawn him before, from the photo with Maka missing. But maybe *this* would work as a watercolor, something she could sell. She didn't notice he'd stopped playing until he rested the guitar in the swing and joined her on the top step to look at her sketch.

She let him see. *I need to sell something.* And she and Kal needed to talk about money. "Kal, I'd like to contribute to your household expenses."

The comment seemed to have come from nowhere. Erika wanted to chip in financially. In the long run, that was a great idea. If he married Erika, maybe he could work five days a week like a normal man. But now... "You're my guest. I don't want your money."

"Please."

"No. Don't say it again."

They both fell silent.

The leaves shifted around them, and Erika took a deep breath just as Kal said, "So, what's this about your brother?"

"Oh." The word came out in two syllables. No need to ask what he meant. "David's first wife committed suicide. She threw herself off the bow of his ship and was killed by the screws. Skye was a very wealthy woman— a publishing heiress—so David inherited a lot of money. People said he pushed her, but no one else was there. Just David and...and his son." She paused. "Chris was three."

She didn't mean to say more, but a motor inside her refused to stop running. "He's married again. The first time wasn't a good marriage. Actually Skye was the driver of the car that hit me. I was driving David's car. She thought I was him, and she hit me on purpose." *Stop, Erika. Stop, now.*

Hit her on purpose? Kal's first reaction was disbelief. No one would do something like that. Maybe Erika was one of those people who liked to dramatize, who made things up....

His instincts said no. Telling him had upset her, he could see. The way she was trembling, yet seemed unaware of trembling, struck him as honest. He wanted to touch her, to soothe her, but she was holding herself, locking herself up. *I need to know more. Tell me everything, Erika.* He encouraged with a statement that was a question, a question to which he already knew the answer. "Your injury was temporary."

Erika had known he was bound to ask sooner or later. She turned off her emotions. The shame was too painful to feel. "There was a temporary injury, but I also developed something called a conversion disorder. The reason I stayed...paralyzed was psychological."

A stillness went over him. Kal slipped into his thoughts for a while.

Erika needed to explain. *I'm not unbalanced. I'm fine.* "The accident was quite traumatic."

He could buy that. But... "You really couldn't feel anything?"

"No."

She was defensive now. Backing away from him on the step.

Kal said carefully, "I just want to understand. Stay with me a minute, okay?" He tried to catch her eye. She wouldn't meet his. "How did this...psychological thing work?"

She drew a breath. It had been a long time since she'd put herself through these kinds of explanations. It hadn't gotten easier. "It's called a conversion disorder. It works like avoidance. Say, hypothetically, that a person has made a lot of sacrifices to take care of people. Then, suddenly, she gets sick, and when she's in bed she realizes that if she stays there she doesn't have to take care of people."

Kal's eyelids dropped to half-mast. In the moonlight, Erika was blue-black. "So, what were you avoiding?"

Her mouth opened slightly. Averting her eyes, she wet her dry bottom lip with her tongue. She looked back at him.

Beyond the trees, beyond the blue beach house, the ocean crashed.

"I'm not sure. There was some suggestion it might be…"

Kal lifted his eyebrows, inviting her to continue.

She murmured, "Sex."

Talkin' story bin get interesting. "Why's that?"

Erika hugged her calves, pulling her knees up to her chest. "Oh, I was engaged when I had the accident. My fiancé, René… He was French, but I met him in Australia. We lived together for three years before we were engaged, and he…" A quick, almost silent exhalation as she picked her words. "He was used to my diving with him and…doing physical things…"

Like sex, thought Kal.

"He latched right onto the doctors' saying it might be temporary. He kept talking about when I'd walk again. And then he slept with my sister-in-law. Skye."

"The one who killed herself?"

"Yes."

Again Erika felt the anger, an anger related to what she knew was appropriate guilt. She would not accept responsibility for what Skye had done. *I was angry. What did she expect me to say? "I know you didn't mean to hit me—you thought it was David...." "Oh, the incident with René? Yes, I understand. Sure, sleep with my fiancé."*

She sponged clean her conscience. But streaks remained.

"So," he said slowly, "does this have anything to do with why you answered my ad?" He wanted to be more direct.

Erika wished she'd brought a sweater outside. It was too cool for just cutoffs and a faded pink tank top. "Not exactly."

"Your accident?"

"No."

"Why don't you want a sex life?"

His eyes, midnight blue as the sky, gazed right into her, as though trying to see all her secrets.

Why not tell him? thought Erika. Who was more entitled to know? "I don't like it."

Kal drew in a breath, shifted. *Doesn't like sex...*

The chatter of the leaves filled their silence until he spoke. "Were you raped?"

"No." How awful he'd wondered. "Nothing like that." Rushing, before he could leap to other wrong conclusions, she said, "Look. With this guy...Skye wasn't the first. But that's not it, either. In fact, that has nothing to do with it."

Kal lined up his spine against the porch post opposite hers. Forearms across his knees, he waited. Burning with curiosity. Thinking she was pretty.

Erika saw no reason to say more.

Was it right to grill her? Kal didn't think so. She didn't like sex. End of story, as per their agreement.

He wanted to kiss her, but he only watched her until she looked at him.

Once she met his eyes, Erika found it wasn't hard to

keep hers there. His expression was intelligent, direct and sensitive, and reminded her for no reason of her brother, David. A fact that calmed her.

He's different.

She shook inside and didn't look away.

Kal said, in that low sandpaper voice, "Just for the record, Erika Blade, I think sex is beautiful. If you love each other."

Later it occurred to her that the comment should have made her jealous of Maka, who had known his love. It didn't. Because he was speaking to *her,* and he was sharing something. Like a friend. A very good friend.

But not long after he'd said it, he got up and retrieved his guitar and went inside.

When the screen door swung shut behind him, Erika shivered under a trade-wind gust. Her head felt suddenly feverish. What had they been saying to each other? Why had the subject come up?

The prospect of a celibate marriage should have erected barriers between them. Instead, it had opened dialogue.

On a subject she discussed with no one.

The discussion had just begun, but it had already taught her some things about Kal. That he wasn't going to tell her she hadn't made love with the right man. That he didn't believe in Band-Aids for wounds of the spirit.

And that he had the potential to be what he'd seemed in those moments when he looked into her eyes and told her he thought sex was beautiful.

Her very good friend.

WHEN ERIKA GOT HOME from a predawn walk on the beach the next morning, Kal was on the swing eating cooked plantains and something that looked like library paste.

"What's that?" She peered into the bowl before going inside.

"*Poi*. Mashed taro root."

He seemed tense. Hurried. Dressed for work, shaved, already eating. Though he didn't have to be in Hanalei for forty-five minutes.

"Can I taste it?" asked Erika

He dipped his spoon into the *poi* and held it up.

Erika leaned over the swing. She tasted and swallowed. Bland, she decided, but quite edible. "Thanks."

"There's more inside. Hiialo loves it." He shifted on the swing, feeling only half-present, trying to look forward to the day on the water. It was a good job. He was lucky. And he didn't have to take Hiialo to day-care. She and Erika were going to the gallery.

He ate some more *poi*.

"Want coffee?" Erika looked at him.

"No, thanks."

She hesitated. He'd asked her about sex the night before. She could ask this. "What do you have to do for your ulcer?"

Change my life. He couldn't—any more than he already had. He'd actually felt good when he went to sleep the night before. The alarm clock had ended that. "Eat right. Take antacids. It's a stomach ulcer. I'll live." His smile glanced off her.

"Are you seeing a doctor?"

"Yeah."

Erika nodded. She'd asked enough, but when she went inside, she put on water for tea, instead of coffee. Kal liked kona. She wouldn't tease him with the smell.

His day pack was on the counter, a lunch bag and a cheap plastic thermos on top of it. Thursday was his day off. The rest of the week—and the weekends—he belonged to Na Pali Sea Adventures.

Stressful.

And then, of course, he had a new housemate. A stranger.

Erika could see his back through the window as he sat on the swing. He was still eating. Still tense. Plantains and *poi* and antacids for breakfast.

She wanted to help and realized she could.

She'd answered Kal's ad because of what she wanted. To mother a child. But he must have placed it because of something he needed. Erika saw now that it was something more complicated than a stepmother for Hiialo.

Kal was in desperate need of a partner.

That, she could be.

SHE AND HIIALO TOOK HIM to work, then drove home, played with Barbies, and returned to Hanalei and the gallery at eleven.

"I thought you could work over here," said Mary Helen when they arrived. She showed Erika to a corner created by a wall partition. An artist's table and stool were already set up under a skylight beside French doors opening onto a veranda and the courtyard beyond. Across from the gallery, the back door of Na Pali Sea Adventures was propped open. "Let me know if there's too much wind from the doors. It's nice and cool over here."

"This is perfect," Erika said. She was going to paint from the sketch she'd made of Kal the night before. For the first time in months, she really felt as though she had something.

"Our routine on Tuesdays is that Grandpa takes Hiialo out for a fruit smoothie, and then in the afternoon she and I go to the library and for a swim at the beach. Is that all right with you?" Kal's mother asked.

It was—and with Hiialo, too.

Erika's project absorbed her completely, and while she transferred the sketch to watercolor paper, drawing faint lines for Kal's face, the folds in his T-shirt, the shadows on his guitar, it was comfortable to think about him. And, strangely, comforting.

Hiialo left with her grandfather for a smoothie, then returned, and at lunch Erika took a break to eat Chinese take-out on a picnic table outside with her and Mary Helen.

After lunch, she began actually painting, and a few customers, tourists from the mainland and also from Japan, stopped at her table to observe. While Mary Helen took care of several framing jobs, Erika visited with a couple from New York who debated on and then rejected one of her prints.

At last Mary Helen came over to see her work in progress. "That's Kal."

"Yes." Erika knew she had captured him. His intensity. His absorption with his music. The grief that was part of him.

The watercolor was neither happy nor sad, but it was real.

Mary Helen stood back for a time, watching her paint, and Hiialo, who had been practicing *hula kahiko* nearby—some ancient hula Danny had taught her—stopped and asked, "Will you paint a picture of my dad for me?"

No request had ever pleased Erika more. "Yes, I'll do that, Hiialo."

"Thank you."

Mary Helen touched Erika's shoulder, and when she looked up, Kal's mother was turning away with a smile. "Come on, Hiialo. Let's go for our swim."

When they returned, Erika had finished the watercolor, and as she cleaned up, Mary Helen came over to admire it.

"You did that so quickly. I'm amazed."

Erika was elated. For years she'd seen other artists convey depth of personality with their subjects. Others were able to show what lay beneath the surface. Emotions. In contrast, her people always seemed flat. But the watercolor of Kal and his guitar… This was what she wanted to be able to do—what she'd told Adele she hoped to do. Standing, stepping back to look at it some more, Erika said, "I'll take it home and press it tonight."

"I can cut the mats for you," Mary Helen volunteered. She frowned at the picture.

"What's wrong?"

Kal's mother laughed. "Nothing. I want to buy it."

Really? But she couldn't take money from Kal's mom. She would give her the painting.

Tired of looking at the picture, Hiialo stood in the French doors slurping the remains of a soft drink from a paper cup. Erika glanced at her and saw her blow through the straw, spraying red pop out the door and into the flowers just as Kal came up the porch steps. He gave her a tired smile.

Erika supposed blowing pop at plants was harmless.

"Kal," said Mary Helen, "look at Erika's painting."

He came inside. The watercolor was beautiful. He found a place to stand and stare, and Hiialo trailed after him, making bubbling noises with her straw and soda.

Then she blew through the straw into the cup. The drink sprayed out the top, and Erika saw red liquid spatter her paper, across Kal's face. Involuntarily she cried, "Oh!"

Kal turned. "Hiialo!" He snatched the cup and straw from Hiialo and crumpled them.

Hiialo began to cry.

"Hiialo," Mary Helen said, "that was very naughty. Oh, Erika, can you fix it?"

Hiialo cried louder. "I want my drink! I want my drink."

Kal told her, "Get your things together."

"Nooo!"

He picked her up and took her out of the gallery.

Her face etched with anguish, Mary Helen gazed after them before she turned back to Erika's watercolor.

The worst was in some shadows on Kal's face where the paint was still wet. The pop had made the colors run together, dark areas streaking across the untouched highlights. Erika carefully dabbed at the affected area with a sponge. The pop and the paint came up, but the result was blotchy, dirty-looking, and Erika doubted she could make it right again. Her only successful piece of art in months, and Hiialo had ruined it. Erika could still hear her shrieking outside. Anxiously recalling Kal's anger, she asked Mary Helen, "He won't spank her, will he?"

"Oh, no." Mary Helen's eyes softened on Erika's. "We don't hit children or dogs." She smiled sadly. "Though we might occasionally want to. Oh, Erika, I'm so sorry. You must let me reimburse you."

"It's not *your* fault. It's my fault. I was supposed to be watching her." Erika stifled a choked sound. She could attempt the watercolor again—or try to fix it—but it would never be as good.

Kal's mother said, "Well, let me write a check for having you in today."

"Oh, please, no." How embarrassing. Did Mary Helen guess that she had no money? She'd never mentioned paying her till now. "Really, I can't accept payment."

Kal came back in the door with Hiialo on his hip. Mary Helen looked as though she wanted to argue more, but at last she turned to her son and granddaughter. "Hiialo, what are we going to do with you?"

Hiialo sniffled. "I'm sorry, Erika. I didn't mean to wreck the picture."

Erika knew it was true. Just an accident. "That's all right, sweetie. We had a good day, didn't we?" She smiled at her, trying to cheer her up. "And tomorrow

you can watch me try to fix it. Remember I said sometimes you can fix mistakes?''

Something made her turn her head, and she saw Kal's
blue eyes on her, and they lingered the way they had
Sunday morning on his parents' couch. He didn't shift
his gaze as he said softly, ''Ready to go home?''

And Erika felt, for one moment, that his home was
hers, too.

IT WAS A TENSE EVENING, and Hiialo was slow going to
sleep. She got up repeatedly for drinks of water and to
go to the bathroom and to gaze at Erika and Kal with
dark eyes, as though suspecting them of having a good
time without her.

Erika sat on the couch, waiting to talk to Kal, to ask
what he liked for lunch and offer to prepare it for him
the next morning. Unfortunately he was standing at the
sink eating antacid tablets, holding his guitar in one hand
and growing angrier at Hiialo.

When Hiialo's-face appeared between her curtains for
the fourth time, he said, ''Get back in bed *now*.''

Hiialo started to cry, returned to her bed and wailed.

With an unemotional glance at Erika, Kal went outside.
She heard the swing creak, but no sound from the guitar.

Hiallo sobbed behind her curtain door, and Erika
couldn't help going in to see her. A tear-streaked face
peered up from the bed.

Erika sat down on the edge of the bed and picked her
up. ''Honey, don't cry. Your daddy's just tired. That happens to grown-ups, and it doesn't have anything to do
with you. But when he asks you to go to bed, your job
is to get in bed and stay there.''

Hiialo sniffled, wiped her nose on her nightshirt, one
of Kal's T-shirts. She didn't answer. She looked very
sleepy.

"Maybe we can go somewhere special tomorrow. Is there a place you like to go?"

Hiialo nodded. "The *heiau*."

Oh, yes. The old hula platform. She'd mentioned that on Sunday. "Okay," said Erika. "That'll be fun. And remember, tomorrow night's your dad's birthday, and we'll go to Grandma and Grandpa's and visit the puppies, and you can give him your present. Now go to sleep, so we can have fun in the morning, all right? That's a good girl."

Hiialo lay down and whispered, "Thank you, Erika. I like you."

"I like you, too." She'd try to fix the watercolor, and if it didn't work, she'd paint something else, something just as good. But the thought was like a prayer.

Erika covered Hiialo, tucked Pincushion and Fluff on each side of her and went out to the front room, just as the screen door opened again.

Kal came back in, bringing the wind. Apologetically he said, "I'm going to sleep."

He looked pale. Tired. He had to work again in the morning.

"Kal?"

He'd started toward the hallway but stopped.

Erika leaned against the paneling where the hall met the living room. He was just a foot or so away, still holding his guitar.

She asked, "Is there anything I can do?"

About what?

Her eyes answered the unspoken question. Kal saw himself reflected in their expression; he was strung too tight, worn too far. His gut twisted. The pain increased. "I'm fine." He smiled at Erika, then moved by her into the darkness of the hall and pushed through the beads in his doorway. Without turning on a light, he hung the

Gibson on its hook and pulled his shirt over his head. *Is there anything I can do?*

There were things a wife could do, things Maka had done. Not all of them were taboo between him and Erika.

Shirtless, he went back through the beads and out into the front room.

Erika stood by the kitchen sink, staring at his day pack on the counter. Seeing him, she started, and he saw her cheeks flush. "What do you like for lunch?" she asked.

"Lunch?" He ran a hand over his hair absently. "Oh, tabouli. Tofu. Brown rice..." He couldn't think. "Why?"

"I thought I'd make it for you." Erika glanced at him, afraid she might actually be staring at his skin, his taut stomach muscles. René, her fiancé, had been five-nine, slightly built, and he'd put some effort into reducing a nascent beer belly.

Kal...

He was the kind of man who could make her think sex might be different with him. Might be good.

But men had never been the problem. *She* was the problem.

And Kal wasn't looking for a lover.

"Hey, that's really nice of you."

She remembered she'd offered to make his lunch.

He opened the refrigerator. "Okay, well, that leftover blackened tofu and stir-fry would be fine for tomorrow. Stuff with garlic is good for me. Easy on the dairy products—milk produces acid. There's Tupperware in the cabinet down there." He shut the fridge. His eyes raked over her.

Erika's legs felt like long rice.

His speculative expression made her wonder if he was going to ask if she did windows. But what he said was, "So, Erika. Do you give back rubs?"

CHAPTER EIGHT

SHE FOLLOWED Kal into his bedroom, where he flicked on the lamp and lay down on his stomach on the purple-and-lavender quilt.

Erika wondered if she should have excused herself to change. She was wearing a wraparound knee-length sage-colored skirt and a crocheted sleeveless cotton sweater. Well, she wasn't going to straddle his body in any case. Sitting carefully on the edge of his bed, she put her hands on his lower back, above the waistband of his indigo blue cotton shorts.

She'd never had trouble touching men. What she didn't like was their touching her.

But touching Kal was scary.

Smooth sun-browned skin.

He shifted on the bed under the motion of her hands, laid his cheek on the quilt.

Outside, leaves rustled.

She tried to think of something to say. Something impersonal. Nothing came to mind. Except that he was beautiful.

Making herself look away, she studied the quilt. There were letters stitched on it. MAK... Both their names. The quilt must have covered their bed.

Distracted, she massaged his back more deeply, feeling the muscles, imagining what Maka must have felt, losing herself.

To Kal, the change felt erotic. As his sudden erection

tried to carve room for itself in the mattress, he moved slightly, trying to get comfortable, and closed his eyes. To blot her out.

Her hands felt so different from Maka's. And so good.

"Hiialo wants me to take her to the *heiau* tomorrow. Can you tell me how to get there?"

Her voice made him jump. The *heiau*.

"Um…you follow the main road to the very end, to Ke'e Beach. Hiialo can show you from there." This way he wouldn't have to go with them and remember Maka dancing on the hula platform.

Erika's hands slipped down the sides of his chest. He wanted to roll over. Wanted her to touch him. Wanted someone to touch him. *I'm lonely, Erika. I can't help what's happening. I know you don't like sex.*

After a long time her hands gave his back a last stroke and went away. "How's that?"

"Great. I don't want to get up." If he did, she'd see…

"Don't then." She turned off the lamp on his desk. "Good night, Kal. Sleep well."

He heard her go out, the beads clacking behind her. He needed to brush his teeth, but he lay in the darkness until he thought he heard her sit down on the couch. Then he got up and went through the beads.

They collided in the hall, Erika's arms full of art materials. Him still aroused.

Erika saw, and her heart gave one explosive beat.

"Excuse me," she gasped, and hurried past him. When she reached her room, she shut the door and leaned against it in the dark. *Oh, Kal…*

She knew how sex was supposed to be. When she'd begun recovering from her accident, she'd found herself in a relationship with an acupuncturist. Missing David and Chris, seeing their happiness with Jean, Erika had been determined to make things work. But sex was bad. So bad she'd given up, and in the ensuing months, when she'd met someone else she liked, a film director, she had read up on female sexuality. She'd studied the mystery of orgasm, considered taking up tantric yoga, and dosed herself with herbs to increase her sex drive.

No luck.

Like the first, her second attempt at a sexual relationship had repelled her. It disgusted her to have a man touch her body with its scars, her body that had been flaccid and useless in a wheelchair.

In her mind, she saw Kal as she'd seen him in the hall. Something stirred in her, something that felt right. But she couldn't believe in it.

Sex would be the same with Kal. She was sure of that now.

In fact, it would be worse.

Because it would matter much more than it ever had.

WHAT ERIKA HAD DONE to him wasn't going to let him sleep unless he dealt with it. The solitary orgasm was release, but afterward he was lonelier than he'd been before.

And he couldn't remember Maka's face.

With a sense of panic, he turned on the light, reached down and opened the desk drawer. Knocking off the top of the shoe box, pushing aside the tape case, he found a photo. Maka grinning from the edge of the crater on Diamond Head.

It was easy to remember then.

He touched the picture, his eyes filling, his throat swelling. Swiftly he switched off the light so that if Hiialo or Erika came out of their rooms neither would see him cry; and he lay in the dark with the photograph as though it was her.

The other pain came as well, uninvited, the pain of dreams unfulfilled, of ambition stifled by practical necessity. He would turn thirty-one tomorrow. Time slipping by. *Too late, Kal. Let it go.* Blind in the dark, he opened the drawer again and felt for the tape case, and then he got up and found his headphones, so he could listen to his voice and his songs.

THE NEXT MORNING, Erika took Hiialo to Ke'e Beach, and they walked up the path to the *heiau.* The trail, which led through a fantastic garden of wild foliage, was narrow and muddy, and stones formed stairs that led up to the grassy terraces. Pausing on the path shadowed by palm fronds and large oblong tropical almond leaves, Hiialo said, "Eduardo, you must be respectful at the *heiau.* If you're good, maybe Erika will buy us shave ice later, 'cause it's Daddy's birthday."

Though Kal wasn't with them. *Working.* It made Erika hot all over whenever she remembered the night before. Which happened often.

As a gray-and-red bird suddenly took flight up into the trees, Hiialo called, "Aloha, Mr. Cardinal."

It must be a Brazilian cardinal; Erika had read about them in her Kauai guidebook. Her skin was dewy with sweat, and she hiked cautiously. Rocks that looked like good footholds were as slippery as algae-covered stream boulders, treacherous because they made tempting stepping stones. But Hiialo was a nimble hiker.

So were the elderly man and woman coming down the path toward them. The couple smiled in recognition of the little girl, and the woman said, "Hello, Hiialo. Do you know me?"

They were of Japanese ancestry, and Erika recognized them. These were the Johnsons's neighbors, the picture bride and her husband.

Hiialo pursed her lips, looking thoughtful. The woman held out her hand. "We are Mr. and Mrs. Akana, and we live next to your grandparents."

"Hello." Hiialo shook hands with her and then with Mr. Akana.

Erika stepped forward. "I'm Erika Blade. I'm a friend of Kal's."

"Oh, yes, his mother told me." Mrs. Akana beamed. Her skin was thin and smooth, the wrinkles draping gracefully around her fine bones.

Had Mary Helen told her neighbor how she and Kal had met?

"We were just taking some flowers up to the *heiau*," said Mrs. Akana.

That morning, Kal had told her to be sure to look at the offerings at the *heiau*. People, especially dancers, left *leis,* lava stones wrapped in ti leaves and other gifts for the hula goddess, Laka. Erika asked Mrs. Akana, "Do you know hula?"

"Oh, yes." She smiled. "When I was young. But just *bon* dancing now."

"*Bon* dancing?"

Mr. Akana spoke for the first time. "You don't know *bon* dancing? Kal should bring you over to learn. All the Johnsons used to go to the *bon* dances. Family thing. Very Hawaiian."

"Can I go?" asked Hiialo.

"You maybe little," said Mrs. Akana. She told Erika, "*Bon* dances are part of *obon*. It's a Buddhist religious festival, the Feast of the Dead, when our departed loved ones come back to visit us and we celebrate that they have achieved a higher state. A joyful time. Goes July and August. But *bon* dancing is for everyone. All you need is a kimono. *Happi* coat for men. Required attire."

The Feast of the Dead. Departed loved ones coming back. Did Kal see *obon* that way? Erika was fascinated. "I'd love to learn a *bon* dance."

"Good." Mr. Akana smiled in satisfaction. "But be

sure you come before *obon*. We belong to a *bon* dance troupe, and we travel all through the *bon-odori* season.''

''It is very nice to meet you, Erika.'' Mrs. Akana took Erika's hand in both of hers to say farewell, and then she and her husband continued down the path.

Her thoughts on *obon* and Kal, who loved a dead woman, Erika asked Hiialo, ''Shall we go?''

Soon they rounded a bend in the path, and the stone-rimmed terraces came into view.

Walls of black lava stones supported gradually rising narrow grass terraces. Erika paused at the foot of the first terrace and turned toward the sea. The sun, still low on the horizon, shone through a strip of filmy clouds in an otherwise immaculate sky. The ocean was turquoise, the palms dark silhouettes in front of it. To the south was Bali Ha'i, the cliffs filmed in the movie *South Pacific*. Kal had pointed them out from the outrigger.

Erika followed Hiialo up to the wide platform on the highest terrace. This had been the *halau hula,* hula school. Against the cliff wall stood a rectangular altar built of shoe-size lava stones. It was perhaps six feet long, five deep and two feet high, and all along the wall beside it were shelves made of lava stone. On top of the shelves lay sun-browned *leis* and stones wrapped in ti leaves. Offerings.

Hiialo walked over to look at them, then skipped back to Erika. ''Want to see the hula Danny taught me?''

''I'd love that.'' Erika sat down at the edge of the grass, beside the lava-rock rim.

Hiialo stood in the middle of the grass with her hands on her hips. Carefully she said, ''Hula tells stories. This hula dance tells visitors to enjoy Hawaii.'' She crouched, sweeping one hand slowly down in front of her, then raising both, then pressing them down to the earth. Standing again, she pointed the tips of her fingers toward her lips, then sent one hand out to the side. She moved with a natural grace haunting in one so small. Erika was enchanted.

Hiialo completed an entire dance, concluding with one foot pointed on the ground in front of her and both hands forming a point, reaching toward the mountains.

Erika clapped, and Hiialo ran over to her. Erika gave her a hug. "That was wonderful, Hiialo. You're very good."

"Thank you. I'm going to practice more."

Erika watched her, delighting in her grace but also envying the woman from whom Hiialo must have inherited that grace.

Envy...

I'm not supposed to feel this way. He warned me. He said explicitly that he did not want another lover.

She tried the old formula. Think of the reality of sex. Think, *Yuck.* But instead, she saw the reaction of Kal's body the night before. She thought of him and imagined him touching her. She'd envisioned it before, her first night in Haena, but only embraces. Growing friendship. Now she pictured something more sexual. His hand on her bare skin. On her breast.

It wasn't distasteful.

But the reality would be. Horrible.

Her skin felt as though it was starting to burn, and she opened her day pack to look for sunscreen and to take out a sketch pad. She sketched Hiialo and memorized colors—Payne's Gray for the lava rocks, Hooker's Green Dark for the grass—while Kal's daughter practiced hula. *She really loves it.* Erika hoped Kal would encourage Hiialo to continue hula, perhaps go to a *halau.* He should like that she took after her mother.

The envy came back.

Get over it, Erika.

After some time Hiialo collapsed on the grass beside

Erika like a little rag doll. "That was fun," she said. "What are you drawing a picture of?"

"You." Erika showed her.

"Oh. I like you," said Hiialo. "I don't have to go to day-care anymore. There was a mean dog there." She squatted on the grass and began trying to catch a bug. In a singsong voice, almost as though she didn't care whether or not Erika heard, she said, "And maybe my daddy won't be so sad anymore. He cries sometimes." Musingly, practically to herself, she said matter-of-factly, "And once he threw up blood."

Erika choked on a breath. Kal really did have an ulcer, didn't he?

"Then he had to go the hospital, and I stayed with Grandma and Grandpa for a whole week. I watched *Cinderella*."

"When was that?" asked Erika.

"I don't know. I was three." Hiialo sat down again. "Can we get shave ice, Erika?"

"Yes, darling." Troubled, Erika closed her sketchbook and put it away in her day pack. Hiialo needed her. And Kal needed her.

She had to get rid of these disturbing feelings for him. They had to make this relationship work—and within the boundaries they'd set.

Because even if those limits broadened by mutual agreement, sex would fail, and she would leave in the end.

And Kal would want her to go.

THAT AFTERNOON, she tried to fix the watercolor, showing Hiialo what she was doing. When she'd finished applying new paint to the affected areas, Hiialo exclaimed, "You *did* fix it."

Erika didn't have the heart to tell her that it was no

longer good enough to sell or even give away. At least she could use it as a guide to paint another.

She asked Hiialo to play on her own, and she transferred a sketch she'd made at the *heiau* to watercolor paper. But her thoughts distracted her. From worry about her future as an artist and about money, she began to wonder what she would do if Kal decided he didn't want her to stay. Tension held her body stiff, but when she'd finished sketching in the faint lines, the composition was right. She saw the promise of a good watercolor.

And she prayed there would be no accident this time.

A TURQUOISE-AND-WHITE Sunbeam was parked outside Kal's parents' house when he and Erika and Hiialo arrived for his birthday dinner. Kal said, "That's my sister's car. Niau."

Hiialo skipped ahead as they made their way to the front door. Kal carried a huge salad Erika had made, their contribution to the meal, and Erika carried a paper bag containing Hiialo's gift and her own birthday present for Kal, a good stainless-steel thermos.

When they entered the roomy kitchen with its pale green spackled walls and maple cupboards, Niau, a strict vegetarian, was advising her father to feed an aggressive dog brown rice.

Teasing, King said, "No. Raw meat. Red meat. Hi, folks." Erika was closest, and he embraced her like one of the family.

The warm gesture increased Erika's disquiet, her sense of urgency about her future on Kauai. "Hi, King. Hi, Mary Helen."

She was introduced to Niau, whose smile glowed with romantic speculation. *So this is the woman who answered my brother's ad...* But after "It's nice to meet you," Niau turned swiftly away, as though looking for some-

thing to break the awkwardness. She pounced on Hiialo.
"There's my favorite *keiki*."

Hiialo said, "Niau, Erika is an artist."

"I know. I can't wait to talk about art with her over
dinner." Niau ran the Okika Gallery in Poipu, on the
south side of the island. She winked at Erika with a sales-
woman's smile. *Isn't this the cutest kid you ever saw?
Isn't my brother wonderful?*

Erika liked her immediately.

"Erika, were you able to fix the painting?" asked
Mary Helen.

"Yes," said Hiialo.

Erika gave Mary Helen a private look, an answer that
differed.

Mary Helen said, "Well, King and I have decided you
can't sit in the gallery again unless you let us pay you.
We know how it is for artists."

Kal glanced at Erika. Was she having money problems?

"That's very nice of you." She smiled at his mother.
"Okay." Her eyes flitted toward his, then away.

Then, she *did* need the money.

Kal didn't understand his own response. A need to set
her at ease. *I'll take care of you.*

"Grandpa, can I see the puppies?"

"Well, I think we can manage that." King picked her
up. "You want to see them again, Erika?"

"Sure."

They went out, the kitchen door swinging shut behind
Erika, and Niau said, "I saw Jakka and Danny in Hanalei. They want Kai Nui to get together again. Is Erika
into it?"

Kal's stomach churned. "We're not getting together
again." Quickly he said, "I'll still play at your wedding,
though."

"I don't think *I'll* be the next one getting married."

"Niau, would you please pour drinks?" asked Mary Helen.

His mother stood on tiptoe, searching the cupboard for birthday candles, but Kal saw the worry lining her face—for him. He moved close to the chair to spot her. "You shouldn't be climbing up there when you've got tall people around, Mom." He held the chair as she climbed down, and when her eyes silently assessed him, he smiled. "I'm going out to see the dogs. And Erika."

His mother said, "Good."

But Erika wasn't with his father and Hiialo and the Akitas. When he pushed open the kitchen door, she was right there, ten feet down the shadowed hallway, contemplating a photograph on the wall. The door closed behind him.

She made a guilty movement, shifting her focus to a different frame.

Kal joined her. He stared at him and Maka in Fern Grotto, Maka in her white dress.

Erika thought, *You look so young.* Both of them. He must have been nineteen or twenty. But they'd had a good marriage, a normal marriage. Two people perfect in body. "What happened in the accident, Kal?"

"The other guy was driving too fast, passing on a corner. He was in her lane."

The other driver's car had had air bags. Theirs hadn't. It was a thousand-dollar car that was all theirs. *Poor but happy.* That night had made him rich and sad. A year and a half later, when he'd gotten the insurance money from the hurricane damage, he'd used that and Maka's life insurance to buy the bungalow from his parents. Start over in a place that didn't remind him of her.

What hurt most of all now was realizing how many of his memories didn't have her in them.

Life just went on.

"Was the driver prosecuted?" asked Erika.

"Twenty hours of community service." He looked at her. "What about your brother's wife?"

"Oh…" It was a startled word. "Oh, we didn't do anything." Maybe if she'd pressed charges, as David had told her to do, things would have turned out differently. Maybe she wouldn't have said—

"Erika? Are you okay?"

She lifted her face, and his eyes were concerned.

"Yes." She turned her head away. "I'd like to go see the dogs."

They went out to the kennel and leaned on the half door of the whelping shed and watched the puppy who looked like Jin. Kal said light things, talked about the Akitas and about Jin, and the obedience titles she'd won, but all the time his arm was touching Erika's and neither moved.

All the time, he wondered how it must feel to Erika that her sister-in-law had made a selfish wild mistake— had hurt Erika in an automobile accident—then slept with her fiancé. And finally, as though the guilt had caught up with her, she'd killed herself.

While Erika watched Jin's puppies, especially the one that she liked the most, Kal let himself examine her. Her thick hair sweeping the side of her face. Her slender muscular arms and small breasts.

Eventually she glanced up, and he was staring, but he didn't look away. He just gazed into her eyes until someone rang the dinner bell. She was flushed, and he felt that way, too. Tingly.

He wanted to say something, but he didn't know what, so they moved away from each other in silence.

THE PRESENTS WERE both successful. Kal seemed genuinely delighted by Hiialo's picture and told her exactly where he was going to hang it in his room. Unwrapping Erika's thermos, he said, "Now, this is what I need."

When they got home that night, they put Hiialo to bed, and then Erika went into her own room and changed out of her dress and into a tank top and track shorts. She had time to paint before she went to bed.

But there was a knock at the door to the hallway, and she opened it.

Kal asked, "Want some more birthday cake?" Mary Helen had made a coconut layer cake.

"No, thanks." Erika had stringent personal rules about sugar and fat. When she'd realized how hard she was going to have to work to get her legs back, it had seemed sensible to go all the way. Good diet. As few cellulite dimples as possible. She still hated her body, but at least she wasn't fat.

She stepped back from the door, an invitation.

After a moment Kal came in, wandered over to her art table to examine her drawing of Hiialo at the *heiau*.

"We met your parents' neighbors today," said Erika. "The Akanas? They were coming down from the *heiau*."

"Oh, yeah? Mrs. Akana looked after us some when we were kids. Taught us *bon* dances. My folks used to take us to *bon* dance clubs on weekends in the summer."

"I'd like to do that," Erika said, sitting down on the edge of her bed, on his quilt.

"You'd like the Floating Lantern Festival, too. That's part of *obon*. People send paper lanterns out on the water to guide the souls of the dead back to the other world." With his toe Kal nudged one of Hiialo's crayons, which lay against the baseboard. "I wanted to take part in *obon* the summer after Maka died. My dad and I practiced the dances. But…" He shrugged. "I didn't go." It had been too hard.

To Erika, it sounded like something he should have done. "Couldn't you still go? Couldn't you do it this year?"

"Oh…" Why did he feel threatened? "Yeah. Sure."

"Mr. Akana said he'd teach us the dances. But you probably know them."

"A few." He didn't want to talk about *obon*. He wanted to talk about why Erika didn't like sex. What she'd said the night they discussed it hadn't satisfied him. *And what happened last night...*

He crossed the room and sat down near her. Drawing a knee up onto the mattress, he faced her. "You rubbed my back last night. It was nice."

"I'd...do it again." She swallowed, hoping he didn't know she'd seen that hard unmistakable bulge under his shorts. Hoping that if he did know, he would assume she'd taken it for what it was. Meaningless. Without significance.

"Thanks for making my lunch, Erika. And the thermos."

"You're welcome."

"So," Kal proposed carefully, watching her face, "what do you say I rub your back tonight?"

Erika stilled. *Him touching her...* "No, thanks."

He was silent.

She had to explain. "I really don't like getting massages."

"Had a lot of them?" She must have been in rehab a long time.

"Yes."

They sat stiffly beside each other, and he wondered if she'd noticed his hard-on the night before, if that had anything to do with her answer. Because she didn't like sex.

Ah, Erika... He turned to her. "We'll go to the Blue Room tomorrow night, yeah? The place I told you about in Waikapalae Cave?"

She nodded, making a wordless motion with her mouth.

Nervous. He said softly, afraid of his own voice and

of what he was saying, "I'm pretty gentle." He'd meant the back rub, or intended to mean the back rub. But he knew he was saying something else.

Erika knew it, too. Almost sick with tension, but unable to turn away from the wonderful thing she knew others enjoyed, she whispered, "You can rub my back."

SHE WAS NERVOUS. When she lay down on her bed, her arms near her head, she turned her face to the mountains, away from him. But Kal knew she trusted him. He touched the middle of her back.

Erika swallowed, feeling the heat in her face, not bothering to try to talk.

Kal knew she needed him to talk. He grabbed the first topic that came to mind. As his hands slid over her, over her tank top, he said, "Do you know anything about *obon?*"

Her jumpiness eased. "Just what I learned today. Mrs. Akana said it's a Buddhist festival that celebrates the temporary return of the souls of the dead."

Kal massaged gently, as he'd promised. "Right. It has other names. *Bon, bon-odori, urabon.* Supposedly *bon* dancing started in India with a dance performed by one of Buddha's disciples. He was allowed to see his mother in another realm after death, and she'd been reborn among the Hungry Ghosts of Hell. She'd eaten meat and denied it, so she had to hang upside down as punishment. She couldn't eat because food and water would turn into fire. So the son earned merits to help her, and when he saw her freed from her suffering, he danced for joy, and people around him joined in."

Earning merits for the dead. Erika liked the idea. Some people died too soon. Maka. *Skye.* If anyone could use some extra merits, it was David's late wife. *If I could help Skye...*

Kal saw her eyes drop shut. Completely relaxed. It wasn't fair to take advantage of this moment.

But it was necessary.

"So, Erika. Have you had any lovers since your accident?"

Erika's muscles went tight. Upset, she rolled away and sat up. Her throat felt dry and full of ridges.

Kal's hand was still on one of her shoulders as they faced each other.

She shrugged it off. "You don't have a right to ask that." And then—knowing her reaction was beyond her control, because she heard her own voice and knew how she must sound to him—she started to cry.

"Erika…"

She dragged her arm across her eyes. "Yes, you do. Yes. Yes, I have. I don't know what you want."

Kal swallowed, his chest heaving at the sight of her tears. Distraught tears. He didn't know what he wanted, either. She'd spoken the truth. He had no right to ask.

He risked it. Put his arm around her, drew her against him. She allowed it. Stiffly. He said, "I'm sorry. I'm sorry. Ah, Erika…"

He hugged her for what seemed like a long time, and then he said again, as though it was a solution, "We'll go to the Blue Room tomorrow. You'll want to paint it."

Erika was soothed by the thought. And by his arms around her body and his head against hers.

And by his voice, rough and smooth and familiar, saying, "We're still friends, yeah?"

THE NEXT NIGHT, after dinner, Kal drove down the road toward Ke'e Beach and parked on the shoulder, not far from the yawning mouth of a wet cave. As he turned off the ignition, he told Erika, "They say these wet caves are where the goddess Pele tried to build her volcanos when she first came to the islands. But her sea sister,

Namakaokahai, whom she'd come to Hawaii to escape, destroyed them with groundwater.''

Erika gazed out the window at the cave. "Are we there?"

"No, this is a different cave. We've got a little hike to Waikapalae."

That made sense. He'd suggested she wear her hiking boots.

Hiialo unfastened her seat belt. She was out Erika's door almost before Erika and raced toward a wide gravel path that led up into the woods in the direction of the mountains.

"Hiialo, please wait for us," Erika called.

Hiialo slowed her steps to a creep, then skipped over to a nearby rock, her fancy caught by a plant or a creature.

Wearing a neoprene knee brace and hiking boots, her swimsuit and a sarong, and carrying her waterproof 35-mm camera and her mask, Erika limped to the place where Hiialo stood. Hiialo had brought her mask, too. But Kal carried only an underwater flashlight to guide them down a short underwater tunnel to the Blue Room.

Though the sky had grown cloudy, it was warm out, balmy low seventies, and it wouldn't be dark for hours. As they climbed the path, the gravel disappeared, and the trail became rocky, twisting back toward steep cliffs. "I don't see how you two can hike in just flip-flops," Erika said.

Behind her, Kal corrected, *"Slippahs."*

"What?"

"Slippers. In Hawaii, they're slippers. *Malihini,*" he added, turning the word to a caress.

The kind of caress his hands had lavished as he'd embraced her the night before. Erika remembered his fingers on the back of her neck, his palm skimming her spine, his arms squeezing tightly. *Friends, yeah?*

Yes, thought Erika.

The road below vanished, and the air became quiet, as though the three of them were the only people on earth.

Kal said, "Here we are."

About seventy-five feet down a rocky slope was the curved dark entrance of a wet cave. Hiialo started scurrying down the slope with the ease of a squirrel, but then her foot went out from under her.

Erika gasped.

Hiialo fell hard on her rear end and let out a howl.

Kal scrambled down to pick her up. "Bet you'll be more careful next time."

Seeing Hiialo's face, hearing her sobbing, Erika wished he'd warned her *this* time.

With Hiialo in his arms, he returned to her side. "You can hold on to me, Erika. It's steep."

She opened her mouth to say she was fine, she liked to do things alone. But then she assessed the slope. Hiialo wasn't the only one who could fall. Without meeting Kal's eyes, she grasped his arm. "Thanks."

She had to take small steps, compensating for the weakness of her left knee, but he never rushed her, and she remembered when she'd been learning to walk again and had held on to David. Kal was as strong and sure-footed as her brother. Like a pillar that would never topple.

The walk down seemed long, and the whole way her throat swarmed with feelings. *Friends.* He was a good friend. And the slope was so rocky, so slippery, it was as though she and Kal and Hiialo were on a dangerous sojourn together. Going to the underworld to meet with their own ghosts.

At the bottom of the slope, the cave looked about that inviting.

They set down their towels, took off their shoes and went in. The water was colder than the breakers off the north shore, and Erika shivered as she waded through the mud, then lowered her whole body and dunked her head. "Brrr!"

Kal grabbed the back strap of Hiialo's swimsuit to keep her from swimming away into the shadows, and she turned and clung to him, shivering. Watching Erika clear her mask, he said, "I bet you've dived all kinds of places."

"Yes." Everywhere. In Australia with sea nettles. In Hawaii, in water teeming with sharks, where she'd watched a *longimanus,* an oceanic whitetip, bite her brother. She rarely dived anymore. Trying it again with David and Jean six months before, she'd been unreasonably afraid. Since the accident, she'd been afraid of a lot of things that had never bothered her before.

But David had said she was just getting older. Naturally more cautious.

Kal said, "Okay, we have to swim down a tunnel for about ten feet. Are you up to that?"

"Sure."

Hiialo let go of him and dog-paddled back into the cave, and Kal and Erika followed.

At the back wall the top few inches of a tunnel arched above the surface of the water. Erika pushed her mask up on her forehead. It was so dark that Kal's blue eyes looked like charcoal smudges, and the cave seemed huge around them, the pool bottomless. Hiialo hung on to Kal's right shoulder. In contrast to her small hand, he seemed big and sturdy. Erika knew the feel of his shoulders. Briefly she imagined their silhouette above her body in the dark.

"I'll go first," said Kal. "Grab my ankle if you want as you're going through. The tunnel's really short. Then you come up in the Blue Room."

"I'm ready." She cleared her mask again.

"Okay. Count of three, Hiialo?"

Hiialo said earnestly, "One…two…three."

She took a breath, and they went under together. Erika watched the black outlines of their bodies in the light Kal had switched on. They swam quickly through the tunnel, Hiialo in front, and Erika followed easily, carrying her camera and watching Kal's muscular legs and the fabric of his surfing trunks moving with the water. Without wanting to, she remembered again the night she'd seen the shape of his erection under his shorts.

The natural light in the pool beyond was blue—a mix of Cobalt Blue and Turquoise—not as dark as the water in the tunnel. Realizing she'd emerged from the passage, Erika rose to the surface. As she gasped a breath and caught, through her mask, a water-streamed glimpse of blue, she felt a warm solid touch, Kal's hand at her waist.

"You okay?"

Until you touched me. His leg brushed hers underwater. Her body tingling, Erika shoved up her mask and peered about in wonder. Even their skin was washed an eerie ghostly blue. "Oh, Kal—your eyes."

He was looking at hers and at drops of water on her lips. He swam away from her, over to a ledge where Hiialo could stand. Hiialo began using her mask as a bucket to scoop up water.

Erika was sure she was going to drop the mask, but said nothing and swam to the far wall where she could brace her foot on a slimy narrow shelf and focus her camera. "Kal, let me take your picture. I can paint from it." Her voice echoed through the chamber. "Sit up on that ledge."

He climbed up on the ledge, and Hiialo handed her mask to him, then abandoned the rocks and swam toward Erika. "Can I take a picture?"

"Sure. Then will you be in the picture with your dad?"

As Hiialo came near, Erika reached out and two small

hands grabbed her arm. She pulled Hiialo over to the shelf and helped her find a place to stand.

"I want you to be in the picture with my dad."

"Not this time," said Erika.

"Why not?"

Erika decided to be honest. "I don't think we should both be so far away from you in this dark pool."

Hiialo's forehead creased with worry. "What might happen?"

Kal wanted to know, too. More than once after Erika had cautioned her about something, he'd seen his daughter look worried and fearful. Then, fortunately, her adventurous spirit took over again.

"Well, if you were to get a cramp and go underwater, it would be hard for us to find you."

Kal thought, *I'd find her.* He could tell Hiialo thought so, too. No wonder Erika didn't like sex. A person had to relax to enjoy it.

Then he remembered her tears.

Not that easy.

Hiialo tried to focus the camera on Erika. "Which button do I push?"

"The yellow one, honey. Right there."

He was the one who'd advertised for a celibate marriage. It was something he forgot more and more often lately. In the blue space of the cavern, Kal admitted it was something he no longer desired.

Celibacy was a way of clinging to Maka after her death.

But he wasn't dead. And watching Erika and his daughter figuring out the camera together, happy, liking each other, Kal knew he wanted to live. It was going to be hard to convince Erika. Hard to get to the bottom of whatever she didn't like about sex. But he would try.

He'd found someone who needed him as much as he needed her. And he didn't want to let her go.

CHAPTER NINE

BACK RUBS SEEMED a safe approach. Again that night he asked her for one, then lay on his bed while she stroked the muscles in his back. It was just right. Her touch stirred him, but this slow friendship was what he needed.

What she must need, too.

"Hey, Erika."

"Yes." Her voice faltered on the word.

"Let's do this every night. We'll trade off, yeah?"

Heat tingled in Erika's chest. Every night? It would become a ritual, like her making lunch for him, like tucking in Hiialo at night.

He might ask her about sex again.

Friends, she thought. In the deepest place inside her, she knew she needed a friend like Kal. A back-rub friend. A close friend.

She couldn't say no.

THE NEXT DAY he didn't have to be at work until noon, and Erika took advantage of his being home to get some time alone to paint. At the art table in her room, she completed a watercolor of Hiialo at the *heiau.* It was good, and when it was dry she tacked it high on the wall, out of reach of disaster. Then she took another sheet of paper, her drawing board and the ruined painting of Kal playing guitar and went out her back door. Sitting on a warped damp bench among the mock orange bushes, she drew.

Somewhere a band began to play rock and roll, but she scarcely heard. The drawing was as good as the first one she'd made, and by the time she finished, the sun had risen high over the mountains. Erika noticed the live music. It wasn't just Kal. She heard a drum, too, and another guitar inside the bungalow. Danny and Jakka? She climbed the steps to her door.

Inside, Erika consulted the clock on her nightstand. Eleven-thirty. She'd been working since eight.

Her bedroom door was closed, but she heard the song end, heard male laughter. Danny's voice said, "You gotta go to work?"

"Yeah. Where's Hiialo?"

Erika took her art supplies to the drawing table and paused there. Something wasn't right.

Then she saw. Gray goop spilled on the table, running into the bristles of four of her brushes. Dried.

The lid was halfway on the bottle of masking fluid.

Erika set down her drawing board, stored the drawing in her portfolio, then opened the door of Hiialo's room.

Hiialo was sitting on her floor, her head down, playing with Fluff and Pincushion. Though she must have heard Erika, she didn't lift her eyes.

"Hey, Hiialo?" Kal stuck his head in. "There you are."

Erika wasn't sure who to kill first. "Hiialo, were you in my room?"

Hiialo jerked her small round face up, her eyes big. She didn't answer. The terror of the guilty.

Kal came into the room. "What did you do, Hiialo?"

Her chin trembled, and she gazed down at her stuffed animals.

"Hiialo?" He bent down, picked up Pincushion and Fluff and tossed both on her bed. "Look at me."

Hiialo raised her head, met his gaze. "What?"

She was impossibly brave—or impudent, depending on

point of view. Erika didn't know which way she felt. She was torn between wanting justice and wanting to protect Hiialo from Kal's anger. She was tempted to ask him, *Well, where were you?* But Hiialo shouldn't have to be watched every minute. She was old enough not to get into someone else's belongings.

Her mischief had been very expensive.

Kal asked, "What have you been doing?"

Hiialo began to cry. She rubbed her eyes and wouldn't speak.

Feeling the anger mounting in Kal, Erika said, "Hiialo, that was wrong to get into my things. You know I would have let you use the masking fluid if we were together."

Hiialo sobbed.

Kal stepped over her and around Erika and into her room. In a minute he was back. The muscles in his neck were tight, but Erika understood the expression in his eyes. Helplessness. *Why can't I control you? Why do you do these things?*

Erika had a good idea why. Because Kal loved Hiialo to distraction, and he didn't know how to discipline her. Maybe he only understood dogs. Disapproval for undesirable behavior, praise for good. It wasn't a bad place to start.

But it wasn't enough.

"Hiialo," said Erika. "Please get up."

Hiialo looked at her.

Erika stared back.

Hiialo bowed her head, picked at a scab on her knee. Then she slowly rose to her feet.

As Kal slipped back toward the window, Erika held open the door to her room and gazed expectantly at Hiialo. Hiialo went in.

Trying to stay calm and not to think about her last three hundred dollars or the watercolors she hadn't painted, Erika stood over the art table. "I would like you to clean this up. You'll need to peel all the masking fluid off the table.'' That would be fun; the rest was not. "And then you'll have to get it out of the bristles of these brushes. Now, you must be very gentle. This brush cost eighty dollars, and once a few bristles start coming out, the rest will come out, too. The brush is probably ruined, but you're going to try to save it and the others. And if it can't be done, we'll have to figure out a way for you to work to help pay for them.''

Hiialo's eyes filled.

In the doorway, Kal thought, *That's unfair. She's too little.*

But he remembered the photos of Maka all over the floor of his room.

"Now please do what I asked,'' Erika said, and turned and crossed the room and opened the door to the hall. She went out.

Hearing her walk into something and swear, Kal remembered the amp was in the hallway and winced.

In her pink shorts and tank top, her face tear-streaked, Hiialo gave him a glance of appeal.

"Don't look at me.'' He went after Erika, took a minute to move his amp and found her on the lanai. She was sitting on the steps, her head in her hands.

Kal contemplated her slender athletic body, her back, her defeated posture, before he came and sat down beside her. "I'm sorry.'' He had to say that first thing. "It was my fault. Danny and Jakka came by. They'd stopped at Na Pali and knew I wasn't working.''

"She's old enough to know better,'' Erika said. Kal couldn't be expected to spend every free minute with his daughter. It was just that he had so few. She moved her hair to see him. "Maybe you should take an antacid.''

He smiled a little. His stomach was bothering him less today. The last few days. "I think you're my antacid, Erika. That sounds trivial. But it's not.''

She knew.

"I'll pay for the brushes," he said. "I mean, she should do some work, but that's not really going to help you now."

There was no point, Erika decided, in assuring him that his four-year-old daughter *was* going to do one hundred and sixty dollars' worth of manual labor. She could fold laundry. She could sweep. They'd make a chart. And when those jobs were done, Hiialo would never ever again touch anything that belonged to someone else without asking.

"Hey, Erika, I know this set you back, so let me do it, yeah?"

It didn't seem right. She wasn't just a houseguest. She didn't want to be. If she was Hiialo's stepmother... "No, Kal." She had signed up for this. *At least Mary Helen said she'd pay me for going into the gallery.*

"You're not leaving, are you?"

"No." Did that mean— He didn't want her to go. She saw it in his face. He wanted her there. "I'm not leaving. Now," she added.

"I have to get to work, but there's an art store at the mall in Lihue. I'll take you there tonight, eh? I'll get a baby-sitter. We can have dinner."

Heat stole over her, and her emotions pulled on each other. Butterflies in her stomach. "Let me see what I can do with the brushes I have." Panicked, she met his eyes. "I don't want to... I'd rather stay home."

The moment was interminable, even the air immobile.

"I see," Kal answered finally. "Sure." And then he got up, as though he couldn't stand to be near her anymore, and hurried inside.

THE BRUSHES WERE RUINED.

That afternoon, Erika made a work chart for Hiialo, assigning dollar amounts to certain tasks. Sweeping the front room and the lanai was worth three dollars, folding two loads of laundry, five. If the jobs weren't done well, they wouldn't count.

Hiialo asked if she could start by sweeping, and she went to work, and soon Erika heard her singing a song from the Disney version of *Cinderella*.

With her remaining brushes, Erika tried to paint the watercolor of Kal, using a sponge for the wash because her good wash brush had been destroyed. But the effort was frustrating and eventually she stopped.

Why hadn't she agreed to have dinner with him? It had sounded so lovely. Perfect.

He likes you, Erika. He's held you when you cried. He said you could hold onto him when you walked down that slope to the wet cave. He said you're his antacid.

"How romantic," Erika murmured to herself.

But here she was, trying to paint with four small brushes, the wrong brushes, and she'd hurt Kal and he'd hardly said another word to her before he left for work, just tried to act very casual, like it didn't matter.

She abandoned her painting on the table and went to the bed and lay on it. What would it've been like if she had said she'd go? He would've bought her new brushes, bought her dinner.

And I would have been sponging. Because I can't be his lover.

Kal would be horrified if he thought she perceived the invitation that way—gifts in exchange for sex. But Erika knew that was what it always came down to in the end. Even her staying in this house…

Friends, yeah?

"Oh, Kal," she whispered into his quilt. "Let's just be friends."

She couldn't be more. With anyone.

HE CALLED HER at four and he sounded distant. "I need to do some stuff after work. Don't fix dinner for me, okay? I'll see you by ten at the latest.''

"Okay.'' She wanted to apologize. She wanted things to be as they had before she'd refused his invitation to go to Lihue. "Kal, I feel bad about today. I—I don't know where we stand.'' It sounded so trite. What if he hadn't meant anything? What if he was just asking her to go with him as an extension of their friendship?

Then why get a sitter?

On his end of the phone, a car passed. He must be in the gallery with the doors open, or maybe at the pay phone in the park across the street.

His voice said, "Let's talk about this when we can see each other.''

Her heart thumped.

"Is everything okay there?'' he asked.

"Yes. Hiialo's been working. She's earned off ten dollars so far.''

The sound he made might have been a laugh. Then, silence. After a time he said, "I'm not very good at that kind of stuff. That's why I asked you to come.''

Erika felt bad for him. "She's perfect, Kal. You're a good dad. I love her.'' Who couldn't love a girl who sang Cinderella's work song while she was being punished by her wicked stepmother? Well…maybe *future* stepmother.

This silence lasted longer than the first, but eventually Kal spoke again. "Ten o'clock, yeah? Kiss Hiialo for me.''

Erika agreed, and then they hung up, neither saying goodbye, as though if they did they might not see each other again.

Hiialo was out on the porch with her stuffed animals. "We're having a *luau,* Erika.'' One of her animals, who had the misfortune to be a pig, was covered with a layer of dirt. Erika was sure he'd been buried—cooked underground.

Laughter bubbled inside her. The last of her anger drained away. She didn't have room to be angry at Hiialo. She was too upset about Kal.

Trying to take her mind off it, she sketched and photographed Hiialo playing, and then she made dinner for the two of them. Hiialo asked for pancakes and supervised Erika's making them, pointing out when each began to bubble and the edges to pucker, and when Erika tucked her in bed that night, Hiialo said, "I'm sorry I was bad."

"I know you won't do it again. Now, here's a kiss from your daddy." Erika kissed her forehead.

Hiialo asked, "Are you going to live with us always?"

Always. She couldn't answer that alone. "I don't know, Hiialo."

Hiialo pulled her covers up to her chin.

"Good night, sweetheart."

"Good night, Erika."

SHE WAS STRUGGLING with her small brushes when she saw headlights in the driveway and heard the car. Leaving the painting of Hiialo's *luau* on the art table, Erika got up and gathered her brushes to take out to the kitchen to wash.

Kal was just coming in the front door with a paper bag in his arms, but he stopped when he saw her.

Neither moved.

The screen door swung shut behind him.

Erika said, "Hi."

"Hi." She'd changed clothes, and his eyes saw more than her tank top and shorts. Long legs and scars and brown eyes... It felt too long since he'd seen her. *Do this right, Kal.* He moved toward the counter, toward her, and set down the bag. "I got you these. I think they're like what you had."

Brushes. They were wrapped in tissue, and Erika

watched his rough hands unfold the paper to show her. She studied the golden hairs on his wrists and forearms. She smelled his sweat.

She touched the fine camel hair of the brushes. She never used sable; the Siberian mink were endangered. Kal must have noticed her preference.

"They're just like what I had. Thank you." No need to look at him. She could feel him there beside her.

"I also got you this."

She couldn't see his hands anymore—or what he held. Had to turn.

It was a *lei,* made of pale green moss.

Erika's gaze crept up his chest and throat, stopping at his mouth. Looking in his eyes would make her head swim.

"In Hawaiian culture," he said, "the head and the shoulders are considered sacred. To give a *lei* is a sign of respect. And affection."

Erika had to meet his eyes then. His peered into her heart as he said, "And that's where we stand."

Placing his hands on her shoulders, he gently kneaded her muscles. "I think it's my turn to do this to you tonight."

She quavered. But she could smell the sweet earthy scent of the *lei*—and she'd never forget his words.

They went into her room, and she removed the *lei* so she could lie down without crushing it.

This time he didn't mention past lovers. He just caressed the tightness from her back and sang to her.

IT WENT ON LIKE THAT for almost two weeks.

Each day Erika awoke before dawn, practiced twenty minutes of yoga, did her isometric exercises and slipped out of the house and down to the beach in the dark. There, she walked the shore alone, two miles west along the sea and back, and she was lulled to peace by the inside-a-conch-shell churning of the waves, a roar louder than her thoughts, clearing her mind of everything but Kal.

Because each night they touched.

In between those mornings and nights came the long days without him, while he was at work. Hiialo had almost finished working off the paintbrushes she'd ruined, and Erika had completed several watercolors, which Kal's sister, Niau, had driven to Poipu to be photographed and made into transparencies for Adele. Now the originals hung in the Hanalei Okika Gallery.

On Thursday, two weeks after Kal's birthday, as Erika was returning from her morning walk, she spotted a shirtless man in loose indigo blue cotton shorts walking toward her. The papaya-colored ball of the rising sun was just a sliver creeping over the horizon, but she recognized Kal.

Instantly she was afraid something was wrong. Why wasn't he home with his daughter? When he reached her, she asked, "Where's Hiialo?"

The waves crashed.

"My mom took her to Lihue for the day. Relax." He was holding four mangoes. "Breakfast."

Relax, Erika. He said it often. When Hiialo ran ahead of them into the ocean. When she was quiet in the bathtub for too long. When she wandered away in the grocery store. When she went outside to play without telling anyone. When she practiced hula alone in the courtyard outside the Okika Gallery, just out of sight of where Erika was painting.

Kal stretched, his skin the finest color of the morning, a dilute wash of Yellow Ochre and Burnt Sienna. The pink-filtered dawn glowed over the ocean-facing side of his body, lightening his eyes, turning the irises the aquamarine shade of the sea. The line of dark hair dipping from his naval to beneath the loose waistband of his baggy shorts was an invitation to stare.

He tilted his head toward the high-tide line, gesturing her to sit down with him. "Want some mangoes?"

There was a mango tree behind the house, outside Kal's window. They ate a lot of mangoes. Mango ice cream. Mango bread. As they sat down together, Erika asked, "How long does mango season last?"

"July?" He lay back in the sand near her, and Erika could smell the juice of the fruit he was eating and the scent of the ocean and his body. The last brought familiar confusion. Earthy feelings she recognized as desire.

He wanted her, too. She'd seen him aroused more than once after she'd rubbed his back or Kal had rubbed hers. He knew when she noticed, too, and he smiled a little tensely and said something light. Once it had been, *Yeah, that happens.* Another time he'd said, *I guess you can tell I like you.*

She'd said nothing. She didn't want to tease him. She was afraid.

He knew that, too.

A black-and-white dog bounded up the beach barking, then splashed into the water and began swimming in the gentle surf. Erika saw his owner a few hundred yards away, throwing a stick for another dog, a golden retriever.

"We ought to get a dog to walk with you in the mornings," said Kal.

He said it as though she was going to stay. As though he took it for granted. Relief rushed through her, but she was still afraid to feel secure. His house already felt too much like home. And yet she always half expected to discover that her own ship would soon be weighing anchor, that she'd have to leave him and Hiialo.

But a man didn't talk about getting a dog with a

woman he wanted to send away. "I'd like to have a dog, Kal."

His eyes explored her face. "Yeah?"

"Yes."

The surf broke, and the froth crept up the shore toward their feet.

Kal bit into his second mango, eyeing her. "You want to drive around the island with me today? I thought we'd go to the Menehune Ditch and Barking Sands. You said you don't surf?"

She used to surf well, by Santa Barbara standards. But her knee wasn't what it used to be, and Hawaii drew the best surfers in the world. "I can still do it. But I can't handle anything too hairy."

"During summer, it's tame here. We could put the rack on the car, try Polihale." He smiled. "I'll take care of you."

A lump formed in her throat, and her eyelids opened and shut hard, trying to keep the tears in. He was only talking about surfing. "Okay."

His eyes were sober, lingering on her face as though he was searching for something. Suddenly he sat up, turning his back to her. Patches of sand covered his smooth skin and sifted with the rippling of his muscles as he took another bite of mango and watched the Pacific.

Facing forty-five degrees away from him, Erika kept a vigil of her own, staring at the horizon, telling herself, *It's going to be okay.*

She needed the reassurance.

She knew what staying with him would require from her. Her only comfort was that he had the patience of the sea. And more gentleness than anyone she'd ever known.

Her fear was that she would disappoint him.

And break all of their hearts.

CHAPTER TEN

"IT REALLY BARKS!"

Kal grinned at her as they carried the cooler between them and a surfboard each across the warm "barking sand." It was a good day at Polihale, few people, no nasty kona winds.

He picked an isolated spot near some sloping green cliffs with rocky bases. They set down cooler and surfboards and shed their day packs. Clouds had floated in, cooling the morning, but Erika immediately fished in her pack for a tube of sunscreen.

The frayed edges of her loose faded cutoffs hung white against her tan. She pulled her T-shirt over her head and tossed it onto her day pack. Jade green bikini underneath. She squirted sunscreen into her palm.

Without asking, Kal put his hand over hers, collecting the lotion, and rubbed it into her shoulders and her back. His hands slid up her sides, and she stood motionless, a warm statue with soft skin... Moving down to the waist-band of her cutoffs, he imagined unbuttoning them for her. *"I Wanna Be Your Man..."*

"Do you like it when I touch you, Erika?"

"Yes. But..."

His hands left her. He was done, and he moved to see her face.

In his, Erika saw the person who had become her closest friend. Because Adele was far away. Kal and Adele were like two sides of the same coin. Each knew things about her the other did not. Kal could never understand what it had been like Before and During. Adele could not share this magical part of After. Kal cared about her as a man for a woman, and Erika couldn't remember knowing his kind of caring before.

He waited, gazing down at her face, his chest just a few inches from hers.

"We said we were going to be celibate, Kal. Has that changed?"

"What do you think?"

She felt his hand push back her hair, stroke her cheek. She answered the question, not the touch. "I think I'm frigid."

The word stopped Kal. It was ugly. He dropped his hand. "That sounds like something someone else said."

Her head shot up. "No. It's not like that. The men I've dated have been kind people."

His throat tightened. "I don't want to hear about them."

Erika clasped her arms about herself. He'd asked once. And she'd cried in his arms. A lot had changed since then. What she saw in his eyes and felt radiating from him was primal. Desire. For her.

"Why are you so afraid?"

How could she explain? It was so complicated. She could remember when she couldn't feel parts of her body. And sex was... She looked up into his eyes and told him the truth she thought he deserved and that she knew would push him away. "I'm not afraid, Kal. I'm repulsed."

He didn't move. "By...?"

"Sex." Because he didn't, she stepped back and turned away. She stripped off her shorts and picked up her surfboard.

"Wait. Just one thing. Are you repulsed by *me?*"

She turned and stared at him. His eyes were sky-water, translucent blue. "Of course not."

"Then I have a suggestion. When you wake up in the morning and when you go to bed at night and about twenty-five times every day, say to yourself, 'Sex is beautiful. When you love each other.'"

"You don't know how bad it is."

Her sister-in-law had nearly killed her, then slept with Erika's fiancé and killed herself. And Erika had spent three years in a wheelchair, her mind paralyzing her body. Now she was "repulsed" by sex. "I think I can guess." He picked up his board. "Let's hit the breaks, yeah?"

"WE SHOULD KEEP an eye on each other and the shore. The bottom drops right off here, and it's easy to get sucked away by the currents. See that knife-edge point at the end of that valley? Let's not go past it."

Erika nodded.

They had paddled out beyond the breakers. In the noonday sun, they'd found a spot of their own with easy peaks and hollows, fun for novice or advanced surfers. But Erika had butterflies in the pit of her stomach, re-action to being far from shore, surfing an unfamiliar spot, in a swell that seemed too big for summer. She started thinking about sharks.

Kal eyed the scars on her knee. "Feel okay?"

"I'm nervous."

"Just go whenever you want. I'll wait."

Erika took comfort from his voice. He was like the ocean for her. Necessary. Sometimes healing, sometimes too scary.

Together they watched the incoming set. It looked all right to Erika, and when she glanced at him question-ingly, he said, "Go ahead."

She began paddling, and Kal watched soberly. Had he pushed her too much? It was summer, but the waves were overhead.

She was paddling.

The surf rolled under him, and then he couldn't see her anymore.

This is good for her.

Fear on her behalf was not something he allowed himself to feel. Accidents, destiny, could not be stopped.

THREE SHAKY RIDES and one battering wipeout were enough. Two hours later, Erika lay on her back with her shirt over her face, her left shin wickedly bruised, her body enervated, trembling with exhaustion. Overhead, the sky was cloudy. It smelled like rain, but the heat was intense.

Kal, still dripping from the ocean, lifted up her shirt, offered her some *mochi,* cakes made from pounded rice, that they'd bought in Waimea with their Japanese box lunches.

"Thanks." Erika sat up and took the chewy delicacy. Her hand was shaking, which embarrassed her. She rested her arm against her knee to steady it. She shouldn't feel sheepish about being unable to keep pace with a man who'd been surfing Kauai's waves since he was a kid. But she did.

He didn't, she noticed, ask how she was feeling. She was glad. She felt a little like throwing up. And if she opened her mouth she would say the words in her head.

I'm too old for this.

She didn't want to be too old.

For him.

ON THE WAY HOME, they stopped at the Menehune Ditch, an ancient irrigation ditch supposedly built by a mischievous race of little people with supernatural powers. It was raining, and when Erika got out of the car at the overlook, her legs ached.

When they were enclosed in the Datsun again, Kal reached across her to find the latch to put the seat back.

"Oh, that's great." Erika shut her eyes. She'd changed out of her suit in the bathroom at the beach, and her T-shirt felt soft against her skin, like sleeping clothes. Kal started the car, and the windshield wipers squeaked in a soft steady rhythm. As the Datsun began to move, Erika stretched her arms over her head and yawned. "I feel so relaxed."

"Mmm." It was a speculative sound. "Hey, I think I'm going to Jakka's tonight to jam. Is that okay with you?"

"Sure." Sleepily she turned in her seat.

Kal switched on the radio, low. Reggae was playing. "You Can Get It If You Really Want." Slowing the car to turn onto the Kaumualii Highway, he manually flipped the broken turn indicator back and forth.

As he pulled onto the road, Jimmy Cliff faded out and the DJ said, "And now we've got an old one from Hawaii. And I'll take a call from anyone who can tell me what happened to these guys. Kai Nui. 'Pau Hana.' For all the *malihinis* out there, that means 'quitting time.'"

Erika sat up, straightened her seat back. Had he said *Kai Nui?*

Kal murmured, "This should be interesting." Hearing what someone thought had happened to him.

The car filled with music Erika recognized. The song he'd played on the guitar that first Sunday when they'd gotten home from breakfast with his parents. "You have a single."

"More than that. We recorded a whole tape. Ten cuts. We used to get a lot of airplay."

Staggered, she gazed at his profile. His voice played in the car, coarse and beautiful. A voice that should be on the radio. Had she been oblivious or what? "Why hasn't anyone told me? Why haven't *you* told me?"

"It's not my favorite subject. It's past." He shrugged it off.

Erika listened to the song. God, he was good. They were all good. Jakka's backup vocals were spooky owl calls. Danny's drum was rock and roll and hula rhythm beating as one. It was a song for people who couldn't wait for five o'clock. *Pau hana.* Quitting time.

As the last notes faded out, the DJ said, "And we've got a caller on the line. You're on the air. What's your name?"

"Danny Kekahuna, drummer for Kai Nui."

Kal made a sound of irritation. But a smile twisted the corner of his mouth as he watched the road, driving with his hands loose and relaxed on the wheel.

"*Shaka!* So what happened to you guys, Danny?"

"A hurricane and some personal tragedy, Jim. I think you know we were slated to play on Letterman…"

Erika choked.

Kal listened to his friend tell every listener that "the tide always comes back in." High tide. Kai Nui. Shaking his head in disgust, he switched off the radio.

"You were going to be on David Letterman?"

"Yeah. The date was three weeks after Maka's death. And like he said, we had a hurricane in the meantime."

"Was there any way to reschedule?"

"That's the last thing I was thinking about. My wife had just died. My family didn't have food or drinking water. I didn't have a house. I had a baby girl who'd never drunk out of a bottle."

Oh, Kal. She ached for him.

"Is Hiialo why you stopped playing?" As she saw it, his band had never really broken up.

"I guess. And… I don't know. You get bad luck like that, and you see the writing on the wall." He shrugged.

"Would you want to play again? Professionally?"

"Um... *Sure.*" Twist my arm.

And now that I'm here, thought Erika, *he can.*

But she kept silent, for the most selfish reason of all.

If he asked her to stay in Kauai with him, she wanted it to be for herself.

THAT NIGHT, after Hiialo was in bed, Kal loaded his guitars and amplifier into the Datsun to drive to Jakka's home in Kalihiwai, twenty minutes away. When he'd left, Erika sat on the couch to rough out some sketches of the Haena Store, playing with photos she'd taken. Boys hitchhiking, an aging surfer selling plumeria *leis,* and a sumo wrestler on a picnic bench across from the gallery wolfing a pizza. Erika wanted to incorporate one of the images into a painting of the store.

She worked at the coffee table because the breeze from the trade winds was so pleasant. Time passed quickly, and soon she began to finalize a drawing on watercolor paper. By ten-forty-five she was ready to paint.

"Hello, Erika."

She started at the familiar voice, peered through the screen, then leapt up and ran to the door. "David!" Banging open the screen, Erika hurled herself at her tall bearded brother. "What are you doing here?"

"Visiting you. Thawing out." His face was windburned. In his long-sleeved rugby shirt, chinos and running shoes, he was overdressed for Kauai. But he'd been in Greenland.

He came inside, and Erika couldn't get over it that he was really there. "Where are Chris and Jean?"

"At Haena Villas. I walked over. We just got in, rented a condo, wanted to surprise you. But it's past Chris's bedtime, so Jean said she'd stay with him. She's a little worn out herself."

Erika saw a quiet gleam of pleasure in his eyes. It made her suspicious. "Is she pregnant?"

David nodded.

Because of Hiialo sleeping in the next room, Erika mellowed her cry of excitement. "How far along is she? When's the baby coming?"

"Valentine Day."

"How wonderful." Erika's joy was genuine, only slightly tinged by envy of Jean, who was going to know the experience of pregnancy and childbirth.

But I have Hiialo.

For now.

What she and Kal had discussed on the beach echoed through her. *Sex is beautiful....*

She'd try out the new mantra later. "Sit down, David. Do you want something to drink?"

"No, thanks." He glanced at the brown chair with the threadbare armrests and sat down. Casually he surveyed the front room, checking out his sister's home. "So, where are your housemates?"

Erika's windpipe seemed to develop a crimp, cutting off her air. "Oh." She perched on the edge of the couch. "Hiialo's sleeping. She's just four. And Kal's out playing music with friends. He plays guitar."

David missed little. "You're living with a man?"

She folded her arms across her chest. "Well...not the way you mean."

He grinned. "Jean thought it was a man. She said, 'Look, there's not a personal pronoun in this whole letter. It's a guy.'"

Erika wished David's wife would stick to marine biology.

But her conscience needled her. Kal had leveled with his family. She should do the same. "I answered a personal ad."

"*What?*"

"I answered a personal ad. In *Island Voice* magazine. That's how I met Kal."

Her brother sat back, rested one ankle over the opposite knee. "I thought you said it wasn't like that."

It took her too long to answer. "We're friends. Hey, want to see what I've been doing?"

"Sure. "

They went to her room, where Erika switched on the track lights, illuminating her studio. Her best work was hanging in the Okika Gallery. *Hiialo's Luau* and *Haole Guitar Man,* the painting she'd done of Kal on the swing, a copy of the one Hiialo had ruined. She had painted it with gouache, and, as with the first, Mary Helen had wanted to buy it, but Erika had refused to take money for it. She was less panic-stricken about finances now. Mary Helen and King paid her fifty dollars every Tuesday, when she came in to paint at the gallery, and Erika had sold an original watercolor of the Hanalei Bridge for three hundred dollars. She wanted *Haole Guitar Man* to be her gift to the Johnsons. That was where the matter stood, but Mary Helen had insisted that Erika prepare a slide to send to Adele. The piece had potential for a print series.

Erika wished David could see it, but it would have to wait till morning. Nonetheless, on her wall she'd taped up several other watercolors. A mother and two children selling bouquets of flowers at a roadside stand. The mango tree in the yard heavy with fruit. Two paintings of Hiialo at the *heiau.*

David examined the watercolors. "Has Adele seen them?"

"Not these. I've sent her some other slides." But what if Adele didn't see anything she wanted to publish? *I'll be all right. I sold a painting. I'm getting by.* "Tell me what you think, David."

"I like them." He was scrutinizing her now. "You look great, Erika. Relaxed."

"I ought to. We went surfing today, and I could barely walk afterward."

As they returned to the front room, headlights lit the bamboo window blinds. Tires crunched on gravel. Erika glanced at the clock. Eleven. "That'll be Kal."

She heard the engine go off, the door of the Datsun shut, Kal's tread on the stairs. He was singing. Not a cover, someone else's music, but a song he played at home, a song he'd written, called "Kona." The melody always stayed with her when he was through.

Erika heard Kal pause on the porch. Perhaps he'd seen David's shadow, the shadow cast by the lamp beside the couch. After just a moment, he opened the door and came in, smelling faintly of cigarette smoke, carrying his amp and the electric guitar case. Setting them down, he looked from Erika to her companion with the kind of black stare locally called "stink eye." He did not say hello.

"Guess who stopped by," said Erika. "My favorite man in the whole world. This is my brother, David."

Looking fractionally less irritated, Kal held out his hand. "Kal Johnson."

David shook it. "Good to meet you. Sorry I didn't warn anyone before coming by. We just had a long plane flight—a few of them. We checked into our condo, but I wanted to surprise Erika. I'll get out of your hair now. It's late."

Kal regretted being surly. "Don't go. I just came in, and—"

"I know."

Kal saw that he did.

David said, "What's your phone number here, Erika?"

"Oh, I'll write it down for you. How did you find the house?"

"Asked the right person. The woman who works the

desk at Haena Villas had seen you at some gallery. Knew who you were and where to find you.''

She squinted at him warily. And he hadn't known she was living with a man?

Unnoticed, Kal picked up his amp and guitar and took them to his room. He was about to step through the beaded doorway when the thought hit him that David Blade might know he and Erika weren't sleeping together, had planned not to. Or he might not know it.

It shouldn't matter.

It was juvenile to feel mortified at the thought of Erika's ''favorite man in the whole world'' learning that he and Erika weren't lovers. Did David know sex made her sick?

He went into his room without turning on the light, knowing the light would illuminate the nest of a widower. David Blade would recognize it. Kal set the guitar and amp on the floor and returned to the living room.

David stood with his hands in his trouser pockets, smiling at something Erika had said. She turned and bent to close her sketch pad, and Kal saw the backs of her thighs, tanned brown, sleek with muscle. With a slight yawn, he wandered to the couch, only glancing at her brother.

As Erika straightened up, sketchbook in hand, he touched her spine, the center of the muscular back he'd watched as they'd paddled surfboards that day. The back he'd rubbed with sunscreen.

''Get some work done?''

Erika met his eyes, remembering that morning, everything they'd said.

Sex is beautiful. When you love each other.

Now he was touching her. *Oh, Kal, you do scare me.*

She almost forgot her brother was there. She wanted to talk to Kal, just to ask him how it had gone with the band, to exchange news of the hours they'd spent apart.

He had asked about her art. After too long she said, "I did work. I want to show you."

"I want to see." His arm was still around her, and his gaze slipped from her eyes to her mouth. As though he wanted to kiss her.

David cleared his throat. "Well, I'll undoubtedly see you both later."

His smile was contented, showing quiet satisfaction at something.

Her and Kal. *He thinks we're in love,* thought Erika.

Kal's faded green T-shirt had a picture of an outrigger and a Hanalei moon on it. She could smell the laundry detergent. She had washed the T-shirt with some of his other clothes and with Hiialo's things three days before. Hiialo had folded them. The washer and dryer were in a shed alongside the bungalow, outdoors, hidden by a flowering plumeria tree. Erika liked doing the laundry, helping him. His ulcer was bothering him less; she hardly ever saw him popping antacids anymore.

Kal released her and turned to David. "Well, it's good to meet you. Come for dinner tomorrow, eh?"

"Sounds great. We'll give you a call in the morning."

Erika stepped around the coffee table, hugged her brother again. "I'm so glad you're here, David. I can't wait to see Chris and Jean."

"They'll be glad to see you."

They migrated out to the lanai. The trunk of the Datsun was open, and Kal went down the steps to get his other guitar.

David murmured, "Erika, I think someone else wants to be your favorite man."

Erika put her bare foot on his instep and dug an elbow into his ribs. But he'd made her think, and she wished she hadn't called him that.

It wasn't true anymore.

Kal came up onto the porch with his guitar case, and

David said, "Well, good night. Good to meet you. And good to see *you*."

He hugged Erika, meeting her eyes. In his she saw the memory of their shared past, shared pain. The three years she'd spent on his ship in her wheelchair. The years before he'd met Jean.

He was all right now. Happier, in fact, than she'd ever seen him. And Chris could talk again, and he loved Jean. It was only Skye who...

Kal said good-night to David and took his guitar into the house. When her brother had left and Erika came in a moment later, she heard the shower running.

She went to check on Hiialo.

Hiialo had kicked her covers off and looked ready to roll out of bed. She slept with her mouth partway open. She wore one of Kal's T-shirts as a nightgown, and it was twisted around her little legs.

Carefully Erika picked her up and moved her to the center of the mattress where her head could rest on the pillow. Hiialo stirred just a little, and Erika said, "It's all right. It's just Erika."

Just Erika.

Suddenly weary of the uncertainty in her life, Erika straightened Hiialo's sheet and quilt and covered her, then retrieved Pincushion from where he was wedged against the wall and put him in Hiialo's arms.

In her sleep Hiialo murmured, "Thank you, Erika."

Erika's heart went warm. This was worth more than anything she had. For this she could live with her future unsettled. She whispered, "You're welcome, sweetie. Good night."

WHEN KAL CAME OUT of the bathroom, he saw light under Erika's door. He slipped into his room and pulled on some shorts and a T-shirt, then rapped on the door that adjoined their rooms, the door that was seldom opened.

"Come in."

He did.

Seeing him, she laid aside a drawing she'd been studying. "Hi, Kal."

"Hi."

He sat on the bed beside her, as he had many times before giving her a massage. David's appearance had made her forget their nightly ritual. It was her turn to be touched by him tonight.

She tried to relax. "How did it go? Playing?"

"Great." The jam session at Jakka's had made him euphoric, like a condemned man suddenly paroled. But they'd gotten into another argument over whether to start up the band again. He needed to wait and see if Erika stayed.

"I want a copy of your tape," she said. "Where can I buy it?"

"I'll give you one. I have a few."

"Let me pay you."

"Erika." Shaking his head, he stood up and went into his room. He returned a minute later with a tape case still wrapped in cellophane and handed it to her. "It's a gift."

"Thank you." The cover illustration looked like an acrylic. Kal and Danny and Jakka swimming through water wearing seaweed *leis.* And nothing else. "You had long hair."

"For a while."

She unwrapped the cellophane and took out the tape and the folded song sheet with the illustration. Inside were pictures of Kal and Jakka and Danny, looking four years, one hurricane and a death younger. Erika touched the picture of Kal's face. *You're so beautiful.* Remembering he was beside her, she read some of the lyrics, instead. All the songs were by K. Johnson or K. Johnson/ J. Bennee. It was like holding his soul. She carefully

folded the paper and returned it and the tape to the case.
"Thank you, Kal."

"You're welcome." Why had she touched his picture
that way? *She likes you, Kal. You like each other.* He
liked Erika enough that it had bothered him to come
home and find a strange man in the house with her. Coming inside, he'd wondered if he was about to meet a part
of her past she'd kept hidden. But it was just her brother.

Still, if he was going to be out at night much... "So,
you said this morning you'd like a dog, Erika?"

He couldn't know how much. "Yes. Like I told you,
I've almost always lived on boats. I couldn't have one."

The same way he couldn't have one until she came
here. It mattered to him that there was something she
wanted she'd never been able to have—and that he could
give her.

"Akitas are independent," he said. "You have to work
with them a lot and be assertive. It brings out the best in
them."

One of his parents' beautiful Akita puppies... Erika
frowned. "Do you think it's safe to have a dog like that
around a child?" Then she wished she hadn't spoken. He
would just belittle her fear.

"Depends on the kid—and the dog. You start with a
good puppy and do the right things, and you should have
a good dog. But any dog needs respect, and Akitas need
ongoing obedience training. They're protective, and you
don't want an animal who keeps your friends from visiting. If we got a puppy, we'd need to make sure it
learned to accept commands from all of us, including
Hiialo. And—like I said—the obedience work never
stops. If you're really interested, let's borrow some of my
folks' training books, eh?"

"Okay."

He eyed her sketchbook. "Show me what you did
while I was gone."

"Oh. This."

Erika shared her drawing—three adolescents hitchhiking outside the Haena Store.

"That's good. I can't wait to see it when you're finished."

Her cheeks, flushed from the day on the beach, ripened more from his praise. Kal wondered if he'd ever tire of looking at her—or being around her. She was fingering the Kai Nui cassette case.

"Hey, Erika…"

She turned her head, her smooth brown hair moving in one sheet.

"Have you been doing what I suggested this morning?"

His eyes explained what he meant—*Sex is beautiful….*

"I don't believe it, Kal. What you said. Sex doesn't have anything to do with love, whatever people say. I can be crazy about someone, and it doesn't make a difference."

"Yeah, but that's not the kind of love I'm talking about."

The wind rushed past outside, carrying leaves.

Erika looked at him, and his eyes were intense. Serious.

"I'm talking about giving," he said. "You care about someone and try to make that person feel good. Sometimes it's better than other times, yeah? But it's a gift every time. It's not like, you have an orgasm, I have an orgasm. It's…being involved. Being close."

Her heart twisted. What did he mean? It wasn't like anything she'd read about sex.

But it sounded wise.

His eyes searched her face, studying her. Erika knew that expression, the one she probably wore when studying a nearly complete watercolor. Thoughtful. Preparing to act.

Her insides folded and turned on themselves with heat, unraveling.

Kal studied her mouth as he had earlier that night, and then he brought his face near hers and kissed her, his nose brushing hers in a light Hawaiian kiss to match the distant sound of the waves and the scents wafting through the window.

His hands circled her wrists, holding them, and she felt the calluses on his fingers that had come from making music. She smelled the soap on his skin, shampoo in his damp hair.

Give?

Give to Kal... Erika let her lips move slightly, bare millimeters, against his. She tried to kiss him more, but he eased gently back from her, his hands sliding up her arms, caressing her.

The touch of those hands had become familiar. And Erika realized she'd known all along that he could touch her like this, too. That he'd always been touching her this way.

Giving.

"Kal..."

He watched her eyes, waiting to find out just how much she hated sex. Her soft scared breaths whispered against his face, but she didn't try to move away, and Kal realized that something had shifted inside him. His tired craving for the impossible, for the dead to rise, had vanished.

"Baby..." It wasn't the word that was supposed to come out.

Erika heard it. Nobody had ever called her that.

Kal wanted to brush her brown hair back from her eyes, to slide his hands into it and hold her head as he kissed her again. He throbbed with wanting.

But this was like the back rubs. She dispensed her trust in thimblefuls. She'd just given him another one, and he should collect it and put it with the rest and not count it for more than it was.

Kal put his feet on the ground and stood. He tried to slip back into the platonic mode, tried to conjure up the distance of friendship.

Too late.

And he was the one who'd sworn he would never love anyone else after Maka. Stupid thing to say. To write. To believe.

"I'll get some books from my folks about dog training so you'll know what you're getting into."

"Thank you." A dog. They might get a dog.

He had kissed her.

Kal wanted to touch her again. Kiss her more. He edged toward the door to his room. "Good night."

Their eyes met again, and then he went out, closing the door behind him.

Erika locked her arms around herself and whispered inaudibly, "Oh, God. Oh, God." She was praying and didn't know what for.

CHAPTER ELEVEN

WHEN HE GOT HOME from work the following night, a woman and a boy he didn't know were visiting with Erika and Hiialo, and music was playing. His.

He'd barely come through the door when the beautiful athletic-looking woman on the couch got up and said, "Hi, I'm Jean, David's wife. Boy, your music's really great."

Kal recognized the model from Erika's prints. "Thanks." It was good to hear the tape—in a way that it hadn't been for many years.

After Jean introduced Erika's nephew, Chris, Kal ate some antacid tablets he'd forgotten to take to work, then helped with dinner. Putting on the rice, he noticed Hiialo huddling close to Erika's legs, never more than a few inches away from her.

"Hiialo," he said, "why don't you go play with Chris? Erika's going to fall over you."

Erika turned from cutting mangoes into halves. She touched Hiialo's hair. "She's fine, Kal." Hiialo's face showed so much consternation and uncertainty that Erika put down the knife and picked her up.

"Erika." A sandy-haired boy with a deep resemblance to his father got up from where he'd been folding paper at the coffee table with his stepmother. "See what I made you."

A paper crane. Origami. "How beautiful!" said Erika.

"Thank you. I'm going to put it right here on the windowsill."

Hiialo buried her face in Erika's neck, and Erika hugged her more tightly. She'd been surprised by Hiialo's sudden possessiveness of her, first evidenced when David's family stopped by that morning. But at the moment Hiialo's attachment to her was comforting.

The day had been emotional, her happiness slowly deflating like an old balloon. She hadn't expected it to be so hard to hear Chris call Jean "Mom." She hadn't expected to feel such envy of Jean's pregnancy. Seeing her at all was difficult.

Her sister-in-law's thick curly hair swirled down her back like ribbons of gold. Her complexion was flawless, her body supple and slim. Jean's youth and beauty made Erika feel old in comparison, and she had dreaded Kal's coming home and seeing them side by side. He was like the dreams of her childhood, dreams she'd forgotten until she saw caring for her in his eyes. She didn't want to wake up.

Footsteps tromped on the lanai.

Kal said, "Looks like your brother found my mom and dad." David had gone down to the Haena Store to pick up some *shoyu*.

Through the front window, Erika saw King telling Raiden to sit, to lie down and to stay. "Can't Raiden come in?"

She was still holding Hiialo. Kal thought, *Erika, I want you.* "I think Dad's putting him on a long down. It's an obedience thing." He hoped his parents had brought over one of their dog-training books. Kal had called them from work that day and asked if Erika could borrow some.

Chris, still standing near Erika, peered out the window. "Oh, cool! It's an Akita. We saw some in Japan."

At nine Chris was already well traveled.

Turned sideways, talking to Mary Helen, David came

in the house. He was saying, "The ship we'd chartered had ice problems, so we decided to cut our losses. We'll go back, but we thought we'd spend a month here first."

"I'll bet Erika's glad to see you," said King, who was holding three books. He smiled at her, his granddaughter and his son, then looked back and forth across the room, ready to meet Chris and Jean. Kal introduced everybody.

Recognizing her son's music, Mary Helen said, "Is that the radio?"

"Tape," Kal answered.

"It sounds nice." Mary Helen gave Erika and Hiialo a quick shared embrace. "How is everyone? I came over to peek at your paintings, Erika. Kal said you've finished quite a few."

Erika was pleased. "I'd love to show you. Can you stay for dinner?"

"We'd be delighted."

King handed the books to Kal. "Here you go. Let me know if you want me to hang on to one of Jin's litter for you. Kumi's are all sold. Danny bought one."

Erika's knee was starting to hurt. "I have to put you down, Hiialo." Setting her on the floor, she asked, "Would you like to help me make drinks for everyone?"

Chris bobbed up from the seat he'd just taken in a chair two feet away from Erika. "Can I help?"

"No," said Hiialo. "This is my house."

Her rudeness embarrassed Erika. Kal just lifted his eyebrows, but Mary Helen gave Erika a sympathetic glance and said, "Hiialo, dear."

Hiialo's face showed her acute insecurity. Erika crouched beside her and whispered so that no one else could hear, "Don't you want to show Chris what a good hostess you are? We can let him take the ice out of the ice trays."

Her eyes brimmed with tears. "No."

Kal and King exchanged looks of resignation.

Chris, showing the maturity of the older child, said, "It's okay, Erika. I'll make more origami."

David set the bottle of *shoyu* on the counter and looked inquisitively at Erika and Hiialo. Even at four, Chris had never behaved that way. But at four, Chris had been trapped in silence.

As Erika straightened up, King said to Hiialo, "How about a hug for your grandpa?"

Kal saw that lines of concern had creased Erika's forehead. He came over to the window to be near her. That night after Hiialo was in bed, they should talk. It occurred to him to ask David a few things about his sister. But it was David's first wife Erika's fiancé had slept with before she killed herself.

They ate on the porch, spreading out on the glider and on a bench under the window. Kal and Erika sat on the top step, with Hiialo huddled at Erika's feet, subdued but well behaved.

After dinner Erika took Mary Helen back to her room to share her most recent work, including the newest watercolor of the hitchhikers at the Haena Store, which she had painted that morning. Kal's mother was enthusiastic about all the pieces, especially those of Hiialo.

"You've really caught her vibrancy."

The word made Erika smile, and Mary Helen smiled, too, as though conjuring a mental picture of her granddaughter's "vibrancy."

Would Kal's mother have insight into his parenting style? Erika decided it was a safe topic. "You know, Kal and I have some disagreement over how to treat Hiialo."

Mary Helen lifted her eyes.

"I'm a person who always tries to foresee what's going to happen in the next moment. With a child, I try to anticipate possible accidents so that they can be avoided. And Kal..." Erika's sigh was the buildup of weeks of frustration and anxiety. She didn't finish.

Mary Helen turned back to the watercolors, focusing on the hitchhikers. Her lips curved into an expression both thoughtful and wise. "You know," she said, "I think I know just how you feel."

Erika started. *Did* Mary Helen know?

"Look at this painting." Kal's mother regarded the hitchhikers. "Now, my parents always taught me that hitchhiking was dangerous." She faced Erika. "King, on the other hand, grew up hitching rides from tourists. And so you can just imagine the confrontation the day Leo first thumbed a ride home from Hanalei." She echoed Erika's earlier sigh.

"Erika, this is very difficult to accept, but in Hawaii it helps to remember the original meaning of the word *haole*. It didn't mean Caucasian. It meant foreigner. The longer I've lived here, the more I've seen that there are many ways to do things. And they aren't necessarily better or worse. Just different." Thoughtfully she regarded the *hau* tree outside the window. "If you look at Hiialo, for instance. She's wildly spontaneous and sometimes very naughty. But I also find her refreshingly brave, in a way none of my children were with the caution I tried to instill in them."

Erika twisted her hands together. Brave was all right. But children needed protection.

"The other part of it, I'm afraid," said Kal's mother soberly, "is Maka." Suddenly she blinked quickly, dug a tissue from her pocket, and dabbed at her eyes.

Horror crept over Erika. She'd made Mary Helen cry. But no, it was Maka. She stepped forward, wanting to offer comfort.

"I'm sorry. It was just so sad, so hard for Kal." Mary Helen sniffed and put away the tissue. "That accident— and Iniki, too, and what happened with his music—made Kal just a little bit fatalistic, Erika. I don't know what else to say." She arranged her face in happy lines and concluded the discussion. "Except that I'm glad you're here. You're so good for both of them."

Erika pondered Mary Helen's feet in their casual slippers. A woman from the Midwest who had made Hawaii her home.

Raising her eyes, she said, "Thank you. For saying all of that."

Mary Helen answered, "I just wish there'd been someone to say it to me." She gave Erika a quick hug, and together they left the room.

WHEN KING AND Mary Helen had departed with Raiden, the others put on swimsuits and went down to the beach. As usual Hiialo ran into the water without waiting for anyone else, and Erika saw her brother wearing a faint frown of disapproval.

"Can I go in, too, Dad?"

"Yes," said David.

Erika watched Chris approach the water and scan the reef for urchins and stingrays. His caution was in marked contrast to Hiialo's full-speed-ahead confidence, and after her talk with Mary Helen, Erika found herself appreciating the latter. Kal's way of doing things had merit, too.

Not wanting to invite comparison between her body and that of her sister-in-law, Erika wore her sarong as she sat on the beach talking to her brother. Kal went into the water with Hiialo and Chris and Jean.

David said, "I like him, Erika."

So do I.

The waves roared, broke on the shore.

"The kid's a live wire."

Hiialo had done her jet-rocket imitation several times since he'd been there, running through the house, leaping off the porch. Sprinting for the sea and plunging in splashing. "She has a lot of energy. It's the way she is."

David smiled. "I wasn't criticizing. I'm glad you like

her. And she seems to like you.'' The sun turned his face Burnt Umber as he squinted at the others playing in the surf.

Kal dove for something under the water and come up holding a hermit crab. It bit his finger. He yelped, over-dramatizing, and Hiialo and Chris had hysterics. Erika glanced at her brother, but David's eyes were on his wife, full of adoration.

He said, ''I think I'm going to get wet.'' Soon he was out in the water with Jean.

Erika saw them playing, splashing…kissing.

Kal was entertaining the two kids by letting them take turns diving from his shoulders. Standing up, Erika removed her sarong and walked down to the water.

Chris yelled, ''Hey, Hiialo, want to build a sand castle?''

''Hooray!''

As the children ran in, leaping over the foam, Erika dove into a wave and swam away from shore. The sea was like paint water, a Hooker's Green and Cerulean Blue wash.

Spotting Erika, Kal swam toward her. Somewhere behind him, Jean was wrapped around David in the water, the two of them glittery sunset wet, kissing. He'd held Maka like that a few times in the ocean, her legs embracing him. They'd been young.

Water beaded on Erika's lashes. What would it be like to hold her that close, only swimsuits separating them?

He moved nearer her, and they both stood on the sandy bottom, the ocean trying to push their feet out from under them as the surface spread around their shoulders. ''Your brother and sister-in-law seem pretty crazy about each other.''

''Yes… Well. They have a lot in common. For instance, they're both marine biologists. And martial artists.''

"Really?"

"Tae kwon do. My dad did it, too." Erika admitted, "I never took to it. I don't like getting hit."

"I wouldn't like your getting hit, either. We have some things in common, too."

She turned away in the water. "Some things."

Kal's hands touched her bare waist. Wet. Soft. It reminded him of Maka. But the memory hurt only a little.

Erika let him draw her closer, and he spun her slowly around to face him. She saw water clinging to the edge of his scar. She saw her own image in his eyes.

He kissed her.

Feeling swelled her throat. She glanced toward the beach and the children and slipped away from him, swam farther from shore.

Kal followed her. Treading water beside her, he said, "So, your brother thinks Hiialo's pretty naughty."

"No, he doesn't!" While Kal dove beneath the surface and came up, Erika reached a decision. She ought to tell him about Chris. Once it had seemed too personal. Now she wanted him to know. "Kal, from the time Chris was three until he was six, he didn't talk."

Floating on a wave with her, Kal stared.

"He saw his mother go over the bow rail. Afterward he forgot everything. And he was mute."

The boy on the shore was dumping a bucket of water into a moat he and Hiialo had dug. Watching him point to something and speak to Hiialo, Kal recalled Erika saying, long ago, that Chris had hung around her while she painted. He remembered her telling Hiialo that she couldn't have a conversation and paint at the same time.

Now her mouth was bent with unhappiness and pain. Chris had seen his mother kill herself. The thought made him sick. Whoever David's first wife had been, he didn't like her. He'd never known anyone like that. "This woman sounds evil."

"She wasn't. Just…selfish. And messed up. She wasn't strong." Erika frowned. "I think each of us is the product of our life experiences. My childhood was good. Hers… Well, none of us know what it was." Why had Skye killed herself? What was the final trigger? A hastily spoken accusation that had sent her back into painful feelings born in childhood?

Erika shivered. She couldn't even discuss it with David anymore. He'd moved on. He was happy now.

This was her own burden. It always would be.

Fooling around in the water, eyeing the fuzzy silhouette of a dogfish two yards below, Kal considered what she'd said. Selfishness. It was what he and Maka had accused each other of when they fought. His music. Her hula. They'd both wanted to work nights. They'd compromised often. He'd become better because of her and she because of him. That was love.

Erika… Could he learn different lessons from her? Sure. But her past upset him; he recoiled from anything sordid. And what she'd told him was the stuff of horror.

She'd drifted away, twenty feet or so, and he swam over to her. "So how did Chris communicate with you?"

"Some sign language, but mostly just in his own way." The conversation had brought back those days on the *Skye,* the wheelchair, her prison. As the surf washed over her shoulders, Erika watched the children in the sand, one who had never completely been hers, one who might never be. "I think I'm going to go play with them."

"Sure." He swam with her toward the shore, but lingered in the foamy shallows to watch her limp out of the water, a goddess in human disguise. Namakaokahai of the ocean. But in fact, Erika the woman was more noble. A human who had triumphed over ugliness. *The battle's still going on, Kal.*

Sex.

She wouldn't have to wage that one alone. If she could learn to trust him...

Chris called, "Are you going to help us with our castle, Erika?"

From the surf, Kal watched Hiialo scramble to her feet and position herself in front of Erika's legs like a miniature Akita defending her own.

In a voice for the world to hear, she told Chris, "This is my new mom."

On the beach Erika swallowed, her heart racing. Hiialo hadn't really said that.

Chris, a bright boy with a stepmother of his own, asked, "Erika, are you going to marry Kal?"

"Oh, Chris..." She faltered. Where were David and Jean? Where was Kal? Had anyone else heard?

Yes, Kal had. Spinning her head toward the low breakers, she saw his face. Dumbfounded. Then, catching her eye, he shrugged and grinned before ducking under the water and swimming farther from shore.

Hiialo tugged on Erika's hand. "Pick me up."

Absently Erika said, "Magic word."

"Please."

Lifting her, in her wet and sandy swimsuit, Erika saw that Hiialo's eyes were fastened defiantly on Chris. She didn't really believe what she'd said; she couldn't. It was just a challenge, a way of marking her territory.

But Chris was watching Erika, waiting for an answer.

"I don't know." She eyed the round face of the little girl in her arms, and there was nothing to do but sigh.

And secretly wish that what Hiialo had said would come true.

"Do you think I should straighten her out tomorrow?" asked Erika as Kal rubbed her back that night.

He slid his fingers under the straps of her tank top,

noting her slight shiver at the touch. Massaging her shoulders gently, he wished he could say the words in his mind. Soothing love words. Gentling sex words. His fingers slipped down her sides.

More quivering.

"Do you?" she repeated.

Think she should tell Hiialo that she wasn't her new mom? Kal said carefully, "That might be premature."

Premature? Did that mean he wanted to marry her?

She felt him move, the mattress sinking beside her, and rolled onto her side. "Kal?"

He lay facing her. They stared at each other, bodies inches apart.

Kal waited until he was sure she wouldn't move away. Then he reached up and smoothed back her hair. "I want to kiss you."

The words were soft, but she knew what he'd said. She shifted closer on the mattress, and so did he, and he kissed her.

Erika shook. *Give,* she reminded herself. It wasn't hard.

Sensing trust in her lips, Kal wrapped his arm around her, pulling her close. But he hadn't lain in bed with his body against a woman's since Maka, and it was Maka who came to him, a soul-vision filling up his mind, making his eyes burn.

The emotion shocked him. He'd thought it was over. Upset, he pulled away.

Erika saw his face, his confusion, as he rolled onto his back. His hand groped for hers on the mattress, and their fingers wove together.

"Kal?"

Think about her, he thought. *Think about Erika.*

He sat up, searching for something appropriate to say. Some excuse. But when he saw her brown eyes watching him, he didn't want to lie. And the truth was unspeakable.

You couldn't tell a woman that kissing her had made you miss your dead wife.

He stroked her hair and bent to kiss her forehead. "I'll see you in the morning."

"Is anything wrong?"

"Not with you." He hugged her. "Everything's fine."

He got up, and Erika stared at his back and saw the door close behind him as he went out.

What's wrong, Kal?

Had she done something wrong? That had to be it: he didn't like the way she'd kissed him. It was too awful to ponder, that after all this *she* repulsed *him*.

To get rid of the thoughts, she crawled across the bed and took one of the Johnsons's dog-training books from her nightstand. *The Art of Raising a Puppy* by the Monks of New Skete. It took her a long time to focus, to shake off what had just happened with Kal, but soon she was absorbed, and she read the introduction and three chapters.

By then it was past eleven and her eyes were drifting shut. Kal was probably already asleep. She should go to sleep, too.

Erika got up and opened her door to go down the hall to the bathroom.

A bed creaked. It was in Kal's room, and she heard his feet hit the floor. Starting down the hall, she schooled herself not to glance through the beads into his room.

But as she reached the bathroom, she heard a drawer open, and her head jerked toward his door by its own volition.

Through the beads she saw him.

There was a photograph in his hand. He was putting it into a shoe box in his desk drawer, a box full of other photos.

He must have known she was there, because he turned his back as he shut the drawer. Erika quickly did the same, to pretend she hadn't seen. She pushed open the bathroom door and slipped inside.

When the closed door hid them from each other, she drew a breath. But her heart was pounding and she felt sick. The knowledge was so crushing that she clung to one of the towel racks, drawing deep breaths.

He wasn't over Maka.

THROUGH THE DANGLING bead curtain, Kal looked at the closed bathroom door. She hadn't seen. Wouldn't think anything if she had. It was his guilt doing this.

The ancient Hawaiians had believed you shouldn't keep a dead person's possessions close to you, that it caused their souls to stay near in an unhealthy way. Was that what was happening to him?

But these were only photos. Iniki had taken everything else. Everything but the quilt in which he'd wrapped himself and his daughter those nights at the shelter.

Casting another glance toward the bathroom, Kal opened the drawer again and removed the shoe box. He slid the closet door open and put the box on the highest shelf, on top of some photograph albums and videos of Maka dancing—the remains of their past.

He shut the door, and when Erika came out of the bathroom, he stepped out into the hall and said, "Hey, good night." He put his arm around her and hugged her, and she smiled before she hurried down the hall to her room.

He watched the light disappear as she closed herself inside, and he stood in the hallway and told himself again that she hadn't seen him with Maka's picture.

ERIKA COULD SEE no change in his treatment of her, and she tried to forget what had happened Friday night. Saturday, after Hiialo was asleep, she massaged his back, and when she was done they embraced, cheek to cheek, and he kissed her briefly and warmly, looking long into her eyes.

He's still getting over Maka. It's not going to happen all at once. She told herself that whenever she remembered the shoe box in his drawer.

Sunday night David took the three of them—Kal, Hiialo and Erika—out to dinner in Hanalei with his family. They were going to the Hunakai, a seafood restaurant and bar. As they waited for the hostess to return from seating some people, Hiialo exclaimed, "Look! Hula! Can we go watch?"

She was gazing out the front window at a park across the street where two men in short sarongs were running along the walkways lighting torches.

Kal picked her up. "Sorry, Ti-leaf, we've got a dinner reservation."

Jean leaned around them to peer out the window.

"Please," begged Hiialo.

The hostess arrived to seat them.

"Blade, party of six," David said.

Kal shook his head at his daughter.

"I wouldn't mind seeing some hula myself." Jean shrugged at Erika. "I guess they'll be gone when we're done eating."

"Yeah." Kal kept his back to the window, though even from across the street they could all hear the long eerie blast of a conch shell.

Hiialo's face began to quiver, to melt into unhappiness.

The hostess led the way into the shadows of the restaurant, and David waited for the women to follow. Erika went ahead. Outside, behind her, the hula drum beat. *It must make him think of Maka.* There was no way it couldn't. Did it bother Kal to see hula now? How did he feel about Hiialo's interest?

When they reached the table, David pulled out a chair for her and another for Jean. As she sat down, Erika heard a familiar sound—sniffling—and saw that Hiialo, in Kal's arms, had begun to cry because she couldn't see the dancers.

Kal said to David, "Excuse me. We're going outside for a minute."

Erika hoped he wasn't taking her to the park; she'd been told no.

But he was carrying her in the opposite direction, toward the back door. When Hiialo realized this, she began to scream. Patrons all over the restaurant gaped. Her wail rose and fell like a siren as Kal slipped out the back door. Sitting quietly in his seat, Chris stared after them with an expression of amazement that anyone could behave so badly.

Jean and David opened their menus, and so did Erika, but her heart and her thoughts were outside, and she barely heard the conversation around her for the next fifteen minutes, until Kal and Hiialo returned.

THE FEELING AT THE TABLE wavered from relaxed to tense while Kal and Erika tried to keep Hiialo happy, giving her anything she asked for to preserve the peace. But whenever the adults began talking, she grew bored and misbehaved, blowing the paper on her straw across the room—much to Chris's amusement—playing with her silverware, kicking the legs of the table.

She had eaten half her dessert and was looking cranky again when Kal felt hands on his shoulders and looked up.

The owner of the Hunakai, a guy who'd gone to school with his brother Keale, said, "Howzit, Kal?" He smiled at the other guests. *"Ono?"*

Tasty.

"Very," said David.

Seeming satisfied, the owner turned to Kal and spoke quietly. "Hey, I saw Jakka Bennee the other day. He said you guys are getting Kai Nui together again. How 'bout a Fourth of July gig?''

Erika's eyes were riveted to Kal's face. She saw his surprise, but he hid it fast.

"Love to. Let's talk about it."

"Good." The owner clapped him on the shoulder, nodded to the rest of them and left the table.

Kal stared at his plate, wondering why Jakka had said they were a band again. They'd talked about it Thursday night, but nothing had been decided. Now he'd accepted a gig—without even discussing it with Erika.

Erika...

He looked across the table, trying to catch her eye.

Erika smiled. "Good," she said, and then turned to the fish on her plate. But her appetite was gone.

Because of her, Kal could play music again. He would be grateful. But how would he ever separate that from his feelings for her? Would he even try? Or had he simply accepted what he'd said in his letter, that he would never love another woman the way he'd loved Maka?

"Hey, Erika."

His low voice summoned her from her thoughts.

Across the table he smiled, and his eyes were a kiss.

But the timing was all wrong—too soon after he'd gotten the gig—and it intensified rather than extinguished the doubts in her heart.

As HE RUBBED her shoulders that night, he said, "Sorry about the Fourth. Saying yes without asking you."

"It's fine."

It wasn't fine, thought Kal. It was complicated. She'd been with him three weeks. He'd promised her three more to make up her mind about Hiialo. And since then everything had changed. One gig was no big deal, but he knew Jakka and Danny wanted more. It was a commitment he couldn't make. Not till he knew Erika would be there for Hiialo.

He stopped rubbing her shoulders and lay down beside her as he had two nights before. She rolled onto her side to look at him.

Kal wasn't afraid of the Maka feeling coming back. He'd figured out the problem. Firsts. Most of them had happened in the year after she died. First Christmas without her. First birthday without her.

But he'd forgotten about first kiss.

First sex would be something else.

Just part of going on.

As he hugged her, Erika let her body slide alongside his. It felt good. Only her doubts bothered her. When she felt his lips touch hers, she wondered if he wished she was Maka. It wasn't something she could ask.

His mouth formed a word on hers. "Erika…"

"What?"

He shifted, and she felt the shape of his erection through their clothes. His hand touched her jaw, and she saw his eyes and spun in them.

She'd never felt this way before, when all she wanted was to gaze into a man's eyes and never stop. Helpless, she knew the truth.

I love you.

He was talking. "I know how I asked you to come here. We both know everything's changed." He moved his face against her cheek, getting closer to her, and his nose stroked her skin. "I don't want you to leave."

Heat saturated her body, pouring into her legs, one of which was somehow between his, skin to skin. What was he saying?

"But I can't have a celibate marriage to you." He pressed his lips to her jaw, let them creep up her face. Her mouth was looking for his, too, and they kissed again, drawing closer. When he looked at her, those brown, almost black eyes were open, wholly present.

He said, "I love you."

Her breath stretched. *He loves me.* The arms around her, the face so near to hers. The friend who'd seemed too faraway ever since that night she'd seen him with a photograph. But this was Kal, who had told her that love was giving. And he loved her.

He kissed her again.

"Kal…" It felt like the beginning of sex, but she didn't care. There was no man she trusted so much.

Kal turned his head, coaxed her mouth open with his. *It's all right, Erika. This is how we go farther.*

His tongue slid inside.

She kissed him back, and he knew she didn't know she was rubbing against him, trying to get closer. It lasted quite a while, and he wanted much more. As he pulled his mouth away, he watched her. She didn't move her hands from his shoulders. Her lips were flushed, her face bright, too. Her eyes were misty.

"You," he said softly, "are not frigid."

"I don't want to get hurt." She didn't mean to say it, but it came out.

"There you go again," he said softly. "Worrying. Why don't you think, instead, that here's this guy who loves me and maybe it'll work out?"

Her heart heaved, and she placed one of her hands in one of his.

Kal kissed her again and did not say what *he* was thinking. That if anyone got hurt, it would probably be him.

CHAPTER TWELVE

AFTER HE'D SAID good-night to her, he went out on the porch to play guitar, but he ended up laying aside the instrument and staring out at the hot humid night. She'd said, *I don't want to get hurt.*

She'd been hurt before, by her fiancé. Maybe by other guys.

Kal had married Maka when he was barely twenty, after she'd been his girlfriend for more than a year. He'd had sex once before that, on the beach after a party, with a girl who liked his voice and the way he played the guitar. In a half-drunken state, he'd realized what he was doing. He still remembered feeling, *This is intense. This is real life.* Then he'd looked into the blurred face of a stranger and pulled out and said, "I don't want to do this."

Maka hadn't changed him that way; she'd proved him right. Sex was like...getting a puppy. You were inviting someone to fall in love with you, and if you turned your back...

He wasn't going to turn his back on Erika. He knew that already. But unless they made some real promises, he wasn't sure she wouldn't do that to him.

She wasn't Maka.

And her feelings about sex differed from his in more ways than one.

THE NEXT DAY Adele called to say that she wanted to publish three of Erika's paintings as prints. Erika met Kal after work with an ecstatic hug, and his parents, hearing the news, decided to host a spur-of-the-moment potluck to celebrate her success and Kal's new gig. It was the start of a busy two weeks.

On evenings when he and Erika and Hiialo weren't busy with David's family, Kal played music with Danny and Jakka at Jakka's house in Kalihiwai, on the other side of Hanalei Bay. When he was home, he practiced with the band tape they'd made. He wanted the Fourth of July show to be great—the start of a comeback.

If all went well, it would be the start of something else, too.

Something more important.

Erika.

On the Fourth of July, she would have been in Haena more than five weeks.

ON THE FOURTH, he and Erika and Hiialo gathered on the beach to light fireworks with David's family. The kids would be going to his parents' house for the evening, Hiialo to spend the night because he'd be out so late. Chris would stay only till midnight; David and Jean wanted to see Kai Nui play, but because she was pregnant, they wouldn't stay till the end.

When the last sparklers had been lit, David and Jean corralled the children into their rental, and Erika and Kal got into the Datsun to drive to Hanalei to the Hunakai.

Kal was wearing white cotton twill pants and a beige aloha shirt with navy blue guitar players on it. Erika wore a thigh-length emerald green silk dress with no sleeves. It was Kal's favorite of her dresses—and the color seemed like a good omen. The same shade as something he wanted to give her. The small square box weighed down his shirt pocket. He'd lock it in the trunk before the show. And afterward...

As he turned the car down the street beside the Hunakai, planning to pull into the back lot, Erika spotted a
sign in front of the community center. Bon Dance Club.
''Kal, what's that?''

Obon. It was that time again. It hit him as it did every
year, perhaps because his parents used to take them all
bon dancing in the summers. The festival marked the
years. Since Maka had died, it had marked the years without her. He didn't know why.

''What did you say?'' He couldn't remember what Erika had asked.

''What's a *bon* dance club? They have clubs? I thought
it was a Buddhist thing.''

''Well, the dancing has become pretty secular. People
still go to temples to dance but also to these clubs. *Bon*
dance clubs have musicians or taped music for the
dances. Sometimes they have dancers who perform alone.
Sometimes the dancers travel, like the Akanas. You can
join a *bon* dance club and go every weekend.''

''Do you think we could go visit the Akanas?'' asked
Erika. ''I'd really like to do that.''

''I'm sure they're traveling with their troupe now.''

Erika was disappointed. *Obon* appealed to her. Her life
had been altered by death. Her parents'. But even more,
Skye's. Maybe honoring it somehow would help. Help
to shed the guilt.

And maybe if Kal went, he would stop missing Maka.
He loves you.

He'd only said it once, and sometimes Erika wasn't
sure she believed it. For the past two weeks, he'd been
wrapped up in the band, sometimes coming home too late
for their back-rub ritual.

But she treasured the memory of a night she'd awakened in the dark to find him covering her up. He'd kissed
her good-night, with soft words and a brief embrace that

left her able to drift easily back into sleep, his voice and touch imprinted on her mind and heart.

As he turned into the narrow lot behind the Hunakai, Kal noticed her silence. *Bon dances.* She wanted to go. He should take her. His parents knew several dances. They could teach her, and he could take her to a *bon* dance club some weekend. It didn't have to mean anything; it never had when he was a child or a teenager. It was just a thing his family had done.

He parked behind the restaurant, and Erika gathered her purse and pulled on her door handle. Kal almost reached out to stop her, just to say, *I'll take you bon dancing, Erika.*

But the grief, the hurt of the past, stopped him.

He knew what the *bon* dances meant. And he couldn't dance with joy that Maka had moved on. He wasn't that generous.

He'd never wanted her to go.

He opened his door, and the trade winds gusted in and brought her voice into his mind, answering him.

That's why I've never gone.

Erika was already out of the car. Kal paused, gazing at a hole in the interior of the driver door.

Bon-odori.

Maybe this was the way the souls of the dead came back. By speaking through the subconscious of the living. But it felt like Maka in his heart. Real Maka, loving him.

In that moment Kal knew that she *was* there, had been there since the day she died. Maybe she slunk through his house in a *mo'o's* guise as Eduardo, playing with her little girl. Maybe she hovered around his head and shoulders, keeping close to him in his pain. But Kal knew now the power of his own love for her, of the love they'd shared.

She'd never turned away.

And she never would—until he let her go.

"IS EVERYBODY HAVING a good time?"

The screams and shouts from the dance floor were deafening, muted only slightly by the earplugs Kal had given her. It was after midnight, and Erika stood against the wall, some distance from the stage. David and Jean had already left, and now she was alone, a spectator because she didn't dance.

From the shadows, she watched Kal at the microphone. He was sweating, his hair wet with perspiration, as he grinned at the responsive crowd.

"One more song, and then we're gonna take a break. This is a dedication."

Erika hadn't thought he knew where she was standing, but his wink hit her with the accuracy of a laser, and when he strummed that first chord, she recognized the song. "I Wanna Be Your Man."

Her heart swelled, the way it did when he kissed her. The way it had when he said he loved her. But as he played, his joy seemed more intense than love, than anything Erika had known that could happen between a man and a woman. She wondered again if it was *her* that he loved.

Or simply the freedom to be where he now stood.

She watched his body, his touch with the guitar, the grin he rained on the crowd, the way he moved. He seemed like some god, unattainable, whose attention to a mortal woman could only end in tragedy.

She wasn't like him. She wasn't beautiful enough. Her body was ravaged. And the way she'd lived in that wheelchair. The indignity. She didn't ever want him to know how she'd been. He would be disgusted. Even if he *didn't* feel that, she did.

Watching him on the stage, she faced what she'd known the first time she'd seen his picture.

That the highest love was for the beautiful.

And that she was not among them, while Kal was.

If he loved her, as he'd said, it was for his daughter and for his life, his music. He could not be *in love* with Erika Blade.

AFTER THE SHOW Erika helped Kal get his equipment together in the back room and waited while he loaded the car. Although Jakka and Danny were friendly, she felt out of place. What did she know about music, about this late-night scene? It was obviously something they'd all done many times before, and she pictured Maka with them, knowing which electrical cords belonged to Kal, helping coil them.

Or maybe just knowing how to speak pidgin with Jakka and Danny.

Erika only knew better than to try.

But when she climbed into the Datsun with Kal, when the doors were shut, the tension rolled off her body and evaporated. This was Kal, her friend, who rubbed her shoulders at night, who hugged and kissed her before he left for work, who had, just two days before, left a note on her pillow that said, *Sex is beautiful.*

Her doubts faded into the night.

"You're so good, Kal."

"Thanks." He grinned at her as he started the car, and then he leaned over and kissed her mouth. "Gonna be my number-one fan?"

I want to be.

I Wanna Be Your Man.

She had to believe. She'd been reading to Hiialo. When the fairy godmother came and provided a dress, you put it on. You could worry about the pumpkin coach and the midnight curfew later.

"Yes," she said. "I think I already am."

He didn't put the car in gear. He maneuvered over the stick shift to hug her. "I love you."

Wear the dress, stupid. "I love you, Kal."

Their eyes locked and the stars swirled and the waltz began. Erika felt the warm skin of his neck against her cheek and knew that she'd never known anything so divine. *He does love me. He's not a man who would lie about love. This is Kal. Kal...*

He sang as he drove toward Haena, stopping in the middle of songs to ask her questions. "Did you hear that weird bass thing in the middle of 'Kona'?" And, "Were the lights too bright?"

She pushed back the seat and felt as relaxed as she had after surfing Polihale. It was so easy.

Before they reached Haena, Kal pulled off the road and parked the car.

Erika sat up. "What are we doing?"

"Introducing you to a new beach." He grabbed an old wool blanket from the back seat. Erika waited, accepting his quick kiss before she opened her door. Close by, waves crashed.

As she stood hugging herself in the breezy night, Kal rustled around in the trunk, undoubtedly checking his equipment. "Ready?"

"Yes."

He came around the car to collect her, to take her hand. She clung to it tightly, and sometimes to his arm, as they hiked down a rocky trail to the water. Kal spread the blanket in the sand on a vine of *hunakai,* white beach morning glories, and they both sat down.

Erika drew a breath, inhaling the night. Overhead a sprawling ironwood tree leaned toward the sea, dividing the view of sky, but between its limbs she could see the stars. "This is beautiful."

"Thanks. I told the Visitors' Bureau to make it just for you."

He was teasing. Affectionate. When Erika turned to give him a look, she saw the box in his hands.

"Except I hope you're not just a visitor."

Her heart thudded too hard. She forgot to breathe and couldn't help glancing at the box again.

"It's what you think."

She lifted her eyes.

His tilted up a little at the corners. "Want it?"

Erika edged back slightly. *Just ask, Kal. Don't do this to me.* But he *was* just asking. She should just answer. "Yes."

Kal moved to surround her with his legs. Erika's own stretched out under his bent right knee. She studied the shadows in the folds of white fabric. He was silent, and at last she looked at him.

"Will you marry me, Erika?"

Her eyes got hot. Dammit, couldn't she ever keep from crying? "Yes."

Kal held her, tears and silky strands of her hair under his cheek. His hands found her spine through her dress, found all the muscles and hollows he knew. "I'm asking you to make love with me, Erika. To be my real wife."

Real wife. She quaked, made herself small to be closer to him. "Yes. I want to be your real wife."

His legs pressed around her, all of him holding her, and it was safe, the safest place she'd ever been. She tried to wipe her eyes and he pulled back. "You can use my sleeve. I empty my pockets before shows. I don't have a handkerchief."

"I have a tissue." She found it, and she laughed as she blew her nose. "I'm sorry I always do this."

"I'm not." Smiling, Kal opened the lid of the box and sang some words from a David Lindley song, asking for her hand.

Her left hand. Erika couldn't remember giving it to René. She recalled how she'd received that ring at a jewelry store. It had been a conscience gift. She'd gone months with no symbol of their betrothal, only his words, which were worth little.

Giving her hand to Kal was different. He held it and kissed it before he slipped something cool and metallic over her finger. Erika looked down. In the moonlight, she saw an emerald. The ring was thick, textured, gold.

"It's a *haku lei.* I had a guy in Kapaa make it."

"It's beautiful, Kal." Not wanting to take her hand from his, she leaned closer to examine it.

His musician's fingers stroked her cheek. Then he gently twisted the band against her skin. "How does it feel? Too snug?"

"I think it's right. It won't come off." *Ever,* she vowed silently. Kal was not René. And she would fulfill the promise she'd made.

Fear stole over her.

What *had* she promised?

All of love.

Panic-stricken, she repeated the words he'd taught her. *Sex is beautiful. When you love each other. Sex is beautiful. When you love...*

How soon? When would it have to happen?

Kal read the fear on her down-turned face, like Hiialo when she was nervous or uncertain. But Hiialo had the sense to lift her brown eyes to him, to say the name she called him.

Erika had forgotten how to love or trust like a child.

I can teach you, he thought. But all he said was, "So you still owe me a back rub."

Her eyes did look at him then, just like Hiialo's. *You won't make me do it tonight?*

He treated her as he would have Hiialo when his daughter was avoiding a scary inevitability. Never releasing her left hand, he used his other hand to smooth her hair away from her eyes and gently told her again that it would really happen. "We'll have a nice long honeymoon."

She nodded, frozen-faced, and Kal had to quiet more than a ripple of misgiving in his own heart.

What if she never learned to love sex?

"DADDY, YOU WOKE ME UP," Hiialo said, rubbing her eyes the next morning.

"I know. I want to talk to you before I go to work. Erika made some mango bread last night." At three in the morning. She'd told him she couldn't sleep. He'd played the guitar while the bread baked. "She said we could have it for breakfast. So get up, sleepyhead."

"Okay, Daddy." Hiialo gathered Pincushion, Fluff and her favorite blanket and got out of bed. She followed him into the front room.

Kal heard Erika stirring in the back of the house, and a song rose in his mind, one that had tried to write itself while he lay sleepless on his bed. Rejecting some lyrics, trying to make others wait till after his conversation with his daughter, he collected the pieces of bread he'd cut for himself and Hiialo. "Can you carry that cup of juice? Let's go out on the swing."

The sun wasn't yet poking through the branches of the trees. About now it was probably starting to show above the ocean's horizon. Too bad the bungalow wasn't on the beach. When he'd bought it from them, his parents had asked if he wouldn't rather have the oriental beach house. That house had seemed big for him and Hiialo. But now there were three of them. Something to think about.

Beside him on the porch swing, Hiialo helped herself to a piece of mango bread.

"So, Hiialo. How would you feel if Erika lived with us always?"

Hiialo squinted at him thoughtfully. After a moment she said, "Okay. Would she be my nanny, like Mary Poppins?"

"Ah…no. Remember that day on the beach when you told Chris Erika was your new mom?"

She didn't look at him. Caught making things up. She hadn't known *he'd* heard.

Kal let it sink in. It never hurt to let her think he had the powers of Santa Claus. "Hiialo?"

"Yes. I remember."

"It turns out you're right. I'm going to marry Erika. She'll be your stepmother."

Hiialo peered up at him anxiously, and then her eyes filled with tears.

Kal's heart gave one hard thump. "What is it?" She was the one who'd said Erika was her new mom. He gathered her up, mango bread and all. "What's wrong?"

"She'll make me do all the housework. I don't want a stepmother!"

"Do all the housework?" He thought. "Didn't you finish paying for the paintbrushes?"

"Yes." Hiialo still looked troubled. She closed her mouth and wouldn't talk.

"Tell me what you mean. Does she make you do housework now?"

Hiialo simply shook her head, her lips drawn tightly together.

"Well, I am going to marry her. We love each other. And we both love you. I wouldn't marry someone who didn't love you."

Hiialo began to cry, not a screaming tantrum, but quiet deep sobs as though she was afraid she'd be overheard. "No, Daddy. Please don't make her be my stepmother. I don't want a stepmother."

Kal heard Erika in the kitchen putting on water for tea. "Why don't you want a stepmother? I thought you wanted—"

"She'll be mean. And you might…" Her voice trailed off on another incoherent sob.

Erika came out onto the lanai to see if Kal wanted something to drink. She was sleepy but happy—until she saw Hiialo's tear-streaked face. "Hiialo, what's wrong?"

Hiialo took one look at her and buried her face in her father's shoulder. She sobbed softly and continuously.

Erika searched Kal's face in the dim light, and he tilted his head toward the seat, inviting her to join them on the swing. Erika sat down. She put a hand on Hiialo's back. "Can I hold you, Hiialo?"

Hiialo shook her head hard and hugged her father convulsively.

Kal said, "Hiialo, let's finish our breakfast, yeah?"

"I don't like it."

Erika knew Hiialo was trying to hurt her. And there could be only one explanation. Kal must have told her they were getting married.

But she told Chris I was her new mom. She loves me.

"Hiialo, do you need to go back to bed?" suggested Erika. She usually wasn't up so early.

Hiialo shook her head.

"I think that's a good idea." Kal stood up with her in his arms.

"Nooo!"

The tantrum began, and Erika tensely rocked the porch swing, hugging herself, heartsore.

The last thing she'd expected was that Hiialo wouldn't want her.

DAVID STOPPED by the bungalow that afternoon while Hiialo was sleeping. She'd had another tantrum at noon, throwing her plate lunch on the floor.

When Erika saw David at the door, she wasn't sure if she was sorry or relieved. They sat out on the steps of the lanai in humid sunshine filtered through clouds, and she told him she was going to marry Kal.

His eyes shone. ''That's great. That's really great, Erika.''

''Hiialo's not happy about it.''

He quirked his eyebrows. ''No?''

''She cried.''

David rubbed his chin, ran his tongue along his teeth thoughtfully. ''Chris wasn't too happy when I told him I was marrying Jean.''

''He loved Jean.''

''Sure. But getting a new parent is threatening. Hiialo will come around.''

A skink raced over a boulder beside the step. Erika tried to believe her brother's words.

''I'm really happy about you and Kal, Erika. I've worried. For a long time.''

Erika knew since when. She had no secrets from David. He'd been privy to everything. Not just her private struggles on his ship, things no one else knew. But what had happened with Skye that day in the hospital.

He had said, *Don't even think about it. Her decision, if she ever consciously made one, had nothing to do with you.*

Erika still couldn't quite believe that. Her chivalrous brother would say nothing else. But if she owed him anything now, it was to set him at ease, the way he'd always tried to do for her.

''Everything's fine.'' She smiled like a newly engaged woman.

And tried not to wonder what would happen when she and Kal tried to make love.

THEY DECIDED to be married in the Awa'awapuhi Valley on the Na Pali Coast. They would get there by Zodiac and be married by Kroner, Kal's boss, who was a mail-order minister; he'd sent away for a license from an ad in the back of *Rolling Stone*. Kal had said he'd like to write the vows—did she want to help? No. Erika felt incapable of planning. Trying to help plan made it too real.

After the ceremony Kal's parents would host a party at their house. In Hawaii, Kal explained, hardly anyone attended the wedding; but everyone came to the reception.

And that night…

Kal had ten days off, two before the wedding, a week after. Mary Helen and King would be looking after Hiialo. And they'd offered the beach house for a honeymoon getaway. Erika hadn't objected when Kal asked her. There was nowhere more beautiful than Haena, and it didn't matter where the honeymoon took place, anyway.

She couldn't hide from him.

On Monday, the week after the Fourth, Erika was washing dishes at the sink and wishing she could break through Hiialo's moodiness, her strange anxiety about the wedding, when a white rental car came down the driveway and pulled into the Datsun's empty space. *David or Jean,* thought Erika.

But when the driver door of the automobile opened, the person who stepped out was a heavyset woman with spiky burgundy hair and enormous yellow-and-black art deco earrings. Chrome Yellow blazer over a Lamp Black dress. Erika squinted at the visitor for three seconds before recognizing her.

She limped quickly to the door, banged open the screen and made fast time down the steps. "Adele!"

"Hello, Erika!" Adele burst out. "You look like an engaged woman. All aglow."

The two friends embraced, both talking at once.

"I didn't expect to see you yet."

"As the matron of honor, I had to come and make sure

everything's set for this wedding. Do you have a fabulous dress yet?''

Erika rolled her eyes. ''I've heard enough about fabulous dresses from Jean. She keeps taking me shopping. Try this on for size. We're going to land on the Na Pali Coast and hike up into a place called the Awa'awapuhi Valley. There is no fabulous dress involved. I'm going to wear ti leaves.''

Adele broke into laughter. ''If I had your body and was marrying the Haole Guitar Man…''

My body. No, you don't want that.

Pausing in the middle of the sun-splashed little lawn, Adele regarded the bungalow. ''It's so cute, Erika. Now, I just have to know this. Didn't you and I read some personal ad from an SWM in Haena?''

Erika couldn't help smiling. ''Yes.''

''I see.'' Adele threw back her head and laughed again. ''Well, you didn't do too bad for yourself, and neither did he. Where's the *keiki?* And is your intended home?''

''At work.'' Erika opened the screen door.

Hiialo was coloring at the coffee table. Just fifteen minutes before Adele arrived, Erika had tried to talk to her about the wedding, to ask what was bothering her. Hiialo had clammed up and shaken her head, refusing to talk.

All Erika could do was love her. Try to make her happy.

''Hiialo, I want you to meet my special friend, Adele.''

Hiialo got up, her face still puckered with worry.

''How nice to meet you, Hiialo,'' said Adele. ''You just call me Auntie Adele. I love to spoil little girls. Are you going to help me find a wedding dress for Erika?''

Hiialo swallowed, looking frightened. ''Okay,'' she whispered.

Adele lifted her eyebrows at Erika like, *What gives?*

Erika shrugged. To divert attention from Hiialo, she

said, "Adele, I've been out with Jean three times this week looking."

"Jean schmean. You don't shop for a dress with Cindy Crawford, you know what I mean? I can't even sit at the same dinner table with your sister-in-law. Too beautiful. Adele is in charge now."

Erika brushed Hiialo's hair, and the three of them went out to the rental car. Hiialo brought her blanket and Pincushion and Fluff and sat in the back seat sucking her thumb, looking troubled.

"Now, tell me where you've been already," said Adele. "Rest assured, if we don't find it on this island, I'm taking you to Honolulu."

"I am not going to Oahu for a dress." As they passed the Haena Store, Erika said, "Okay, we've looked in Kapaa, Lihue and Poipu."

"Have you tried Hanalei?"

They visited a Hanalei boutique that sold cotton and silk imports. Exploring the racks, Erika tried to imagine getting out of a Zodiac in a dress.

Adele corralled a petite salesgirl with a long dark braid, who asked Erika, "You're from the mainland?"

"But she's marrying a local guy," said Adele to Erika's dismay.

"Who?"

No hiding it. "Kal Johnson."

The girl's eyes widened. "Kalahiki! He some *ono.*"

Adele laughed richly. Even Erika had picked up enough Hawaiian to know the word for "tasty."

In the corner of the store, Hiialo sat placidly on a chair, sucking her thumb, holding her blanket and stuffed animals. Erika sighed without sound. What on earth was wrong? She told Adele, "Let me browse."

When Adele and the salesgirl began searching together, she joined Hiialo in the corner and crouched beside her chair. "Darling, please tell me what's wrong. Why are you so worried?"

Hiialo took her thumb from her mouth. Her face tightened painfully. She swung her legs under the chair, as though contemplating whether she should speak.

"Please tell me. I thought you wanted me to be your new mom."

"Mom," said Hiialo. "Not stepmother."

Erika blinked, startled by her confusion. "Honey... I can't be your mom. You grew inside Maka before you were born. She'll always be your mom. But if I marry your dad, I'll be your stepmother. And I'll take care of you like a mom."

Hiialo's eyes grew tearful, and her mouth and face crumpled. She turned her face toward the wall, trying not to cry.

"Honey, look at me."

She did. And whispered anxiously, "Will you make me do the housework?"

"What?" Was this about the paintbrushes? Had she been too harsh? Erika didn't know what to say. She couldn't promise Hiialo that she wouldn't have to do any chores. "Well, we all do some of the housework. You're such a help to me when we fold laundry together."

Hiialo bit her lip. "What if my daddy dies?"

Erika opened her mouth. "Why would that happen?"

"I don't know." She clamped her lips shut, hugged Pincushion and resumed swinging her legs.

The salesgirl said, "You like this?"

Erika glanced up in distraction. She had an impression of a pale yellow dress. She couldn't wear that color.

Adele made a polite indecisive sound. "Don't worry, Erika. Your fairy godmother will take care of all."

Fairy godmother...

Erika felt like slapping her head. "Just a minute. I'll try something on in a second."

Adele slipped away to confer with the salesgirl, and Erika turned back to Hiialo.

"Honey, are you thinking about Cinderella?"

Hiialo nodded gravely.

"Oh, no no no." Erika took her in her arms and embraced the little body. "I love you, Hiialo. Nothing like that will happen to you. Stepmothers don't have to be mean. Why, Jean's a stepmother." She pulled away to see Hiialo's worried face.

"Really?"

"Yes. Yes."

Hiialo seemed to think it over. At last she picked up Pincushion and her blanket again and leaned closer to Erika, asking to be held.

Erika picked her up and sat down in the chair, hugging Hiialo on her lap. *My little girl now.* She'd answered a personal ad, and now this small person was part of her life. She felt thankful. "You talk to your daddy about it when he comes home tonight, okay?"

"Okay," whispered Hiialo.

"Will you help me pick out my dress?" Softly Erika confessed, "I want to look special for your dad."

Hiialo handed Erika her blanket and stuffed animals, then slid off her lap. "Okay, Erika. I will help. But my daddy already thinks you are very pretty, and that's why he kisses you."

Leaving Erika, she began to wander through the store, touching dresses. After a moment she found Adele, plucked at the edge of her jacket and said, "Auntie Adele, I'm ready to help find a pretty dress for Erika."

CHAPTER THIRTEEN

HIS LIPS WOKE Erika Sunday morning.

She smelled coffee and saw his blue eyes and his naked shoulders and remembered what day it was. "What are you doing in here? It's unlucky. I shouldn't see you till the wedding."

He shook his head, smiling, and climbed over her on the big bed. "Paid attention to all that stuff the first time. This is the lucky way."

Her eyes began to focus. Sunlight flooded through the screen door to the outside. She'd begun to sleep with the door open because the evening breeze was so pleasant. With Kal so close by, she felt safe.

He was very close now.

She'd seen those worn-out cutoff pajama bottoms before. They always seemed on the verge of falling off his slim hips. They were all he wore as he lay on his stomach and propped himself on his elbows to face her. "Your coffee's on the nightstand."

She looked. Two cups. "How's your ulcer?"

"I forgot I had one till you said something. Must be getting good medicine."

She touched his arms, his biceps. She couldn't help it.

Bending his head to kiss one of her hands, Kal thought, *It's going to be fine.* Whatever the problem, at least she was able to get aroused. Phrases like "repulsed by sex" he barred from his mind. There were better things to consider. Day-to-day happiness. He and Hiialo had a secret from Erika. A good one.

Her hair was messy, a sexy halo on the pillow.

"Like having me in your bed in the morning?"

"Yes," said Erika. "When I came here, I wondered why you'd made it so big."

"You had good legs. I could tell from your picture."

Erika searched his eyes. Good legs. He didn't mind her scars. "Really?"

He shrugged. "Well, I don't know why I made your bed big. But I do like your legs. All of you." He didn't want to talk about how he'd felt before she came. He didn't want to think about it. He had hurt so much without Maka every day. Thinking about that time brought it back. He slid his hand to Erika's side, against her breast, and laid his head on the pillow beside hers.

Her brown eyes wouldn't meet his. They seemed to be trained on his throat as she asked, "Are you going to sleep in here, then?"

"That's the idea."

What about the quilt on his bed? she wondered. What about the photos of Maka in his bottom drawer? She didn't want to look at those things in his room day after day.

She didn't want *him* to look at them.

As he kissed her again, a shadow cut out the sunlight from the door.

"Ahhh!" screamed a voice as the screen creaked. "What's *he* doing in here?"

It was Adele. Erika giggled as her friend came inside, clutching a paper grocery bag. The older woman waved her free hand at Kal. "Scat! Get out. You're bad luck."

"I'm the groom." He gazed into Erika's eyes. "Go away, Adele. We'll be done in a minute."

"Oh, good grief. It's your funeral. I mean, your wedding." Adele opened the door to the hall and went through to the kitchen. "Hurry up!" she called over her shoulder. "Erika has to get dressed."

From the bedroom, as Kal kissed her again, as she allowed the now familiar touch of his tongue against hers, Erika heard Adele's voice soften. "Why, good morning, Hiialo. Are you ready for the wedding?"

"Kal…" whispered Erika.

"I love you," he said. "It's going to be a good day."

KAL SHOWERED and left in a car with his brothers to go Erika knew not where. She and Hiialo and Adele sat on the lanai and ate the croissants and fresh pineapple Adele had brought in the paper bag. Hiialo seemed ready to burst and finally said, "Auntie Adele, I have to tell you a secret about Erika. Two secrets."

Erika rocked dreamily on the swing while they went inside. The fairy tale hadn't stopped. This was how a wedding day should be.

It didn't matter that she'd seen Kal before the ceremony. He was right. It was a good omen.

Hiialo took a bath and put on the tie-dyed cotton-jersey dress she'd picked out in Hanalei to wear to the wedding. It matched Erika's tank dress, which was tie-dyed as well—her wedding clothes. *Why not?* Adele had said. *You're young, you're skinny. And it's cute that you match.*

More to the point, Erika loved it that Hiialo wanted to dress like her. Looked up to her. Maka would always be important to Hiialo, but each day Erika recognized the influence *she* was going to be in Hiialo's life.

If only it was the same with Kal.

But where Kal was concerned, it would take her seven years to catch up with Maka.

Adele was blow-drying Erika's hair when Jean showed up. David and Chris had gone down to the beach, she said. Erika slipped into the bathroom to take off her robe and put on her dress, and when she came out, Jean was in the hallway, staring into Kal's room.

Strange that for Jean—who must have worried once that David still loved Skye—Erika found herself making things up. "We'll probably use that as a spare room. Or a music studio for Kal. Maybe Chris could sleep in here if he comes to visit alone."

Jean's slanted blue-green eyes regarded her curiously. But she betrayed no suspicion that all was not right when she said, "Maybe you'll have another kid."

"Oh." Since Kal had asked her to marry him, she'd forgotten to want a baby of her own. She had Hiialo. "I'm thirty-six."

"Thirty-six works," said Jean. "Hey, your dress is beautiful."

They all walked down to the beach. Erika expected to see a Zodiac; instead, she found Kal's outrigger, draped in blossoms. Danny held the paddle, and David waited at the water with a maile *lei* for her hair and another *lei* for her to give Kal. The *leis* made of the fragrant leaves of the maile plant were highly prized for all special occasions. Erika carried Kal's *lei* over her arm. *Leis* for other people were not supposed to be worn by the giver.

Only she and Hiialo were to ride in the canoe with Danny, and as they left the shore, Erika noticed that, though hot and humid, the morning was also tranquil and clear. That would change; north shore rain came daily. Erika sat with Hiialo nestled against her, the matching fabric of their dresses blending together like flowers in the same bed.

Hiialo held on to both of Erika's hands. "My daddy planned this. He wanted you to ride in an outrigger like a princess."

"I love you, Hiialo," Erika whispered.

Near Hanakapiai Beach, a Zodiac passed them, familiar faces on board. Kal's parents, Adele and Kurt and their son, Jean and Chris and David. The outrigger had almost reached the steep lantana-green walls of the Awa'awapuhi Valley before Erika spotted a canoe coming from the other direction. As it drew nearer, she recognized Kal's body, the way he moved. He and another man were paddling the canoe, and two others were with them. The Zodiac was already beached with a little group of people gathered around.

As Danny landed the outrigger, jumping out to hold the gunwale, King and David waded through the water. "Hi, beautiful," Kal's father greeted Erika, then picked up his granddaughter to carry her to shore.

Accepting the support of her brother's arm, Erika stepped barefoot into the low breakers, holding up the shin-length skirt of her dress.

Soon she was on the beach, beside green cliffs like skyscrapers. The other outrigger was landing. Kal had rolled up the legs of his long white pants to pull it onto the beach. He unrolled them before he took some *leis* his brother Keale had been holding and walked down the beach toward Erika.

It felt like a lifetime since Erika had seen his face. But as she moved toward him on the hard wet sand, the crash of the surf echoed the pounding of her heart. *I'm crazy to be doing this. What if I never learn to like sex?*

Of course you will. Look at him, Erika.

They met midway between the canoes.

"You look beautiful." He touched her dress, then put *leis* of maile and of pikake, jasmine, over her head, around her neck. Drawing her near, he touched her hair, her head, with both hands and kissed her cheek. "How do you feel?"

Her stomach yawned, turned on itself.

If worse came to worst, she could fake it.

No, not with him. Not with Kal...

"I'm fine."

A PATH EDGED WITH LAVA rocks led up into the green valley. The steep slopes rising around it were covered with vegetation; it wasn't the dark green of the north shore but more vibrant, Hooker's Green Light, new grass in spring. From a distance the valley seemed to be lined with emerald velvet. Up close, Erika discovered that all that grew there were air plants and thorny lantana. The ginger for which the valley had been named was gone, eaten by goats.

Kroner, in cutoffs and a Na Pali Sea Adventures T-shirt, led them to a place under a dry falls where a lush hanging garden of watercress and maidenhair grew. In the muggy air Kal and Erika held hands, the others gathered in a semicircle around them. Adele was beside Erika, Kal's oldest brother, Leo, beside him.

Kroner said, "We're here today to witness the wedding of Kal and Erika and to let them know that we, representing the larger community of their *ohana,* will be with them throughout their marriage, ready to offer support."

Erika felt the salt spray that had dried on her skin. The sun beat on her bare shoulders through intermittent clouds. The air had grown oppressive with the threat of rain, and each time clouds passed over the narrow valley, the walls of the landscape, the mossy cliffs too steep to be scaled, seemed to press in a little more.

Kroner read from a piece of paper in his hands the words Kal had written. "Do you, Erika, take Kal as your husband and mate, to love by giving and receiving, by growing with him and respecting him, in married faith and devotion, till death divides you?"

Erika's eyes blinked against the sun. Kal's hands wrapped around hers, and the clouds shifted impatiently in the sky as though waiting for her promise.

"I do."

His face was near hers, his eyes holding a soft smile

full of love as Kroner repeated the question, substituting Kal's name for Erika's and hers for his.

"I do," he said.

All was silent, the valley still.

Kroner pronounced them husband and wife. "Kal, you may kiss the bride."

Erika saw the light sheen of sweat on her husband's upper lip as he met her eyes. He put one of his hands over the back of her hair, over her neck, and he murmured, "We're really good at this."

Trying to stop the nervous sickness in her stomach, Erika gave herself to the sensation of his lips on hers. Lips she had tried to recreate with her paintbrush. Lips she had watched as he sang. Lips she had seen kiss away Hiialo's screams, her tantrums. Lips that had made her believe in the love of a good man. They were kissing her mouth, saying, *Trust me now. Give yourself to me.*

She did. He was strong, and she felt all the muscle and power in him as he held her. All was relaxed, but his strength felt like security, like permanence.

She believed in their love.

IN HIS PARENTS' YARD, long tables covered with floral sheets held sushi, chow mein, *lumpia, kim chee,* long rice, squid *luau* and *kalua* pig, which Danny and Jakka had roasted in an underground oven. Foreboding of the night ahead made it almost impossible for Erika to even look at the food, particularly the glazed pig. But after the hula chant and blessing by Danny's dance troupe, she helped herself to everything on the tables, saying, "Oh, how wonderful." The start of a headache thrummed in her temples. Maybe she'd feel better after she ate.

Maybe Kal would be tired after the reception. Maybe he'd drink a lot and pass out, and...

Remember what it feels like to lie against him and kiss him. Sex won't be so different.

But it always was. It was hideous.

She and Kal had barely sat down at the head table when the guests began banging silverware on glasses.

For Kal, the sound echoed the past. His first wedding. Heeding the custom, he leaned toward Erika and kissed her. His bride's pallor cut through the memories of Maka, the sense of her all around.

"You okay?"

She nodded, sick with apprehension. "There are a lot of people here," she said, as though that was the problem.

Time crawled. She was introduced to dozens of people and spoke to others she'd met only briefly. The Akanas had made a point of getting back to Kauai for the weekend, and they came up to congratulate Kal. Danny introduced her to the men and women in his hula troupe.

They cut the cake and fed it to each other, then sat down with mango ice cream. Trying to take her mind off her nausea, Erika told Kal, "I really didn't know there were so many ways to eat mangoes."

He lifted his eyebrows, touched his tongue to his lips. "I know another way to eat them. I'll show you when we're alone." His eyes reached into hers. "Now that we're married."

It was a gentle flirtation. She knew he intended something sweet...sweet as mangoes.

But her nerves, her fears and too much unfamiliar food, triumphed. Remembering the sight of the *kalua* pig, she stood up abruptly, trying not to fall over the chairs, and limped toward the house.

"Erika?"

She heard his chair bang behind her.

Her mouth filling with bile, Erika headed blindly in the direction of the kennels.

"Erika."

Kal's shadow was beside her. She pushed her hand at

him, wanting to tell him to go back to the table, but if she opened her mouth she'd throw up. Which she did, in the first flower bed she saw. And on her beautiful *leis*.

One of the Akitas began barking at her.

Kal said, "*Toshi*. Enough." He touched Erika's back and she waved him away.

"Please…go."

He didn't, but he discouraged his mother and sister and a few other people from approaching. And tried to tell himself it wasn't the thought of sex with him that had made his bride vomit.

He *had* been talking about sex, hadn't he? Mangoes… There was a hurt inside him.

Too much excitement, that was all. He stuffed his hands in his trouser pockets and waited for Erika to turn to look at him. She didn't. She was taking off her *leis,* dropping them into the flowers as though she didn't know what else to do.

Kal remembered that Leo had handed him a handkerchief that morning. It was still in his pocket, and he gave it to Erika. "Here, baby."

Erika couldn't face him. She needed to go in the bathroom and cry. "Thank you." Weak, she turned from the heliconia and from the party.

Sliding an arm across her shoulders, Kal guided her toward the kennels. They'd go in the house the back way.

"Kal, don't…" The tears began streaming. To throw up on her wedding day, at his parents' party.

"Shh. It's all right. You're a trooper to eat everything at your first *luau*." *Not sex. Don't let it be the thought of sex that did that to her.*

Erika wiped her eyes on his handkerchief. They'd reached the kennel runs, and the puppies in Jin's litter were barking at her. She searched for the one that looked like Jin, the one she'd liked. But the puppy was gone.

She started crying again. Dumb to hope Kal would

really get that dog for her. He would pick a dog for other reasons. He'd pick the one that was right for them.

Oh, God, she needed to think about how *he* was feeling.

Kal watched her pull herself together, dry her eyes. Face him.

She was bedraggled, but still beautiful to him.

"I need to wash up."

"Sure. I'll ask my mom to find you some clothes. She's worried about you." He pulled her against him, hugged her tight. He was worried, too. "I love you, Erika."

Each of her breaths fell hard against him, gradually evening as he stroked her hair. "Kal…" she whispered. "I love you. Don't ever leave me."

"No…I won't. I won't." He subdued his own fears, told them to go away. Hers mattered more.

THERE WAS A LOT of traffic upstairs. Mary Helen brought Erika bath towels, a new toothbrush, one of Kal's T-shirts and a pair of his gym shorts with a drawstring waist. Grateful, Erika took a shower in the bathroom that had been Kal's. When she emerged, comfortably dressed in his clothes, Niau and Mrs. Akana and Jean and Adele and Mary Helen were all in the upstairs bedroom waiting for her.

Jean, looking a little green herself in early pregnancy, said, "Don't feel bad, Erika. My sister, Cecily, threw up on a runway in Paris."

"Before takeoff or after landing?" asked Niau.

"Cecily's a *model*," explained Adele. "She means she threw up at, like, a Ralph Lauren show."

Mary Helen put her arm around Erika's waist. "Enough about throwing up. Erika, what can I do for you?"

"Nothing." She met her mother-in-law's eyes.

"You've been so good to me, and I'm so sorry about this, Mary Helen."

Kal's mother looked at her sweetly and corrected, "Mom."

Erika tried not to cry again. In no hurry to leave the comfort of the room full of women, she moved toward the window to gaze out at the party. People were playing volleyball. She couldn't see Kal.

Mrs. Akana smiled up at her from a striped wing chair beside the window. Noticing her, Erika said, "I'm so glad you could come today. I was disappointed I didn't learn *bon* dancing from you before you went away on tour."

Rising gracefully to her feet, the elderly woman touched Erika's arm comfortingly. "Mary Helen and King know *bon* dancing good. And I will brush up with you in the fall, yeah?"

"Okay. Thank you." A peace settled over Erika. These were nice people. Kal was a good man. She was going to be all right.

On the other side of the room near the door, Adele was laughing at something Niau had said.

Mrs. Akana smiled and told Erika, "I threw up at my wedding, too. Maybe something picture brides do."

Erika took the older woman's hands in hers and met her eyes and knew she'd found a friend.

She began to leave the room, and she saw the tall figure in the threshold, his blue eyes waiting for her, and when she went into his arms again, she knew he was her dearest friend of all.

She hoped that she could be the same for him.

That she could be the lover he needed.

THE AFTERNOON was a celebration of *ohana*, of family. Within a few hours, Erika was almost able to laugh at the recollection of what had happened earlier. She enjoyed last moments with Adele and Kurt and sixteen-year-old Jason, who would all be returning to the mainland the following day, and with David and Jean and Chris, who were ready to head back to Greenland.

Talking to David near the volleyball net, Erika said, "You know, I'm sure Kal and I can arrange to see you guys next week before you go."

Her brother's lips twisted upward, amused. "Erika, I want your husband to like me. I'm not going to pull you away on your honeymoon."

She started to object, to say it didn't matter. But she knew it was right that she and Kal have that time alone. And she was going to do her best to make it right—for him.

She told David, "I'm going to miss you."

"We'll be back. At least you live by the ocean. Besides—" he glanced about the garden, his eyes softening "—you've got quite a family here."

As the sun began sinking in the sky, the band—which was Kal's band, playing without him but with his brother Keale—began tuning up.

Kal found Erika. "I think we're wanted." He steered her toward the area in front of the band.

She said, "Oh, I don't dance."

"Mmm. You're not good for much, are you?" The misty *pali,* the cliffs, loomed above them as Kal took her left hand in his right and put his other arm around her.

They danced slowly to two songs. On the second, others began dancing, too. Then Kal led her up toward the band and sat her down on a folding chair and took the guitar Jakka handed him. His Stratocaster.

He spoke into the microphone, to Erika but also to the crowd, as he had in the bar on the Fourth of July. His ragged, distinctive voice, that sweet low voice, came through the mike. "Okay, no more jokes about my beloved eating that *kalua* pig. She does good, yeah?"

Everyone laughed and cheered and whistled, and Danny gave a drumroll. Erika would have buried her face in her hands, but Kal's eyes were holding hers. Their expression cherished her.

She couldn't look away.

When the guests were finally quiet, Kal said, "I guess it's no secret how Erika and I met. Through a want ad in *Island Voice*. We sent our pictures and our stories to each other, and I asked her to come here. This is a practice that has a history in Hawaii, a history some of our guests have experienced firsthand, the old way. Erika and I did things a little differently. But I wrote this song about our way of finding each other. And about her."

The blue of his eyes went through her eyes, into her heart and soul. *You really love me,* she thought.

He and his band spent a couple of seconds tuning, then broke into the song.

Mainland girl
I thought you'd turn your back
on me and my life,
but you'd sold your Karmann Ghia for a plane ticket here
You were running like me,
running to me...

He knew things he'd never revealed, but he was telling them all now, telling everyone. Erika had believed that her feelings were secret from him, that he hadn't known when she'd fallen in love with him. But he knew. He sang about lying in the dark thinking about her and seeing her in the kitchen in the mornings and knowing she was afraid to look at him, afraid to let him see she loved him. He watched her as he sang, and the song got sexier and more personal, and his voice was doing that thing to her, playing her. Erika sat on the stage, flushed, knowing she was going to have to go home that night and make love with this man who was telling their secrets.

Knowing she wanted to.

As she gazed out over the dancers, her eyes stopped on two figures near the edge of the crowd. Mr. and Mrs. Akana were dancing slowly in each other's arms, gazing into each other's eyes, smiling the shared contentment of lifelong friends.

The sight gave Erika courage as nothing else could.

Except Kal's voice singing "Picture Bride."

CHAPTER FOURTEEN

"Shouldn't we get groceries first?" asked Erika as Kal turned down their driveway. The headlights illuminated the foliage and the familiar dirt road, but they passed the bungalow and continued to the blue house on the shore. In the moonless night the drive seemed long and dark.

"My brothers stocked the house for us." Telling himself she wasn't really stalling, that she'd lost all her lunch and was just hungry, Kal took his hand from the steering wheel and squeezed hers.

Erika clung to him. She had cast off from a safe port and headed for open sea. She'd said goodbye to Jean and Chris and David. In this new land she had one friend. Kal. Her husband.

Who wanted to have sex with her.

He parked, they got out of the car, and the breeze rushed at them from the sea the night had swallowed. The waves roared invisibly. "Want to go down there?" Kal asked. To the beach.

"Okay." The blackness and the ocean beyond seemed safer than the house, a bed with expectations. Sex could be easy without expectations.

Kal was swinging the key to the rental, which was on a ring with a plastic pineapple on it. "Let me check some things in the house. I'll meet you out here."

Erika nodded. In the blackness he crossed the patio and unlocked the glass doors of the beach house. Barefoot, still wearing his old clothes, Erika wandered through the deep sand and scooped out a seat for herself near the dark shape of Kal's outrigger. The wedding gift from Maka had brought them back home together from their wedding ceremony.

After several minutes Erika heard a dog breathing and the faint sound of a leash and collar, and she looked about the beach to see who was walking a dog. Fur brushed her arm, and she started as something bounded around her, kicking sand. The tall shape standing over her, sitting down beside her, was Kal.

"What is this?" But then she knew. The puppy explored her hands, licked her. Feeling its thick fur, Erika made out the markings. It was the one she'd wanted, the dog who looked like Jin. "Kal! Does Hiialo know?"

"She and Chris were playing with him in my parents' den all day."

The excited puppy squirmed, then settled down under her hands.

Erika turned her head to say something, and Kal's mouth was there, kissing hers.

"I want to make you happy, Erika."

His voice wasn't quite steady. Was he nervous about making love, too?

He has to be. I told him I find sex revolting.

And Kal wasn't arrogant enough to assume he would be different for her than other men. He had told her only that love would make the difference.

I need to love him. To give to him.

The puppy contentedly licked Erika's hands, shifting only occasionally in her lap, showing no signs of going anywhere. The sea made its long slow beats in breaking waves.

His arm behind her, his hand resting in the sand, Kal said, "He's got a Japanese name a yard long. What are you going to call him?"

"I don't know." Kal hadn't yet turned on any lights

in the house to shine to the shore outside, but her eyes
had adjusted to the dark, and she could see his legs on
the beach beside her. She could make out the pattern of
his aloha shirt. "His mom is Jin." She thought it over.
"Kin?"

"Like family. That's nice." His foot held down the
end of Kin's leash. He'd asked his brother to bring the
dog out to the house a half hour before, so that it would
be there for Erika. A distraction to calm her. *Baby, I
won't hurt you....*

What was that aching in his heart?

He put both his arms around her and eased her back
till her head was cradled on the sand. The puppy climbed
over his body and moved away to explore.

"He won't run away..." said Erika.

"I've got him."

His leg settled between hers. The beach felt soft under
her, the sand a cushion that molded to her body, and there
was relief in the intense blackness of the night. Kal's
hand touched her cheek, and he eased against her so that
she felt his erection. A dark confusion swirled inside her.
It felt good. They'd come this far before.

She let her left hand reach up and touch the front of
his shirt, then grasp his arm.

Kal moved closer to her. "I love you, Erika."

Magic words to peel away the last tension in her limbs.
Then there was only his mouth, gently kissing her, starting something that might go on for hours, unrelieved for
seven days. His voice, rough and quieter than the ocean,
whispered soft things to her, the gentle murmurings of a
lover. Things about sex, about her getting wet and pressing up against him. Erika felt as though she'd become
the earth beneath her body, become the rocking tide before the waves hit the beach in that slow steady rhythm.

She loved how he smelled and tasted. His mouth didn't
seem to be driving things toward an inevitable end. His

mouth seemed unconscious of time. His body had melted into hers, so that they were both part of the sand, except she wanted to be closer to the top layer of sand that was him, heavy and warm and hard above her.

"Kal…"

His hands were in her hair, cradling her head. He didn't want to let go, didn't want to stop being so close to her. He brushed his face against hers, feeling her smooth skin. Her head went back, and he touched her face, touched her lips with his tongue.

"Oh, Kal…"

No protest, just saying his name. She was ardent. Her breasts pushed up against him. She held the sides of his chest, his arms, his shoulders, in turn, trying things. His lips kissed hers again, and then he felt the puppy walk over his back.

He moved carefully, not wanting to roll on Kin.

Erika felt his weight shift, leave her. He caught the puppy, letting Kin kiss his face. Erika sat up, knowing there was sand all over her, that she was wearing a man's clothes sizes too large, not caring because Kal had transfigured her, made her beautiful.

She was chilled without his body.

He asked, "Want to stay out here for a while or go inside?"

Inside… She wished they could stay on the beach forever. He wouldn't make love to her on the beach. And on the beach they couldn't quite see each other. Erika couldn't see the lines on her own hands when she touched him.

He gave her the puppy, set Kin in her lap, and then he hugged her tight from one side, held her as though she was something he had wanted for a long time. "Let's go in."

Kal opened the patio doors of the oriental beach house, and he and Erika went in, Erika still holding the end of

Kin's leash, not tugging at all because the puppy wanted to go in, too.

Ahead of her in the darkness, Kal turned on a light above the kitchen stove. The front room was filled with gifts. Leo and Keale had brought over the gifts and one of Kal's guitars, too. Even the crate for the puppy and its leash and brush and food were there.

The gifts made it all terribly real to Erika. *Married*...

Returning from the kitchen, Kal glanced at the presents without interest. "Want a tour?"

"All right."

"Pick up Kin. We'll put him in his crate soon."

Erika collected the fluffy puppy and unclipped his leash, which she dropped onto the couch.

The floors were ceramic tile, as in his parents' house. Off to one side, a bar separated the kitchen from the rest of the room. A window room divider cut off the sleeping area, with its king size bed, from the living room. Folding koa blinds could be drawn across the opening in the partition for privacy. Matching doors closed it off, as well.

"The bedroom," said Kal. The clothes they'd packed for the week were in suitcases at the end of the bed. Kal led her down the hall. "There's another bedroom here." With two full-size beds. "Bathroom across the hall."

As they made their way back to the glass-fronted room opening onto the patio, Kal said, "Let's get Kin used to his crate."

"I can't believe your parents let us bring him here. Aren't they worried about accidents in their rental?"

Kal was taking the crate into the bedroom. He emerged and picked up an old bedspread his brothers had dropped off. "For one thing, the only rugs in here are area rugs. For another, my parents feel that if a puppy has more than a couple of accidents, you're housebreaking wrong." He folded the bedspread. "They also consider dogs first-class citizens."

Erika followed him into the bedroom, stroking Kin. Kal took the puppy from her and coaxed him into the crate. It was a large crate, the size for a full-grown Akita.

Kin sat nervously at one end and looked out at them.

Kal didn't shut the door. He said, "Good boy, Kin. You're a good dog. Kin, stay." The puppy started to come out.

Kal put him back in. "Stay."

The puppy sat down.

"I love him, Kal. I really wanted a dog. Thank you. And thank you for the song. I don't have anything like that for you."

He sat back on his heels, eyed her. "You have something for me."

Erika was glad for the darkness. The only light on in the house was the kitchen light. "Kal, I... I'm still uncomfortable about sex."

"I know." He changed the subject. "I'd like a shower. If you want to sit in the tub for a while first, I'll watch Kin."

Relaxing in the bathtub sounded good. On the nightstand, the glowing numbers on the clock read nine-thirty-three. She picked up her tote bag and set it on the bed.

She had packed it the night before, but when she opened it, the first thing she saw was an unfamiliar garment. Who had put it there? Adele? No. Though he wasn't looking at her, though he was on the floor reassuring the puppy in the crate, she knew Kal was paying attention to everything she did.

She pulled out the fabric, which was coffee-colored silk, sheer enough to show every shadow. A thigh-length chemise. Simple, with slits six inches up the sides. "Kal, do you..."

He told the dog, "I like lingerie."

He had packed it, on top of her other clothes, like a word. *Please.* She took it out and started to leave the room, but Kal, at her feet, playfully nipped at her calves. His eyes were loving, and Erika swallowed.

I want to please him.

She went down the hall. The bathroom had been stocked with soaps and bath salts from the Island Soap Co. On the edge of the tub was a bottle of papaya-scented shampoo. She drew a bath, using some salts, and as she soaked in the fragrant water, she tried to relax her mind. *It will be okay. Just try to enjoy it.*

When she got out, she dried off in front of the mirror and saw the hard-won muscles in her arms and legs, saw her tan lines. She put moisturizer on her face and looked closely at her eyes and her face and did not find the wrinkles many. She removed the towel from her hair and drew the coffee-colored chemise over her body. It fit, and the private shadows showed as she had known they would. *How do I really look?* It was hard to step outside herself and tell. But the chemise was clothing; it masked her.

Nudity… *I'm going to hate it.*

She emerged from the bathroom with wet hair and smelled popcorn. She followed the scent and the sounds of popping to the kitchen. Kal's back was to her. "Kin's in his crate. I shut the door. He seemed happy. We should check on him in about ten minutes."

Erika said, "It's like having a baby."

When he turned around, her face was red, as though she'd made a blunder. Kal switched off the burner. She was the woman he wanted, and it made his blood rush just to see her muscular legs and arms, her firm body, her proud features, faintly lined with age but sexy to him. Beautiful.

"Come here." He took her hand, led her down the shadowed hall to the living room, which still lay mostly in darkness.

She sat on the couch while he wandered through the

presents, too many presents, too many good wishes for them. He found a large package with no corners. Heavy. Sitting on the couch, he laid the bundle across both their laps. Erika knew it was a quilt.

She opened the inexpensive floral card. "A wish that all the gifts of love will shower you from heaven above." Beneath the printed message was scrawled, "With love to Kal and Erika from Mary and Jessie Kekahuna and the Makanalua Quilters."

"Maka's mom and her aunt," said Kal. "They wanted to come to the wedding party, but Aunt Jessie is sick."

Erika pictured the old quilt on Kal's bed, the quilt he had shared with Maka. Would the quilt in this package ever look so old and tattered? Together she and Kal unwrapped it. It was green, yellow and white; the flowers were anthurium, lilies.

Kal unfolded it and laid it over her. He pulled her legs up onto the couch and rubbed her feet before tucking them under the quilt. As he kissed her lips, there was a whine from the bedroom.

Kin.

Erika's glance followed the sound.

"He doesn't have to go out. It's too soon. This is when we let him cry for a little bit. Like a baby," he said just as she thought it.

For a moment their eyes held.

He broke the connection between them. "Want to watch old surfing movies?"

It sounded good.

"Let me have a shower first." He stood up, opened the doors on an entertainment center, then went into the bedroom. Erika heard him talking to the puppy. "You want to come in the bathroom with me? Or you want to go see Erika?"

He brought Kin out to her, and she cuddled the puppy, stroking his fluffy body, while the shower ran. She couldn't see the ocean through the plate glass, but the surf was audible, and the trade winds periodically gusted through the screen doors.

The dog licked her hands.

She heard Kal come out of the bathroom, then go into the kitchen. When he joined her, he was carrying the bowl of popcorn and wearing a pair of baggy cotton shorts that looked new. They hung low on his lean hips, and when he sat down beside her it was hard not to stare at his skin.

Kin sniffed at the popcorn.

"No," said Kal. "Time to say good-night."

Erika hugged her dog, gave him a kiss, wanted to take him to the crate herself. But Kal said, "I'll do it," and then he was gone, and she heard him putting Kin in his crate.

Erika fished a large flat package from the stack of presents. Obvious. Not half as sweet as a puppy. When Kal sat down with her again, she handed it to him. "Here's your present."

"Thanks." He tore off the white envelope containing her card. The card itself was a small original watercolor, an outrigger on a beach. Kal opened it and read the message.

Dear Kal,
I love you, in the giving way. I want to make you happy.

Erika

He closed the card and gazed at the front. He said, "Receiving, too. Did I mention that?"

"No." The look on his face—strong and vulnerable at once—caught her heart. "But you gave me Kin. I received him."

Yes, thought Kal, *but what about my fingers between your legs, my tongue licking you?*

Repulsed by sex.

He hadn't expected those words to come back now.

And scare him.

Concentrating on her gift, he removed the paper and found an oil painting similar to a watercolor that was hanging in his parents' gallery. His favorite, *Hiialo's Luau.* The oil was better. He knew it was worth more money, but it was the other that she'd decided to publish. This one was just his. "Thank you."

He set the picture at the end of the couch and gazed at it for a while. "There's a skink in it that wasn't in the other one. The pig looks better in this one, too."

The pig reminded them both of the pig at the wedding party. Of Erika's throwing up. Of what Kal had suggested just before.

"Erika." The quilt shifted as he drew her closer, met her eyes. "Were you just nervous today? I know what I said was... I didn't mean to scare you." Or make you sick. *Tell me it wasn't me.*

"I was just nervous. I still am."

It was easy to kiss her then. It made him excited, and he thought of just taking what he wanted. A reasonable pace. If she wouldn't be seduced, she would at least let him...

Cool it, Kal.

He got up to go to the VCR.

Watching, Erika saw the front of his shorts distended, hiding nothing.

She shut her eyes, surrendering to the dizziness, the yearning that mingled with uncomfortable things, that went into the world of nakedness, a teetering place between the beautiful and the grotesque.

Since neither of them would be watching it, Kal didn't ask her opinion about the movie. It was a distraction for her. If it didn't work, he'd bring out Kin, another distraction. A ball of fur she could touch—so she could forget that a man was touching *her*.

Carrying the remote control, Kal went to the kitchen and switched out the light, then returned to the couch. He turned the volume very low before he sat down on her left near the end of the couch. In the faint glow from the television, everything was blue. Kal put one leg against the back of the couch and reached for her.

She accepted the warmth of his bare chest, his legs surrounding her. Rolling on her side, she stared at the TV, the waves, the start of the film. Kal covered her with the quilt, held her beneath it. She felt every muscle, every hair, every line of his body. She felt his penis.

All of it seemed safe. He made her safe. She pressed her face to the smooth skin of his chest.

Kal wasn't hungry, but he grabbed a handful of popcorn and passed her the bowl. "No butter," he promised.

Erika took some popcorn and feigned interest in the movie, as though he wasn't holding her waist, stroking beneath her breasts. He was doing everything right. But it would make no difference.

She said, "I can't have an orgasm. I've never had one with a man."

He dragged her closer, his arms and legs speaking the language of affection and security. "I'll have to send you back to the mainland."

Erika buried herself deeper in the den of his body and the quilt and touched his leg, moving upward.

"Erika, don't." He caught her hand, the hand moved by practice rather than passion. By what she thought he wanted. They had to talk, and it should happen in the bedroom.

With luck, something else would happen there, too.

He picked her up, her and the quilt, and stood. Erika closed her eyes and let him carry her to the bedroom. He left open the shutters that separated the king-size bed from the next room, from the soft sound of the television. Setting her at the foot of the bed, he drew back the spread and the sheets and blankets.

Erika crawled up to the pillows, where he joined her and pulled the covers over them. They turned toward each other.

"Tell me what you like," he said. "What you don't."

I've already told you! Why did you marry me? "Maybe we should just…do it."

Well, it wasn't the worst idea. But he shook his head.

He kissed her mouth, and Erika's breath went away. She kissed him back, slowly. His ribs were against her hand. His skin was warm. She wanted to touch him. He was beautiful like no man she'd ever known. But her own body felt tight as a spring.

When he drew her near, she tensed.

Kal took a silent breath, eased his hold on her.

"It's okay," she said.

He didn't answer.

In the next room the television talked low. Through the partition, the trade winds, carrying a breath of plumeria, blew over their skin.

"Really," said Erika. "I can just do this. Let's not try to talk about it."

"Okay."

But all he did was make a place for her in the crook of his arm, intimate with the scent of his skin. It would be so comforting to roll over and put her face against him in the night. She could get used to his lips resting half-parted against her forehead, as though he drank her like a sleeping draft.

She must be making him crazy. He was tense now, too. Pained, she crunched up her eyes, her forehead. This was her wedding night. Where was the magic?

The clock had struck midnight. The pumpkin was smashed.

Kal felt her small tense breaths. Under his hands, her back knotted. *Relax,* he thought. *Relax, Erika.*

"Hey, Erika. Just remember the stuff about love, yeah? I want to try to give to you. Just…let it happen. It's okay if you don't get excited. But just know that I'm doing it because I'm in love with you. Humor me."

She nodded, strangely glad. No decisions to make, except to love him.

"I'm so in love with you." His mouth kissing her jaw, her throat, her closed eyes, he rolled her onto her stomach, and she resisted only slightly, then lay tensely with her face to the pillow. Kal rubbed her shoulders and arms, territory they'd covered before. Then places they hadn't. The backs of her legs. Her naked bottom.

She moved beneath his hand with the restless stirrings of pleasure. *Good.* "That's right. Just relax." He drew her chemise up her body, and she sat up and let him take it off.

There was a horrible gulping feeling in her throat, alien qualities at war. She huddled back under the sheets, hiding. *You don't have to have an orgasm. He doesn't care.*

Kal took off his shorts and reached for her again, sliding down the sheet.

"Kal…"

"You're so pretty. You make me so hard, Erika."

She'd heard words like that before. They were different coming from him. Kal she believed. Not that she was pretty. But that he found her so.

And his hand felt so good against the skin of her back. His body settling against her, pressing close, cradling her.

It didn't feel as she'd imagined. It was earthy. Body hair. Muscle. Heavy male body. The smell of sex. It was in the air already, and it brought a choked feeling to her throat.

Suddenly she wanted to escape. *I hate this. I hate this.* "I love you."

Give, she thought. *Let him.* But, oh, the feeling inside her. It would be easier to touch him, and she tried to roll over. He wouldn't let her. He kissed her shoulder and rubbed her spine, gentle-hard. "Don't move."

"No," she said, trying to move again.

He slid away from her and she from him.

Her eyes were big, desperate. Like Hiialo waking up from a nightmare. "Let me give to you," she said.

Kal knew she was choking on her feelings. She hated it. Had hated having him close to her. He shook his head. "No." Like her, he couldn't talk. Except the most familiar words, the only safe words for this moment. Gently he leaned over and kissed her cheek. "I love you."

And he got up and left their bed.

THE PUPPY WOKE THEM in the middle of the night. At the sound of his whining, Erika remembered where she was, what had happened. Kal was beside her, and though it was dark, though the light from outside was the blue shade of night, she didn't want to get up because she was naked. Bleary-eyed, holding the sheet, Erika searched for her chemise on the bed.

Kal sat up, crawled to the foot of the bed and opened the door of the crate, catching Kin's little collar as he came out.

"Let me get him, Kal." She hunted for her chemise and couldn't find it.

Observing her panicky movements and figuring it out, Kal said softly, "Come on. It's all right. I think you're beautiful."

Naked in front of a man. Oh, well, it was hardly less than her bikini. She let the sheet fall, and without meeting Kal's eyes, she stood up and walked around the end of the bed to take the puppy.

Cool air all over her skin, she carried him out the
screen door to the garden area in the starlight. Kal followed, drinking a glass of water, and when she turned
from the puppy, she found a big beach towel waiting for
her.

He slipped it behind her, but didn't close it. Erika saw
him stare at her breasts in the dark, saw his eyes drift
down. This was part of what she didn't understand about
sex, why it should excite her to see him look at her, to
see it give him an erection.

She swallowed.

He closed the towel and met her eyes, and they both
remembered how she'd gone to sleep alone.

She said, "Please…I want to try again. I won't be that
way."

"Oh, we'll try again," he assured her, not quite lightly.

But they didn't just then.

They sat on the patio and played with Kin, throwing
him a rubber ball. Finally they took him back to his crate
and got back into bed together, and Kal tried to forget
that he had an ego. He knew it would get in the way in
a hurry if he couldn't make her respond.

Just kiss her. You've kissed a lot. She likes it.

Erika sensed his tension, a kind of tension she'd seen
before. The inevitable. Frustration. She closed her eyes
and begged of forces she didn't trust that she could make
love with her husband.

And then, desperate, she thought rationally again. *I
love him. This is loving.* But now there was a double
enemy against them. Experience. What had happened
earlier that night. And fear of its repetition.

Kal touched her face and kissed her. A voice spoke
inside him. *Open your heart, Kal. Stop thinking about
you and fantasies of making her come. Just tell her how
much you love her.*

"Erika…" He kissed her with his tongue, keeping his

body a little apart from hers. "Just let me touch you. I love you. That day we went to Polihale, I just wanted to take off your shorts, take off…"

He told her more, and he kissed her, and she drew nearer. The weather was gathering inside her, the sticky hot of hurricane season. Her mind tried to find a thought to hang on to. She deliberately stopped it and felt his tongue against hers and his hand on her breast.

"It's all right," he said. More kisses.

She lay back, but when his hand slid down her front, she was nervous and rolled onto her stomach. "Don't stop touching me," she said.

"I won't." Her back, her sides curving to her breasts. Lower. The backs of her thighs.

She responded.

He touched the insides of her thighs, slid his hand up, pressing his lips to her shoulder. Wet…

Erika felt his fingers stroking her, and the room became a cloud.

"Kal…Kal."

"You're all right. Shh. We'll just do this for a while." A long while.

She forgot about him, about anything. It felt good. So good. It was a long time before she wanted to turn, and then they were kissing again and she reached out to touch him.

"That's right," he said. Her hand on him, stroking. Shaky hand. Like his touching her. Petting like teenagers afraid to go all the way.

"I want to make you come," she said. "Show me what to do."

He kissed her, held her tight, until he found the power of speech, and sometime later they knew their first shared climax, which was his.

And as she lay in his arms afterward, Erika felt like his wife.

WHEN SHE AWOKE in the morning, it was with an awareness of Hawaii, of the warm air, of the smells and the
humidity, of the hue of the light—the faintest dilute wash
of Payne's Gray and Alizarin Crimson. The windows in
the beach house had invited the outside in.

Smelling something frying—plantains, she thought—
she started to get up, but Kal came in, naked, and said,
"Don't move." He brought her Kin, who had been in
the kitchen with him, and said, "Watch over this guy, all
right? I've already taken him out, so he should be okay."

Erika propped the pillows up behind her, and the
puppy crawled over the blankets, exploring. After a moment she caught him and stroked him while he looked
into her eyes.

Kal carried in two plates, handed her one, set the other
on the bed and picked up the dog. "Back to your crate,
Kin." He got in bed beside her, and they ate plantains
and eggs and drank guava juice.

After breakfast she washed the dishes and they put on
their suits and went out and swam together, a quarter mile
along the shore.

The sun was coming out, and Kal said, "This is really
nice. I never have time off like this, without Hiialo."

The sea was the color of his eyes.

Erika said, "I've never had a time like this, ever."

They stopped swimming and stood in the sand, a wave
riding over Erika's shoulders, washing his chest. He held
her tightly, a bear hug.

When they returned to the beach house, they fed Kin
and took him outside and trained him, working on teaching him to come, to answer to his name. Then Kal sat
under the gathering clouds and let Erika sketch him for
a painting of the Blue Room.

After lunch he put Kin in his crate and said, "Want to
lie down for a while?"

The wonderful nightmare that would never go away.

Erika had pushed it out of her mind all morning, but now it was back.

They were salty from the ocean, still wearing their swimsuits, but they went into the bedroom. He unmade the bed she'd made that morning and they lay down. Soon he was hard, stiff, wanting sex. The way they were kissing made it more intense, and he reached for the zipper at the back of her high-necked aqua maillot. He pulled it down.

Erika swallowed the sound she wanted to make. She didn't want him to stop.

It's going to be okay, he thought.

He nudged her swimsuit off her shoulders, tugged it down her front, revealing her breasts. His yearning mounted.

Sitting up, Erika slipped the maillot off her arms. But she could see herself in the light, and—

Kal pulled her against him, kissing her, his hands sliding under her arms, rubbing her shoulders. But she was rigid, tense.

Their eyes met.

Instinctively Kal raised the sheet to cover her.

Erika closed her eyes, closed him out. *I hate my body.* "I think it's because I was in a wheelchair." *I don't want to say this. I don't want him to know.*

"I think so, too. Tell me what it was like. You can tell me anything, Erika." Her eyes opened, and he moved his head closer to hers. "We live together. I'm going to know more about you than anyone, and you're going to know more about me. That's the beautiful thing about being married. You know each other's weaknesses, and you love and are loved, anyhow."

"Character weakness is one thing…" Erika began.

"It's uglier than anything on your body. Just like goodness is more beautiful. You know that."

She knew it. But only because he'd said it.

"I love you," he said. "And nothing you say is going to disgust me."

And so he held her and she told him. She told him what it had been like every day, the horrible ways her body had not worked right, things she'd never discussed with a lover. About falling on the ship, between her wheelchair and her bunk. About feeling half-human yet knowing she was fully human.

Kal never let her go, and her words moved from matters of the body to the spirit.

"I didn't know what to do. I was a diver. I was an artist, but I was an athlete, too. I was so ugly suddenly, and René couldn't even stay in the hospital room with me. When Skye came, I wished she was there, instead of me. I told her she was a self-centered bitch and the world would be a better place without her. I said why didn't she do us a favor and get out of our lives? I said my brother would be happier without her. I told her she was ugly inside...."

Whispers. No tears. Erika, who cried so easily over flowers, did not cry about this, he saw.

"Then she slept with René. And then— Oh, Kal, it wasn't better without her. It was horrible, for David and for Chris. I never stop wondering if what I said was the last straw. What if she killed herself because of me? I can't stand it. I think about it every day. I always will. I want to believe she's moved on to a higher place, but I *don't* believe it. She was a weak woman, and she chose a weak way out. I think she's in hell, and I put her there. She could have stayed on earth and become a better person—"

"Erika." Kal sat up. "Wait. Stop. This woman tried to ram your brother with a car. She was trying to hurt him, and she hurt you. You got mad. That's all that—"

"I shouldn't have. It doesn't matter what she did. I have to think about what *I* did. I want to participate in *bon-odori,* Kal. I want to do things for her. I want to try to be good for her. If anyone might be with the Hungry Ghosts of Hell, it's her. I need to close this somehow. I need peace.''

Obon.

Kal wanted to groan. Of all the ways she could deal with her guilt, she had to ask that.

Gone was any hope of experiencing the *bon* dances in a secular context. Erika understood the symbolism of the festival, and it held meaning in her life.

Unfortunately, the same was true for him.

If it wasn't, he would have encouraged her to rejoice for Mr. and Mrs. Akana and learn some *bon* dances. He would have taken her to the temples, where the slow enchanting rhythms floated on the summer night.

But he didn't want to rejoice for the souls of the dead.

He didn't want to feel Maka leave on the last night, to see her as a candle afloat on the water, a flame that could no longer be held.

Angry, knowing there was no chance in *hell* that he was going with her, knowing Erika was going to have to do this one alone and without his blessing, he said, ''Yeah, I hear you.'' And he scrambled to the end of the bed and opened Kin's crate. ''Come on, boy. Come on out.''

CHAPTER FIFTEEN

THE AFTERNOON WAS HUMID and sultry, billowing clouds choking the sunlight without cooling the day. At six Erika and Kal pushed the outrigger down to the shallows and out into the surf and paddled toward Keʻe Beach. It was crowded, full of tourists and, sweating, they went on to Hanakapiai. They paddled until their arms were sore, and when they reached the beach it was nearly deserted.

"We're going to be alone soon," said Kal. "Maybe we can have a romantic time." *Instead of talking about the bon festival.*

They dragged the outrigger far up into the sand, then went into the water, swimming down to the wet caves at the southwest end of the beach. A lava boulder protruded above the surface near the caves, and Kal paused behind it. The placid water was still translucent under the dark sky. But he and Erika were alone, as he'd wanted. He watched her rinse the sweat off her body and dive down to touch the sand, and he dove after her, grabbing her beneath the surface as they came up.

Erika relaxed in his wet embrace. When the water cleared from her lashes, she saw how dark the sea and sky had made his eyes.

He kissed her, touching her face, the way he always did. "Put your legs around me, Erika."

Shaky from the emotion of the afternoon, in which she'd learned to depend on him, she put her hands on his shoulders and did as he asked. Her legs around his waist.

Kal's hands on her bottom drew her all the way against his penis, which was trying to penetrate barriers of cloth.

They kissed again.

"Kal...this feels good. I like it in the water." The ocean was hers, the blue wash in which they floated a part of her. She had been born in it and raised in it like a thing of the sea.

"Does this feel good, too?" A taste of how it would feel...

"Yes."

Kissing her salty wet mouth, he whispered, "I love you even more than I did at noon. You're brave. It's okay, Erika. All that stuff is okay."

Skye... That would never be okay.

"Feel what you do to me, Erika. You've got me so turned on."

He said more. The tension left her body. All that remained was natural response to him, to his excitement. She let him take off her bikini and set both pieces on the lava rock, out of the way of the tide. His shorts, too. He reached for her again, wrapped her around him. All the barriers between them had vanished. She felt only his skin. And she trembled.

He kissed her lips again, teasing her with his erection, feeling like he was going to come from the sensation. "This could make a baby."

"Not now." She liked the smoothness pressed close to her. She wanted him inside her and couldn't remember ever feeling that way about anyone.

"That's not a very reliable method."

Erika just looked at him. She knew her own cycles.

He pushed into her and she opened to him, letting him guide her, grateful for the buoyant salt water to support her. It felt good. It felt life-giving, like his tongue in her mouth. Making love.

Her awfulness—the ugliness she perceived in herself—

passed over her and through her. She shuddered, shaking it off. "Kal..."

"Don't think." He couldn't think, either, or he'd think about Maka. Hard to have another woman. Hard to be inside her, feeling her wetness. Beautiful, too.

But this wasn't *a first time without.* It was all Erika. It was exactly what he wanted.

Bride, he thought, and he held her tighter, wanting to protect her and give her everything. Her mouth was against his shoulder, kissing him, pressing hard with her lips as she made love to him. He held her tighter, went deeper, his own urgency making him half-crazy. "Oh, God, Erika. Just..." The next sound was a quiet moan.

It was hers.

"There, baby..."

She was lost, different from how he'd seen her before, and he was different, too. They were in the same place. Adrift.

Erika buried her face in his shoulder, and he held her down on him, moved gently against her, his blue eyes half-closed. She cried, and a small wave, a tingling baby breaker, swept through her. What happened to Kal was stronger, more intense. His lips bit down on her wet hair, arms crushing her. Shaking. "Erika..."

They held each other afterward in the water, and Kal wished they were back at the house in bed and never had to get up. Because he wanted to tell her things, as she had told him.

"Let's go sit on the beach," he said.

They put on their wet swimsuits and swam around the lava boulder and back to the beach. Their towels were in the outrigger. Wrapped up in them, they sat on the still-warm sand, and Kal told her about the night the police cars came and when he had to go and identify her and crying at night with Hiialo. He told her about the hurricane that came eight days later and tore apart the rest of his life and ravaged the island that was his home.

In the end, as the sun became just a dome on the horizon, as he felt the urgency that they must leave, he told her the truth. As close to the truth as he could speak.

"Erika, I can't go to the *bon* dances with you. They mean something to me, and I don't want to go. That time was too painful. If I participated in *obon,* I'd live it again."

Maka's death. Erika understood more than he'd said. He didn't want to face Maka's death again because he had never let her go.

Silencing the cry inside her—that he was saving parts of himself for Maka, that he was putting a dead woman before his wife—she said the only thing she could. "That's fine, Kal. The last thing I want is to cause you pain."

Unfortunately the price of saving him pain was accepting it herself, by living with the ghost of Maka, not a beloved memory, but too strong a presence in his heart.

THEY MADE A PIZZA for dinner, with a thick whole-wheat crust loaded with vegetables. Afterward they walked Kin on the beach in the dark of the new-moon night, beginning leash work.

"You've got to understand," Kal said, "that this dog is going to grow. He'll be big and powerful, and it's his nature to want to be in charge. But *you* have to be in charge. Never give a command unless you have the time to make sure he obeys it. If you let him disobey, he's one up on you."

He didn't apply the same rules to Hiialo. Erika remembered Hiialo's heedless behavior. And she remembered Kal's face above her the morning of their wedding, the bad luck of her seeing him before the ceremony. Even though he said it wasn't bad luck at all. For no reason a shiver ran over her.

They played with Kin in the sand in front of the beach house, working on getting him to come when his name was called. Erika loved his three-colored coat. He was a good dog, a baby who looked up at her with concerned brown eyes.

When the sky grew dark, they took the puppy inside and put him in his crate where he lay down to sleep. Erika and Kal opened wedding presents, and Erika wrote down who they had come from. Many people had given them money, and Kal counted it with satisfaction. There was almost six hundred dollars. "What do you want to do?" he asked. "We could go to Honolulu and stay at the Royal Hawaiian. Eat and dance and order from room service and go to the aquarium and Pearl Harbor. Or we could be practical and trade in the Datsun. Buy another car. I have a thousand dollars in savings."

Erika had almost that much herself. "Where do we get a new car?"

"Lihue, if we want to trade in the old one. Or we can check the papers, see if there's something we want to buy."

They decided to go to Lihue the next day. Erika asked, "Are you going to practice with your band this week?"

Kal shook his head. "It's our honeymoon."

"Kal."

He lifted his eyebrows, waiting.

"It's okay with me. The music. I just want you to know. It'll be hard—with you gone at night. But I'll stay with Hiialo." Erika stopped speaking. She realized the truth, and it was ugly. She was doing what she'd never done before they were married. Bribing him—to love her.

Love me like you loved Maka. Love me more.

She got up from the couch where they were sitting and

went into the kitchen to get a drink and regain her dignity.

Kal's voice called to her cheerfully from the couch. "Thanks."

And she knew suddenly that while she had been bestowing a gift, it was actually something he had been planning to take all along.

LATER, WITH THE PATIO doors open and a light burning in the front room like a night-light, they went into the bedroom. The bed was unmade and a little sandy from that afternoon.

Erika began hesitantly to remove her tropical-print rayon dress.

"Not yet. Come here." Kal wrapped his hand around hers, coaxed her toward the bed. When they lay facing each other, heads on the pillows, he said, "It's just like the ocean."

She moved into his arms and it was.

"I didn't let you take this off because I wanted to." He unbuttoned her dress. Beneath, her bra was of some fine navy blue fabric, sheer enough to see through. Like her dress, it opened in front. He pressed his face to her. "I loved that today."

Erika's eyes were closed. *Don't wake up from the dream. Don't think about During.*

Kal kissed one breast, one nipple. She put her hands on his head, in his hair, and imagined the ocean around them. As he touched between her legs, she stayed in that sea of blue, a sea that had become his eyes. She didn't know when she'd opened hers again. He made her sit up and helped her out of her dress.

Then he was touching her, talking to her, sliding off her underwear. *I'm going to die of this,* thought Erika. She heard him taking off his clothes.

"Look at me, Erika."

She did and saw in the half-light what she had not seen in the water. She swallowed. "Kal."

He was moving against her body, embracing her, rolling her onto her stomach. He rubbed her spine as he had so many nights, then lay tenderly against her, cradling her, protecting her with his body. Erika could feel his heart, his mouth on her neck and her jaw, his weight on her.

She wanted to be one with him. He put on a condom—"I don't trust your method"—and touched her as he pushed inside.

Erika gasped softly, and her eyes watered. He cradled her with his arms and went in deeper.

"I love you," she said. "I'm so in love with you."

"Two of us are in love." Deeper. "God, Erika." He held one of her breasts, and he pressed his mouth against her shoulder, then the side of her face. "I love you."

He kissed her jaw for a long time while he tried to get as close to her as he could. He felt that place inside him that remembered Maka, too, and he knew that loving her—and losing her—had allowed him to love this woman more. But he expelled Maka from his thoughts.

His cheek to Erika's, he asked, "Are you all right? Comfortable?"

"Yes." The sheet swallowed the word. She'd never before known what it was like to be in love with someone and to have him inside her this way.

Kal covered one of her hands, which had twisted into a fist. He talked to her quietly, exciting her. He was going to make it happen, just like before. Erika felt the loss of control approaching, and she didn't fight it, just felt the closeness of their mating, of their movements against each other.

"Kal…" Her voice was odd, too high. Sounds came from her and she couldn't think. There was just a feeling like waves crashing in her head. She tried to hear the surf, and when she listened she did, but then she just felt Kal and the hot liquid sensations he was making inside her.

"I love you," he said again, moving inside her.

He heard her gasping lightly, and that made it hard not to come. He had to focus on holding on, on not letting it end. But when he heard her deep cry and felt her clench around him, he surrendered. They were both shaking hard, coming, and the tears were released from his eyes because he remembered what it was like with Maka and this time it was so completely different.

They separated, and Kal pulled off the condom. The end was broken.

"And you don't trust my method," said Erika. "Where'd you buy that thing?"

He dropped it in the trash, grabbed her, tickled her till she screamed and begged him to stop. In the dark he said, "Do you want to have a baby, Erika?"

She was practicing never lying to him. "Yes."

The next second was long. She had no clue what he was thinking, but finally he hugged her tighter. "Let's get busy, then. *Hana hou.*"

THEY WENT TO LIHUE the next day, traded in the Datsun and spent two thousand dollars on a rusty twenty-year-old aquamarine Thunderbird, then messed around a nearby shopping mall. They bought a T-shirt and a new Barbie doll for Hiialo, a new paintbrush for Erika and three CDs for Kal. On the way home Erika spotted a red-and-white-striped bandstand in the middle of a courtyard outside a Buddhist community center. Around the tall square bandstand was printed BON DANCE CLUB.

Kal saw it, too.

Neither of them said a word.

WHEN THEY GOT HOME, they made dinner, took a hike to Waikapalae Cave and swam in the Blue Room, naked,

until they were both cold. Back at the bungalow afterward, Kal played his guitar and Erika tried more
sketches, using a photograph she'd taken the first time
they'd gone to the Blue Room. In the picture Kal was
sitting forward on the ledge talking to Hiialo, who was
out of camera range. As she was working, a gecko
crawled over the arm of the couch. Erika stopped sketching and stared at it, trying to make out its features. Without daring to turn the page, she roughed out a sketch of
the lizard.

In her mind something clicked. She remembered weeks
before, at the gallery. Hiialo had asked for a picture of
her father. Suddenly Erika knew what she was going to
do. When the gecko moved away, she got up to try to
see where it had gone, but it had disappeared. She went
to the bedroom and collected watercolor paper, palette,
paints and brushes.

Kal had been sitting across from her, figuring out a
song, repeating the chords he'd learned, experimenting
with finger-picking, but when Erika returned to the room
and started working, when she actually began painting,
he stilled his hands and watched her face.

She didn't notice that the music had stopped.

She was gone far away.

He absorbed her presence. How long would it take him
to shake the little whispers of disloyalty and guilt, the
pining for Maka? After a bit, he put the Gibson in its
case and went to the bedroom to let Kin out of his crate.
He took the dog outside and played with him in the dark
in the sand, and when he came back in, Erika was still
working. She painted as the hours crept on, and he didn't
disturb her, though sometimes he came near enough to
see what she was doing.

It was him. He must have been talking to Hiialo when

she took that photo. He hadn't known he seemed so earnest when he spoke to her.

In Erika's watercolor he wasn't talking to Hiialo.

He was speaking with Eduardo.

He wanted to put his hands in Erika's hair, to touch her. Instead, he let her be. He went back to his guitar, taking breaks to stare at her, to watch her eyes, so deeply focused on the paper. Taking a long break to walk back to the bungalow and collect some of the last mangoes of the season from the tree.

She finished at two-thirty in the morning. She set the watercolor on the coffee table, and they both stood over it, studying it.

Kal said, "It's great."

"It's for Hiialo. She wanted a picture of you."

"She'll love it."

Erika was amazed he was still awake, still there, waiting for her. When she was painting at night, René had always gone downtown to the bar. Where there were other women...

She cleaned her brushes and they went to bed. She knew that was what Kal had been waiting for, to make love again.

He tried to take things further. He'd tried in the Blue Room, but she had known what he wanted and had dodged him, trying to say every way but with words that she didn't want it. She'd just gotten used to making love with him, to feeling desire.

In bed with him she couldn't swim away.

"Shh..."

"No," she said. "I really don't like it, Kal. Please don't."

His mouth was on her flat stomach, on the slender area that, though she was thirty-six, had never grown full with a child. He kissed the hollow beside one hipbone. He nudged her thighs apart.

"Please don't, Kal."

He sat up, touching her.

She wouldn't look at him.

He couldn't say to her, *Why doesn't it excite you?* He couldn't say that Maka had liked it. He couldn't even remind her that love was giving.

"Erika?"

She opened her eyes, stared in the dark.

"You know Sam-I-am, the guy selling green eggs and ham?"

"Yes." She looked wary.

"Try it, you might like it?" He lifted his eyebrows. "Two minutes?"

I know what it's like, Kal. Been there, done that. She didn't want to remind him.

Give. As he was trying to give to her. It was, she knew, a sweet act of love. But she hated the exposure, the intimacy. It was almost more than she could bear. As soon as one level of closeness was reached, Kal went deeper.

"Okay." It was a whisper.

Kal pressed his cheek against hers, kissed her mouth. Then he bowed over her, and she saw his shoulders in the dark. She wanted to shut her eyes, but he was too beautiful. Unable to look away, she saw his head go down and his mouth kissing her, and there was so much love in him that something changed inside her. She dared herself to look at the body he kissed, her hips, the juncture of her thighs. Herself. Seeing herself as the object of the love he bestowed, she thought with stunned pleasure, *I'm beautiful.* It was the first time in five years, perhaps in her life, that she had loved her body. Seeing what he was doing. His hands opened her. His tongue probed her, caressed her.

Erika's breath grew ragged, and the dark world came, the sex world that was as out of control as she had been during those three years on the *Skye*. She hadn't been able to control the feeling in her body, to get it back.

She couldn't control this, either.

The only control was to choose not to do it, to tell him to leave her alone.

Or to give the control to him. To let him play her like one of his guitars.

She gave. Love. Trust.

"Kal..." His name became a cry, and she tossed, enjoying a body she had forgotten how to do anything but hate, feeling suddenly proud and beautiful, as beautiful as he said she was. The sounds she made didn't matter to her, but he soothed her and held her, controlling her, not letting her escape, as though she could have escaped.

Kal felt her reborn in his hands, from the love he gave with his mouth.

And the night was so good and so long that in the morning, after he'd taken the puppy outside and brought him back in, he wasn't afraid to go into the kitchen and retrieve the mangoes he'd picked the night before. When he returned to the bedroom, Erika's dark eyes were watching him as though she wanted him.

Crawling onto the bed with her, he said, "At our wedding, it just for a minute crossed my mind that the thought of oral sex with me made you throw up."

"Well, it did."

He kissed her smile. "Guess what we're having for breakfast in bed, *ipo*." Sweetheart. Lover.

Erika welcomed him into the sheets, and together they learned more about love and joy.

CHAPTER SIXTEEN

"YOU TWO LOOK WONDERFUL," said Mary Helen, when they came to pick up Hiialo on Sunday night, one week after the day they were married. She kissed both of them, and Erika wondered if Mary Helen, too, had feared that Kal would never really get over Maka.

An inarticulate unhappiness tugged at the edge of her mind, and she pushed it away. *Don't think about his room, about the quilt on his bed. Think about the room and the bed you're going to share.*

Hiialo was eager to see Kin again, and though it was past her bedtime when they got home, they let her play with the puppy for fifteen minutes before bed. During that time, Erika walked down the hall to her room, the room she would share with Kal.

On the way she paused beside the beads in his doorway. He was unpacking. The purple quilt lay smooth on his bed.

It probably didn't mean anything. She should just suggest he pack it away somewhere, for Hiialo.

Oh, right. And how are you going to word that request?

But Erika slipped between the beads.

Shutting the closet, Kal saw her. "Hi." He grinned and came nearer to hold her. "We can try out your bed together when Hiialo's asleep."

Their lips touched. It gave her courage. "Do you want

to move your things in there? We could use this room for...I don't know." She shrugged, wishing she hadn't gone so far, hadn't actually suggested taking apart his room.

Kal glanced around. "I've got a lot of stuff. It's probably better for me to keep using this closet. We'll see."

It's not important, she thought. *Let it drop.*

But the feeling, the twinge of jealousy, had become an entity inside her and it would not rest. After Hiialo was in bed, Erika went into the room that had been hers to find Kal spreading their new wedding quilt on the bed. The older one, his birth quilt, he'd folded and set on a chair.

A better chance would never come. "I love that quilt," said Erika, nodding to the one his grandmother had made. "Maybe we could use it on your bed."

Intuition pricked Kal. There was something in her voice that told him she wasn't just talking about redecorating. Or maybe his own guilt made it sound that way. The purple quilt on his bed...

He turned. "You're right. Good idea."

Surprised by his agreement, Erika watched him take the yellow-and-red quilt through the door that adjoined their rooms. She looked in to see him folding the purple quilt and opening his closet.

A gravity fell over her, and she moved from the door. *He knows. He knows how I feel, so he put it away.*

But the action of changing the quilts on the bed hadn't accomplished what she'd hoped. It had only, for some reason she didn't understand, confirmed the belief that bled inside her.

He could strip all signs of Maka from his room and his house, in courtesy to her, his new wife.

But Maka would still be there, first in his heart.

DAVID AND JEAN and Chris had gone, returned to Greenland. Adele was back on the mainland. Erika resumed her schedule of painting at the gallery on Tuesdays, with Hiialo, and sold two more watercolors, after which she asked Kal if he wanted to shorten his work hours some. Gladly he arranged with Kroner to have both Wednesdays and Thursdays off, yet Erika saw no more of him than she had before.

He had become a professional musician again, with a dedication that showed her how much it meant to him—and that increased her niggling suspicion that he'd married her so she would be there for Hiialo and he could play with his band. It had to be at least partly true.

But he did love her. Erika believed that, because there was no room for that kind of lie in the double bed they shared. She slept well in his arms. But when the sun shone outside or when the lights still burned in the house, he played music. And Erika kept waiting for the joy to end, for the tragedy that would explode her happiness.

Kai Nui had a gig in Honolulu, at a popular club in Waikiki, on the third weekend in August.

Tragedy came two weeks before, on August first.

It wasn't the tragedy Erika feared or anticipated, that Kal would cease to love her.

It was something she'd forgotten to fear.

The first was a Thursday, Kal's day off. Erika took Kin with her on a painting trip to Wailua Falls, halfway around the island. She would've liked to take Hiialo, too, but Danny had promised to come over and teach her some hula that day.

Kin seemed fifty percent bigger than when Erika had first received him as a wedding gift from Kal. A family dog, the Akita possessed deep affection for Kal and especially for Hiialo, but most of all he responded to Erika and she to him. She loved him as she'd never known a person could love an animal, and driving home from the falls, she worked on his automobile manners. Sit. Stay. He sat patiently on the seat, and Erika was feeling happy when she turned down the driveway in the rain and steered the huge Thunderbird into the spot beside the garden shed.

As she was getting out of the car, Kal walked out onto the lanai. Erika told Kin, ''Go see Kal.'' Tail wagging, the puppy trotted to the porch. Gathering the tote bag that held her art supplies, Erika checked to see that the watercolor she'd completed was protected from the rain.

Barefoot, Kal came down the steps and across the lawn. He held the car door open for her.

''That was fun, Kal. Thanks for letting me get away for the day.'' When she kissed him, she saw in his eyes that something was wrong.

''Kal?''

The rain beaded on his hair and his eyebrows and nose. ''Come inside.''

She was scared. ''What is it?''

The car door was still open.

Kal held her arm, looking into her eyes. ''Kurt just called. Adele had a heart attack yesterday. She's dead.''

''Oo-ooh.'' The wavering sound had nothing to do with words, just with pain. Kal couldn't take it away. He wasn't Adele, who could laugh at the antics of men and children, who could tell Erika that René had never been worth a single tear, that Skye had charted her own course to self-destruction, who had said all the right things Before, During and After. Who could always make her laugh. Who had saved her with art.

''No. No...''

She didn't remember going inside. ''Where's Hiialo?''

"My folks' house. It's just you and me." He took her to what at first had been only her room, to the bed they now shared, to lie down and feel numb.

"Kal…"

He could hold her against him as though she was Hiialo. Sobbing woman.

"She's my best friend. I need her… Oh, God, what about Kurt? And Jason?" Their son.

Kal's hand held her hair, her head.

After a while Erika lay back, staring vacantly at the ceiling. Where was Adele? "I have to see her. I have to go to California."

He was holding her hand. He knew all those things.

He hated death.

"Kal…"

They both wanted to make love, to make death go away. They joined their bodies while the rain poured off the eaves and the sky darkened with the end of the day. Then they drank *mai-tais,* Erika to try to blunt the pain, and they made love again. After that, Erika called Kurt and talked to him for an hour and a half.

When she got off the phone, her eyes were hollow, and Kal saw her walking around trying to function, an imitation of how he had been four years before.

Hiialo was going to sleep at his parents' house, but once it was dark they went over, anyhow, walking Kin through the rain. When they went in the door, Raiden approached to sniff the puppy and Mary Helen emerged from the kitchen and embraced Erika.

"Oh, darling," she said.

Erika began crying again. "Mom."

She went into the kitchen with Mary Helen and Kal, and she told them about Adele and how when she couldn't walk, Adele had been there, always ready with a wisecrack and never with pity. *Why should I feel sorry for someone who can paint like you? Get outta here.*

King came in and leaned against the counter with Kal.

Mary Helen told of when her friend Lou had died of breast cancer. Talking story.

Talking story.

Kal thought about when Maka died, but none of them mentioned it, because it was too hard to think about how she had looked. They'd all seen her in the casket, fixed the best the funeral director could do. After a while Kal left the kitchen and went down the hall and looked at the photo of them in the Fern Grotto, and the hurt caught him and made him cry.

Death was a fishing net, and it gathered up all the old deaths, too.

He went outside and lay on the wet lawn with Raiden and cried, holding his stomach, trying to forget.

He would never forget. He had a new wife, and he loved her, but Maka would never go away.

"Kal."

It was his father.

Kal sat up, found. He shook off the tears and stood.

"Erika's looking for you." There was a quiet warning in his voice.

Kal didn't hear it. He straightened his face, dried the tears, glad it was dark. "I love Erika," he said, in case his father got the wrong idea, that he didn't. "I really love Erika."

King pressed a hand on his shoulder and said nothing.

A man who'd been happily married thirty-five years might doubt that you could love a new wife as much as an old one.

But in some ways, I love her more. Instinct pulled his eyes toward the house.

Sickness crept over him, and he knew why his father had not responded.

Erika stood on the patio, watching him through the twilight.

His stomach felt like lead.

It's nothing. You were just crying.

No, he'd been sobbing. And Erika would know it hadn't been for Adele. He felt like throwing up. Like she'd caught him in bed with another woman.

His father slipped away into the night, walking toward the kennels as though fleeing the scene of a disaster.

On the patio Erika was motionless.

Raindrops hit his face.

He walked toward her.

Erika saw his dark form, the tall broad-shouldered body. The sound of his sobs was still with her, would never leave her, nor those words of denial he had cried to his father. *I love Erika. I really love Erika.*

As though he needed to convince them both.

This was not the stroke of twelve. This was not Cinderella locked in the tower while her stepsisters tried on the glass slipper downstairs.

This was real. Water spilled on the painting of her life, flooding the colors to gray.

Her husband faced her, and she saw his features wet with rain. She saw the pulse at his throat, evidence of the heart that had pounded against hers when they made love.

She had never seen infidelity till now.

He spoke her name on a breath. "Erika..."

No reason to answer. *Adele. You could have made me laugh through this.*

No. Not even Adele.

She turned from him, because there was nothing that could be said. Sick, disgraced, Kal followed her inside, followed her up the stairs of his childhood home to see Hiialo sleeping in his old bed. As Erika covered her, he felt the enormity of his error.

Of not letting go of the dead.

It had cost him the living.

Without meeting his eyes, she walked past him to the door, and he tried the plea of the unfaithful. Grabbing her arm. "Erika. It doesn't mean anything. It's death. It's just death."

The room was dark, but her brown eyes were the eyes of Pele, the goddess of volcanos, who could turn men to ashes. With a steely strength he'd never known she possessed, she said, "Don't ever lie to me again."

And when she had gone downstairs without him, he stood frozen, leaning against the doorjamb, half clinging to it. He had lied.

And she had known.

His fear, the enormity of the knowledge between them, made him want to sink to the floor, to cover his head with his hands, to pray for it to be undone. How could he have been so stupid? Clinging to Maka was pointless. She was gone. She was utterly gone and would not comfort him and did not care.

Erika, alive—Erika, his lover…

Oh, shit. Oh, shit. He tore his hand through his hair, thinking he would go mad.

His breath grew weak, imperiled by recollection of his face against her thighs, of her cries, of their intense promises of devotion. *I love you so much. I'll never leave you.*

The hideous part was, he knew she wouldn't. She would stay.

For Hiialo.

Because she would never hurt his child.

WHEN HE CAME DOWNSTAIRS, she stood in the living room with his parents. Kin explored at the end of the leash in her hand as Kal's father remarked, "It's still *bon-odori*."

Erika had seen Kal in the arch at the edge of the room. She ignored him.

Bon-odori. Adele. Skye. If she could deal with the deaths, if she could put them somewhere, she would find a way to go on. Oh, she couldn't think about Kal now. She had to go to California. The funeral. Horror returned.

Obon would end sometime in early August. She asked King, "Does it take long to learn the *bon* dances?"

"Well, there are lots of them. But I could teach you a few. Mom and I have done them many times. So has Kal."

From the arch, Kal saw his father's eyes. King's were saying, *You messed up, son. Hope you can make it right. Better start now.*

His stomach felt wrenched, and he remembered that once he'd had an ulcer. Without her. Before her.

Erika tried to think through her numbness. "Could I learn enough to participate? I'll be in California a few days. Maybe longer. But when I come back…"

"Weekend after next is the last, I think," said Mary Helen. "You could certainly learn some dances by then. I have a kimono you can borrow. You'll need one. But oh, mine will be short on you."

Kal ventured into the room and took Kin's leash from her hand. Relinquishing it without a glance, Erika said, "I'd like to learn the dances. I haven't made a plane reservation yet. But maybe I could come over tomorrow morning?"

"Sure," said King. He squinted at Kal. "You'll be at work, won't you?"

Kal stiffened inside, knowing the price his father thought he should pay. Because they'd practiced the dances together the summer after Iniki, after Maka had died. But when *obon* came, he couldn't face it.

Coldly, resenting the interference, he said, "Yes. I have to work."

A short time later, he and Erika left in the rain. She limped in silence, and he didn't try again to explain. He was shamed. And when they went to bed, she turned away from his love, from his hands touching her, needing her. He begged, pleaded for forgiveness without confessing his crime. But no longer denying it. "Please. I love you. You're here. Erika, I need you."

Her body was something he craved, and he'd never known before that she was his nourishment, that he would grow sick without her. "Please. Erika, I love you so much."

His voice reached her ears, and she had never heard a voice like that before. Even when René had begged forgiveness, she could perceive his falseness, that though he was sincere, he was also fickle.

With Kal it wasn't like that.

Wind banged the blinds gently in the windows as she turned to him. Her heart vacillated between hurt and distrust and the dreadful fear that, if she didn't forgive him, it would be over. That he would not come to her like this again.

She had forgiven in the past. But Kal mattered to her too much. How little she knew his character. How deeply she believed in it. She staked her heart on that faith and she told him, "Sorry isn't good enough."

They did not make love.

He got up and went outside with the Gibson, which he couldn't play. He slept on the lawn, rolled up in the quilt his grandmother had made before he was born. And when he came home from work the next day, Hiialo was at his parents' house and Erika was gone.

HE BROUGHT HIIALO HOME and slept alone in his and Erika's bed, her scent all around him, making him crazy with pain. He tried to lose himself in his music, and on Saturday he called Jakka and Danny to come over and practice. While Hiialo played with Kin, Kal poured his mind into the Stratocaster, forgetting everything until Jakka remarked, ''Hey, where's the *keiki?*''

''Hiialo?'' In the front room, where they'd been playing, Kal unfastened his guitar strap and set down the instrument. ''Hey, Hiialo.''

They all three began wandering through the house, and it was an eerie echo of the past. He and his two friends and a little girl. No mother. Hiialo wasn't inside, so Kal went out on the lanai and called for her.

She didn't come.

He searched the yard and the shed where the washer and dryer were. The dog was missing, too, so he called for them both. There was no response, and in his mind were Erika's worries about all the dangers he had said would never find Hiialo. He was scared, ready to call 911.

But first he jogged down the driveway to the beach, and there they were, Hiialo teaching the puppy to lie down.

Kal spent a long time catching his breath before he spoke. Even then, he yelled. She cried, threw a tantrum, reminding Kal of how it had been before Erika. It had been a long time since Hiialo had thrown a tantrum.

Kin comforted her and growled at Kal, behavior Kal

had to discipline aggressively. They couldn't have an Akita who growled at them.

Band practice was over for the day.

He needed antacids, and he took them.

When Hiialo was in bed, Kal went into his old room, put Pink Floyd's *The Dark Side of the Moon,* side two, on the turntable.

The night was lonelier than before Erika had come.

He went into the room where they slept together and stared at the watercolors on her wall. In his mind he saw her hands and how she looked when she painted. Missing her, wanting just to see things that brought her closer, he opened one of the drawers under the bed and looked at her clothes neatly folded there. She folded his clothes perfectly after she washed them. Much better than he ever had.

From the next room he heard a bittersweet tribute to the passage of time, to late starts and missed chances.

He shut the drawer with his knee and fell on the bed, his head in his arms. *Sorry isn't good enough.*

Maybe it would have been, if not for the way things had begun between them. With the ad. And his letter.

Recollection gnawed at him.

Oh, God, that letter.

Did she still have it?

He sat up, scanned the room.

She must have it somewhere. Erika didn't throw things out, especially anything he or Hiialo had given her. There were dried *leis* hanging on the wall and all kinds of little paper things from Hiialo.

Possessed, he got up from the bed and began hunting, turning the room upside down in search of that fateful epistle he'd sent her. The first letter.

He felt no sense that he was violating her, because

everywhere he looked he had a greater sense of Erika, a greater knowledge that she had made herself his completely.

As he should have made himself hers.

He found his letters on her art table, in a mahogany box he discovered also held ribbons from art shows. He read all the ribbons, all the things she'd won. His heart whispered, *I love you. I love you. Erika, I can't lose you.*

The letters were underneath, and he took them out and went to the first one. He knew it because it was addressed to Ms. Aloha, instead of to Erika Blade.

When he pulled it from the envelope, something fell out, and he remembered the cropped Christmas-card photo. Sweet Maka's arm.

He looked like a kid.

You wouldn't know me, Maka. Things have happened without you.

A hurricane happened.

And Erika, who had let him lick mango juice from her body, who had shown him a happiness that took him higher than he'd gone before. Higher. Deeper.

He unfolded the letter and read it.

…If you are still interested in Hiialo and me, please write back. But understand that even if a permanent domestic arrangement is possible, your relationship with me would be platonic. Maka and I were married for seven years, and no one can replace her in my heart. I want no other lover, and I would prefer to live alone, if not for Hiialo. Please understand this, because, as you said, we all need to be kind.…

She had been kind.
She had saved his life.

And she still had this letter, in which he'd written that no one could replace Maka in his heart, which was true.

He hadn't known there was so much room in his heart.

He read the other letters he'd sent her, too. He looked at all the photos. When he was done, he put them away and went back to his old room and fell to his knees on the floor. Burying his head in his arms, beside the instruments on which he released his finest gifts, he begged and vowed to be a better man.

THE NEXT DAY was Sunday, and he made some bread and took Hiialo and Kin and the loaf to his parents' house for breakfast. His father was out walking Raiden, but Niau had come up, and Kal and Hiialo ate breakfast with her and his mother.

Afterward Kal caught his mother when she was alone in the kitchen. "Mom, would you mind watching Hiialo for an hour or so? I have something I want to do."

Her eyes were curious, but she didn't ask. "That's fine. If you're looking for your dad, he walked Raiden down to Ke'e."

Kal was not looking for his dad. However, he could keep King off his back—with a confession, via Mary Helen. It was a system that always worked for averting those father-son top-dog confrontations. "I'm going next door."

Her eyes fluttered. "Oh." After a beat, "I'm not sure they're home."

Kal shrugged as though it didn't matter, as though he just hoped for a cup of tea.

The day was hot and muggy, hurricane weather, and he shook the damp cotton of his T-shirt from his body as he walked down the drive to a slot between the flame trees, a path to the property next door, a secret passage from childhood.

They're probably not home.

Next week was the Floating Lantern Festival. They'd probably been asked to dance at the Judo Mission in Haleiwa, on Oahu.

But he saw the glint of the Akanas' silver-blue Buick, and as he scanned the tangle of flowers, the riotous garden in front of their graceful sprawling home, he caught sight of a man amid the ginger. Mr. Akana straightened, staring at Kal from beneath thick white eyebrows. Then he smiled and waved.

Brushing an insect from his neck, Kal made his way through the flower beds. When he reached the old man, Mr. Akana was removing his gardening gloves. "Good morning. Nice surprise."

"Good morning. Your flowers look good."

"Thank you. You want to come inside and see June? Where your little girl?"

"She's next door. I'll go get her," Kal offered. He made a motion of departure, but then he stopped. "Actually I'd like to ask a favor." Awkwardly he faced the man who seven decades before had sent across the sea for a bride he'd never met.

In halting words, as courteously as he knew how, he asked for what he wanted.

Mr. Akana leaned on his hoe, wearing the sober face of a veteran of the Second World War, of one of the bravest and most decorated Allied regiments. He said, "In Japan, we have belief called *giri*. I do you favor, you owe me."

"Yes. I understand that."

"I old. What you going to do for me?"

"I'll dance for you, sir."

Mr. Akana laughed, clapped him on the back. "Ah, good. Go get little Hiialo, though. We want to see her."

NERVOUSLY ERIKA WATCHED the shrubs rush past as the plane descended to the airfield. It felt like a lifetime since she'd first landed in Lihue two months before. How could things have seemed simpler then?

Oh, Kal.

She missed him.

The funeral had been depressing, and she had felt helpless to do anything for Kurt and Jason, who had lost the sun of their world. She had longed for Hawaii, for the quality of light in the morning, for the scents of pikake and gardenias and the advance of rain. For shave ice and mangoes and long rice. She wanted Kal and Hiialo and to forget that drizzling night, to forget Kal sobbing on the lawn.

Far away in California, where she could not hold his body, it had seemed unimportant, her reaction overblown.

It was going to be okay. They'd talked briefly the night before to arrange for him to pick her up at the airport. She'd heard his heart in his voice. *I really miss you,* he'd told her. *We've got to talk when you get home.*

Before she left, sorry wasn't enough. But into the phone she'd said, *It doesn't matter. I love you, Kal.*

He was there, right inside the door, when she stepped into the terminal. He grabbed her in his arms, and they held each other as though there had been no hurt between them.

"I love you," he said. "I love you, Erika."

But they did not kiss.

On the way to the car, carrying her garment bag, his free hand in hers, he explained that Hiialo had gone to watch a hula festival in Princeville with his mother. Anxiously he unlocked her door and let her in, and when he'd put her garment bag in the trunk, he came around and got in, too.

Erika gazed at him in the hot interior of the car. "I'm sorry," she said.

"I am." From the back seat, he brought forward a gift-wrapped box. The paper was oriental, like a bamboo-screen design.

There was no card.

Erika knew about conscience gifts. This wasn't one. She unwrapped the paper and lifted the lid on the box. Folding back the tissue inside, she saw silk.

It was a kimono.

For *obon*.

Kal said softly, "I bought a *happi* coat for me."

Erika saw and felt his hands cover hers, hold them tight.

"And I've been practicing the dances."

The box was crushed in their embrace.

MARY HELEN AND HIIALO had returned from the hula festival by the time Kal and Erika reached Hanalei. They picked up Hiialo and Kin at the gallery, and Mary Helen showed them two oil paintings of Erika's that she'd framed while Erika was gone. *Shave Ice* and *Talk Story,* which was a picture of two local women smoking ciga-rettes and gabbing at a table in the Haena Store. "I really want you to think about a show, Erika," said Mary Helen. "To celebrate your new style. And we really have to get some of your work into shows in Honolulu, too."

Erika liked the idea of a show of her own in Hanalei, surrounded by her *ohana*.

When they left the gallery, they took Hiialo for shave ice, then headed home. As the familiar drive came into sight, Erika's heart beat irregularly, and she experienced what she never had before.

This was her home.

But time had passed. There was a pungent tangy smell in the air, oversweet, almost like garbage. She sniffed.

"Rotting mangoes," said Kal. Mango season was *pau,* finished.

Heat hung in the air.

They went up on the lanai, Hiialo dripping shave ice. Kicking off his slippers at the door, Kal asked, "Want to go swimming?"

"Hooray!" shouted Hiialo, taking her melting treat inside.

But Kal paused suddenly on the porch and took Erika's hand. She followed his gentle lead into the house. Carrying her bag, he led her toward the hall but paused at the door of his room.

"Come in here a minute."

The beads clattered around their bodies. Kal set her garment bag on the floor. "I moved the stereo out into the front room," he said. "And I cleaned out the closet. I thought you might want to store some of your paintings in here."

The closet stood empty and he said, "I put my clothes with yours. I'm kind of a slob," he warned her.

Erika hugged herself. *Yes. But you're mine.*

THEY WEREN'T QUICK about putting on their swimsuits, though they had got them on and were lying on the bed kissing when Hiialo bounded into their room in her neon green suit, jumping up and down. "Come on, come on," she said. "It's time to go swimming!"

Kal and Erika got up, and they all went out onto the lanai.

"Let's go, Kin," Hiialo said. She climbed around the porch railing so she could jump over the heliconia to the lawn.

Slinging a faded towel over his shoulder, Kal slid his fingers into the back of Erika's swimsuit, stroking her skin. They took their time crossing the lawn while Kin watered the traveler's palm and the autograph tree.

In the shade of that tree, Kal paused to scratch one of the leaves with a twig: I LOVE ERIKA.

"Come on, Kin! Let's go swimming!" yelled Hiialo, skipping ahead down the driveway.

Erika followed her with her eyes, welcoming the familiar sight of the ocean at the end of the drive. Turquoise and green, teal like Kal's eyes. Kal walked beside her, holding her hand. He dropped it to retrieve Kin's Frisbee from the shrubs growing alongside the blue house. Erika waited.

Hiialo had disappeared.

Kal whistled for the dog, ready to throw the Frisbee.

Kin didn't come.

"Kin!" called Erika.

A moment later the Akita ran up the driveway from the beach, barking.

Kal threw the Frisbee.

Kin ignored it. He barked, then turned and ran back toward the water.

Intuition made Erika hurry down the driveway.

But Hiialo was fine. She was waiting for them before going in the water. "Hurry up, Erika! Eduardo and I want you to come swimming!"

Still barking urgently, Kin ran into the froth at the edge of the water. He stood between Hiialo and the sea.

"Go away, Kin," Hiialo ordered.

The puppy continued to bark.

Kal trudged across the sand to get the Frisbee the dog had ignored. It had landed at the high-tide line.

"Kin, be quiet," said Erika. "Come."

He did not respond at once.

"Kin. Come."

Taking advantage of the puppy's distraction, Hiialo bounded around him and into the surf. She dove and came up splashing. "Come on in, Mommy!"

Mommy. Erika stared, her eyes stinging.

Yards away down the beach, Kal watched her till she looked at him. He smiled, blew her a small kiss. Hiialo had asked him if she could call Erika that.

Bending over, he scooped up Kin's Frisbee and started to straighten up. Then he looked down again.

Within the circular imprint the disc had left was a fist-sized blob, whitish-clear except for the sand clinging to it. Kal straightened up, scanned the wet shore.

"Hey, Hiialo! Get out of the water."

Her scream tore through the sounds of the wind and tide, and he ran, easily dodging all the box jellyfish washed up on the beach. The fleet was in.

Erika, limping, was already in the surf, where Hiialo was screaming hysterically, brushing at lines of red welts on her chest, where jellyfish tentacles still clung. "Daddy!"

Knowing what had to be done and what would happen to her from doing it, Erika pulled the tentacles off Hiialo's skin. Burning shot through her fingers, weakening her legs, clenching her stomach. Some of the tentacles remained stuck to Hiialo, some to her own hand, causing the most excruciating sensations she'd ever known. Moving on autopilot, she put that hand in the water and tried to wash the rest of the tentacles off Hiialo, holding the shrieking child with her other hand.

Her hand was burning.

Hiialo's little face contorted. Her limbs went strangely rigid. As a wave washed her little body forward against Erika's legs, Kal's arms came down to gather her up. "I've got you. I've got you."

Erika staggered after them out of the water, trying to think beyond the agonizing fire in her hand.

Hiialo convulsed, fighting Kal's arms. He had to set her down, and she lay on the sand going rigid, doing strange back bends, terrifying him.

"Call 911!" said Erika. "I'll stay with her."

He ran.

Kin circled Hiialo, whining in concern.

Helplessly watching her convulsions, Erika didn't even realize that she could turn from Hiialo and put her burning hand in the ocean to try to cool the pain. There was only this child, her child, *and nothing she could do to help her.* "Hiialo, I'm right here. Your dad went to call the doctor. I love you, Hiialo." *Oh, make my hand stop hurting, make it stop.* She wanted to scream. The world seemed fuzzy, tilting unreal, and she wanted to throw up.

After an eternity Hiialo's spasms slowed. Ceased.

"Hiialo, can you hear me?"

She lay motionless, and Erika scooted toward her on her knees. With her left hand, she felt for the pulse in Hiialo's carotid artery, so close to those blazing red-and-purple welts. She could not find it.

And Hiialo's small chest neither rose nor fell with breath.

CHAPTER SEVENTEEN

IT HAD BEEN YEARS since Erika had taken a CPR class. She couldn't remember anything about resuscitating children.

Airway, breathing, circulation.

Airway. Airway.

Erika tilted the small head back and used her left hand to open Hiialo's mouth to clear her airway, move her tongue. *Mommy...*

Oh, God, don't do this. Don't do this.

She didn't know she was gasping from the pain in her hand.

Kal skidded onto his knees in the sand beside her, and Erika moved out of the way, watched him do the things she had begun. Watched him start CPR on his daughter.

They heard sirens immediately. Erika sat motionless, breathing raggedly, holding Kin's collar with her left hand, sick from the pain in her right, praying and watching Kal's steady movements.

He was still working when Erika saw the lights of the ambulance.

She started to sing softly, sing away her own fear. Sing about Puff.

"Yeah, yeah, do that," said Kal, still counting.

He felt Hiialo's chest stir beneath him.

She gave a small cough.

He picked up the words from Erika, sang about the dragon who'd lived where they did.

She was breathing.

She was breathing.

Erika released Kin's collar without thinking, and the puppy went and sat down beside Hiialo, watching her face, waiting for her to open her eyes.

"YOU CAN'T DRIVE," said Erika. "Get in the passenger side."

Kal didn't argue. He walked around the Thunderbird and got in, but when Erika reached past the steering wheel with her left hand to start the car, he said, "What's wrong with your hand? Erika!" He pushed open the door again and ran into the house, emerging seconds later with some gauze pads and three bottles. He opened the driver's door. "Move over."

She unfastened her seat belt and slid over. Kal got behind the steering wheel. The welts on her hand crossed the insides and backs of three fingers and her thumb. Painting hand. Turning sideways in the seat, Kal laid her hand, palm up, across his knee. He made a paste of meat tenderizer and vinegar and used the gauze to apply it to her wounds. In his mind he saw the welts on Hiialo. There would be scars.

Stupid, Kal. You're stupid.

"Better, baby? Not yet. I know." He opened the bottle of Tylenol and handed her three. There was a water bottle on the floor of the car, and he fished it out and uncapped it.

Erika swallowed the pain relievers, drank some water. She felt as if she'd lost quarts of fluid. She tried to go away from the pain, to fly out over the ocean. "I'm fine.

Let's go to Lihue.''
   To see Hiialo.

THE HOSPITAL LET THEM spend the night in Hiialo's
room. Kal couldn't sleep, so Erika lay on the extra bed.
A doctor in the emergency room had prescribed codeine
for her hand and she fell asleep, and Kal sat in the dark
listening to the night sounds of the hospital, looking at
small Hiialo in the dark, with the IV in her arm.

She had woken up crying in the ambulance, he'd
heard, and he'd listened to her wail in the emergency
room. It was a long time before they'd moved her to a
regular room, longer still before she'd gone to sleep.

He couldn't stand being inside his own mind.

If he'd told Hiialo to check for jellyfish on the beach...

But there hardly ever were jellyfish on the beach.

He wasn't a worrier.

Maybe he'd worried some when she was a baby, about
her smothering at night, things like that. But after Maka's
accident...

You just can't stand to think in what-ifs, Kal.

Erika shifted on the bed, turning over.

Kal wished they were all at home, that he was in bed
with Erika where he could hold her close.

CPR. Counting. Hiialo not breathing. *Can't lose her...*

If he hadn't spent the last two years working as a tour
guide, renewing his CPR and advanced first-aid certifi-
cations every year, she would be dead.

Deep breath. Take a deep breath.

The electronic equipment on her IV pole made intermittent beeps.

A nurse came into the room on silent shoes. She
touched Kal's shoulder. Her voice reminded him of
Maka's. ''You can curl up with your wife on that bed if
you want. You don't have to sleep in a chair.''

"I'm fine. Thanks."

She smiled and moved around Hiialo's bed, switched on the light. Hiialo didn't stir, and Kal checked again to make sure he could see her chest rise and fall under the white bandages. Erika had pulled the tentacles off. Brave Erika. Christopher Blade's daughter must have known better.

The nurse tried to take Hiialo's vitals without waking her, but her eyes opened and she began to cry, trying to rub them, befuddled by the tube coming from her arm.

He stood up and went to her side. "It's all right, Tileaf. I'm here."

"Daddy, I want Pincushion and Fluff...."

Kal found Pincushion wedged against the bed rail and tucked him in Hiialo's arms. Fluff was under the covers. His parents had come to the hospital earlier bringing clothes for all of them, and Pincushion and Fluff and Hiialo's blanket.

Kal stroked Hiialo's hair. "Go to sleep, *keiki*."

In her bed Erika grew restless as sound and sensation penetrated her mind. Her hand was stuck to a hot skillet on the stove. She couldn't pull it off....

With a moan she opened her eyes and saw Kal standing over her. She glanced at Hiialo's bed to see a nurse switching out the light. As the young woman left the room, Erika said, "Kal?"

Hiialo had gone back to sleep.

"Here, baby." Kal gave Erika a glass of water and two of the pills from the bottle he'd stuffed into the pocket of his shorts. Erika wasn't a hospital patient, just a visitor, like him. Parent of a sick little girl.

Erika took the pills and lay down, and Kal kicked off his slippers and got onto the single bed with her. "Hi." She lifted the sheets to welcome him, and soon his arms were around her, holding her. He wouldn't go to sleep. Had to be awake for Hiialo.

Had to stay awake.

Waiting for the hurt in her hand to lessen, Erika clutched Kal's big hand, his musician's hand, which lay across her opposite arm. His fingers wound with hers, and he pulled her closer, hugging her tight.

"Erika," he said softly, drowsily.

A few minutes later, she felt him drift off to sleep.

SATURDAY NIGHT was the last night of *obon,* and there would be a Floating Lantern Festival at the temple in Waimea. Hiialo had been home from the hospital for three days, and by that afternoon she was well enough to visit her grandparents.

As Erika and he kissed her goodbye in the Johnsons's den before setting out for the south side of the island, Kal eyed the welts that reached up above the neck of Hiialo's T-shirt. There would be scars, though not as bad as he'd feared, thanks to Erika's pulling the tentacles off so quickly. But he knew he'd never forgive himself.

He would never again take the same attitude about Hiialo's safety—that mishaps could not be prevented. He hated that he had learned the lesson at her expense. A kind of sickness held him, death sickness.

Tonight he would take the cure.

He was ready—to let Maka go.

And he felt a strange relief that tonight's event was leading him back to Waimea, which had been their home.

THE HILLTOP CEMETERY in Waimea, which was largely Buddhist, showed the care relatives had taken of the deceased during *obon.* Many of the graves were freshly swept and bedecked with floral arrangements. Throughout the cemetery, the plumeria trees were blooming, sending off their sticky-sweet heady fragrance.

Kal parked the Thunderbird under a tree with cerise blossoms. The Waimea sky was brushed with faint white clouds, and he didn't bother to roll up his window, just looked over at Erika in her jungle green silk dress, the dress he loved on her. Her kimono and his *happi* coat, protected by a plastic dry-cleaner's bag, dangled from hangers in the back window. "You come with me, yeah?"

Their eyes met with the certainty of love, and she nodded.

He leaned across her to open her door, because of her hand. Gathering up the flowers from the seat between them, he opened his own door, and they both got out. As the trade winds blasted their hair, he went around the car and shifted the bouquets to his left hand to hold Erika's uninjured one with his right.

"It's up this way." He remembered the layout of the cemetery. Sometimes, when Hiialo spent the night with his folks, he had driven down to Waimea in the middle of the night and sat on the lawn on the hill and played his guitar for her.

Now he came in daylight, like a sane man. With Erika.

They reached the headstone, the piece of granite with her name and the dates with not even three decades' gap between them.

MAKANOE-PALI KEKAHUNA JOHNSON
MEA ALOHA

My beloved.
Kal knelt beside Maka's grave, fit the bouquets into the two places set for them in the ground. *Miss you,* he

thought. *Won't ever stop missing you. Won't ever forget the way you laughed.*

Erika touched his hair and he felt her moving away, drifting off to look at other places, to leave him alone.

He sat by the grave and tried to talk to Maka, tried to believe she could hear. *You used to dance for me. Tonight I'll dance for you.*

He closed his eyes and remembered her face and the way she moved, and he opened them and saw the letters etched in the stone. The engraved evidence of the permanence of death.

He could not have her and had learned it was wrong to want her.

The only right thing was to let her go and to dance with joy for the good life she had lived and for her right to let her soul part from him and go to a sweeter place.

THEY PARKED three blocks from the temple in front of an empty lot. The sun had set, and the sky was lavender with fiery stripes.

Standing outside the car, Kal put on his *happi* coat and Erika her kimono.

He told her, "Maka and I lived on this street."

"Where?" She looked about.

"We'll walk past. The house is gone. Someone has a trailer there now."

He took her hand, and they crunched along the gravel street in their slippers. They could smell the food already.

But it was eerie to walk past the trailer where someone else lived and remember when a white house had stood there.

Erika put her arm around him.

"The hurricane wiped it all away. Like we have no history."

"I know. I know."

It hurt. But this wasn't the guilty hurt of lying on his parents' lawn, sobbing over ugly longings. This was grief, in the open presence and with the blessing of his beloved.

But it was so intense he had to stop in the street he'd strolled with Maka and hold his head back, tip his face toward the dimming sky, to make the tears flow back into his eyes. After a moment he started walking again, his arm around Erika. They passed the places that hadn't changed, the laundromat where he and Maka had washed clothes and the gas station where they'd bought shave ice.

The lost past.

In the next block, as they turned at the main road and walked on the cracked and chipped sidewalk, Erika saw the first of the food stands and the people in kimonos and the bright paper-ball lanterns hanging around the perimeter of the temple grounds. The lanterns cast a white glow against the sky, luminescent as sparklers on the Fourth of July.

Kal heard instruments playing from the *yagura*, the musicians' tower. He heard the *taiko* drums and the gongs, and they resonated inside him so that his flesh and his breath became notes, too. His heart beat music, instead of blood, and *bon-odori* spoke the language he understood, which was song.

Erika's first impression was that all the people at the festival were Japanese. But then she saw the *haole* faces in the crowd and those of other races, as well. She glanced at Kal beside her. His teal eyes alert, taking in this world that was part of his childhood.

"Let's eat something," he said, and Erika knew the

words meant more than, *Are you hungry?* Kal meant, *Let's be here. Let's live.*

They had passed a shave-ice booth, and Erika saw another which sold sushi. "That's what I want."

"Say please." He put his arm around her.

The faces were bright with smiles, voices laughing and talking in English and Japanese and pidgin. Erika and Kal stood in line together and bought sushi with something mysterious inside and devoured it and moved on and bought teriyaki sticks, saimin and *mochi.* Kal loved to hear Erika's voice, her good manners. *Please* and *Thank you* and *Wow, that looks good.*

The people serving the food smiled at her and liked her, and Kal stayed close to her. She was as precious to him as song.

As the sky grew dark, the lanterns glowed brighter. The *yagura,* the red-and-white-striped square tower where the musicians played, dominated the center of the open temple grounds, and the round lanterns reached out from the ornate oriental roof with its up-curved edges. The glow they cast matched the music as the *bon* dancing began. He and Erika joined the other dancers, who had formed several concentric circles around the *yagura.* Kal felt the slow beat of the music inside him.

Oh, Maka…

Beside him, Erika forgot his presence. The dance was Yagi Bushi, from the Fukushima prefecture in Japan, which had once been the Akanas's home. She found she could follow the steps, and she remembered Adele, her friend, and felt joy in her heart, felt Adele's joy.

Then darker thoughts came, and with them came Skye. Erika made the apologies and vows of her heart, and the mystery of a mutual forgiveness enveloped her.

There was only the music, the dance for the souls who

had left the pain of earth and also its joys. The smells and the tastes and the sounds.

The tone of the gongs vibrated in Kal's veins, and he was with Maka as he had never been since her death. Her voice spoke inside him and her smile reached behind his eyes as he moved, as he manipulated the *tenugui,* the small hand towel, lifting it over his head, sliding it behind his neck.

Kal, we're not in the same place anymore. You must let go.

Maka...

You'll be fine. You'll be so happy. I want you to be happy. I like her, your picture bride. You love her and enjoy many mango seasons, yeah? And don't forget the sweet plums in Kokee; they should be ripe now. It's already August, so wiki-wiki, Kalahiki.

He cried.

Remember what you tell her, Kal? Give...

The struggle raged inside him, separate from the joyful faces around him. He was a wrong element, out of sync.

Another dance. Fukushima Ondo.

Give... Let go. He separated himself from Maka, tried to look at her from far away, and she was smiling in the way that would never leave him. And with that gift from him, the first step of separation, he knew the first glimmer of her joy.

The dancing went on for hours. He and Erika knew only three dances, and there were many, some of them old. Bound by invisible silken threads, husband and wife, they stood together watching and eating more until the time of the service to honor the deceased.

They went into the temple then, to a ceremony that was otherworldly but of his world, too, of Hawaii. Buddhist incense filled Kal's head, and the gong purified him, clearing away all other music. He took Erika's hand and held it tightly. She was alive—and his.

THE NIGHT AIR on the beach, the ocean's own, was a welcome bath on their skin. Erika inhaled deeply as she carried the candlelit lantern down the hard wet sand to the shore. The lights floating on the sea would guide the spirits back to the netherworld.

Nearby she saw men and women filling a straw boat with food and other articles. Already lanterns were setting out on the ocean.

Erika waded into the water, remembering the stings on her hand, remembering the jellyfish. She set the floating lantern on the water and pushed it out, away from her. *Goodbye, Adele. I love you!*

Goodbye, Skye...

Her eyes leaked, crying at the beautiful sight, the lights reflected against the water, bobbing their way toward Niihau, the Forbidden Island, and beyond, to the Paradise of the Western Regions.

When she glanced over to where she'd seen Kal before, he was crouched at the water's edge, the legs of his long white pants dragging wet in the sand. He looked beautiful with the glow of that one candle lighting up his face. Erika knew the gift that single light, that Maka, had given her by being loved and making love with Kal and bearing sweet Hiialo.

Thank you, Maka, she thought. *I love them so much.*

Kal's eyes were on the candle, the light inside the lantern, casting its glow onto his hands and the water and the sand. Holding what represented Maka's soul, he stood up and waded deeper into the sea.

Maka, I can't say goodbye. I can't say goodbye....

Kal, you know what to say.

The candle blurred with the water, with all the lanterns everywhere, the loved and lost, the ancestral spirits, the souls who had left the living behind. He set the lantern on the surface of the water. It floated well, and he nudged it away from him, pushed it farther away.

"Aloha, *ipo*," he whispered. "Aloha."

He watched it drift till the current caught it and pulled it away from him. Then he turned his back on the lantern and waded out of the summer water to Erika, who was holding their slippers. Her arms went around him, all warm, and they turned away from the temple and walked back along the beach to their car parked on the street where he had lived and loved with Maka.

And she was really gone.

THAT NIGHT in their bedroom, they made love in the comfort of cool darkness, and each knew the reassurance of the other's body, of heartbeat and breath and the trust of love.

"I needed you," he whispered. "You must have known when you read that first letter, the letter I wrote when you answered my ad."

"I guess that's true. It made me cry."

"*That* doesn't surprise me."

"I needed you, too, Kal. You know, I used to tell myself that only desperate people have anything to do with personal ads."

Their eyes met. Simultaneous laughter. *Who could have been more desperate than us?*

Kal's arms could have broken her with their embrace. He remembered something they'd talked about on the way home from Waimea, a surprise for Hiialo. "She's really going to make us crazy.''

Erika smiled against him in anticipation of Hiialo's joy.

THEY'D BEEN INVITED to breakfast at his parents' house. Hiialo was awake when they arrived. She ran out into the foyer to see them, and when she saw the flat package wrapped in Cinderella paper, which Erika carried under her arm, her eyes grew big.

Kal smiled. ''Come on in the living room, Hiialo. Where are Grandma and Grandpa?''

''Right here!'' Armed with a camera, Mary Helen found a place beside the plate-glass windows while King leaned forward in his easy chair, petting Raiden. Kal had called to warn them that morning.

He and Erika sat down on the couch on each side of Hiialo.

''It's not my birthday,'' she said, clearly excited nonetheless. And she was already opening the envelope that held the card.

''Look, it's Kin!'' She held up the card to show her grandparents. ''Mommy painted Kin for me.''

Then she unwrapped the package and turned over the special teal blue frame flecked with black and green.

''Oooh,'' she said. ''Oh, Mommy, look what you made me.'' She hugged the picture, frame and all.

The camera flashed.

Everyone laughed.

''Look, Daddy! It's you and Eduardo.''

The *mo'o's* head, neck and front feet were emerging from the dark water in the Blue Room. In the watercolor, Kal leaned forward from the ledge where he sat, as though listening for wisdom from the giant black lizard, whose tail just showed above the surface of the pool.

''I love this picture. I want it right by my bed.''

"Hiialo," said Erika softly. "Your daddy and I talked about this. If you want, my publisher—" Her voice caught. Just Kurt was her publisher now. "We can make that picture into prints to sell and use the money for you to go to a *halau hula* when you're bigger, if you'd like."

"And I can be a hula dancer?" Hiialo asked, eyes wide.

Erika nodded.

"Oh, Mommy." Hiialo cuddled against her, gazing at the watercolor. "But would I have to give away my picture?"

"No, no, no. They make something called a plate and use the plate to make pictures like yours. Then other people can enjoy your daddy and Eduardo, too."

"Okay." Hiialo smiled big and kicked her feet on the couch. "I love my picture. It's the best picture you ever painted. And it's a good thing it's of Eduardo, because now I can remember what he looks like."

Kal stilled. Erika looked at him.

He gazed down at his daughter. "What do you mean, Hiialo?" A strange feeling crept up his spine, and he felt his parents—his father who'd never known anything but Hawaii and his mother who loved all things Hawaiian— staring, too. They all understood the same things. They all knew about *mo'os*.

Hiialo smiled happily at her picture. "Oh, he left. Last night."

The four adults in the room exchanged glances.

King reclined in his chair and levered the handle to pull out the footrest. His hand on Raiden's head, he observed, "I think that's probably a good thing."

Shifting her back against Erika, asking to be hugged, Hiialo said, "I don't need a *mo'o,* anymore. Now I have a mommy."

Kal caught Erika's eyes. He said, "We all have each other."

EPILOGUE

Two years later

"IT'S GOOD TO PLAY for a local crowd."

The revelers in the gym yelled back.

They were, as he'd said, mostly locals, from all the islands. But others in the audience were from the mainland. One listener was a producer from a growing independent label based in Seattle, a man who made his second home in Haena. Ever since he'd landed in Kauai for his annual two-week vacation, he'd been hearing the same voice on the radio. He was hearing it again, and he saw that the voice went with good looks and charisma. With star quality.

"We had to come back to Hanalei, because my wife, she *hapai*."

The crowd roared enthusiastically at this personal news.

In the back of the gymnasium Niau touched Erika's rounded stomach. "He obviously wanted to tell everyone that."

Erika thought the shaking on the floor was going to start her labor. "I think I need some air."

"I'm supposed to get him if you go into labor," Niau reminded her.

"No, I'm fine. I'll be back in a while." She made her way to the rear door and slipped out into the evening to

look at the painted sky and the mist-laden *pali*. The night
was warm. She could hear the music perfectly, and she
lay down on the lawn on her side, putting her hand on
her stomach against the cotton of her oversize T-shirt.

On the front of the T-shirt was a stylized reproduction
of the cover art of Kai Nui's first CD, *Mo'o*. The picture
was a reprint of the watercolor she'd given Hiialo two
years before, *Blue Room Meeting*. Her father-in-law liked
to joke that Hiialo could start her own *halau hula* with
the money from that one picture. Two hundred and fifty
lithographs had sold out, and a new poster series was in
production. The *Mo'o* CD was gaining popularity in Los
Angeles and San Diego; in Hawaii, it was first on the
pop charts. Disc jockeys throughout the islands were
spinning ''Picture Bride'' and ''Mo'o'' every hour.
Everyone loved Kal. He was a *kamaaina,* a child of the
land, one of their own.

On the lawn Erika listened to the music drifting from
the gym, to his haunting voice, to what his fingers could
do to a guitar. She lay on the grass through the whole
first set. When she knew they were taking a break, she
got up and went to the door behind the stage. It opened,
and Jakka came out with his cigarettes. He smiled
broadly at Erika, ''Howzit?'' He stuck his head back inside. ''Eh, brah!''

Kal came outside, drenched with sweat.

He grabbed Erika and hugged her, adjusting his body
to her shape. ''You okay?''

''Fine. I just want to kiss you.''

His lips covered hers before the words were out.

They spent the break together in the privacy of the
Thunderbird. When it was time for the next set, Erika
said, ''I'm not going back in the gym, Kal. I can hear
fine outside. It's too hot in there.''

"Okay."

Welcoming the solitude, knowing such moments would be increasingly rare in the future, she lay down on the lawn again, listening to the songs she knew so well. The second set crept on. They played "Kona" and "Lanterns."

Then came "Picture Bride," and it sent shivers up her spine.

Shivers...

Cramps.

She sat up and got to her feet, limped barefoot over the warm lawn. Lihue was an hour away.

ERIKA HAD WAITED till the end of the second set to go into labor, but now Kal wanted to get away, to be with her. He left through the closest door of the gym and found her outside, with his mom and dad and Hiialo. Niau had called his parents on the phone. Everybody wanted to go to the hospital. Keale had promised to come from the Big Island as soon as the baby was born, and Leo was down in Poipu already, seeing a girlfriend. Even Jean and David and Chris and toddler Cecily were expected soon, coming by ship from Australia.

Couldn't have a baby without the whole *ohana*.

"Kalahiki," said a voice behind him.

Kal glanced back. A man had come out the door after him. A *malihini* in an aloha shirt. Expensive wristwatch. Big smile.

"I know you're in a hurry, but here's my card. I'll be in Haena for a couple of weeks. Give me a call."

Kal took the business card and pocketed it without looking at it. "My wife's having a baby. I have to go." He was already reaching for Erika's hand, and his dad

was getting behind the wheel of his parents' new Land
Rover, where Kin was looking out the window.

Danny peered out the door of the gym, grinning. "Eh,
brah, we see you at da hospital, yeah?"

Kal returned his grin.

The man who had given him the business card waved.
"Aloha."

NOON SUNLIGHT shone through the window of the birthing room.

"Look at her, Hiialo." Though at six she was getting
too heavy to carry, Kal held Hiialo against his hip, reassuring her while they gazed down at Ano, his infant
daughter in Erika's arms.

"You can both sit on the bed," said Erika. "I'm really
fine." She scarcely noticed that her bottom was sore.
She'd almost forgotten fifteen hours of labor in the happiness of holding Ano.

Kal set Hiialo on her feet, and she climbed up on one
side of the bed. He walked around and sat gently on the
other. He kissed Erika, touched her hair. "I love you.
You're amazing."

Erika asked Hiialo, "Do you want to hold your sister?"

"Okay." Hiialo bit her lips together uncertainly.

"Now, don't let her head fall back. She can't hold it
up on her own." Erika carefully moved the baby to Hiialo's arms and helped settle her. The baby winced, then
shifted in her sleep. Erika hugged Hiialo and whispered,
"I love you, Hiialo."

She felt Hiialo's body relax. Afraid of being sup-
planted by the baby. Hiialo said, "I love you, Mommy."
Like a person making a decision, she said, "I love Ano,
too. Oh, look. She's making a face. I think her nose is

cute. Look at her cute nose, Mommy. Her hands are so small.''

''I haven't even seen her eyes open yet,'' said Kal, one arm around Erika, the other hand on her leg. ''Have you?''

Erika shook her head. She hoped they would be blue, like his.

King, Mary Helen, Leo and Niau all crowded in the door, looking in.

Niau said to her parents, ''Hiialo's turn, I guess.''

''Yes,'' said Hiialo. ''I'm holding my sister.''

The others went out, and after a while Hiialo yawned and said, ''Is it Daddy's turn?''

''Are you done, Ti-leaf?''

''For now. I'll get to hold Ano lots.''

Kal lifted his arms for the baby. Hiialo got down off the bed and went out into the hall. Erika heard her exclaim, ''Danny! Is that a present for the baby? I got to hold her.''

Kal held Ano, infatuated with her, seeing features that might have come from Erika or from him. It took him a moment to remember something he'd wanted to do when he and Erika were alone.

''I have a present for you.'' He glanced at Erika, then bent his head to nip at the shoulder of her hospital nightgown. When she lovingly nipped him back, he said, ''It's in my shirt pocket. You've got to get it out.''

Something they'd talked about before. She wanted it, too. He *hoped* she still wanted it.

Erika reached across, touching his chest, feeling his heart, before she dug into his shirt pocket and pulled out a key on a ring she had seen many times before, a key ring with a plastic pineapple on it.

It was just the key to the blue beach house, the key

they gave David or Jean or whomever when they came to visit Kauai.

Erika started to reach into his pocket again.

Kal laughed, and the baby opened her eyes. "Look! Her eyes are going to be blue." He prodded Erika very gently. "Like our house."

"Kal!" She slid her arms around his neck and hugged him and kissed him.

Mary Helen and King looked in the door again, and Erika saw Hiialo beyond them in the hallway performing *hula kahiko* for an audience of aunt and uncles. She rested against Kal's shoulder and closed her eyes, embraced in the fold of her family.